Dream Makers

The Stairway Press Collected Edition

Charles Platt

Other books by Charles Platt
The Silicon Man
Free Zone
Protektor
Blood Crazy
Anarchy Online
MAKE: Electronics (Learning by Discovery)
Encyclopedia of Electronic Components
MAKE: More Electronics

Print ISBN   978-1-941071-00-7
eBook ISBN 978-1-941071-01-4

STAIRWAY≡PRESS

www.stairwaypress.com
1500A East College Way #554
Mount Vernon, WA 98273

Cover image by Charles Platt
Cover Design by Guy Corp, www.grafixCORP.com

Dedication

To all the people who extended so much
friendship and generosity to me
during my 30 years
in the science-fiction field,
from 1965 through 1995.

I received more than I deserved.

Contents

Contents...1

Introduction 3

Isaac Asimov 11

Thomas M. Disch...20

Frederik Pohl..35

Kurt Vonnegut...49

Algis Budrys...61

Philip José Farmer...73

Frank Herbert..89

Ray Bradbury..104

A. E. van Vogt..118

Philip K. Dick...134

E. C. Tubb 155

Alfred Bester 165

Brian Aldiss..180

J. G. Ballard 194

John Sladek 211

Harry Harrison..224

Dream Makers Collected Edition

Theodore Sturgeon 235

Jerry Pournelle 248

Piers Anthony..266

Keith Laumer...280

L. Ron Hubbard (?) 292

Arthur C. Clarke...312

Stephen King...321

James Tiptree Jr. 335

Charles Platt, by Douglas E. Winter 356

Charles Platt

Introduction

FROM 1978 THROUGH 1982 I interviewed almost all of
the best-known science-fiction writers in the United States and
Great Britain. From these interviews I derived fifty-seven profiles
that were collected in two books, *Dream Makers* and *Dream Makers II*,
published in 1980 and 1983. Twenty-four of those profiles are
reprinted here with afterwords that I have written for this edition.

It's fortunate that I interviewed the writers when I did,
because many were at their peak, financially and creatively. What
none of us foresaw was the long-term impact of changes in science-
fiction book publishing that were already occurring. These changes
would be beneficial to some, but catastrophic for others. In many
ways the field was never the same again, and when you read the
profiles here that I wrote so many years ago, some historical
context may be helpful.

The Readership

During the 1950s, very few people took science fiction seriously.
Payments were meager, critical recognition was nonexistent, and
writers were scorned for "juvenile escapism" and "wacky ideas."

By the 1970s, writers such as Asimov, Heinlein, Herbert,
Bradbury, and Clarke were no longer considered wacky. Some of

3

them even found themselves on *The New York Times* bestseller list.

By the 1980s, some books that had sold originally for around $2,000 had spawned sequels that sold for 100 times as much.

Alas, the rising tide of popularity did not benefit everyone equally. For most writers, the trickle-down from huge financial successes of Heinlein or Clarke turned out to be relatively disappointing. This was only just becoming apparent when I started interviewing people for *Dream Makers*.

The Editors

Prior to the mid-1960s, science fiction had been primarily a short-story medium molded by magazine editors such as John W. Campbell (at *Astounding Science Fiction*, later renamed *Analog*) and H. L. Gold (at *Galaxy*). They exerted a strong stabilizing force and demanded stories that made plausible sense. These demands were not always entirely satisfied, but at least there was a shared goal which I would define as rigorous extrapolation.

By the late 1970s, control over the content of science fiction had mostly diffused among a miscellaneous assortment of book editors, many of whom had shallow roots in the field and little interest in rigor. Few had time for the type of editing that used to be done, where concepts were developed interactively with writers.

The long-term effects of this transition were just beginning to be felt when I conducted my interviews.

The Content

The changes in the field were catalyzed by a movie named *Star Wars*. It opened up a huge new potential audience for science fiction.

Personally I regarded it as a disappointing mélange of second-hand imagery compiled by a facile idiot-savant. It tapped the collective unconscious of science fiction without displaying any comprehension of its higher brain functions.

Worse, it was implicitly anti-science. This became painfully obvious at the climax, when a young protagonist with a winning grin and a mall-rat haircut pushed aside his computerized bomb sight, preferring to "go with the flow of the force." That is, he spurned technology in favor of delusional wishful thinking. As George Lucas said in a *Rolling Stone* interview at the time: "I just wanted to forget science...I wanted to make a space fantasy."

Fair enough, but *Star Wars* ripped off the iconography of science fiction, and looked like science fiction, and therefore it was seen as science fiction. For an entire new generation, it defined science fiction. Even if they had understood the idea of rigorous extrapolation, they would have had no interest in it.

This did not go unnoticed in book publishing. Judy-Lynn and Lester del Rey led the way, serving as enablers for George Lucas by publishing tie-ins that were not just derivative, but were derived from something that was itself derivative. This was a smart long-term investment; by the beginning of 2014, between 400 and 600 *Star Wars* tie-ins had been published (the exact number is hard to determine), about half of them by Del Rey Books.

The del Reys also pioneered an entire new intellect-impaired category of fiction inspired by the unexpected commercial success of a whimsical Luddite named J. R. R. Tolkien. They broke new ground by launching an imprint solely devoted to fantasy, and populated it with medieval adventures by Terry Brooks and the cheerful nonsense of Piers Anthony's *Xanth* novels.

Science fiction traditionally had appealed to a relatively small audience of technophiles. By contrast, *Star Wars* and heroic fantasy reached out to a much larger audience of people who didn't understand science and were sometimes even hostile toward it. Since they outnumbered the nerds by at least ten to one, editors who had no special loyalty to science fiction responded accordingly.

To clarify the division that opened up, consider a book such as

Michaelmas by Algis Budrys, which was published in the same year that *Star Wars* was released. This was a genuinely predictive tour-de-force, displaying a breathtaking understanding of the potential of distributed computing power and artificial intelligence. Budrys had high ambition, formidable intelligence, a sensitive understanding of human relationships, and an ethical purpose. These attributes earned his book a flattering review in *Newsweek*, but its relentless realism was of little interest to readers who wanted laser-sword duels, a beautiful princess, villains in silly costumes, and space "fighter planes" with wings that somehow worked in a vacuum. *Michaelmas* was not a big success.

In 1985, a few diehard writers were still honoring the old imperative to build a future that worked, using technology that made sense. *Schismatrix* by Bruce Sterling was an example. Complex, challenging, and uncompromising, the book was singularly dense with ideas, but did not enjoy great sales, as it was incomprehensible to the popcorn-multiplex crowd whom Lucas had seduced with vapid nonsense and eye candy.

After *Schismatrix*, Sterling dabbled in journalism for a while, shifted into writing techno-thrillers, and became a prognosticator on the lecture circuit. As for Budrys, he wrote only one more novel during the thirty-one years of his life following *Michaelmas*.

The Outcome

This, then, was the context in which I interviewed writers for the *Dream Makers* books. The changes in science fiction were visible, but their long-term consequences were not yet clear. No one realized, for instance, that when an enlarged potential readership provoked an editorial obsession with bestsellers, the diversion of money to the bestsellers would eventually starve the midlist—those books which were above the level of formulaic fiction, but lacked mass-audience appeal.

Likewise, a few more years passed before everyone saw that

the "singular" novel (that is, an individual book that had no sequels) was becoming an endangered species. For decades, they had been the norm in science fiction. From Robert A. Heinlein to Philip K. Dick, everyone wrote them. But as publishers generated more titles, and the battle for bookstore shelf space became more intense, the advantages of a trilogy became obvious. A reader who bought the first volume would be likely to buy the second, and the second could help to keep the first in print. By comparison, singular novels began to look like orphans.

For publishers and retailers, an open-ended series was even better than a trilogy. A new sequel to an old book would also be welcome, and if the creator of the original work was uninterested in writing more of the same, a new species in publishing known as a "packager" would hire a lesser-known writer as a stand-in.

In this environment, relatively few writers managed to flourish by doing what they had always done. Frederik Pohl was a fine example. Others tried to survive through adaptation; thus Brian W. Aldiss stopped writing singular novels long enough to create his *Helliconia* trilogy, Thomas M. Disch conceived *The M.D.* as the first of a series, Philip José Farmer wrote more *Riverworld* novels, and Michael Moorcock recapitulated Elric of Melnibone.

Even aging and death could not interfere with this process. When Frank Herbert died, his son perpetuated *Dune*, and when Arthur C. Clarke became too old or tired to embark on a new series, John Baxter was ready to do the heavy lifting.

Writers who were less willing or able to adapt became marginalized as they found their audience shrinking and their advance money diminishing. Harlan Ellison, Norman Spinrad, Algis Budrys, Robert Sheckley, Keith Laumer, Poul Anderson, Alfred Bester, John Brunner, and Fritz Leiber all had a presence in the field when I interviewed them. The 1970s had been the summer of their careers—an Indian summer, perhaps, but still, a benign time. Twenty years later, those who were still alive were struggling. A few, such as Norman Spinrad, persisted in writing work that was iconoclastic and challenging. They paid a heavy price financially. Others, such as Budrys and Bester, simply gave up.

About this Book

Let me now deal with some practical matters regarding this edition of *Dream Makers*.

First and most obviously, a reader may wonder why it includes such a small subset of the original fifty-seven profiles.

This is a matter of economics. Stairway Press felt disinclined to publish a print version that contained more than 120,000 words, and my editor had to make some hard choices regarding the names to include. He wanted writers with name recognition and profiles that he felt were memorable. I added a couple of requests but generally acquiesced to the author list because I respect editorial decisions that are influenced by practicalities.

The list of writers who have been included will inevitably rouse criticism on grounds of gender imbalance. I say "inevitably" because the original *Dream Makers* was targeted with this criticism, and the new edition is even less balanced than the old. Twenty-three of the authors here are male, while only one is female.

The reason is obvious. Most people who wrote science fiction in the 1950s, the 1960s, and even the 1970s were male.

In *Dream Makers II*, I regret that I yielded to a female editor's demand for an ideologically driven quota system. The result was that I interviewed several people whose work did not happen to appeal to me personally.

This was a mistake. A memorable interview requires a rapport between two people, which becomes vanishingly unlikely if the interviewer has no great affection for the work of the writer.

Personally I don't see why it should matter that a writer is male or female, any more than it matters whether the person is fat or thin, young or old, or white or nonwhite. So far as I'm concerned, people are people and writers are writers.

The content of each profile in this edition has not been updated. My precept was that the personality of a writer is relevant to our understanding of his work, and the environment of the writer is relevant to his personality. Each profile was therefore a snapshot in time, using a wide-angle lens. The only way to create an updated version would be to re-shoot the whole thing from scratch, which is impossible.

As for the sequence of profiles, I have done my best, this time around, to make them strictly chronological. I was able to determine this with some confidence because I spoke the date at the beginning of almost every interview tape, and those tapes are still playable. In the first edition of *Dream Makers*, approximate dates were included, but they were the dates when I wrote the profiles, not the dates when the recordings were made.

Over the past three decades, many people have suggested that a third book of profiles would be desirable. It would include important writers such as William Gibson, Greg Bear, Kim Stanley Robinson, Richard Kadrey, Rudy Rucker, Bruce Sterling, Michael Blumlein, and many others who emerged in the 1980s and subsequently.

Unfortunately, in today's book business, a project such as *Dream Makers III* would not be economically viable. I received royalty advances of $6,500 and $12,500 respectively for the original Berkley editions. Those advances were necessary and sufficient to enable me to visit many people scattered across Britain and the United States. Allowing for inflation, I would need perhaps $30,000 for a similar project today.

The idea is absurd. I doubt that any publisher other than a small press would want the project, and I would be lucky to receive a royalty advance of $5,000.

The changes in book publishing have affected me along with everyone else. The *Dream Makers* books were midlist titles. It is possible that a third volume could be financed using a crowd-funding system such as Kickstarter, after which I would self-publish it. My daughter Rose Fox, who is a reviews editor for *Publishers Weekly*, has offered some creative ideas along these lines.

I think it could work if various incentives were offered, such as MP3 interview clips for the major donors, but to do it successfully I would have to be a different person. I've never been good at the financial aspects of business, and I derive no pleasure from them.

Therefore, I strongly suspect that the profiles from the 1970s and 1980s are the only ones I will ever write. This is not such a bad thing. Having complained that writers should do something new instead of creating endless sequels to their old work, I should probably follow my own advice.

If more profiles are really desirable, perhaps someone else will write them.

—Charles Platt

Northern Arizona, April 2014

Charles Platt

Isaac Asimov

New York City, June 21, 1978

OF ALL SCIENCE-FICTION writers, none is more prolific than Isaac Asimov. From science-fiction novels (*Foundation, The Caves of Steel*) he moved on to science-fact articles (more than 300 for *Fantasy and Science Fiction* magazine alone) to an endless proliferation of nonfiction books demystifying microcosm and macrocosm for the masses. He has authored exhaustive reference tomes, little pieces in *TV Guide*, quixotic items such as three volumes of "lecherous limericks," *The Sensuous Dirty Old Man*, a new annotated *Don Juan*, and a 640,000-word autobiography (this work alone is as long as a dozen science fiction novels put together; longer than Nixon's memoirs).

He is so prolific, in fact, that some reviewers decided his name must be a pseudonym shared by a consortium of authors pooling their collective energies. In truth, there is only one of him, and he works entirely unaided, typing the first and the final draft of each manuscript himself, handling his own mail, answering his own phone. He does it all with a very modest little reference library, a cheap pocket calculator, and a remarkable memory.

He lives in an expensive but characterless New York high-rise—one of those modular towers with little fountains out in front and plastic chandeliers in the lobby. The sprawling penthouse

11

apartment that he shares with his wife Janet is on the thirty-third floor, overlooking Central Park.

There is a comfortable, contemporary living room, but no time for more than a glimpse of it. With vague, awkward gestures (he is not a graceful man) Asimov ushers me quickly down a hallway to a door with his name on a plastic plate beside it, like an M.D.'s office. "In these two rooms is where I work," he tells me. "Even my wife must knock on this door, to come in. I always do say 'come in,' but she has to knock anyway."

This private Asimov zone is less fulsomely furnished. His writing room is almost primitive. A cheap gray metal desk stands in the middle, facing a blank white wall. There are stacks of neatly labeled metal drawers. Very tidy, very bare. The shades are down over the windows, obscuring what must be a fabulous view of the Manhattan skyline. "I prefer working by artificial light," he tells me. In truth, this guide to distant galaxies, this seer of stars and spaceflight, doesn't like heights, won't ever fly in airplanes, and generally keeps as close to Planet Earth as possible. It's no deprivation, because he isn't interested in travel anyway. "In my mind I have gone all over the universe, which may make it less important for me to make piddling little trips. I did visit England, by ship, in 1974. I did enjoy seeing Stonehenge." He shrugs. "It looked exactly the way I thought it would look."

We sit in his "library" (which contains fewer books than the living rooms of most authors I know). He makes himself comfortable in a wrinkled undershirt, as if deliberately wanting to seem unimpressive, uncharismatic. Still he has a conscious Presence, an obvious pleasure in being Isaac Asimov. He's blunt ("I hate giving interviews," he says, as I turn on my tape recorder), but in the forgivable manner of a crusty middle-aged eccentric. He makes me feel an intruder in his precisely scheduled working life, but at the same time he obviously likes to be available. In the years before he turned himself into a corporation, his name was openly listed in the phone book. He can even be gregarious in his own way, to the extent that work permits:

"I work every day from the time I wake up to the time I go to sleep—with plenty of interruptions. For biological functions: eating, eliminating, sex." He counts them off on his fingers. "For social interruptions: well, you have to go out and see your friends." I comment that he makes it sound less entertaining than staying home typing. "If that's how it sounds, maybe that's what I mean. Then there are business interruptions, like business lunches." He looks at me. "*You* count as an interruption."

His social ambivalence and self-imposed work ethic go back a long way. "I had in many ways a deprived childhood...I had to work in my father's candy store, I didn't play with the other kids much, I wasn't accepted by them. But what I chiefly wanted to do was read, anyway. So it didn't bother me much."

Perhaps to compensate for the alienation that he never recognized or admitted, the teenage Asimov started a meticulous diary. At first it was purely to keep track of baseball—"A whole series of double-entry bookkeeping devices"—but when he sold his first science-fiction story at age eighteen, the diary—"filled with microscopic writing"—started logging his career instead, still with the same obsessive attention to detail, constituting a private reality where everything was neatly organized and itemized.

His first sale was to John W. Campbell, Jr., editor of *Astounding Science Fiction* magazine. "I fell under his spell. He filled me with enthusiasm. He made science fiction the most exciting thing in the world. I celebrate my fortieth anniversary of my first sale on June 21." And now, as we talk, he suddenly realizes: "Oh my goodness!" His voice rises in pitch. He slaps his cheek. "Is *today* June 21? Oh my goodness! Today is the fortieth anniversary of the first day on which I walked into a science-fiction magazine— *Astounding*—and met John Campbell! Oh my goodness." He sits back in his chair, looking stunned. "Oh that's frightening—I might have—I have only four hours more to remember it in!" (During our whole conversation this was the only time he showed any emotional reaction or loss of equilibrium.) He shakes his head and pulls himself together, with some effort. "Well, anyway, June 21, 1938 was the day I first walked into John Campbell's office, and this is June 21, 1978. Well, gee."

Writing mainly for Campbell, he quickly gained a reputation among science-fiction readers. Many early stories were about robots; paradoxically, he admits he knows nothing about engineering, couldn't fix his own typewriter if it went wrong, and was never good at laboratory work. "I'm strictly an ivory-tower person. I can explain things but I can't do things."

His ability to explain things was what finally made him well-known outside of science fiction; but it didn't happen quickly. "It wasn't until I was past forty that it was at all clear I was going to be, quote, successful, unquote." And he says he was never aiming for success anyway. "I was, if anything, less ambitious than my friends. In a way I aimed low. I was perfectly satisfied to write science fiction knowing it would pay very little, that it would be seen by very few people."

In his recent collection *The Bicentennial Man*, he wrote: "My only large interest is in writing. Selling is a minor interest, and what happens after that is of almost no interest." Sitting with him in his library, I quote this to him with some skepticism, but he remains adamant. "I don't care for instance if a book of mine is sold to the movies," he says. "I don't care if a book of mine is advertised or promoted. No, I really don't care. If my publishers for their own reasons are anxious to enlarge my audience, I won't stop them. But I'm not sufficiently interested to goad them on to do so. I'm much more interested in writing my next book. As long ago as twenty years my first wife said to me, 'You can make a living if you just type for half a year, and we can have a vacation for the other half,' and I said, 'Sure but during the vacation, just to give myself something to do, do you mind if I continue typing?' When I was in the hospital with my coronary for sixteen days, my wife brought in my manuscript of my autobiography so that I could edit it in pen

14

and ink while I sat there. As soon as I was finished with that they had to discharge me because it was clear that sitting there with the job done was not going to be good for me."

I ask him how it feels to be *prevented* from working. "I suppose partly I feel guilty, because I should be writing. The writing is clicking away in my head and piling up, and unless I get it on paper somehow it's going to create uncomfortable pressure in my skull." Not a very clear explanation, from an expert in the biological sciences; and he seems to realize this. "It's difficult to say; I don't generally analyze how I feel," he apologizes.

He's much more lucid about objective matters. The facts and figures of the future: "My feeling is that the chance of our surviving into the twenty-first century as a working civilization is less than fifty percent but greater than zero. There are several items, each one of which is sufficient to do us in. Number one is the population problem. If we multiply sufficiently, then even if everything else goes right we're still going to ruin ourselves. Unfortunately it's difficult to make people see this, but I imagine that the time will come very shortly in which a third child will be outlawed, by prohibitive taxation, or forcible sterilization after the second child. Only two things will prevent this. One: If nonviolent means of reducing the birthrate prevail; in other words, if human beings *choose* not to have too many children. Two: If the population problem overtakes us so that the world is reduced to chaos and anarchy before we can even try drastic measures."

Is he generally pessimistic? "I'm pretty *optimistic* as far as the solving of problems that *don't* primarily involve human beings. For instance I believe it's not going to be very difficult to set up solar power stations in space to supply us with all the energy we need, if we're going to consider it as a technological problem. But if you say, 'Do you think we will be able to persuade Congress to supply the money for it?' And, 'Do you think we will be able to persuade the people of the world to drop their competitiveness and cooperate on a task which is perhaps too great for any one nation?'

Then you see the problem is perhaps impossible of solution."

I ask what people should do on a grass-roots level. He sighs. "Oh, join organizations...I can't participate in a nuts-and-bolts way partly because I don't have the style, the manner of life for it." He looks uneasy and, again, I feel his estrangement, his preference for solitude and retreat. "I tend to send money to lots of people who ask me to send money. I belong to almost any population organization that you can name: Zero Population Growth, the Population Institute, National Organization of Non-Parents, and so on. Also I support women's rights, which I consider essential to our survival, because I think the most logical way to reduce the birthrate is to raise the social status of women."

He recites all this quickly and precisely, in sentences that are always grammatical and devoid of the hesitations that one hears in most people's conversation. He must have said it all before, in lectures, in print. It's probably all in one of his 300-odd books.

Before I leave he insists on showing them to me, each volume neatly numbered and placed in chronological sequence: tangible evidence that you can make a private obsession become a public reality, that you don't need ambition or avarice so long as you have the willpower to apply your talent unrelentingly enough.

Yet it's not really a matter of willpower. Asimov's daily diary may sound like conscious self-surveillance, monitoring his own performance, and he does seem impelled to work by guilt and a sense of obligation; still it would require willpower for him *not* to work. The work is both his hunger and his feast. He enjoys the occasional diversion—he says he watches TV and his favorite sitcom is "Laverne and Shirley"—but you can tell that ultimately his true delight is retreating to his expensively spartan penthouse workroom, artificially lit at all times, like a basement. There, avoiding interruptions, evading self-analysis, he gets on with the job. He doesn't have to tell himself to keep at it, any more than he has to tell himself to keep breathing.

Work first, social obligations second, everything else third. This simple, rigid set of priorities is the "mystery ingredient" in Isaac Asimov's prolific success. For most of us, life is never so simple; our ambitions are mixed, our work lives, love lives, social lives, and fantasy lives compete and conflict, and our priorities fluctuate. Even when we think we know what we really want, we may secretly know that next year we could feel differently. Few can say, *this* is the most important pursuit in my life, and it always will be.

Asimov has apparently been able to say it about his work since he was a teenager. "I started writing in the 1930s when I was eighteen years old. And deep inside me I'm still eighteen and it's still 1938."

Historical Context

Because this was my first interview in the *Dream Makers* series, I was too inexperienced to know how to encourage a reticent person to talk about himself personally, and I hesitated to venture into sensitive areas. Thus I failed to describe some controversial aspects of Isaac Asimov's public persona which contrasted oddly with his body of work yet were well known to those who encountered him at informal events.

Long ago, when I was attending a science-fiction convention in New York, a party in one of the hotel suites became too noisy and hot, so I walked out into the corridor to continue a conversation with a friend. Several other people made the same decision, and were chatting quietly nearby.

A man came striding purposefully toward us along the corridor. He had a regal air and was wearing a black cape, like Darth Vader without the mask. He grabbed the hand of the first person he came to, showing no awareness that his brusque interruption might be unwelcome. "Hi, I'm Isaac Asimov," he said. He moved on to the next person, and the next, grabbing each person's hand and repeating his self-introduction without making eye contact or pausing for a response. We stared after him in stunned silence as he continued into the party suite without a backward glance.

Later, at the same event, I was talking to a female friend when Asimov again introduced himself, this time just to her. She barely had time to say her name when he dragged her toward him and tried to kiss her on the mouth. "What's the matter?" he asked, as she struggled to avoid him. "Do you think I have syphilis?"

Many science-fiction writers are solitary by nature, and tend to become awkward in social situations. I like to think that this kind of behavior was Asimov's way of compensating. The incident above was not unusual—Ed Ferman, who used to be the editor and publisher of *The Magazine of Fantasy and Science Fiction*, recalls that when he and his then-girlfriend attended their first science-fiction convention, "My father introduced me and my date to Asimov, who, instead of shaking my date's hand, shook her left breast."

This brings to mind some text from *The Sensuous Dirty Old Man* (1971), which Asimov wrote under the pseudonym "Dr. A.":

> *Now a lovely girl walks past you with a dress whose neckline is generously loose and under which there is clearly and obviously no bra. What do you do?*
>
> *You can emit a melodious whistle or a snort of pleasure. You can stare openly. You can walk over to get a closer view. You can address the girl in friendly fashion.*
>
> *And how does the girl react? She is pleased that she has created such an obvious stir in a gentleman of such substantial and prosperous appearance. She realizes that you agree with her own opinion of herself and this can't help but impress her with the excellence of your taste.*
>
> *Seeing in you a person whom she can respect, she will think, "What a nice, gentlemanly old man," and will smile at you. From that to a friendly word or two is but a step, and from that to a pat on the cheek or some slight pressure on the upper arm is but another.*

I think he felt that as a well-known (and generally well-loved) author, he was entitled to his eccentricities. He certainly felt that they were harmless.

After I interviewed him in 1978, he continued living in the same apartment and continued to follow the same relentless work habits. He was producing nonfiction books exclusively, which was easy for him, because he had a truly exceptional eidetic memory. All he had to do was write down what he had already memorized by reading other reference books, while making it more accessible to a general audience. His *Asimov's Chronology of Science and Discovery* (1989) is an astonishing example of his ability to digest, sequence, and integrate a huge quantity of information. *Asimov's Chronology of the World* (1981) was equally remarkable, and his *Understanding Physics* series (in three volumes, all 1966) remains one of the best introductions to the field.

The content of his writing changed around 1980 in response to demands from his editor at Doubleday, who begged him to add more volumes to the *Foundation* trilogy. Two sequels and two prequels were eventually written. The first sequel, *Foundation's Edge*, won a Hugo award in 1983. Two new Elijah Baley / "robot" novels were also published, in 1983 and 1985.

During an informal conversation around this time, Asimov told me that he was unhappy about his return to science fiction because each novel required twice as much writing time as a comparable nonfiction book. I think he was happy, though, about getting into the bestseller list in *The New York Times*.

He died in New York City in 1992, at the age of 72. Ten years later it was revealed that the myocardial and renal complications which had killed him were a consequence of an HIV infection that had occurred during a previous heart bypass operation.

Thomas M. Disch

New York City, March 28, 1979

NEW YORK, CITY of contrasts! Here I am on Fourteenth Street, walking past The New School Graduate Faculty, a clean, modern building. Inside it today there is a fine museum exhibit of surreal landscape photography, but the drapes are permanently drawn across the windows because, out here on the stained sidewalk, just the other side of the plate glass, it's Filth City, peopled by the usual cast of winos, three-card-monte dealers, shopping-bag ladies festooned in rags and mumbling obscenities, addicts nodding out and falling off fire hydrants. Fourteenth Street, clientele from Puerto Rico, merchandise from Taiwan. And *what* merchandise! In stores as garish and impermanent as sideshows at a cheap carnival, here are plastic dinner-plates and vases, plastic toys, plastic flowers and fruit, plastic statues of Jesus, plastic furniture, plastic pants and jackets—all in Da-Glo colors, naturally. And outside the stores are dark dudes in pimp-hats and shades, peddling leather belts, pink and orange wigs, and afro-combs...itinerant vendors of kebabs cooked over flaming charcoal in aluminum handcarts...crazy old men selling giant balloons...hustlers of every description. And further on, through the perpetual fanfare of rap

---

[1] Photograph by Ulf Andersen.

music and car horns, past the *Banco Popular*, is Union Square, under the shadow of the Klein Sign. Klein's, a semirespectable old department store, was driven out of business by the local traders and has lain empty for years, but its falling-apart facade still looms over the square, confirming the bankrupt status of the area. While in the square itself—over here, brother, here, my man, I got 'em, loose joints, angel dust, hash, coke, THC, smack, acid, speed, Valium, 'ludes, Seconal, Elavil!

Union Square wasn't always like this. Michael Moorcock once told me that it acquired its name by being the last major battlefield of the American Civil War. Foolishly, I believed him. In truth, there are ties here with the American labor movement: many trade unions are still headquartered in the old, dignified buildings, outside of which stand old, dignified union men, in defensive lunch-hour cliques, glaring at the panhandlers and hustlers toting pint bottles of wine in paper bags and giant twenty-watt ten-band Panasonic stereo boom-boxes blaring hits from radio station WBLS.

Oddly enough I am looking for an address, here, of a writer who is known in the science-fiction field for his civilized, almost elitist, sensibilities. He has moved into an ex-office building that has been converted from commercial to residential status. Union Square is on the edge of Chelsea, which is supposed to be the new Soho, a zone where, theoretically, artists and writers are moving in and fixing up old buildings until, when renovations are complete, advertising execs and gallery owners will "discover" the area and turn it into a rich, fashionable part of town.

Theoretically, but *not yet*. In the meantime this turn-of-the-century, sixteen-story, ex-office building is one of the brave pioneer outposts. I am admitted by a uniformed guard at the street entrance, and take the elevator to the eleventh floor. Here I emerge in a corridor recently fabricated from unpainted sheetrock, now defaced with graffiti, but high-class graffiti, messages from the socially-enlightened tenants criticizing the owner of the building for his alleged failure to provide services ("Mr. Ellis Sucks!" "Rent

Strike Now!") and here, I have reached a steel door provisionally painted in grubby latex white, the kind of paint that picks up every fingermark and can't be washed easily. There's no bell, so one has to thump the door panels, but this is the place, all right, this is where Thomas M. Disch lives.

Mr. Disch opens the door. He is extremely tall, genial and urbane, very welcoming. He ushers me in, and here, inside, it really *is* civilized. A thick, new carpet and new couch and drapes and a fine old mahogany rolltop desk—and a view over Union Square, which is so far below that the dope-dealers dwindle to insignificance. It's charming, and so is Mr. Disch, hospitably offering a wide variety of edible and drinkable refreshments. Not such an imaginative variety as is available from the natives in the square, but he offers them with considerably more graciousness and finesse.

New York, city of contrasts, also is city of high rents, so that even a relatively well-to-do, quite successful writer in his middle years has to resort to unlikely neighborhoods to beat the accommodation problem. But Thomas Disch has traveled so widely and is so adept at living almost anywhere, he makes the outside environment seem immaterial. It is Disch's nature to make himself at home by sheer willpower, never ill-at-ease or out-of-place, regardless of circumstances. Perhaps it is his tallness, perhaps it is his implacable control and elegant manners; he always seems to be both part of the environment and at the same time distanced from it, as if on a higher plane altogether.

Similarly, in his writing: he has traveled widely, through almost every genre and technique: poetry, science fiction, nonfiction, movie scripts, mysteries, historical romances. And in each field he has made himself at home, never ill-at-ease or out-of-place, writing with the same implacable control and elegant manners.

Take, for example, his ventures into the science-fiction field. He has logged quite a few years in this literary ghetto. Yet he has always remained a visitor rather than a member, part of the environment and at the same time distanced from it, with his own ironic perspective. This has not always gone down too well with the ghetto-dwellers themselves—the long-term science-fiction residents. Some of them have been unhappy about an elegant aesthete like Disch "discovering" their neighborhood and using the cheap accommodation for his own questionable ends.

Disch's first novel illustrates the point. Science-fiction readers recognized it immediately as an aliens-invade-the-Earth story, in the tradition of H. G. Wells's *The War of the Worlds* and a thousand others. There was only one snag: in all the other novels of this type, Earth wins and the aliens are vanquished. In Disch's novel (cheerily titled *The Genocides*), Earth loses and the aliens kill everybody. It almost seemed as if Disch was deliberately making fun of the traditional ways in which stories had always been told in the science-fiction field.

Naturally, he sees it differently. "To me, it was always aesthetically unsatisfying to see some giant juggernaut alien force finally take a quiet pratfall at the end of an alien-invasion novel. It seemed to me to be perfectly natural to say, let's be honest, the real interest in this kind of story is to see some devastating cataclysm *wipe mankind out*. There's a grandeur in that idea that all the other people threw away and trivialized. My point was simply to write a book where you don't spoil that beauty and pleasure at the end."

To the science-fiction community, Disch's ideas about "beauty and pleasure" seemed a bit depressing, and they accused him, and have continued to accuse him, of being a pessimistic author. He responds:

"What sort of *criticism* is it to say that a writer is pessimistic? One can name any number of admirable writers who indeed were pessimistic and whose writing one cherishes. It's mindless to offer that as a criticism. Usually all it means is that I am stating a moral position that is uncongenial to the person reading the story. It means that I have a view of existence which raises serious questions that they're not prepared to discuss; such as the fact that man is mortal, or that love dies. I think the very fact that my imagination goes a greater distance than they're prepared to travel suggests that the limited view of life is on their part rather than on mine."

Comments like this lead, in turn, to other criticism—for instance, that Disch is setting himself up as an intellectual.

"Oh, but I've always taken it for granted that I'm an intellectual," he replies ingenuously. "I don't think of it as being a matter of setting myself up.

"My purpose in writing is never to establish myself as a member of a club. I don't feel hostile to my audience, indeed I'm fond of it, but to write other than what delights *me* would be to condescend to my audience, and I think that would be reprehensible. I think any writer who reins in his muse for the sake of some supposed lack of intelligence or sophistication on the part of his readers is...well, that's deplorable behavior."

So Disch has consistently written at a level which pleases himself, and has consistently been misunderstood by many science-fiction readers as a result. His novel *334*, a gloomy vision of America in the future, was if anything less well-received by such readers than *The Genocides*, and was condemned as being still more depressing—even nihilistic.

"Well, nihilism is a pejorative that people throw out by way of dismissing an outlook," he replies. "It was one of [Nixon's vice-president Spiro] Agnew's words. Agnew loved it because it means that someone believes in nothing and, of course, we *know* we don't approve of people like *that*. But it also throws up the problem of what do *you* believe in. God? Is he a living god? Have you seen Him? Do you talk to Him? If someone calls me a nihilist I want the transcripts of his conversations with Jesus, till I'm convinced that we're not brothers under the skin."

And about the book *334* itself:

"I think what distressed some people is that it presents a world in which the macroproblems of life, such as death and taxes, are considered to be insoluble, and the welfare system is *not* seen as some totalitarian monster that must call forth a revolt of the oppressed masses. The radical solution shouldn't be easier to achieve in fiction than in real life. Almost all science fiction presents worlds in which social reform can be accomplished by the hero of the tale in some symbolic act of rebellion, but that's not what the world is like, so there's no reason the future should be like that."

Is this an argument that all fiction should be relentlessly tied to present-day realities?

"I'm not saying that every writer has to be a realist, but in terms of the ethical sensibility brought to bear in a work of imagination, there has to be some complex moral understanding of the world. In the art that I like, I require irony, for instance, or simply some sense that the writer isn't telling egregious lies about the lives we lead."

I reply that it isn't necessarily a bad thing if readers look for some simplification of the eternal problems of real life, or at least a little escape now and again.

"People who want that are certainly supplied with it often enough. Of course there's no reason that artistry can't be brought to bear upon such morally simplistic material, but it remains morally simplistic, and to me it will always be a lesser pleasure than the same artistry brought to bear on morally complex material. The escapist reader wants a book that ends with a triumph of the hero and not with an ambiguous accommodation; I suppose I'm inclined to think that you can't have it that way. I don't know people who have moral triumphs in their lives. I just know people who lead more or less good lives.

"A literature that doesn't try to mirror these realities of human existence, as honestly and as thoroughly and as passionately as it can, is being smaller than life. Who needs it?"

Tom Disch was born in Iowa in 1940 and grew up in Minnesota, first in Minneapolis-St. Paul ("Always my growing-up image of the big city") and then in a variety of small towns. "I went to a two-room country school for half of fourth grade...finished fourth grade in the next town we moved to in Fairmount, Minnesota, which is in the corn belt...."

At the age of nine he had already started writing: "I filled up nickel tablets with science-fiction plots derived from one of Isaac Asimov's robot mystery stories. If we could find those nickel tablets I'm certain that the resemblance would be astonishing. But I think *my* stories were livelier even then." He laughs happily.

"I remember a moment in tenth grade in high school, talking to my English teacher—I was always the pet of my English teachers and made them my confidantes—and I envisioned two alternatives. One of them would have kept me in the twin cities on the paths of righteousness and duty (I can't remember what that would have been, exactly), the other was to come to New York and become an Artist.

"My first job after high school, after taking some kind of test at the state employment center, was with U. S. Steel as a trainee structural steel draftsman. I stuck it out through that summer till I'd saved enough money to come to New York. Then in New York I got the lowest type of clerical jobs.

"I wanted to get into Cooper Union, to the architectural school. My idea was to be Frank Lloyd Wright. Cooper Union did accept me. Even though the tuition was free, I still had to work as well, and in the end I just collapsed from overwork and possibly from lack of real ambition to be an architect. Architects have to study a lot of dull things for a very long time and I probably wasn't up to it."

Disch returned to college later, but: "The only purpose I had in mind then, for any degree I might have acquired, would have been to become an academic, and I thought it would be better to be a writer, so as soon as I sold my first story I dropped out of college."

Supposedly, a major factor that influences people to read a lot of science fiction, and then write it, is a sense of childhood alienation. I ask Disch if he had that experience. He is skeptical:

"*All* young people are prone to feel alienated, because that's their situation in life. Very often they haven't found a career, don't have a social circle they feel is theirs, and they feel sorry for themselves, accordingly. Certainly it is something real that happens to you, but with luck you work your way out of it and soon your social calendar will be filled and you won't complain about alienation any more. You'll get married. Very few married men with children complain about alienation."

Disch himself seems unusually gregarious, for a writer, and many of his projects have been written in collaboration with various other authors. His first collaborator was John Sladek. "We started writing together in New York in the summer of 1965, just short japes at first, and then two novels. One was a gothic which is best forgotten. The other was *Black Alice*." (A mystery/suspense novel.)

"My experience of collaborating with other writers is just mutual delight. One person has a good idea and the other says, that's great, and then what-if.... When you write in collaboration with a person whose work you admire, miraculously, sections of the book are done for you, it's like having dreamed that you wrote something, it eliminates all the real work of writing.

"I've planned other collaborations. I've worked with composers on a small musical and an opera, and I just like the process of it. I would like to write for movies. Other writers complain about the horrors of dealing with directors, but if it's a director one admires I would think that it would be exciting, and if it's not a director you admire then you shouldn't be doing it. It would be difficult to share my own earnest novels; but for comic writing, for instance, I should think it would be so much more exciting to write for *Saturday Night Live* than just to write humorous pieces for magazines, however great your inspiration."

The range of people with whom Disch has worked reflects the range of different forms of writing that he is interested in. "Part of my notion of a proper ambition is that one should excel at a wide range of tasks. I want to write opera libretti; I want to write every kind of novel and story. I've written a lot of poetry and I will continue to do so. I foresee a pattern of alternating between science-fiction novels, and novels of historical or contemporary-realistic character."

I ask if he isn't worried that this will give him too diffuse an image in the minds of publishers, who are generally happier if a writer can be given a single genre label.

"Publishers do feel more comfortable with you if you are, in a sense, at their mercy. They prefer you to be limited as a writer. If you're a science-fiction writer who begins to write a kind of science fiction that isn't to the taste of a publisher whom you've been working with, they will in effect say, stick to what you know best, go back and write the kind of book that has made you successful. If you are a genre writer, then genre editors can dictate to you the terms of the genre. In the long term they're asking for the death of the imagination, and a dreary sameness of invention, plots, and characters is the result."

Since Disch has managed to avoid being typecast in this way, I ask him which matters more to him: success and recognition in the science-fiction field, or outside of it.

"I would suppose that any science-fiction writer would rather be successful in the big world than in the small world. The rewards are greater. Not simply financially, but the rewards of public acclaim. If the approval of your peers means anything, then the approval of more of your peers must mean more. And not all of the palates that you want to tickle, the critics you hope to please, are within the science-fiction field. In fact the big judgment seat is outside of it."

I ask if Disch's best-known novel, *Camp Concentration*, was an attempt to achieve recognition outside of the science-fiction field.

"*Camp Concentration* was a science-fiction novel, and I think it was probably not strong enough to stand on its own outside the genre. Not as a work of literature. It might have been marketed as a middle-brow suspense novel—some science fiction is smuggled out to the real world in that disguise—but I think the audience outside of science fiction is even more resentful of intellectual showing-off, while within science fiction there's been a kind of tradition of it. Witness something like Bester's *The Demolished Man*, which was in its day proclaimed to be pyrotechnical. Pyrotechnics are part of the science-fiction aesthetic, and that's what *Camp Concentration* was aiming at.

"In America the novel didn't receive very much attention and it became the focus of resentment for some of the fuddy-duddy elements in science fiction to carp about. I never had enough success with the book to make me seem a threat, and I'm not much of a self-promoter, so the book just vanished in the way that some books do. And that's not entirely a bad thing. The kind of success that generates a lot of attention can be unsettling to the ego, and the people who have that kind of success are often encouraged to repeat it. It would have been a very bad thing if I had bowed to pressure to write another book like *Camp Concentration*, which was the expectation, to a degree, even in myself. For a while I wanted to write things that were even more full of anguish, and even more serious."

Camp Concentration is the diary of a character who is locked up and given a drug to heighten his intelligence, an unfortunate side-effect being that the drug induces death within a matter of months. The book thus presented a double challenge to Disch: he had to write the diary of a man who knows he is going to die, and he had to write the diary of a man whose intelligence is steadily increasing to superhuman levels. In a way it was a self-indulgence—a conscious piece of self-analysis—in that Disch himself is aware of his intelligence to the extent that it is something of a fetish.

While he was working on *Camp Concentration*, he confided to Michael Moorcock (as Moorcock tells it), "I'm writing a book about what everyone wants the most."

To which Moorcock replied: "Really? Is it about elephants?"

"Elephants? No, it's about becoming more intelligent."

"Oh," said Moorcock. "What I've always wanted most is to be an elephant."

Talking to Tom Disch, I recount this anecdote, if only to check its accuracy. Disch laughs and comments, "Well, I guess Mike Moorcock and I have both realized our secret dreams."

Historical Context

Tom Disch was not good at making predictions. When I first read his novel *334*, which was written in 1972 and described the United States fifty years in the future, I couldn't understand why he insisted on describing a world in which hope no longer seemed to exist. When I asked him about it at the time, he seemed genuinely puzzled. "But this is the best possible future I can imagine!" he exclaimed.

Recently, when I took another look at *334*, I saw the problem clearly. It shows technology empowering the state, but does not recognize that it may also empower the individual. In Tom's vision, everyday people are powerless. Quite often, their aspirations are met with punishment.

The idea that science can help us to transcend our human limits was central to American science fiction when Tom began his writing career. Likewise, countless science-fiction stories depicted a resourceful individual overcoming entities that were more numerous and more powerful than himself. How perverse, then, that Tom's first novels constituted a rebuttal to the field in which he chose to write. It was as if he was trying to *set people straight*, telling the writers who had gone ahead of him that they were mistaken in their fundamental assumptions.

If Tom were alive today, I would suggest to him that when he wrote *334*—or his novel *Camp Concentration*, which retold the story of Faust—he was looking at the past rather than the future. By the 1960s it should have been abundantly clear that a net positive benefit can be derived from science. In fact, rather than being a fatal flaw, hubris can be seen as a prerequisite for progress.

In my imaginary conversations with Tom, I tell him that although he rejected the Catholicism of his youth, and mocked religion in much of his writing, he was perpetually afflicted by the absolutist mindset of the church and its visions of an angry deity who spent an inordinate amount of time punishing people.

Unfortunately, even if Tom were still alive to hear my arguments, I doubt that he would listen to them, because—well, he usually didn't listen very well. During the waning days of our long friendship, when my girlfriend and I invited him to dinner, he was quite self-absorbed. After consuming two bottles of wine in short order, he expounded lyrically about the success of his play, *The Cardinal Detoxes*, and assured me that it was such a seminal work, it would be performed for decades to come. He described himself as the world's greatest living writer of blank verse. And then, on a tangent, he told me that I really should read the story "Apt Pupil" by Stephen King.

I pointed out that I had recommended that same story to him several months previously. "You know," I said, "you don't listen very well."

"Well, why should I?" he responded. "You aren't as widely read as I am, you don't write as well as I do, and you don't even make as much money as I do. Why should I care about your opinions?"

The next day, I waited for an apologetic phone call. Around 10 PM, when no call had been forthcoming, I called him, and he brushed the whole thing aside. "You have to make allowances," he said, "for my extreme ego."

When I first immigrated to New York from England in 1970, Tom had been witty, gregarious, intellectually playful, and extremely generous. He cooked me many meals, introduced me to many people, and helped me to establish myself in the city. When I wrote a couple of poems which I thought were of little value, he tried to persuade me otherwise by quietly placing them in a well-regarded poetry magazine. When he became affiliated with the prestigious PEN club, he saw to it that I was inducted as a member. There were many similar kindnesses.

Perhaps the difficult, bombastic Tom became more dominant as the years passed because his successes were never great enough to satisfy him. Any writer who refers to his own "extreme ego" is liable to find the rewards from the publishing industry inadequate.

His Wikipedia entry is quite lengthy, and I suspect that he wrote much of it himself, because only he could have known all of the minutiae. The catalogue of achievements is impressive—yet there are many ventures which never paid off in the long term.

His science-fiction novels were commercial failures, as he once admitted to me; so he stopped writing science fiction. His attempts to write collaborative gothic and historical novels were not successful enough to encourage more of the same. His story "The Brave Little Toaster" was made into a Disney movie, and spawned one sequel, but did not open a path to screenwriting. His text-based computer adventure game did not do well. His two plays did not ultimately lead to a theatrical career. Perhaps the reason he returned to writing poetry throughout his whole professional life was that it was the one field in which he was enduringly successful.

Back in 1970, when we were all young and had big, vague plans, I remember him talking to myself and Norman Spinrad about a novel that he hoped to write. "Sounds like you want to do a bestseller," Norman remarked.

"Oh, I do," Tom said. "I want that so much."

About fifteen years later, his outlook had soured. He arrived unexpectedly at my Greenwich Village apartment in a state of agitation. He was dressed in a suit and tie, having just come from a meeting with a publisher. He had wanted a lot of money for a project, and his demands had not been met.

Tom paced to and fro. He was palpably angry, denouncing the publishing industry, wishing he could somehow—well, set them straight. "I want to——" He groped for words. "I want to——to make them——suck my dick!" He slumped down on the couch, depleted by his own anger.

While I have never shared Tom's ideas about the inevitability of punishment, or his assumptions about the consequences of hubris, perhaps they seemed valid to him personally. His high ambitions as a writer entailed no small amount of hubris, and indeed he was punished for it, if only by himself.

Frustrated by his own declining value as a novelist, he began writing a public entry on LiveJournal in which he pontificated against the status quo. Most of the entries were pleasant enough, but in one instance he became downright nasty. Upon hearing that Algis Budrys had died, in June, 2008, Tom headed his journal entry, "Ding dong, the witch is dead!" and continued, "what a long wait it's been...I get to dance on his grave." Budrys's great crime had been to write a very negative review of *The Genocides*, more than forty years previously.

By this time, Tom was tormented by health problems, had lost his lifelong lover, and was having difficulties retaining the lease to his New York apartment. Less than a month later, after most of his possessions in a house he owned in Pennsylvania had been damaged by a flood, he ended his own life with a gunshot.

I had not communicated with Tom since 1998, when he had been terminally offended by my response after I received a copy of his critical book *The Dreams Our Stuff is Made Of*. While he seemed to feel that this was an important work, summarizing his personal outlook on science fiction, I considered it intemperate and poorly researched. It paid little attention to what anyone else might have to say, and——yes, it was still trying to set people straight.

I didn't know what to do with it. I don't like to keep books that I don't like, but I don't like to throw them away, either. I couldn't think of anyone else I could give it to. I tried to get the local library to take it, but they refused. In desperation I sent it back, explaining that it wasn't really my kind of book, and he should give it to someone who would appreciate it, because a book should not be wasted.

I should have known what would happen, and perhaps I did know. This may have been a passive-aggressive moment on my part—an opportunity to show Tom what I thought of his writing, since he had felt so free to tell me about my writing. In any case, he stopped speaking to me—permanently, as it turned out.

Fortunately I did my *Dream Makers* interview when he and I were still on very good terms. When I showed him the transcript afterward, he was pleased with it. Normally, he said, he was too annoyed to answer people who complained that his fiction was depressing or nihilistic, but perhaps because I was a friend, and he felt that my motives were honorable, he was able to address the complaints seriously. He felt that he had vindicated himself.

Sometime around that time—maybe in 1981—I remember sitting on a bus with him, heading up Sixth Avenue on our way to see a play. We were talking about friendships, and the difficulty of sustaining them. "Really, it's amazing that anyone stays friendly with anyone," he said, with a sigh. "But you and I, we'll always be close."

Alas, that was another of his predictions which turned out to be wrong. I regret that, because regardless of his bombast, Tom was such an exceptional person. I feel privileged to have known him so well during the 1970s and the 1980s, when he was still full of creative aspirations, before the punishments had become too much to bear.

He died on July 4, 2008. Sometimes I wonder if he had been waiting for Algis Budrys to go first.

Frederik Pohl

Red Bank, New Jersey, April 24, 1979

IN *NEW MAPS OF HELL*, a notorious, eccentric study of science fiction published at the beginning of the 1960s, British novelist Kingsley Amis singled out Frederik Pohl as the best American science-fiction writer.

This choice surprised a few people—not because Pohl had a mediocre reputation (quite the contrary) but because he was less noticeable than writers such as Asimov, Bradbury, Clarke, Heinlein, or even Bester. Pohl did not have such a distinctive voice; indeed, most of his well-known novels of the 1950s were duets performed with C. M. Kornbluth. His prose was always efficient, but seldom stylish. The subject matter he chose, and the worldliness he applied to it—that was what mattered.

Together, Pohl and Kornbluth pioneered and excelled in a completely new kind of science fiction. They invented and played with "Sociological SF"—alternate futures here on Earth, exaggerating and satirizing real-life social forces and trends that most other science-fiction writers seemed too removed from contemporary reality to understand or perceive clearly. This sophisticated material was a powerful but difficult form to write. Few people handle it with finesse even today, and Hollywood has never begun to master its subtleties (movies like *Soylent Green* and

THX 1138 are hopelessly simplistic attempts).

The problem is that good sociological SF requires broad-ranging insights into everything from politics to organized crime, economics to advertising, mass-media to big business. These are the forces that have molded twentieth-century life, and they are likely to endure, stemming from such bedrock motivations as greed, ambition, power, and fear. Pohl and Kornbluth understood it all, better than anyone else around, and so their future scenarios remain the best of their kind, always plausible and often disturbing.

Kornbluth died tragically young, in 1958, but Pohl has continued to work vigorously as a writer, as an editor, and as an activist who has gone out and tried to apply some of his sociopolitical perceptions in the real world. He has written a nonfiction guide to politics, has run for political office himself, has addressed business groups, and has even worked for the State Department, lecturing throughout Eastern Europe.

In the science-fiction world he has edited various magazines, including *Galaxy* and *If*. As an editor at Bantam Books he published controversial novels such as Delaney's *Dhalgren* and Russ's *The Female Man*. Most recently he has written memorable novels (*Gateway*, *Jem*) which are winning at least as much praise as the work which first attracted Kingsley Amis's attention twenty years ago.

Born in 1919, a published writer by 1937, a magazine editor by 1939, Pohl has ended up not necessarily the "best" but probably the most multifaceted and enterprising writer of his generation.

His home is in Red Bank, New Jersey, which is one of a series of smallest towns along the East Coast about forty miles below Manhattan. There is a center of old buildings around the railroad track; further out, there is the inevitable sprawl of gas stations and mini-malls and drive-ins and modern factories that have grown as the population has grown. Once, Red Bank might have been an idyllic retreat; now, it is enmeshed in a long wide, suburban strip.

Pohl's residence is a charming old three-story wooden-sided house, set back a little from a two-lane highway, overlooking the

Navesink River. Traffic moves slowly along the highway and over the bridge that spans the river. Small boats pass by, and occasionally you hear a train on the railroad just across the water. These noises filter into the comfortable old building, as if one is on an island surrounded by methodical, unseen movements of trade and commerce.

Various family members occupy the lower two floors, and Pohl has the whole top story to himself. There are four rooms, and the decor is, shall we say, casual: painted floorboards, faded cream-color walls, dusty carpets here and there. At some point in the past, well-constructed and well-finished bookshelves were installed in each room, but it's been a while since then and things have become less well-organized. Not all the books are on the shelves; in fact they are stacked anywhere they can be stacked, and the place looks like a middle-aged bachelor pad. Odd items of clothing, old envelopes, boxes, empty coffee cups, tape cassettes, mementos, ashtrays, and other bric-a-brac are scattered across floors, chairs, and tables. The roof has leaked over some of Pohl's collection of magazines which he once edited. His shelf of Hugo, Nebula and other awards is covered with dust. But it doesn't matter; he's seldom here anymore—he travels a lot.

Personally I find the place immediately comfortable, a relaxed, lived-in, worked-in space without pretensions. It is a world unto itself (most of the drapes are closed across the windows), obviously the retreat of a man whose imagination is more vivid to him than, say, the view of the river.

In the sort-of living room where we will sit and talk I find a pile of glossy color prints on the edge of a cluttered tabletop. They are photographs of Jupiter and Jupiter's moons—a NASA press release. Pohl himself was down at Cape Canaveral when the data transmissions were coming in from the Voyager probe that took these pictures. He and other science-fiction writers had to wait forty-five years to see images like these, and through most of that time they only had their private faith in an unrealistic dream to sustain them in the face of apathy or ridicule from a general public that didn't believe in space travel until the 1960s.

Looking at these close-ups of the face of Jupiter, a truly alien world of infinite mystery, I feel a twinge of the old so-called sense of wonder that made me start reading science fiction in the first place. And I feel frustrated at the impossibility of ever going out there in person and seeing it with my own eyes. Pohl says he feels the same way, but, "I've just about reconciled myself to it." To judge from his tone of voice, he isn't reconciled at all. He is, I think, an uncompromising man.

He offers me instant coffee made with hot water straight from the faucet ("An awful habit for which I must apologize"), we clear some papers off a once-fancy, now-dusty fifties-style couch upholstered in gold fabric, and make ourselves comfortable. He talks very quietly, chain-smoking, and almost seems shy, which is surprising in view of the time he spends giving lectures and interviews. Indeed, he says he likes the sound of his own voice, and (unlike many writers) is quite happy to promote his own work. "Last fall I did a two-month tour for *The Way the Future Was* [his autobiography] and covered sixteen or eighteen cities. I enjoy doing that, in moderation."

More often, his public appearances have been in some consultancy role. "I've been involved in a great number of symposia and panels and management consultancies in the past. My impression is that the corporations and management groups that employed me wanted to shake them up a little bit and perhaps give them some new perspectives, but they were not inclined to heed what I said very seriously. I remember talking to a group in Chicago once and saying that the primary requisite for achieving a viable relationship between our society and the planet's ecology was individual self-control. They stood up and cheered me. Then the next speaker said exactly the opposite and they stood up and cheered him too.

"As a writer, I don't consciously try to spread a message most

38

of the time, but sometimes in the process of writing a story it becomes clear to me that there is something I want people to feel. I *am* a sort of a preacher. I like to talk to people and get them to change their views when I think their views are wrong. One way of doing this is to write; also, I have actually preached. I've taken the pulpit at the local Unitarian church eight or ten times, and probably twice that number of times at other churches. I was a trustee of the local church for a while. I think if I were not a writer, I would have had to be a preacher."

His most recent sermon in print prior to this interview was a conservationist message in the form of an article for *Omni* magazine, defining growth limits that are imposed by heat that is generated by civilization on Earth. Beyond a certain point, the heat will produce climatic changes, melting the ice caps and inundating coastal areas. Of all the limits to technological growth, this is the most immediate and unavoidable.

However, "An article like the one in *Omni* won't reach very many people who are not already of the same opinion as I am. Many people will say that I'm just telling them more gloom and doom and they don't want to hear it, because surely someone will think of something and there'll be a way around it. People who think like this are wrong, but I don't know how to get through to them.

"Generally, the human race avoids doing *anything* radical until forced into it. Having done it, I think people find they are better off. They don't go exploring until they're forced to, by famine, discomfort, or some sort of political or social force, but then once they get to the new place they kind of like it. This has been true in my own personal life. Most of the changes I have resisted most violently have turned out for the better. So I don't think that any real change in our global lifestyle is going to happen until things get pretty rough, and that part is not going to be a lot of fun. But after that, in the next stage, I have a lot of hopes."

Pohl believes that it may be more effective to preach indirectly, and science fiction can be a tool for accomplishing this.

"In science fiction one can say a great many things that are unpalatable and that people prefer normally not to think about. Because it's expressed as fiction, you can slip it through their defenses. Science fiction can provide all sorts of insights, into technology, natural resources, the grandeur of being out there in space, and they're all valuable. But that's not all that science fiction is good for. It is the only kind of writing that allows you to look at the world we live in and change one piece at a time. What I mean is the process of taking the world apart, taking some elements and throwing them away, replacing them with others and seeing how the thing works after that. I think that that is very valuable."

Certainly this technique, in its purest form, recurs in almost everything Pohl has written. I ask if there are particular themes or obsessions that recur, also.

"There are some doctrines or dogma, I suppose. One is that most of the problems of the human race are human inventions. We don't have severe natural enemies any more—wolves don't come through the streets of London carrying off babies. What endangers people in London or any large city are taxicabs, muggers, and so on. Therefore I think that the solutions to most human ills must be social solutions. I'm not as convinced as I once was that political solutions are possible, but some sort of social solutions are necessary, and that shows in most of what I write.

"Politically I was a Marxist as a teenager and a Democrat for about twenty years. I was a member of the Democratic Party and a committee man here; I ran for office once or twice and helped to elect other people. For the last ten years or so I've been an agnostic politically. I just don't know."

With all his other activities, I ask how he manages to fit writing in.

"I write while I'm traveling. Four pages a day, wherever I am. About two years ago I reinvented the lost art of handwriting; I was getting in trouble with stewardesses, using my typewriter on planes. Since then I've been quite free.

"When I first began writing I taught myself to do first drafts only. The trouble with that was that although I got some of it published, it just wasn't any good. Because I have no willpower, and can't trust myself to continue to do anything for very long simply because I know that it's right, I had to *trick* myself into revising, by writing first drafts on the back of correspondence, envelopes, circulars, any typeable surface that I couldn't possibly submit as a manuscript. So I *had* to rewrite them at least once. Now, I do at least one complete rough draft, and one complete retyping, and I often rewrite sections, some of them over and over again, and then when it's finished I edit it carefully. I spend more time revising than I do writing; I'm not sure why.

"I feel very badly if I don't write. I think I write unless I feel so depressed and miserable that I can't get out of bed, which doesn't happen often. I like to write; it's partly an escape and partly therapy. It's a good way to release tensions and subliminate aggression and dispel hostilities."

I am curious as to whether these purely internal needs were what motivated Pohl to start writing originally, and what ambitions were involved.

"Like most immature and incompetent writers, the principal thing that I wanted was to see a story that I had written in print, because of the vanity and the romantic notion of being a writer. I suffered from that for a long time, but something happens after you've done it for a while, and you begin to feel other desires and other ambitions. I'm not sure that I can articulate them, but they involve saying something that hasn't been said before. I don't know how often I succeed, but I sure as hell try. I've often failed: I have cabinets full of stories and books that are failures and are not ever going to be published." He gestures to a pair of black four-drawer file cabinets. "Seven or eight times," he goes on, "I have been under contract to write a book and have received an advance, and have later returned it because the book didn't work out."

I ask what his ambitions are now. Does he, in fact, have any left?

"It's true, I have very few unfulfilled ambitions. I'd love to be president of the United States but that's not really an ambition, that's only wise counsel to the voters, which they are not prepared to accept. I don't really have urgent ambitions, except to do specific things, like write specific books, and if I live long enough I'll do them. There's nothing that seems to be out of reach, there's nothing that requires the grace of God. It's just a matter of completing projects, rather than trying to attain something that I can't find the handle for."

Through all of this, we have discussed Pohl's personal decisions and preferences. In reality, though, an individual writer has limited free will, if his writing is also his major source of income. To what extent has Pohl's work been influenced by commercial factors?

"I think most of the books that I published up until five years ago certainly would have been rewritten a little more if I hadn't needed to deliver them to get paid. I don't know if they would have been different books. On occasions when I have tried to do something because I thought there was a lot of money in it, it has usually bombed disastrously. The stuff that I wrote for love has worked out much better. All of the science-fiction novels I wrote, alone or in collaboration, are still in print somewhere and are still producing income. The buck-hustles are dead; none of them ever amounted to very much.

"Science-fiction writers as a class, I think, respond poorly to money. If they have too much of it they either become impossible to live with or they stop writing. When I left *Galaxy* it was my own firm intention to spend a lot of time writing, in the spring of 1969. Unfortunately Ballantine Books reissued eighteen of my books and paid me for all of them, so I had no incentive to write, and I didn't, for a year or two. And I didn't feel good about it. I felt unemployed, not doing anything and not wanted for anything. But if I'd had to finish a book in order to pay the mortgage or feed the kids, I would have done it.

"I think during the forties and fifties, in particular, the pressure of getting work written to sell to a magazine for the only check you ever expected to see produced some really good work. The best work of people like William Tenn and Damon Knight, Robert Sheckley and twenty or thirty others, came around that time for that reason. Cyril [Kornbluth] too—he was writing against the mortgage payments all that time, under pressure, and doing some great stuff.

"Today, for some writers, that pressure is not so intense. Science-fiction writers are better-paid than they used to be. I understand the floor [minimum acceptable bid from a publisher] on Heinlein's new novel is $500,000. Incredible. Half a million would have paid every science-fiction writer alive for everything they wrote for ten years, in the thirties." He does a quick mental calculation. "In fact, there would probably have been a couple hundred thousand left over."

Can people be taught to write, in college courses?

"I have mostly negative feelings about such courses. They emphasize the wrong things about writing: how to spell and punctuate, use alliteration, how to take apart a published story. They do not emphasize what seems to me to make one story better than another, which is the personal viewpoint of the person writing it—his own perception of the world. You really can't teach that. People either have something to say or they do not. There are many people who want desperately to be writers and have no talent; there seems to be no way to graft it into them, and they're the ones who show up for writing courses."

Pohl is more positive about the role of an editor in influencing the development of a writer. Like many science-fiction authors, he admires the late John W. Campbell, Jr., who edited *Astounding Science Fiction* magazine (later retitled *Analog*) and strongly imposed his ideas on the writers who sold stories to him. However, times have changed:

"There could not be a John W. Campbell today. He would find some new writer, as he did with Heinlein or van Vogt or L. Sprague de Camp. He would hang on to him for two stories and then Bantam Books or Pocket Books would be bidding for that author's novel and he'd be gone, which would be very satisfactory for him, but would make it impossible for someone like John to change the whole field around as he did. In fact it would make it impossible for him to help writers learn their craft.

"There is no editor in the science-fiction field now who has any real control over what happens. There just is not a place or publisher who defines the field or even defines his part in it. It has become big business, where books are merchandised and promoted and distributed and placed on sale like slabs of bacon or cans of soup.

"One of the reasons I left Bantam [where he had been their science-fiction editor] was that the joys of editing, for me, involve finding something that no one else has seen the wisdom of publishing, and making it go. That is not the skill that's in great demand in major paperback publishing houses. They don't forbid it—I had complete freedom at Bantam and they encouraged me to do what I wanted to do. But I was playing the wrong game for their field.

"What I really like is editing a science-fiction magazine. The big advantage of a magazine is that it should reflect the insanity of one individual, so it has a personality. I would have liked to take over at *Analog* [following the departure of Ben Bova, who inherited the job after John W. Campbell's death]. But I think probably they were reluctant to see any changes in the magazine, and I would surely have changed it."

I remark that in the time Pohl worked for Bantam Books, he bought some remarkably experimental and innovative material, which seems surprising in that during the 1960s some "new wave" science-fiction people had condemned him for being a conservative.

"But back then I was editing for *Galaxy* magazine, and I

published the majority of 'new wave' writers," he points out. "Aldiss, Ballard, Ellison. It wasn't the stories I objected to, it was the snottiness of the proponents. I don't think the 'new wave' has actually died; it still survives in everything that is being written today, just as James Joyce survives. The thing that the 'new wave' did that I treasure was to shake up old dinosaurs, like Isaac [Asimov], and for that matter me, and Bob Heinlein, and show them that you do not really have to construct a story according to the 1930s pulp or Hollywood standards. This is a valuable thing to learn. I don't think I could ever have written *Gateway* if the 'new wave' hadn't happened. And I'm more pleased with that than any other book I've ever written."

I inquire what other influences have affected his work, and what his reading habits are.

"I read most of the science journals and magazines. I average about a book a day, and from time to time I realize there's a big hole in my education that I need to fill. Lately I've been reading nineteenth and early twentieth century writers; and Shaw plays, most of which I had read before when I was a teenager. I found myself with a copy of one in my hand and enjoyed reading the passage from it, so over the last couple of months I've read almost all of them over again. Then from time to time I go back and reread science fiction that I love. Edgar Rice Burroughs, and E. E. Smith. Of the newer writers, I'm impressed by John Varley and George Martin. I think they're very promising."

It all sounds very busy—even the reading seems more like a workload than a recreation. I can't help wondering if he allows himself, or needs, any real leisure. The question causes a temporary halt in the conversation. "Well, I was wholly addicted to watching Kojak, as long as it was on television," he says. "I guess I loaf around a lot, too—my writing time is largely spent sitting at the typewriter mulling over the story and the world. I spend anywhere up to eight hours sitting at the typewriter without hitting one key, before I can find my way out of an impasse."

To me, it all sounds as if work is recreation and recreation is work, and Pohl is equally active in each. He is currently making some attempts to find a retreat.

"I'm shopping around for a new place to live. I'm not really living here," he gestures at the room, in its casual disorder. "I'm only here when I'm not traveling. I haven't yet found the perfect place, but I can describe it. It needs to be warm in the winter and not to have hurricanes or revolutions or civil disobedience or too much street crime, and it should be within reasonable distance of a major airport in case I want to go somewhere else. I've been looking in the Caribbean lately. A couple of months ago I tracked down an island called Grand Cayman, but that didn't work out. I like being isolated. I think I'm overexposed to people because of doing so much lecturing and conventioning, and have become a lot less gregarious. A little isolation knits up my soul."

And I have no doubt that he will find it, and satisfy this need as he has satisfied his others. Frederik Pohl seems a slightly shy man, more self-analytical than other writers of his generation, carefully modest, and extremely complex. But he has a clear, quiet, deliberate determination; despite his low-key presence and his lack of a flamboyant identity he has asserted his will on the world perhaps more than any other science-fiction writer.

Historical Context

Frederik Pohl was the only person I profiled who made no reply at all after I supplied my text for his inspection. I sent him a reminder, to which he also made no reply, and then just went ahead and included his profile in the book. I never knew what his silence meant until years later, when I ran into him at some social event.

"That profile you wrote of me in *Dream Makers*," he said. "Was it complimentary?"

"Yes, I think it was," I said. "But didn't you read the copy that I sent to you?"

"No," he said. "I was afraid that if I didn't like it, I might be tempted to change it, and I didn't want to do that, so I decided that I shouldn't read it."

This, I think, sums up one aspect of Fred: fair-mindedness, governed by a surprising amount of objective detachment.

At another event, in a party in a hotel suite, I was waylaid by a writer who objected to some commentary that I had written about him in a semiprofessional magazine. He expressed his feelings by grabbing my collar and landing an ineffectual punch to the jaw. Such was his reputation for vanity and pugnacity, no one seemed to think much of it—except for Fred, who pushed through the crowd and strode over to me. I think it was the only time I ever saw him visibly angry. "If you decide to press charges," he said, "call me. I will be glad to testify on your behalf."

He was extremely serious in his opposition to any form of violence.

He was also a consummate diplomat. At yet another event, I found myself sitting opposite Fred at one of those big round tables that hotels set up for "banquets," with ten chairs around the circumference. By chance, none of the people at the table other than Fred and myself was professionally involved in book publishing. They were science-fiction fans, many looking a little surprised to find themselves sitting at the same table with Frederik Pohl.

Fred calmly took the initiative. One by one, he asked each person's name and came up with a few sentences of amiable conversation, to put them at ease. It was a masterpiece of diplomacy, and I complimented him on it afterward. He looked disconcerted, probably because he hadn't expected anyone to notice. I think this was the only time I ever saw him at a loss for words.

Many of his novels embodied his politically liberal principles and had social relevance. His novel *The Years of the City* depicted a future for New York which, though not utopian, was an idealized recipe for civilized progress. In 1980 his novel *Jem* achieved a rare distinction in science fiction, receiving a National Book Award.

Despite his interest in progressive politics, his writing stopped short of being sanctimonious. I regard this as a very delicate balancing act which few writers have achieved successfully in any category of fiction.

His memoir, *The Way the Future Was* (1978) remains an excellent guide to the history of science fiction, and he extended it in 2009 with "The Way the Future Blogs," a blog which is still archived online.

He died on September 2, 2013 after being admitted to a hospital suffering respiratory distress. He was 93.

Charles Platt

Kurt Vonnegut

New York City, May 3, 1979

FOR MORE THAN fifteen years, Kurt Vonnegut was a victim of the genre system of modern publishing. His books were labeled "science fiction" and were distributed as science fiction. Bookshops displayed them only on the science-fiction shelves, where respectable readers seldom ventured. During this period, which must have seemed interminable and horribly unrewarding, Vonnegut's novels (including *Player Piano*, *The Sirens of Titan*, and *Cat's Cradle*) were known only to science-fiction fans—and even the reception among them was lukewarm, as they suspected him of poking fun at some aspects of their genre (its jargon, in particular).

Then *Slaughterhouse Five* appeared at the end of the 1960s. Suddenly, everyone knew about Kurt Vonnegut. His early work was brought back into print, and it migrated from the science-fiction shelves to the "modern literature" section—where it was discovered by apostles of the counterculture, who adopted Vonnegut as a bashful new folk hero. His work became mandatory reading in college courses coast-to-coast, he went on lecture tours, and he renounced the science-fiction genre which had trapped him in obscurity. *Slaughterhouse Five* was made into a movie, and he received some of the critical appreciation that had been lacking for so long.

Today, the critics are not always so kind to his new work, but

Vonnegut no longer needs to worry. Each new book, he says, has an assured sale regardless of how it is reviewed, and the old novels continue to earn royalties. He doesn't have to write short stories for a living any more—in fact he *refuses* to write short stories. He is free to produce perhaps one novel every eighteen months, dividing his time between a residence in Cape Cod and a town-house in Manhattan, which he shares with photographer Jill Krementz.

This is where I went to visit him: a fine, imposing residence in the East 40s, renovated and restored in impeccable taste (cream-and-beige decor, unblemished parquet floors, oriental rugs, modern but unostentatious furniture, just like advertisements in *The New Yorker*). Vonnegut himself looks as if he doesn't quite belong here—he could do with a little renovation and restoration himself—but that's his public image, of course, the dissipated Einstein look-alike of literature, in garage-sale clothing of middle-aged style and vintage: sleeveless navy-blue sweater, nondescript shapeless grayish-brownish trousers with cuffs, and decaying sneakers.

He makes himself comfortable on a couch in a room upstairs where there is a large TV set, videotape recorder, capacious soft chairs, and many bookshelves. There are no fancy, leather-bound collectors' editions, or antique library ladders, or gilt-framed oil paintings, or other pretentious frills; everything is functional; this is New York City at its most civilized.

A small shaggy dog stretches out beside Vonnegut's knee and becomes comatose. We begin talking. His conversation is spotted with literary references (a kind of erudite name-dropping); he speaks very slowly, with long pauses, smokes a lot, and often scratches his disheveled curly hair. His voice is dry, and so is his humor; at times it is impossible to gauge how serious he is. He says that this is probably the only interview he will give this year. But there have been many interviews in the past—too many, perhaps—and it must be tempting to invent some new answers to the old questions, to make things more interesting, or simply to be playful. I sense a mixture of whimsy, black humor (he laughs loudest when he mentions death), capriciousness, and craziness; but it's all put across in such wonderfully deadpan style, and with such charm, it's impossible to say where sincerity ends and playfulness begins.

For instance, when I ask him how he feels about science fiction now:

"It's a social milieu. I went to a writers' conference in Pennsylvania years and years ago; they invited me and were glad I came. We got along fine as people, except that I didn't belong to their profession, because I couldn't talk about it. The problem is that I haven't done my homework. I haven't read all the stuff they have read. I'd hang around the drugstore like anybody else, as a kid, and I was always aware of the science-fiction magazines in the racks, but it never interested me much. You see, one thing that kept me from reading those pulp magazines, was that the *paper* was so unpleasant to touch." He pauses thoughtfully. "It was full of brown specks. Very unappetizing." And he chuckles, as if enjoying the absurdist answer he has just given me.

I ask if he feels that any of his books should have won one of the science-fiction awards that are voted each year. "I thought I should have won several times," he says, sounding considerably more serious, now. "I'm proud of *The Sirens of Titan*, and I thought it should have won that year. It was nominated. But Harlan Ellison said, 'You'll never win, the only way you can win is to have the book serialized in a science-fiction magazine, so forget about it.'" He shrugs.

Does he feel that his lack of acceptance by the science-fiction community had anything to do with the unseriousness in his books, which seemed almost to be satirizing science fiction?

"I can't imagine how you would *satirize* science fiction," he says, in apparent puzzlement. "Unless you were to demonstrate how badly written most of it is." There is a pause, as his mind wanders ahead. "There's a guy named Philip José Farmer—I've never met him, but he's a real meat-and-potatoes science-fiction writer, a very nice guy from all reports, and prolific. He asked me again and again, in the mail and through my publisher, if he could please write a 'Kilgore Trout' novel."

Kilgore Trout is a fictitious character whom Vonnegut has included in several of his books. Trout is a wretched, deteriorated, small-town journalist who produces reams of science fiction in his spare time and remains unknown, partly because his work is so atrociously written, and partly because it is distributed only through pornographic bookstores. Farmer wanted to adopt 'Kilgore Trout' as a pseudonym and bring to life one of Trout's imaginary novels.

"I finally told him to go ahead. There was no royalty agreement or anything. I sort of had the dream of giving a whole lot of people permission to write 'Kilgore Trout' novels, so the bookstores and church sales and everything would just have stacks of these shitty things around." He chuckles. "Anyway, the book came out, sold extremely well, but there was no evidence anywhere that *I* hadn't written this. I got a ferocious review in one science-fiction magazine, as though I had written the goddamned novel, and I got nasty letters saying, you'd do anything for money, you're ripping off your fans this way. Farmer refused to break security and admit he'd written the book; the secrecy was terribly damaging to me." [Farmer's recollection of events is different, and is presented in his profile a little later in this book.]

What about the period when Vonnegut was still relatively unknown outside of the science-fiction field? *Cat's Cradle*, for example, had to wait perhaps ten years to be recognized by the literary establishment.

"Yes, it was never reviewed. There was a newspaper strike on, when it came out...but a lot of my books have never been reviewed. A couple of years ago I was at a party for Doris Lessing, and she was talking to me about the book of mine, *Mother Night*, and I happened to tell her it had never been reviewed. So she immediately reviewed it for *The New York Times*, about twelve years after it had first been published."

I remark that he sounds oddly unconcerned about this

prolonged lack of recognition for his work. He thinks about this, carefully.

"I figured it probably wasn't much good," he says, with an ironic smile. "I've met so many people I like, who try hard, and really aren't very good. So I'm willing to believe I'm such a person. *Was* willing—I'm less willing now. But I mean, if that were the case, it would just simply be life. I've always been quite grown-up, or tried to be, about underpayments or failures in this business. I've taken it as routine. I got extremely lucky getting in touch with a publisher named Sam Lawrence, who has as a policy putting back into print any author he takes on. He's done this with Richard Brautigan, with J. P. Donleavy. He's connected to Dell books with a handshake; he simply got them to bankroll him. It's a magnificent policy of his to keep all his authors in print. There are damn few authors in this country who are completely in print. If I wanted to get the collected works of Norman Mailer, for example, I'd be shopping all over town for some of the books, and perhaps that's true of Philip Roth, too."

I ask if Vonnegut's body of work is pointing in any particular direction, and if he always has his future output planned.

"I have known people who live that systematically and rationally. Herman Wouk is a friend of mine; he has known since the end of the Second World War what books he wanted to write, and in all the books he's written so far there's just one violation of the plan, which is a very brief novel which he was so amused by, he had to do it. But I've just finished a book and I have no idea what I want to do next."

Surely *Slaughterhouse Five* is an exception, then, in that it must have been planned over a period of many years?

"Well, that was a command performance. When I found out that it [the destruction of Dresden] was the largest massacre in human history, I said, my god, I must make some comment on this. It was the first truly beautiful city that I had ever seen. I had no idea that such cities existed. No sooner than I had seen it, it was demolished. The Germans, incidentally, don't give a shit about the destruction of Dresden, or the destruction of anything else. It's a little strange that I should have cared and they don't give a damn. I think they're perfectly willing to rebuild anything." He laughs.

To me, the main message in *Slaughterhouse Five* concerns the futility of human life—a message that I find, more or less moderated, in Vonnegut's other work also. I ask him how he replies when people say that his work is too depressing.

He shakes his head. "But people *don't* say that." He smiles, and I feel my question has not so much been evaded, as stopped in its tracks. I start to protest that I can't be the only person ever to find a spirit of futility in Vonnegut's novels, but he goes off into a digression. "I used to speak a lot for money. I stopped when I had the American equivalent of a command performance before the Queen—to speak in the Library of Congress. I had this innocent country-boy manner there, a speech which had worked pretty well, time and time again. Then about halfway through a guy stood up, he was some recent arrival from a socialist country, Hungary or Bulgaria, I never found out. He said, 'What right do you have, as a leader of American youth, to make the young people in this country so pessimistic?' And I had no answer to this; it was such a startling question, and embarrassing in a way, that my speech was ended there. The books are certainly pessimistic...but so much of what depresses me is avoidable. Not by strokes of genius, but by ordinary restraint. A lot of the things that are wrong in the world could be put right by restraint. Just the chance of desolating the whole eastern seaboard with this cockamamie way of generating electricity, this crazy way to boil water...and the weapons we've built and all that...if we just *wouldn't do* a number of things, we'd be much better off."

This leads into my asking about his science background, which is evident in many of his novels and most obvious in *Cat's Cradle*, where one of the main characters is a physicist, apparently drawn from real life.

"Yes, the guy who was Dr. Felix Hoenikker in that book was modeled after Dr. Irving Langmuir, who was one of the few people in private industry who ever won a Nobel Prize. He was a surface chemist; my brother, who is a distinguished scientist, worked with him. But Langmuir was stubbornly absentminded, stubbornly indifferent to worldly matters, and this was a theatrical pose. People don't act that way anymore, because it's no longer fashionable. Fashions change in how scientists behave. When I worked for General Electric and reported on the activities of scientists there, it was fashionable for them to be sweetly absentminded, to have no sense of the consequences of whatever they might turn over to the company in the way of knowledge."

Are there exceptions, whom he admires?

"Well, a scientist I admire a great deal, of the same generation, is Norbert Wiener. At the end of the Second World War he wrote a piece for *Atlantic Monthly* which said he wasn't going to tell his government anything anymore, because they were liable to do almost anything with whatever levers he gave them. I think that's exactly right, that a scientist should be withholding things from a government all the time."

I ask how he got mixed up with science in the first place.

"My father insisted that I be serious about school, and he had an idea about what serious subjects were. My father and grandfather were architects in Indiana; so I might have been third-generation, that would have been terribly respectable, in an architecture firm in Indianapolis, and I wouldn't have minded that at all. But my father was feeling rather sorry for himself because he hadn't done any architecture for ten years because of the great Depression, so he told me to become a chemist.

"I went to Cornell and planned to be a biochemist. I took these Christ-awful subjects and was at the bottom of my class, always. At the same time they had a daily newspaper at Cornell, and it was easy for me to become a bigshot on that. I wrote columns for it, and fantasies, all sorts of irresponsible writing. Writing was something I could always do better than most of my peers, so, later, when I was working for General Electric and had two kids, and the company wouldn't give me a raise, it seemed to me I could probably make more money as a freelance, and that turned out to be the case. Anyone who could tell a story, in those days, was kind of a fool to have a regular job. The magazines that existed then paid so well."

So for some years he made a living by writing short stories, and took time off to write novels only when he had saved enough from the magazine work. Does he regret having had to do so much money-making writing, to finance his serious fiction?

"It makes me mad that I didn't have more money when I was younger, because I would have had a lot more fun, and so would my kids. There's that sort of regret. If I'd had a rich wife, or something, I would have written more novels; but I don't think I've lost anything, and any time you work in a restricted form you're going to force yourself to be more intelligent than you ordinarily would be. One of the wonderful things about structured poetry is that, in order to make a rhyme work or meter work, you use this or that wonderful word that you wouldn't use ordinarily, just to bugger the thing to work, and suddenly it's just exquisite. I think to write a conventional short story for a middle-class magazine is an interesting challenge. All the stories had to celebrate the middle classes in some way, otherwise I wouldn't have sold them. But I don't mind celebrating the middle classes that much. I mean, they must rescue the country; no one else is going to do it."

I mention that many writers I've talked to put their faith in science, rather than the middle classes, when it comes to rescuing us from the future. Vonnegut seems to become mildly irritated by this.

"It's just superstitious, to believe that science can save us all. Absurd. It's youthfulness, I think. It's like the science club at high school—they get excited—go out and capture asteroids—and maybe you can, but these aren't very grown-up people, most of them.

"We're starting to back down on a lot of our technology now. I think the whole country is going to start sorting through our technology to decide what is really good for us and what isn't. That's quite an interesting point to reach."

At the time of this interview, Vonnegut is preparing to go to Washington, D.C. to speak at a rally against nuclear power. I ask about his outlook on politics and economics generally.

"This nonsystem we have here?" He pauses. "Of course, it can't provide nearly enough jobs for people." Another pause. "But we do have these wonderfully motivated maniacs in private enterprise, who will go into, say, the tire business, and do wonderful things with tires, eat and sleep tires. Or TV repair. Or keeping elevators working. This is a very useful sort of nut. Socialism hasn't been able to turn up this sort of person. So I favor a mixed economy where you encourage these nuts to exist and make a few more rubles than their neighbors. They must be paid, although they don't have to be paid as much as they are now—these guys, when they really get going, start working extraordinary extortion schemes and get paid phenomenally for what they do."

The mention of socialism reminds me of an opinion I recently heard from Ben Bova (Executive Editor of *Omni* magazine, at the time of this interview). I mention Bova, and Vonnegut stops me, trying to place the name. He thinks about it for a long time. After much head-scratching he recalls that it was Bova who took him to an *Omni* lunch just a week ago, no doubt hoping Vonnegut might produce a story for *Omni*. Anyway, trying to get back to the subject, I describe Bova's opinion that socialism is "out of gas," and socialist countries will soon be forced to adopt some form of capitalism, in order to survive economically.

Vonnegut laughs. "That's asinine. It's so silly, no, obviously *we're* collapsing, and there's nobody paying attention at all, nobody has even tried to making a drawing of what the gadget is. I think the socialist countries are quite interesting."

He has continued to speak, on these various topics, in the same offhand, laconic style, ironically disengaged from the matters at hand. It keeps reminding me of the amused fatalism one finds in his writing, perhaps spelled out most clearly in *The Sirens of Titan*, where he depicts humanity as a blind mob pursuing high aspirations—which are in fact arbitrarily manipulated by higher forces, to satisfy trivial whims. To what extent does that book reflect Vonnegut's view of reality?

"Oh, it's just a book, people laugh at parts of it, and it has jokes in it," he says, playfully yet deadpan. "See, I got curious about—what if there were a god who *really did care*, and had things He *wanted done*." For some reason this notion strikes him as wildly funny; he goes into a protracting chuckling fit. "And how inconvenient that would be. The whole idea of a purposeful god is comical, I think. You know, what on earth could he want, shoving things around all the time, and giving us things."

Does the book still please him when he looks at it now?

"It's full of typographical errors," he says vaguely. "It began as a cheap paperback, and people have always set type from that original version. I've never changed any of the errors, though it would be the work of an hour to get a clean edition." He ponders for a moment, apparently about errors in other books. "In *Slaughterhouse Five*, I have a person dying of carbon-monoxide poisoning, and I describe the person as blue. In fact the person who dies of carbon-monoxide poisoning is a beautiful golden-rose color." He laughs, at this. "People usually say they've never seen him looking better." At this, he becomes convulsed with giggles.

When the mirth has died down, I try to ask another serious question. Does Vonnegut have a clear idea of his audience? Who, ideally, are his books aimed at?

"A friend of mine, Hans Koenig, a Dutch radical, he's lived here and in London, and he asked me what sort of person I wrote for. It's a person who is more intelligent than his place in society would indicate. Ideally that's the kind of person I would really be proud to have read me."

But was this the audience he was reaching in the late 1960s and early 1970s, when he was a minor hero to the counterculture?

"No, most of those people didn't read. My books and Tolkien's and Heinlein's *Stranger in a Strange Land* were *furniture*, you would come into a person's house and see the books lying around, and immediately know what sort of a person this was."

Going back to the kind of reader Vonnegut would prefer to reach—does he write novels in the hope of changing that reader's outlook at all?

"Oh certainly." There follows a very, very long pause. "I would like them to be better sports about disappointment than they are." He says it carefully and decisively. "I think people are bound to be disappointed in this life. I think this is comical, to be the sort of animal that wants this and wants that...it's not really the animal's fault, it's the nature of the planet, that most such animals are disappointed. I think this is funny, and something to learn to live with. You don't necessarily die from it." He chuckles. "It's an endearing sort of animal that would want all that. It's sweet."

He seems to be trying to strike a cheerful note. I remark that it still sounds a depressing outlook, to me.

"Well, all right." He seems to decide, wearily, to go through an explanation he has given more often than he would like. He starts counting points off on his fingers. "My mother committed suicide. Three months later, I was sent overseas. Five or six months after my mother's suicide I was a soldier in the Battle of the Bulge, which was the largest single defeat of American arms in history. Three whole divisions with all sorts of supporting crap, all lost. I saw that, and I know what it feels like. There was nothing I could do except endure, and try to integrate this sort of catastrophe into my understanding of life. And I got to Dresden and there's this city without even a cracked windowpane, and it was demolished, I saw the demolition of a major art treasure. And then I watched the Russian army come into Germany, in this irresistible wave. The human spirit must somehow be prepared to survive enormous catastrophes like this, and not hold ourselves responsible for it. What the hell was I going to do in the Battle of the Bulge—climb raging out of my hole blazing from the hip and hurling hand grenades in all directions? This idea that if you're down at the bottom of your society, it's your own damn fault, is intolerable to me. Broke, sick, or unhappy, very often it isn't your fault." He pauses for a metaphor. "There are sensational weather systems going around this planet, over which you have no control."

Historical Context

When I was wondering how I might get an interview with Kurt Vonnegut, I consulted a friend who seemed well connected in New York literary circles. "Just send him a letter through his publisher," she said. "He likes to encourage young writers."

I was 34 at the time, which was not exactly young. Still, I followed her advice. I wrote a very brief letter and attached a three-page sample of my writing consisting of the introduction to my profile of Thomas M. Disch. Sure enough I received a friendly response from Vonnegut, inviting me to visit him.

This was where I ran into trouble. While I felt reasonably confident while interviewing well-known writers ranging from Ray Bradbury to Stephen King, there was something about Vonnegut that unnerved me. I still don't quite understand how or why this happened, but my lack of confidence, coupled with his sardonic and sometimes dismissive responses, yielded an interview which never quite seemed to reveal the man and his work.

I had admired Vonnegut's early novels, especially *The Sirens of Titan*, but in truth I cared more for the "badly written" exercises in techno-optimism for which he showed little respect. Maybe that was the real problem: his worldview seemed strange to me, and in some aspects factually wrong. Today, it still seems that way.

He died in April, 1997 from a head trauma incurred by falling down a flight of stairs in his home.

Algis Budrys

Evanston, Illinois, May 10, 1979

I'M A FOREIGNER here; the most ordinary routines are strange. Chicago, is a world away from New York, which is a world away from my small-town British origins. Suburbia is a culture of conveniences, so everything is easy, but still strange.

Close by the airport I collect my rented car from a fenced compound. Then out along a concrete highway, in humid heat, following route directions typed meticulously by Algis Budrys (who is a meticulous man and, like myself only more so, a foreigner here). I traverse run-down Chicago suburbs, toward Evanston, just on the edge of the metropolitan sprawl. Totally mundane but alien scenery drifts past the windshield: Photomat, Wendy's Hamburgers, the White Hen Pantry, Mira-Kleen cleaners, a towel factory, Futuristic Fashions. The bumper sticker on the red Chevrolet ahead of me asks, Have You Hugged Your Kid Today?

As a foreigner, one has no skepticism. One believes anything. Change is an assumption of life. One expects to be surprised. At the same time this breeds a suspicion that nothing is as it seems, nothing is permanent—nothing is, ultimately, real.

This outsider's view of everyday life is a recurring theme in Budrys's writing.

Past a decayed shopping center, and across many railroad

61

tracks, here is Evanston, population 79,300. It looks greener, less industrial than its neighboring urban subcenters. I see tennis courts and baseball diamonds; and on Budrys's block there are ample trees, and grass beside the sidewalks. His front lawn is a cheerfully undisciplined carpet of bright yellow dandelions.

I find him in his basement, amid a jungle of bicycles and power tools, camshafts and dismantled washing machines, stacks of books, garden implements, coiled rope, and old overcoats. It's like a giant thrift shop run by an auto mechanic. He works in a section divided from the rest by bare brick walls. There are stacks of papers on shelves and on the floor. He sits on an office chair, applying an X-acto knife to a cardboard mask which he is making for a large black-and-white photograph. It's part of a promotional campaign for a Chicago jewelry designer.

Budrys, like the thoughtful, gentle men in his novels, has many areas of special knowledge. He applies them methodically. His role today is Freelance Media Consultant; down here in the dusty and cluttered, but cool and quiet basement he has been creating a whole advertising campaign—writing the copy, choosing the markets, supervising the photography, and handling little details like the photographic mask he is now finishing under the fluorescent light of his desk lamp. It's a long way from science fiction; but Budrys actually spends very little of his time writing science fiction, for reasons he explains to me later.

Before he leaves the basement he notices that one of the arms of his spectacles is loose. He opens a drawer and takes out a box of jeweller's screwdrivers. He selects the correct size of blade and carefully tightens the tiny screw in the hinge of his glasses. For a moment I see him as Martino, the prosthetic hero of his novel *Who?*, lecturing on the proper use and maintenance of machines. A gentle touch, and the right tool for the job; every item meticulously maintained.

He is a shy man who falls back on uneasy formal protocol when dealing with strangers; but, as he later tells me, he recognizes

62

a kind of science-fiction brotherhood. So I, a stranger, am welcomed into his home and meet his wife and two of his tanned, blond sons, and a large black cat which has no name, but does have a license—the Budrys family, concerned with local politics, believes there should be a local ordinance making cat licenses mandatory, and they are working to this end. Evidently, they are an active part of their community. And yet, as I say, Algis Budrys labels himself a foreigner. He has no passport. He is a citizen of Lithuania. His identity is as complex as Martino's—or those of his other protagonists, searching for the final bedrock truth in worlds where they suspect nothing is, ultimately, real.

The ground-floor rooms are shadowy and hot, strewn with books. It is a large, comfortable house. After dinner we talk out on the front porch. He speaks very slowly, with constant attention to the function of each word and the precise meaning of each sentence. He talks as if the parts of speech are like mechanical components, which must be selected and assembled carefully, in an exact sequence, in order to function efficiently and elegantly. Later, when I transcribe the interview tape, I find it is almost impossible to trim away any surplus wordage; Budrys only repeats himself when he feels his phrasing was not quite accurate the first time.

I often feel an author's origins are not very pertinent to his work, and in many profiles in this book, I have summarized the person's background as briefly as possible. But Budrys's conversation leads inexorably to his background, because his background not only explains who he is, it explains what he writes and how he sees the world. In his words:

"I'm basically a Lithuanian peasant, and there are centuries of acculturation behind me. I sit here passing for a middle-class American, but I'm not. I was raised by parents who had to endure a hell of a lot and had built in all kinds of cultural safeguards. I think the most noticeable ones were that you should toil incessantly, that you should let no opportunity pass to do something solid, and that there's something essentially rascally, insincere, and impermanent about someone who rises too high. The thing to do is not to rise, but to broaden out and let down more roots. I can laugh at all that stuff, but that does not change what happens inside my head.

"When my mother was eighteen or nineteen she already had an extremely responsible position in Lithuanian military intelligence. She came from a house with a tin roof that belonged to her father, the village tailor and sexton of the local Roman Catholic Church. I don't believe there was any inside plumbing; the source of water was a well outside; all the vegetables, and most other food, they raised themselves. The purpose of her going to the big city and getting a government job was to send money home and keep the land going.

"My father came from essentially the same kind of family, except that his father had already achieved a certain amount of status in the imperial Russian civil service, Lithuania then being a province of the Russian Empire. Dad followed him into it and had all kinds of adventures. When the Russian revolution broke out he was stationed in Vladivostok as a member of the imperial Russian military intelligence; he had to get home to Lithuania somehow, and it took him three years to do it, and he did it by way of China. When he died and I took a look at his insurance papers, it turned out there was a long list of significant scars including bullet wounds and saber cuts that he had picked up along the way, and I know he came extremely close to dying of typhus. His entire motivation was to get back to Lithuania, and do his duty. In fact he's the model for Colonel Azarin in *Who?*; put a little bit more of a smile on Azarin's face, and add the fact that somewhere there was a wife and a child of whom he was fond, though he wouldn't have much time for him—and Azarin is my father.

"My father was transferred into the Lithuanian diplomatic corps after about 1927, and he and my mother were stationed in East Prussia. We always lived in a hostile environment. The only two people that I could talk to intensely day after day were my mother and father; everyone else around me was a German. They were nice, pleasant people, very neighborly, and very loving toward this very Aryan kid. I had ash-blond hair—not merely blond, it was white—and I had these enormous blue eyes and these wonderful clean-cut features. That was before I got to weighing 250 pounds. I spoke German with such an impeccable East Prussian accent, and carried myself like a little soldier, they doted on me. And then they did something that completely changed my life.

"Adolf Hitler drove by our house a couple of times, and they went insane. Hordes of German housewives and househusbands, people that I knew, who were all living in the same apartment complex together, were tearing themselves psychically to pieces all over the sidewalk, just watching the man go by. They weren't simply shouting or clapping their hands or going 'hooray,' they were going through an animal frenzy to the point where some of them were having what I guess were epileptic seizures. Others were defecating in our bushes, couldn't control their bowels. I was four years old. I remember a guy hopping across our lawn with his pants around his knees, tugging desperately at his underpants, trying to get to a bush; and men and women rolling on the ground, writhing, clutching each other. A hell of a thing to see; I'm four years old and I suddenly realize that I know absolutely nothing about the world except that is populated entirely by monsters—werewolves. Naturally, I cling even tighter to my parents. But my mother has the duties that are attendant on her position, and my father is in a hostile country, doing everything he can to keep the Nazi revolution from spilling over into Lithuania. He had a very hard row to hoe, extremely conscious of the fact that with the first bad breeze that blows, Lithuania's going to be reoccupied by the Soviet Union.

"He indoctrinated me with self-discipline and patriotism. I used to hear very long, fervent speeches when I was five or six years old, and the last line was always, '*I* liberated Klaipeda [a seaport he attached to independent Lithuania], *you* will liberate Vilno.' It was going to be my duty in life to restore it to Lithuania, when I grew old enough. [It had been annexed by Poland.]

"A lot of my life when I was a small child was spent in cars, on trains, talking to strangers, speaking a variety of languages, never settling down anywhere, and feeling a great deal of hostility because German governesses hate the kids that they raise, and because I could look out the front window at night and see the Germans out there throwing bricks with swastikas chalked on them. Sitting in the dark on my mother's lap with no lights on in the apartment at all, except for the little green pilot light on the radiogramophone, and my father with a pistol in his lap just waiting for the Brownshirts to break in.

"And then, we moved to New York City, and there was a whole new set of things to learn. My father was consul general of Lithuania in the United States between 1936 and 1964. It was at his knee that I learned what's important about being a P.R. man. He eventually died at his desk, at the age of about seventy-five, having lived a life full of sixteen hour days. He was on his eighth heart attack when it happened. Each time they released him from hospital, he went right back to sixteen-hour days.

"So, I came over to this country when I was six. I very quickly acquired the accent and mannerisms of a born American. I'm almost totally American-educated. I'm married to this nice American lady and I have these fine strong sons all born in this country, and they don't speak a word of Lithuanian. But I do not come from the same place that most people in this country come from.

"I've always had the consciousness that there were larger destinies to be worked out, responsibilities extending beyond one's personal family; you spent your life in the service of an ideal, and toiled for it. I think this accounts for a lot of my naiveté when I was in my early twenties; and it explains to some extent what it was about science fiction that really got to me, that made it a very special thing. It offered me the thought that although life contained some very wild changes, it was possible to live with change.

"My way of looking at science fiction is all wrapped up in a series of quasi-mystical ideas that I gained as a kid, having to do with the nature and the worthiness of science fiction. I'm now forty-eight years old, and I think I read my first science-fiction story when I was eight. The books that I had read before then that I can recall were aviation books and the complete, as-written-by-Defoe, *Robinson Crusoe*—not a child's version. My sister started reading it to me, and I grew impatient with the process and learned to read so I could finish the book.

"Around the age of ten or eleven I decided that it would be a rare and wonderful thing to be able to produce science fiction; this was the very best thing there was to be. I developed the delusion that science-fiction writers were not only a breed apart, but extremely high-cut, and if you were the kind of person who was capable of having his name published in *Planet Stories* or *Thrilling Wonder Stories*, the world would yield up Rolls Royces and homes in California. I assumed that people had cars and homes and girlfriends like that because they were *worthy* of them, not because they had done something that was then paid for, and they converted the money into acquisitions.

"I'm alarmingly stupid in many ways and still to this day I'm equipped with any number of pieces of hard-won practical knowledge which I don't really believe in, because they are not in accord with the instinctive notions I developed as a kid. I'm a romantic. I think worthiness is the key concept behind it all. One of the questions I consider when a story occurs to me is: This story might be all right for somebody else to write, but is it worthy of me?

"When I came to Manhattan from Long Island, as a fellow who had sold a couple of stories, I had absolutely no compunctions about turning to people who were practically strangers, and saying, Do you mind if I move in with you for a while? Because we were all members of the great science-fiction brotherhood. It was as if there was this big house populated entirely by science-fiction people and by right I had a place in that house somewhere, as we all did. It's amazing how tolerant the world can be. My first story had sold to Campbell; I had made it, essentially, first-crack. Somewhere in my mind I equated that with reaching a permanent niche.

"In the 1960s, it was a persistent rumor that I had at that point quit science fiction in disgust. When *Rogue Moon* did not get the Hugo Award [as best novel]...the award went instead to *A Canticle for Leibowitz*, which in that year appeared as a reprint, which I do not believe was eligible. I was extremely angry, because *Rogue Moon* represented a maximum effort and I frankly think it is a better book than *A Canticle for Leibowitz*—as a novel. The original short story, fine; the novel I don't think is that good. I was angry, and in some circles very vocal about my anger. That apparently led people to think that I had renounced science fiction in disgust. Actually I knew my fourth child was going to be born in January 1962, and it was just too much for a freelance to carry; I had to get a salaried job.

"When I get a job, I tend to bury myself in it. From then until essentially January 1974, I was almost always doing something other than science fiction, very intensely.

"When it was my responsibility, for instance, to put out the introductory news-release package for a new truck, I had to work as hard as I think anyone would work in order to completely plot out a novel. A new model of truck can make or break a multi-billion dollar enterprise; it's not like manufacturing family cars at all. If you turn out a product in the truck business that can be proven to be not as good as somebody else's, you are in serious trouble. You may be unable to recover your position, over a period of years. So I researched the news-release package more heavily than I have ever researched a novel. It was intellection and sweat, and some moments in my life that I'm extremely proud of, because by God I worked for them. Whereas in a science-fiction novel, I may put in an enormous amount of labor, but I never regard it as intellection or work. On *Rogue Moon* I would drive myself to a point of fatigue such that I was suffering from auditory hallucinations; but what I was doing was shaping something, I was having some kind of psychic experience. It took me until I was in my forties before I realized: these things are not stories, they're utterances. Some of the time a story comes out without my supervision at all. I just sit at the typewriter and watch my fingers move. A great many times I surprise the hell out of myself with some feature the book will develop.

"I think I have written every science-fiction story that I ever felt was worth writing, at the time that I felt was the right time to write it. I've got to do something with the rest of the time. It's no longer necessary for me to be on any kind of a salary or retainer, thank God, simply because so much time has passed and there are so many properties [books and stories] around that keep getting reprinted. Generally speaking we need less money than most people do, because we set our standard of living at the poverty level, and have been very happy with it ever since! I love doing the public-relations work and advertising copywriting and the other things I do, because I think I'm pretty damn skillful at it. I do it very quickly, glibly, and it comes out better than average because I'm a better observer and reporter than the average person who's working in advertising or P.R. and I've had a lot of training in finding the exact word and the right sentence.

"The only thing that happens is that some science fiction doesn't get finished quite as *soon* as it might, though it gets started when it's ready to get started. *Michaelmas*, for instance: the first sixty pages of a 240-page manuscript were written over a period of about forty-eight hours in January 1965, and if I had stuck with it at anything like that pace, obviously I would have finished it in 1965. It would not have been a substantially different book. As it happens, there was a ten-year hiatus in there, when I was doing something else. But there was no other book clamoring to be born.

"It's a simple test: if a science-fiction idea doesn't make it, doesn't get written, it wasn't good enough. There are no other science-fiction books that I want to write at the moment, although I have the idea that I may in fact write a sequel to *Michaelmas*—which shakes me, because I told a lot of people I never would. But it occurred to me that it would be very interesting to continue the chronology from the viewpoint of one of the minor characters, a very interesting chap who's in there and hardly speaks. Michaelmas is going to die some day, and Domino is going to be looking for his successor.

"I think that all forms of fiction and art are actually survival mechanisms. Far from being frills and decorations on the face of some kind of practical world, they are just about the most practical thing there is. They consist of a series of affirmations or denials of conventional reality, and of tests of various facets of reality. Science fiction has unique capabilities in that respect. I can talk seriously in science fiction about otherwise-unattainable aspects of very important situations.

"When I wrote *Rogue Moon* I was able to talk about love versus death in a way that conventional fiction cannot handle; the whole thing is fueled by a situation in which a man can deal death repeatedly, experience death repeatedly, and can talk about the essential nature of the immortality that love confers, which is that immortality rests in the memory of the beloved. The beloved remembers with love, and confers immortality, without respect to the fact that the object of her love is not in fact the same man that he was yesterday. It is possible to discuss the illusion of reality as an artifact of memory, by having a character in the story who remembers being the same man, but is not in fact the same man. I think that what science fiction is—and this is my definition of it—is drama that has been made more relevant than ordinary drama, by social extrapolation. By which I mean, conditional reality."

His monologue didn't come out exactly like that, all in one piece, but it was coherent to such a degree that I feel it's best presented here without any interruptions.

After leaving the Budrys family, I have some thoughts on what

70

he said. His sense of duty, of course, manifests itself through the main characters of almost every novel and story he has written; and it is obvious, too, in his writing style. Just as his heroes proceed quietly and with dedication, motivated by moral obligation, so Budrys's writing is quiet, careful, and executed with his strange sense of dedication to science fiction as a world apart, a field of worthiness, a brotherhood which claims one's fundamental patriotism.

Paradoxically, the intensity of Budrys's loyalty toward the genre probably accounts for his having written so little science fiction, and so much commercial journalism and advertising copy instead. Despite his very rational arguments (for example, his claim that if a story doesn't get written, it wasn't good enough), I almost feel he avoids writing science fiction much of the time, not because it is too demanding, but perhaps because it is such a special area to him, the work would somehow become devalued if it became part of a frequent routine. It's as if he only allows himself the pleasure of science-fiction writing on birthdays and national holidays; the rest of the year; he has to get his hands dirty and apply himself to the mundane jobs—"doing something solid," as he puts it, "and not rising too high."

Indeed, he has broadened and let down more roots, in just about every commercial writing field. This is frustrating for those of us who admire his science fiction for its unusual depth, humanity, and political sophistication. One hopes that, when he starts his next novel, he doesn't do what he did with *Michaelmas*, and put the half-finished manuscript aside for ten years before coming back and finishing it.

Historical Context

After *Michaelmas*, AJ (as his contemporaries used to call him) wrote only one more novel. Instead he worked for Writers of the Future, the organization founded by L. Ron Hubbard.

He received a lot of criticism for this, some of it from myself. Writers of the Future was ostensibly an organization to provide encouragement and guidance for young writers, yet Hubbard's name was always prominently associated with it. Thus AJ was perceived as helping to renovate the literary reputation of L. Ron Hubbard, and hence (perhaps) the public perception of Hubbard's brainchild, Scientology.

Naturally, AJ rejected the criticism. He pointed out that Scientology was never mentioned in Writers of the Future materials, and he insisted that his public statements or opinions were never influenced by the remuneration he received. Yet he wrote a tribute to Hubbard in which he praised him as perhaps the most influential and important science-fiction writer of the 1940s— an outlook which I doubt any other critic in the field would share.

Several years after I interviewed AJ, when I ran into him at some science-fiction event, he assured me that Writers of the Future was benign. He emphasized the good it was doing for young people, but then rather spoiled the effect by adding in a lowered voice, "And you wouldn't believe how much they're paying me."

Did Writers of the Future help to promote the name (and hence the novels) of L. Ron Hubbard? I think so, to some extent. Did this matter? Probably not. Was the organization useful to aspiring writers? Perhaps, although when I listened to one of AJ's presentations, he seemed to be advocating a very formulaic approach.

Personally I just wish that he had continued writing science fiction. But his intensely realistic, near-future scenarios were incompatible with book publishing after *Star Wars*. I tend to see him as a casualty of the changes that occurred, and since he was a very smart man, he probably understood them long before I did.

His death in June, 2008 was caused by a metastatic malignant melanoma. He was 77.

Charles Platt

Philip José Farmer

Peoria, Illinois, May 11, 1979

TRAFFIC IS AT a standstill all around us. Above the murmuring of car engines, I hear Scottish bagpipes. The music's getting louder. The bagpipes are playing "When the Saints go Marching In." I look at Philip Jose Farmer, sitting beside me. "What the hell is going on?"

"Must be the Shriners," he answers.

I get out and climb onto the roof of the car. The traffic has been held up by police at an intersection a little way ahead of us. Crossing the intersection is a procession which boggles the mind.

First the bagpipers, in full Scottish regalia, including bearskins. Then a phalanx of middle-aged men wearing pastel-tinted, pink-and-orange turbans with MOHAMMED written across them. Then an all-male brass band, followed by a squadron of men wearing business suits and rainbow-striped "beanies" (skullcaps with propellers on top). Then a formation of men in sports jackets riding mopeds, circling one another in an intricate ballet pattern. Then comes a parade of identical dark-blue Volkswagens—at least a dozen of them. Why Volkswagens? Why blue? And why, next, are there clowns riding bicycles, towing painted wooden dachshunds, whose legs move realistically? Why middle-Eastern warriors in garish gold and crimson robes, brandishing silver-painted swords?

73

Why a school bus full of men leaning out of the windows chanting and waving paper flags?

"Where are they all going?" I ask.

"Oh, the Mohammedan Temple," Farmer tells me, as if this should have been obvious.

"But—why?"

"Well, I don't exactly know," he replies, as if he had never stopped and wondered about it.

It's fair to say that there is a strong element of fantasy alive here in this amazingly conventional town of Peoria, Illinois. Maybe the conventionality drives them to it. Either way, that Farmer should live here is appropriate. He is both conventional and bizarre himself.

A very quiet man, he is always respectably dressed, proper, polite, hard-working, conscientious, embodying every Horatio Alger virtue. He is also the man who shocked science-fiction editors in the 1950s by writing stories full of sex. He was the first to give aliens a love life, and have them share it vividly with human beings, in his classic story *The Lovers*; and he wrote *Flesh*, an uninhibited fantasy of lust; and *A Feast Unknown*, in which his two childhood heroes, Tarzan and Doc Savage, are endowed with superhuman sex-drives, described in pungent, pornographic detail.

This brings another scene to mind:

When I first met Farmer, ten years ago, I was in America for the first time, shell-shocked and shy. There were other people in the room who all knew each other, and were talking. Farmer and I sat in silence at one side, like a pair of wallflowers at the prom. Finally I made the most obvious conversational gambit and asked: "What are you working on now?"

He paused, as if wondering whether to take me into his confidence. "Well, you see, Charles," he began carefully, "I really believe that Tarzan existed."

Huh? Oh, really, Phil?

"You see, I think he was related, distantly, to Jack the Ripper."

74

And so on. Farmer, like Peoria, has a rich fantasy life. Most of it goes back to the myths of his childhood, which are as alive for him now as they were then. During my visit to Peoria he refers constantly to the landscape around his house, on the edge of woodland where he used to play as a kid. We walk along a railroad track that has fallen into disrepair, and he talks of a swamp somewhere near here, of which he has special memories—in fact he starts checking each lowland to see if it is the right one. His school friends called him "Tarzan" when he was young; he climbed trees and literally swung from branch to branch. He recalls playing at Indians, too; and building a raft of logs; and being Robinson Crusoe. Even now, in his sixties, he seems very young, and still has an athletic physique; he's a tall, strong, handsome figure. He gives me an inventory of creatures that once lived in the woodlands: wolves, cougars, bears, bobcats, and even, he claims, parakeets. And he says there used to be an Indian tribe which had unique customs—including sexual cross-dressing.

I have to look twice to see whether he is putting me on. He seems not to be. I suppose it makes sense: in a region where local businessmen now dress up in turbans, robes, and kilts, why shouldn't bygone Indian braves have dressed up as women?

The woodlands have largely been built over—with houses such as the one in which Farmer lives himself, with his wife Bette. It's single-story, very modern, with new furniture and wall-to-wall carpets throughout, and in the basement there is a bar with an imitation marble top, and wood paneling and a touch of imitation wrought-iron here and there. The radio in the living room is tuned to a sweet-music station, setting a mellow suburban mood in the house, complementing the furnishings; and there's an air-freshener in every room, complementing the music.

Farmer seems only peripherally aware of these things, which are perhaps orchestrated more by his wife. His working space is down and around a corner in the basement, through a long passageway, to a cool, windowless den at the end. The wood paneling extends here, too, but there are rather different pictures hung on it—erotic art, for instance, drawn to illustrate his early work. And shelves—endless shelves—of reference books, reflecting his fascination with language, myth, and legend; plus a row of copies of his own books, five or six feet long.

In Freudian terms (which Farmer's fiction has often used) this hideaway where he works is buried like a subconscious underneath the conventional American home.

Farmer's literary motives and sources of creativity are equally well-buried, and hard to learn about. Even after talking to him through a two-day stay at his house, I still don't know to what extent he works consciously and to what extent by pure instinct. When I ask him about these things I get very matter-of-fact answers, in terms that are so general, they almost become platitudes. For instance: "You have to keep the reader interested in the story, and even though there's a serious theme you still have to keep it moving. You have to make your characters as real as possible. I never sit down thinking I've got to entertain people, I just write the story the way I want to." And so on.

Partly, I think, it's true: he just does what he does, without analyzing the operation. At the same time, he doesn't talk about himself easily, especially when a tape recorder is running. Before we begin our interview he pours himself some Glenfiddich whiskey and sits down, rather stiffly, saying "I warn you, I tend to get self-conscious in front of these things," as he looks warily at the microphone. And as soon as he starts answering my questions his voice doubles in volume, as if he were addressing an audience, and he chooses his words as if suspecting they may later be used in evidence against him.

What emerges in the end is simply a story of a lot of very hard work, in the face of repeated disappointments; a dedication to acquiring knowledge, as an end in itself; and an idealism so pure, it verges on innocence.

"I was born in January 1918," Farmer begins, formally. "That's the year von Richthoven was shot down," he adds, with a shy chuckle, mentioning another of his favorite legendary figures.

"I was going to be a newspaper reporter, which, as I look back on it, seems pretty ridiculous. Because I don't have the aggressive personality you need for it. In 1936, to put me through college, my father started an extra business on the side, and then went bankrupt. I had to drop out of college to help repay the debts, because, even though he went bankrupt, he insisted on repaying the money he had borrowed. I worked for Illinois Power and Light, repairing electrical lines, fixing high-tension wires in the country sometimes.

"When the war came along I was going to be drafted so I joined the Army Air Corps, as an aviation cadet. But after four and a half months I washed out because of inconsistent flying. So I went to work for Keystone Steel and Wire Company, and waited for the draft. But they never took me. So I was there [in the steel mill] for eleven years, doing some of the hottest, hardest work you can imagine. I could have gone around and looked for another job, but what could I do? I didn't have any real training." He says it matter-of-factly, in his slow, deep voice. Really he is describing an early adulthood of frustrated aspirations and sacrifices. But I can't imagine him ever complaining about his lot in life.

"During those eleven years, I wrote about ten stories, but only sold one, and only two of them were science fiction. See, I had no desire to be a science-fiction writer. I wanted to be a mainstream writer. I sent stories to *The Saturday Evening Post* and *Redbook*. Even there, I wasn't very aggressive. If I got two rejections on a story, I didn't send it anywhere any more.

"In 1949 Bette and I went back to college. I was still working a forty-eight-hour week, doing nights down at Keystone, and also carrying seventeen semester hours of school, which meant that I would work six nights a week, go home, eat breakfast, go to school till about one or two in the afternoon, then I'd come home and sleep, and then I'd study and then I'd go back to work. This went on for a year and a half.

"I was a voracious reader. I even managed to read at work. When I was a billet inspector. Twenty-foot-long rods were sent down a trough; I was supposed to look at the ends of them to see if they had any impurities. There was a little gap in between the time one batch quit coming and the next batch came, so I'd run into the little hut I had there and read maybe half a page, and then run back and do my work, and then run in and read some more. And when I was working the shears, there was a little gap there, too. It was awfully hot and heavy work but still I managed out of eight hours to maybe get thirty minutes' reading. That's how I studied, too. At the end of a year and a half, I came down with what they call a case of nervous exhaustion. So I rested two weeks and then I went out and got a job." He laughs.

"In 1952 I sent in *The Lovers*. It was bounced by John W. Campbell, as being 'nauseating.' H. L. Gold [of *Galaxy* magazine] had somewhat the same reaction. Then I went to Sam Mines, who was editing *Startling* and *Thrilling Wonder Stories*. *Startling* published it.

"I decided I would go into full-time writing. Shasta Publications, a little publishing firm in Chicago, had made a proposal to Pocket Books, to arrange an international fantasy-novel award. The prize would be $4,000, which in 1952 was a lot of money. I sat down and typed anywhere from twelve to sixteen hours a day. Then I'd go over it and correct it, and Bette would type part of it, and a neighbor next door would type part of it, and I got it in just under the wire, and it won."

However, this was just the beginning of a new series of difficulties. Shasta Publications was involved in fraud, which ultimately robbed Farmer of his prize money and the rights to his novel (for many years), and temporarily forced him to abandon the idea of being a writer:

"The publisher of Shasta had kept the money which Pocket Books gave him, and secretly put it into another project, which failed. He not only kept the money, but told Pocket Books nothing about it, so they never got my manuscript, and I couldn't understand why. In the meantime, he kept telling me that Pocket Books wasn't satisfied with my novel and wanted a complete rewrite—which I did. But of course during this time I wasn't making any money from my writing.

"He not only screwed me, but John Campbell, and Murray Leinster, and Raymond Jones. He went bankrupt, so there wasn't any use in suing him. We lost our house—had to sell it and buy a smaller one. And then I went back to work, for a local dairy. Meantime, I was doing a little writing on the side. But not much. It had really shattered me."

Farmer then moved through a variety of jobs. He was a technical writer for General Electric for a couple of years. Then he moved to Arizona, where he worked for Motorola for about seven years. Finally to Los Angeles, where he worked as a technical writer for McDonnell-Douglas. But:

"They had a big cutback of space funds and I was laid off along with thousands of others in 1969, a month before the first moon landing. I'd been helping to put that ship up on the moon, and then they laid me off. Things were really bad. There were engineers with Ph.D. degrees, pumping gas. Some engineers committed suicide. I looked around, couldn't find a job. I decided, well, I'd been writing on the side, on evenings and weekends. I'd try it full-time again. Maybe I'd do better this time. Well, there were some grim periods, and after we moved back to Peoria there were six months when the publishers weren't putting out the money they owed me. But I just persisted, and kept at it. Now in the last five years, things have been steadily improving. And now they're getting pretty good."

Farmer's early novel, which won the fantasy contest, was the first of his *Riverworld* series. "Actually that publisher did me a favor, because there wasn't any market for a 150,000-word novel in those days, in science fiction. So I put it in a trunk. Many years later I took it out and sent it to Ballantine; Betty Ballantine returned it with the comment that it seemed to her just an adventure novel. So I sent to Fred Pohl, who at this time was editing *Galaxy*. He said it was a great idea, in fact it was too big to put into one novel. Why didn't I write a series of novelettes for the magazines, and later put them together if I wanted to. And that's what happened. There's very little of the original novel, aside from the basic concept, in the new Riverworld books I've done."

The books have been Farmer's most popular so far. *To Your Scattered Bodies Go* collected a Hugo Award in 1972. Twenty years after being cheated out of his prize money, he was finally reaching the audience he deserved; and they were showing their appreciation of his work.

"My development in almost anything has always been a lot slower than most people. I don't put it down to a low intelligence. Just the fact that that's my temperament. When I went to high school I never dated. I was just too shy. I never had a drink of liquor till I was nineteen. I was very naive. I was a bookworm. At the same time, of course, I was an athlete. I was a track man. I ran the 440 and the 220, and did the broad jump. But what can you learn from knowing a bunch of jocks?

"I have the feeling that, even though I'm sixty-one now, I'm not the least big fossilized and I'm still developing. And ten years from now, if I'm still alive, I'll be a much better writer than I am now. At present I'm not satisfied by any means, because I haven't really done what I set out to do. I set out to be a mainstream writer, and would like to go back to that, maybe part-time. I want to satisfy myself that I can do it. I think if *Fire and the Night* had got the distribution and the recognition it deserved, when I first wrote it, I might have turned to mainstream then." (The book is an intense story of an interracial love-affair against the background of a steel mill, with symbolic overtones. It is eloquently written. Its theme was controversial, for the time of its original publication.)

I ask Farmer if he is pleased with the work he has done.

"Every time I reread some of my stuff—which I don't do very

80

often, because it pains me too much—I can see where I could have done a lot better. I can see innumerable cases. But it's no good to go back and rewrite them, because if you did you'd lose a certain primitive vigor that they have. The thing to do is to go on and write new stuff.

"There have been cases where I have been just too rushed, not only in the prose but in the structure and characterization, and so forth. I've been too busy making a living writing science fiction, and getting too many contracts, one after the other. But I took my time on some things. *Riders of the Purple Wage*, for instance. [A long experimental story published in the *Dangerous Visions* collection edited by Harlan Ellison.] But of course that was a lot of fun, it wasn't labor. Then when I wrote *Venus on the Half Shell* [under the name Kilgore Trout, who is a fictional character invented by Kurt Vonnegut], I wrote it very fast, but I'm well satisfied with it."

Farmer has more to add about the genesis of this book:

"Vonnegut may pretend to have trouble, these days, remembering my name. But I'm sure he remembers me quite well. We've talked over the phone a number of times. He's spoken about me in at least one lecture I know of. We've exchanged letters. And he's suffered a lot of unnecessary and masochistic anguish over *Venus on the Half Shell*.

"I wrote it (with great enthusiasm and glee) because I thought people would flip their minds if they saw a book by Trout, a supposedly fictional character, on the stands. Also, I did it as a tribute, the highest, to an author whom I loved and admired at that time. And I identify with Trout.

"Vonnegut says that it was his intention to have many people write Trout books. In another publication he said that he'd thought about writing a Trout novel himself. In all the talks and letters between us, he never mentioned these ideas. I firmly believe that they are after-the-event thoughts. Vonnegut is as confused about time as Billy Pilgrim.

"I understand that in his interview for this book of profiles,

Vonnegut's main concern was that I refused to divulge that I was the author of *Venus*. But Vonnegut knows better. When he suggested that I make people aware of who the real author was, I did my damnedest to comply. If he was so anxious about it, why did he turn down my offer to put on the dedication page of *Venus* that Vonnegut was *not* the author?

"Any speculations about Vonnegut's strong tendency to reconstruct the past would be out of place here."

Farmer is now known as a playful writer who has borrowed all kinds of names from history and from famous fiction, and used them as pseudonyms, or told fantasies from their viewpoints. He explains that he got into this when he had a writer's block; he found he could only write fiction if he did it pretending to be a different person. The block soon disappeared, but by this time he was enjoying assuming the other identities.

Most of all, he is still remembered as the science-fiction writer who dared to write about sex, and finally pursued his erotic fantasies to their most uninhibited conclusion, in novels such as *The Image of the Beast* and *A Feast Unknown*. I ask him if he believes in any form of literary censorship.

"No. I believe in total access to all types of material. They worry about the very young being damaged, but in the first place, anything that's too adult is not going to interest the young. They don't understand it. They're bored by it. I think there should be nothing left unsaid. I don't see how pornography of any kind could corrupt people; it's a literary thing. I mean, they're just reading it; they're not going to be aroused by something and go out and rape people."

I ask him how he can be sure of that.

"I can't be sure, it's just my theory."

But he seems to hold the theory very strongly.

"Yep. But so far there's been no way of establishing whether reading pornography or violence will infect people. So it's *all* theory."

82

He willingly admits occasions in the past when he made misjudgments, perhaps because of his faith in human nature:

"In 1953, at the Philadelphia science-fiction convention, I gave a speech in which I did some raving and ranting about our sexual inhibitions and taboos. So what's happened? Our sexual attitudes nowadays are much more liberal and permissive. But at the same time, there's been a proportional increase in sexual crimes, and violent crimes. I had assumed, when I made this speech in 1953, that people would become more sexually educated and would know more about avoiding disease and unwanted pregnancies. What's happened? God, is it one out of every ten teenagers in this country who has an unwanted pregnancy? It's not just in the cities, either."

He sounds baffled, and disappointed, as if he is unable to understand why some people should not want to educate themselves as he has done, and be liberated in a spirit of moderation.

I ask him what he would have become if he hadn't chosen to be a writer.

"I would have tried to go back to college and get a Ph.D. in anthropology and linguistics. I would have liked to be a linguistics professor. Studying languages themselves, their structure, and phonemics, the comparison of various languages. I would have loved to be able to learn an American Indian language. They're so far out from our occidental viewpoint."

I'm running out of questions, and it's obvious that the interview is somehow winding down. He seems dissatisfied. "I feel not enough has been said," he remarks; but seems unsure what's missing.

I decide to mention Tarzan—who, thus far, hasn't featured in my questions at all. I remind Farmer of what he told me when we first met, about the existence of his myth-figure hero.

"Well, in one sense I do believe he existed, you know, because I started reading the Burroughs books when I was very young, and they became a part of my life. I'm a romantic, in some respects, and

I like the idea of the noble savage. Although, actually, Tarzan wasn't a savage, he was really a primitive human being. Anthropologists don't like to use the word 'savage' any more, with respect to preliterate people. Tarzan was raised by the so-called great apes, who were infrahuman. In that respect he was not even a savage. The idea of living off in the wilderness, and making your own laws, is endemic to a lot of Americans. I kind of liked it at the same time that I realized, realistically, it's not feasible. Tarzan was the last of the heroes of the old golden age of mythology. Sometimes I'm not too sure there isn't a Tarzan.

"When I was young I used to play Tarzan a lot. That was my nickname in grade school, because I was always climbing trees. Had a couple of bad falls, too. I lived close to the edge of the wilderness—semiwilderness—and then I used to play deerslayer, used to play Indian, Indian versus pioneer in the eastern forest. That sort of stuff. We used to play John Carter on Mars. But I liked to play Tarzan most of all. I was a real tree-climber, in those days. Used to jump from branch to branch—and sometimes miss." He laughs. "I had a bad fall once, where I was paralyzed for a couple of hours. And—" He breaks off suddenly. "I'm sorry, sometimes I get to rambling."

I think it has been the only time, during the interview, when he has forgotten the existence of the tape recorder.

Later, we go out to dinner. Farmer suggests a new restaurant he's been wanting to try, called the Blue Max. He is fascinated by the fighter pilot legends of World War I, and he's heard that this restaurant is full of motifs of that era. Also, he adds, as an afterthought, the food is supposed to be quite good.

When we get there, the place is quite bizarre. It's the Peoria Shriners all over again—oddball images and weird notions, accepted as if they are not at all out-of-the ordinary. Over the bar hangs a giant *life-size* replica of a Fokker triplane, painted bright red. Against the walls are stacked piles of sandbags, as if this starkly modern building has been commandeered and turned into a sort of

Bauhaus Fuehrer-bunker. There is a garish mural of a burning city—perhaps Dresden?—behind the cash register. While we eat (German cuisine) we sit on chairs whose backs have German military crosses carved into them. Above each table, German military helmets have been adapted as lampshades. And these are not quaint old helmets—the kind with spikes on top. No, these seem to be Nazi helmets. We sit and eat under Nazi helmets turned into lampshades.

Now, maybe life in Peoria is not always as mysterious and deranged as this. Maybe I am overreacting, and it really is a quiet little town, devoid of unusual psychoses. But I think, at this point, it is time to move on, away from scenarists of myth and legend. It is time to head west, to what I can only describe as the relative normality of California.

Historical Context

I corresponded regularly with Phil Farmer over a period of about ten years. He kept me up-to-date about his family, which seemed very important to him, and he asked my advice occasionally about New York book publishing, because I was embedded in it while he remained fairly naïve about it. Our personalities were totally different, as he was reticent and unfailingly polite, while I was outspoken and tended to offend people. Sometimes I wondered why he was always so friendly toward me.

In retrospect I think it was because we were both enduringly naïve. I had grown up with *Astounding Science Fiction*, believing everything I read. When it advocated a study of psychic research and published a feature on dowsing rods that could detect underground objects, I went right ahead and built my own set. When the magazine published a set of plans for a so-called Hieronymus Machine, which could detect "eloptic radiation," I built one of them, too, and tried it on my friends at school.

I remember sending a letter to the editor, John W. Campbell, from my home in England (every bit as dull as Farmer's location in Peoria, Illinois). When I received a personal response from the man himself, on the magazine's stationery, I was stunned. It was like getting a message from God.

As for the fiction that he published, I had no doubt that its core assumptions were accurate. I would be traveling to the Moon and nearby planets within a couple of decades, and might even acquire time-traveling ability, assuming that alien races didn't destroy the Earth first.

During my first meeting with Phil, when he began the conversation by suggesting that Tarzan could have existed, he was expressing a very similar kind of credulity. The only difference was that he had been imprinted about fifteen years earlier, by Edgar Rice Burroughs as opposed to John W. Campbell.

Most science-fiction writers were not so credulous. Did Isaac Asimov seriously believe that one day, there would be a Foundation to protect knowledge during a galactic Dark Age? I doubt it. Did Robert A. Heinlein believe in *The Door into Summer*? Apparently not; he refused to accept cryonics arrangements when they were offered to him for free. (So did Frederik Pohl.)

In fact, most writers, like most readers, only suspend their disbelief during the story. At the end, they return to the unavoidable realities of everyday life. Somehow Farmer didn't do that. Pulp fiction told him there should be no limits, and he believed it. He then applied this mindset to the entire range of human thought and activity.

Sex? Tarzan had shacked up in the jungle with a sexy blonde, so, clearly, sex was okay and marriage was inessential. Race? Farmer had read a lot about aliens. The minor variations in skin pigmentation that distinguished human races from one another were trivial by comparison. Christianity? Just another set of theories about the origins of humanity, less plausible than competing theories that one could find in *Thrilling Wonder Stories*.

So it was that in 1952 he wrote about alien sex in "The

Lovers," making an impact in science fiction that was comparable to that of Henry Miller or William Burroughs in the larger world of American literature. He also showed no hesitation about dealing with religion in "Night of Light" (1957), and then race relations in *Fire and the Night* (1962), before going all the way into hardcore erotica in *The Image of the Beast* (1968) and *A Feast Unknown* (1969).

Fortunately for him, he was an unthreatening man who showed no interest in confronting people who disagreed with him. He had neither the pugnaciousness of Hemingway nor the down-and-dirty, in-your-face offensiveness of Henry Miller. While Lenny Bruce was being dragged off stage for making obscene statements in public, Farmer stayed quietly at home and wrote stories about alien sex for an audience that didn't get upset by that kind of thing. His lifestyle and his choice of publishing markets protected him from adversity.

He did however have a corrupting influence on some of his fellow writers, myself being one of them. I already shared his root assumption, acquired from science fiction, that we should be able to transcend our limits. When I read his erotic novels I realized how poorly I had foreseen the full implications. They were a major influence on me when I wrote my own inexcusably offensive novel, *The Gas* (1970). I was flattered and delighted when Farmer agreed to add an introduction to the British edition. Subsequently, when that edition was seized by the Director of Public Prosecutions, I think Farmer's introduction may have helped to avert prosecution.

Although I believe he remained naïve throughout his life, this certainly did not imply that he was uneducated. On the contrary, when I inspected the library in his basement retreat, I found an astonishing range of reference books, and realized that his insatiable curiosity had led him to educate himself with the same stubborn patience that he applied to other areas of his life.

Like Philip K. Dick, he owned the *Encyclopedia of Philosophy*— and had read it as someone else might read a cookery book, with the intention of borrowing a few recipes. Every world religion was represented on his shelves, along with numerous books on anthropology, history, and geography. He made me feel chagrined by my own lack of education.

The last time I saw Phil was at the end of an unhappy six-month period when I had tried to live with a girlfriend in Los Angeles. I drove back to New York across the country, which enabled me to visit Peoria. Phil seemed totally unchanged by the aging process or by his difficulty in selling his more recent work. He simply continued to pursue his unique fantasies, and if they were no longer in sync with public taste, there was nothing he could do about it except shrug and continue writing.

He died in February, 2009 at the age of 91, after a long illness.

Frank Herbert

Los Angeles, California, May, 1979 and October, 1986

IN THE MID-1960S, his novel *Dune* seemed destined to be a failure. Twenty-two New York book publishers had turned it down, many of them complaining that it was too long and too complicated. When it was finally published, in a small first edition, it received unanimously bad reviews.

But Frank Herbert proved he knew much more than editors and critics about the reading tastes of young Americans. The *Dune* saga has now sold over ten million copies, has spawned the inevitable "major motion picture," and is one of the most lucrative science-fiction series of all time.

Herbert's success story is a real-life enactment of one of his favorite fictional themes: the power of the individual to shape his own destiny, whether it is here in America or centuries hence in outer space. He is a diehard proponent of personal liberty, convinced that a self-taught individual can be more effective than organizations of so-called experts.

His experience with book publishers is a case in point: "It was an alarming shock to me, to be in New York City. I was a native western boy, who believed that God must be in New York City." He laughs. "Well, let's say, I thought the best gravitated to New York City. I arrived there one time, with my satchel in my hand, you know, and my turned-up-brim hat, staring at the tall buildings. And I was asked to sit in on an editorial conference, to decide on the promotion of one of my books. [Some years before he moved to Berkley, his current publisher.] We were ten minutes into this conference when I realized that I knew more about the market, and what was really happening out in the marketplace, and more about what should be done to work in that marketplace, than these experts who were sitting around this table.

"I can still remember the feeling of *betrayal*—a kind of a loss—because I felt suddenly all alone. Here I am in this place, they're supposed to know what they're doing, and they don't! They don't know what they're doing!" He laughs: the laughter turns into diminishing chuckles; finally, it subsides. "So we went our own ways. I just quietly pulled out of all this and went on the lecture circuit, where you really have to be up-front, especially at the university or college level. Boy, do *they* unmask the phonies quickly! So I just did my own, and to hell with New York. They didn't know. Their high-level book tours where you *go* and meet the critics...there is no critic, I believe, myself included, whose taste is the absolute *sine qua non*. They really do not control the market. The market goes on without them, and *Dune* is a perfect example of the truth of that."

Even in modern scientific research, dominated by large budgets and elaborate laboratories, he believes there is still room for the lone outsider to make a significant impact. And he has proved it. His own work as an amateur scientist is a topic he has seldom talked about; he presents an affable, gregarious image in public, with a well-practiced repertoire of quips and aphorisms while in reality he is a very private man who likes to retreat from being a best-selling novelist and pursue small-scale research in his refuge in the state of Washington. This "other" Frank Herbert has tackled ambitious projects ranging from computer design to alternate energy sources.

His home is a large, modified A-frame, with a solar space-heater on the south side, skylights, and an attached greenhouse. Inside, the rooms are spacious, and there is no attempt to conceal the rough-cut cedar wood construction. The house, patio, and swimming pool are surrounded by dense trees that conceal the nearby highway and create the illusion of being at the center of a forest.

Developing a new computer has been one of Herbert's biggest challenges. He has worked on it with the help of Max Barnard, an electronics engineer.

"I wanted a system that was specifically tailored for creative writing," he explains. "None of the systems on the market satisfied my criteria, because none of them was developed by a writer. So I started trying to develop the simplest, fastest, best word-processing computer possible. We're currently in the third revision of the hardware. It's all hand-wired, you understand; you have to wire it by hand to develop the architecture. Once you establish that, then you can etch printed circuit boards.

"Right now, sometimes it works, sometimes it doesn't. But when it's working, we know we're going in the right direction. And when I come back to the primitive present time, and use my Compaq, I know I'm using something less than what is possible."

More than a decade has passed since Apple Computer was started by two kids in a family garage. Personal computers have become big business, and most industry observers believe that large resources are now required to develop any new computer concept. Herbert, of course, disagrees.

"There's just the two of us, and we're entirely independent. And our aim extends well beyond word processing. Our idea is also to create a computer that almost anybody could program, using a graphic programming language. You see a picture, you push that key, and that picture tells you what it's going to do, the way road signs tell you what the road's going to do. This is far more helpful than an orthodox computer language consisting of words. With a picture, what you see is what you get."

Herbert sees this language as a way to take programming out of the hands of the experts and bring computers under the control of people who use them.

"Let's say, at Stanford Medical School, a doctor wants a particular kind of research program in his computer. He hires a programmer, who is not a doctor, and has to get some idea of what is required. He approximates it, and the doctor says, 'No, no, that's not what I wanted, it's got to do *this*.' So the programmer goes back to his drawing board, and comes back with something else, and finally—I've heard some of the doctors admit this—finally they just give up. They say, 'Well, I'll try to make this work.'

"Now, if you could teach that doctor, in four or five days, how to make the computer do precisely what he wants it to do, he would sit down and program it himself."

For a science-fiction writer and an electronics engineer to develop a new computer *and* a new programming language in their spare time seems wildly ambitious. To Herbert, however, it's an exciting game rather than a formidable challenge. His infectious optimism and remarkable vitality tend to belittle any problem, as if he can overcome obstacles by willpower and force of personality alone.

He explains this trait via an off-hand reference to being brought up on a farm. "You can detect self-starting characteristics in this society, of various degrees of strength, and they are strongest among people who have had some kind of rural upbringing at a very impressionable stage. When you come to the time of year when you're making hay, and the hay-baler breaks down, and it's the weekend and the handy little hay-baler repair store is closed, you don't say, 'Well, there'll be no hay this year.' You leap in and repair the thing. You don't even *question* that you can repair it. Obviously you can. My father was a master mechanic; I grew up with a screwdriver in one hand and a pair of pliers in the other— you know, that sort of thing.

"I always had a curiosity about engineering, and no doubt that I could do it. I think that self-limitation is the major limiting factor for most people in the world. People could do far more things than they believe they can."

This attitude has spurred Herbert to tackle other research projects—most notably, a windmill that he designed and developed in collaboration with John Ottenheimer, who was Frank Lloyd Wright's last personal student.

"It occurred to me that wind machines had not been redesigned fundamentally since windmills were introduced in Holland, centuries ago. We've learned a lot since then about the flow of air over laminar surfaces, as a result of designing airplanes. So I started researching that and adapting it to windmills.

"I myself am not an aeronautics engineer, but I can read the research and make my models and test them. And I did; I made a lot of them out of balsa wood. All you need is an alert mind and a new idea; and you go test it, to see if it works."

He first became interested in windmills in the late 1970s, as a possible means of pumping water and generating electricity in his home. The configuration that looked best to him is known as a panamone. It consists of a vertical shaft driven by vertical blades attached to it, the whole assembly resembling an eggbeater pointing upward.

Testing his concept was a problem. It was impossible to build the kind of full-scale wind tunnel used in the aerospace industry. So, lacking any means of moving large volumes of air through the windmill at a steady, controlled speed, he chose to move the windmill through the air instead. He mounted his first full-scale prototype on a pickup truck whose speedometer had been calibrated by means of a radar gun supplied by friendly local police. The truck was then driven to and fro at various speeds, while the windmill's power output was measured.

Results were encouraging, refinements were made, and in 1984 the first working model was installed on the roof of a building in Astoria, Oregon.

"It was four feet in diameter and ten feet tall. In a fifty-knot wind, it developed seven-and-a-half horsepower. This present model is more efficient than any other type of windmill I know of.

"My design is quiet enough to be installed on the roofs of houses in the North-East and Mid-West. This is an application which I think is quite valid. In the winter in that part of the country, the wind-chill factor is just as important to a house as to an individual. It can double the heating bills. But a windmill could generate direct current to power a simple electric-resistance heating system, so that the harder the wind blew, the more the windmill would heat the house."

While the windmill remains the most impressive end product to emerge from Herbert's amateur-science activities, he has conducted smaller experiments that demonstrate the feasibility of other energy sources, including a solar collector and a methane generator.

"I built a passive solar heater, using seconds of thermopane, four feet wide by six-feet-four. They cost me eleven bucks each because each one had a little scratch or something in it. Four inches behind them are banks of beer cans cut in half and stacked like a honeycomb. These panels are tipped in the general direction of the sun. You don't need to make them follow the sun precisely with a tracking system, because it shines into the cans from a wide range of angles. The cans trap the infra-red, so they heat up. Their heat is transferred to air that flows over them by convection. It's very effective."

This system is the one installed in his own home. The methane project, on the other hand, was rigged up temporarily in a shack outside at the back of his house.

"I experimented generating methane from chicken manure in various ways. I wanted to see if it was practical, and it was practical, to a degree. The simplest way was to slit a truck inner tube, insert the manure, then patch the tube. As the manure decomposed, creating the gas, the tube expanded, producing the pressure that you need to use the gas. I was raising chickens then, and we did our own slaughtering. We used the methane for singeing them, to burn off the feathers. So that was like using everything of the pig except the squeal—and maybe even the squeal as well." He laughs.

"There was a spigot and a pipe attached where the valve used to be, in the truck tube. This could also be connected to a small stove, which we sometimes used for boiling water. The whole thing was improvised, and it looked—well, it looked pretty weird."

This kind of primitive farm technology seems reminiscent of communes of the late 1960s, but Herbert doesn't endorse the counter-culture philosophy that suggests we should opt out of society and become wholly self-sufficient.

"People say to me, 'You're trying to build an independent establishment in your farm,' and that's absolutely wrong. The independent, self-sustaining farm is the modern version of building a sailboat and rowing to Tahiti. There's a myth about it. I don't believe in it. You're part of society and you ought to be aware of the necessity for interacting with it."

However, he does agree with decentralization where it's practical, and in dispersing concentrations of political power.

"I believe in putting power in the hands of the people. We have never used the jury system to the extent that we could. Now I'm not saying that juries always do right, and always give you justice. But the people who are governed should be able to say, 'This is the way we will be governed.'

"For example, I would put an automatic jury review, at the local level, on any school-board expenditure over $100,000. Automatically, you'd have twelve jurors who are called up at random from among the people who voted in the last election. And I'd give them subpoena power, so that they can ask for records, and get them, and then say yes or no to the expenditure.

"Now, of course, this brings you head-to-head with the educational bureaucracy, which will say—never in these words, but this is *really* what they're saying—'Surely you don't think some stupid housewife can determine the complexities of these things that we know so much better than they do?' Well, I think that a housewife *can*.

"This would also be an incentive for people to vote. I think they would say, 'If I vote, I may be called on to serve on one of these juries.' I think one of the things that keeps people from voting now is that their vote has very little to do with what's going to happen. So, let's bring the government back where it belongs, into the hands of the governed."

Herbert decided in grade school that he wanted to be a writer, and began his career as a newspaper reporter. Subsequently he worked as speechwriter for a U.S. senator, which gave him considerably more real-life experience of politics than most science-fiction authors, and was a lasting influence on his outlook. He came to the conclusion that large centers of power inevitably attract people who are, he says, "either corrupt or corruptible. I've yet to see a State capital, when I was an investigative reporter, that wasn't a cesspool, and I think the major cesspool in the United States is Washington, DC. So I think we ought to take power away from these centers, and redistribute it.

"But politicians are only part of the problem. We also have to deal with arrogance in the power structure of bureaucracy. I have heard a very high-level bureaucrat in Washington, DC talk of a United States senator who was causing them some trouble, was a threat to reduce their budget, and so on; and he called the senator a 'transient.' Think about the arrogance of that. 'He'll be gone in a year or so, and I'll still be here.' And there's a lot of that in the bureaucracy, especially the higher up you go."

His dislike of bureaucracy makes him deeply suspicious of all large, well-established institutions. And he includes the scientific establishment in that category.

"You get power structures based on bureaucratic demands, rather than on the demands of the research; and the primary demand of bureaucracy is, 'cover your ass.' This is unfortunate, since we need to take chances—take advantage of the fact that wild cards sometimes are playable. Give the odd idea some research money, and let 'em see if it works. Don't say, out of hand, 'Oh, that's crazy, you must be some kind of a jerk to even think that.'

"Most of the major breakthroughs in our history have come from individuals or very small group research-and-development efforts. Whereas, what you get in the bureaucratic system are finance-dominated concepts, where people are more interested in maintaining the life of their system than they are in the original goal, or aim, of the system."

As an individualist and experimenter himself, Herbert feels that scientists should be less constrained by budgetary and bureaucratic controls, even when controversial research is involved. He does not believe we should try to restrict experiments with recombinant DNA, for example—even though one of his novels, *The White Plague*, describes a global catastrophe resulting from such research. His outlook is that legislation to prohibit DNA experiments would simply drive them underground, at which point they would become secret and hence even more dangerous. "Laws to control things invariably strengthen the powers that oppose that control," he points out.

He acquired his views on science and scientists in much the same way as he acquired his political outlook: from personal journalistic experience.

"I found I could approach a very respected person in any particular field and say to him, 'Look, I'm a quick study and a good interviewer, and I'll demonstrate it for you. You must have some papers that you want written; I know a technique for getting them out of you and writing them. In return, I want you to hold individual seminars for me, to give me a quick course in your particular field.'

"The technique for getting the article would be to sit down with a tape recorder, and say, 'Okay, what is the article about?' Because a lot of the time it's just motivation, and dragging the words out of them. I would start asking more and more questions, pertinent questions, getting the language of it. And in return, they would pay off. Once they saw that it worked, I might do three or four papers for them. They became very enamored of this technique—most of them did, anyway. And most of them swore me to silence!" He chuckles.

And so, as in the aerodynamic research for his windmill design, Herbert simply went out and found what he needed. From his personal contact with professional scientists, he acquired a surprising breadth of knowledge, as is evident in the *Dune* books, which are densely packed with detail and are authoritative on topics ranging from ecology to biochemistry.

In addition to the *Dune* series he has written more than a dozen other novels. All of them are science fiction, and perhaps it seems paradoxical that someone so deeply concerned with power and politics should spend so much time writing about imaginary events far from present-day planet Earth. But to Herbert, science fiction offers a way of building social models, like computer simulations, and dramatizing the results. His fiction also reaches a far larger readership than could be achieved by nonfiction tackling the same topics.

Typically, he depicts a powerful central character who creates his own destiny, and changes the fate of a world or even a colonized multiplicity of worlds. In *Dune* itself, an individual rises from obscurity to become the most powerful person in his culture.

At the same time, Herbert shows the dangers of unrestricted personal power, and the folly of slavishly following leaders. He explains: "I created a charismatic leader, a young prince, so that when I inverted it, you would see the dangers of following charismatic leaders, no matter how good they were."

But the legions of diehard *Dune* fans seem to respond more to the power fantasies than the message of moderation, and Herbert finds himself at the center of a cult, even though, in person and in print, he denounces all forms of cultism.

As a result, he has become careful of his privacy. The woods around his home are a necessary barrier between him and his public. Fans of *Dune*, he says, would drive him crazy if they ever found out where he lived. He maintains two unlisted phone numbers, one of them known only to a very few friends and associates, the other monitored by an answering machine that does not mention his name in its outgoing message.

"In the past," he explains, "I've had calls at all times of the day and night, from people wanting to know about *Dune*, and what it all means. I even received a call at two in the morning from Miami, Florida, a bunch of stoned-out fans telling *me* the significance of *Dune*."

He seems uncomfortable when asked to talk specifically about the book and his literary influences. He prefers to speak in general terms—for instance, about the novel's relevance to the role of the individual in society. This outlook, he says, owes little to libertarian authors such as Ayn Rand.

"Ayn Rand is good reading, but pretty simplistic. If I had to name my literary influences, they would be much broader, more Catholic. Ezra Pound's *Make it New* really hit me between the eyes, for instance. And then there's, oh, Shakespeare, Proust, de Maupassant. As regards a system of belief, I'm solidly bedded in Zen."

At the time of this interview, he is gearing himself up to deal with the publicity surrounding the *Dune* movie, scheduled to open in time for Christmas.

For years it seemed doubtful that the film would ever be made at all. Arthur P. Jacobs, producer of the *Planet of the Apes* series, originally bought motion-picture rights, but died while the project was still at storyboard stage. Then Alejandro Jodorowski, writer-director of *El Topo*, an obscure and violent cult classic, became involved, and signed up Salvador Dali and Swiss artist H. R. Giger to do some preliminary designs. The results would have been interesting, but they wouldn't have been *Dune*, and Herbert seems relieved that this attempt to film his book was a failure.

Subsequently, Herbert himself wrote a screenplay, which was never used. Director Ridley Scott (of *Alien*) became involved, but wanted to make it an incest story between the central character, Paul, and his mother. Finally, with Dino de Laurentiis as producer, the writer-director was David Lynch (*Eraserhead*, *The Elephant Man*), and the designer was Tony Masters (*Laurence of Arabia*, 2001).

Herbert renegotiated his contract with de Laurentiis, and became a technical advisor on the film.

"I had no control, but I had very strong influence, because I didn't stand there tearing my hair and saying 'What are you doing to my baby?' I recognized their problems. When you read the book, you create the sets in your head; when you make a movie, you have to *build* those sets. So, some of the sets don't match what I imagined, but some of them do, and some of them are better. What else would you expect from Tony Masters and David Lynch? David is an artist; and I'm not talking about an artist of the camera, he came in through oil painting. He solved how to bring *Dune* to the screen, and he did it cleverly. The real solution, I spotted after he had done it, was the selection of metaphors to substitute for what I had done in the book by using of a lot of words. The fans will see this, and they'll know they've been to *Dune*. It begins as *Dune* begins, and it ends as it ended, too. And I hear my dialogue all the way through it.

"So I can breathe easy. They've caught the essence of it. They don't have every scene that's in the book, but they have not cut out any major character, they have well delineated them, they are real people on that screen, and you feel for them. The love story is intact, the confrontation between good and evil is intact, the sandworm special effects are going to blow your mind. It is *real*."

Inevitably, sequels have been planned. "They're already working on it. In fact they're doing the screenplay right now."

It's all part of the industry that has grown up around *Dune*, creating wealth that Herbert has used partly to invest in projects he believes in. He has already considered expanding his role as "patron of the sciences" to sponsor a private laboratory.

"I wanted to start a research institute, in my little community in the North-West, where you would have think-tank types to dream things up, and you'd also have craftsmen and machine-tool experts in fully equipped machine shops, so you'd be able to see right away if there was any practical application. I wasn't overly ambitious; I thought, maybe, fifty people, eventually, within four or five years, could be working as a basic crew, and maybe I could finance it. I can't start it right now, because of taxes."

In the meantime, despite all his reservations about bureaucracy and the political process, he remains fundamentally optimistic about the American system.

"This country still has an independent spirit, a fix-it-yourself mentality. This is an enormous advantage relative to Japan, for example. We have a lot of screwdriver mechanics around our country. Look at the money that's made by Black and Decker. Who are they supplying—industry? No way, they're supplying basement machine shops, and garages. Now, maybe all that those people want to make is model boats. Fine; but if they were given the confidence to try something else, maybe they'd go do it.

"True, we're not turning out all that many engineers, but engineering is not all that difficult to learn. I believe in never stopping one's education. One of my kids said to me the other day, a thing that really touched me. She said that one of the things I'd taught her was, never to stop learning."

Clearly, this is a motto that has structured a large part of Frank Herbert's life—and accounts for much of his remarkable success.

Historical Context

My original interview with Frank Herbert was inadequate, partly because he was a talkative man who had developed a well-rehearsed presentation for interviewers. He didn't allow me much chance to ask questions.

I had a second chance to talk to him in late 1984, when he was doing a promotional tour for the ill-fated *Dune* movie. I was better prepared, and learned more.

For this edition of *Dream Makers*, I amalgamated the two interviews. While reviewing the texts, I was amused to find that he told exactly the same anecdote in both of them. Supposedly, while staying in a French hotel, he found that the light switch in his room was defective. As a self-sufficient kind of guy, he travelled with a multi-tipped screwdriver. He removed the cover plate from the switch, hoping to fix it—at which point a maid entered the room, saw what he was doing, and exclaimed, "Ah, Americain!"

I think this must have been one of his favorite anecdotes, because on the two occasions when he told it, more than five years apart, he reveled in it, laughing uproariously when he got to the punch line. It was the perfect folksy vehicle to communicate his message about American ingenuity and the capabilities of a resourceful individual.

When I was reading science fiction as a teenager, I accepted this principle uncritically. As the years passed, however, I realized that if a solitary, gifted inventor is going to have any chance of success, he has to choose his problems selectively.

With the wisdom of hindsight, I think it's clear that Herbert's decision to build a better wind turbine was not a wise choice. Aerodynamics is not a simple field, and it has accumulated a huge amount of experimental data from every conceivable design. The prospects for an individual trying to develop a new configuration are not good.

Similarly, his ambition to create an entire computer motherboard, *and* a symbolic programming language, with just one employee, was unrealistic. So far as I can determine, the system never really worked. He had planned to use it to write *Without Me You're Nothing*, an introductory nonfiction book about home computers that was published in 1981. In the end, he used a typewriter.

Perhaps it's too easy to make fun of this kind of thing. Anyone who spends his own money pursuing his own research should at least receive credit for being enterprising. But I think there was a fatal flaw shared among science-fiction writers such as Herbert who were influenced by John W. Campbell, the editor of *Astounding Science Fiction* (subsequently, *Analog*) during the late 1950s and early 1960s. They advocated simple answers to complicated problems.

In his editorials, Campbell suggested quick fixes such as Dianetics (which would eliminate the time-consuming chit-chat of psychiatry) and the Dean Drive (a system of rotating weights that might defy gravity). In the stories that he published, one competent man could solve even the most challenging problem with a set of socket wrenches and a slide-rule. Herbert's novels *Under Pressure* and *Dune* were serialized in *Analog*, and he was a perfect fit for the magazine. Alas, in the real world, problems tend to be less tractable.

The last time I saw Frank Herbert, he was speaking at a science-fiction event where he put on a wonderful show for an audience of about a thousand people. He was noticeably slimmer than in his publicity photographs, and boasted that he had managed to lose a lot of weight in the past year. Everyone applauded, and he beamed at them happily; but in reality, the weight loss was associated with pancreatic cancer.

He died in February, 1986, aged 65.

Ray Bradbury

Los Angeles, California, May 14, 1979

RAY BRADBURY'S STORIES speak with a unique voice. They can never be confused with the work of any other writer. And Bradbury himself is just as unmistakable: a charismatic individualist with a forceful, effusive manner and a kind of wide-screen, epic dedication to the powers of Creativity, Life, and Art.

He has no patience with commercial writing which is produced soullessly for the mass market:

"It's all crap, it's all crap, and I'm not being virtuous about it: I react in terms of my emotional, needful self, in that if you turn away from what you are, you'll get sick some day. If you go for the market, some day you'll wake up and regret it. I know a lot of screenwriters; they're always doing things for other people, for money, because it's a job. Instead of saying, 'Hey, I really shouldn't be doing this,' they take it, because it's immediate, and because it's a credit. But no one remembers that credit. If you went anywhere in Los Angeles among the established writers and said, 'Who wrote the screenplay for *Gone With the Wind?*' they couldn't tell you. Or the screenplay for *North by Northwest*. Or the screenplay for *Psycho*—even I couldn't tell you that, and I've seen the film eight times. These people are at the beck and call of the market; they grow old, and lonely, and envious, and they are not loved, because no one remembers.

"But in novels and short stories, essays and poetry, you've got a chance of not having, necessarily, such a huge audience, but having a constant group of *lovers*, people who show up in your life on occasion and look at you with such a pure light in their faces and their eyes that there's no denying that love, it's there, you can't fake it. When you're in the street and you see someone you haven't seen in years—that *look!* They see you and, that light, it comes out, saying, My God, *there you are*, Jesus it's been five years, let me buy you a drink...and you go into a bar, and—and that beautiful thing, which friendship gives you, *that's* what we want. And all the rest is crap. It is. That's what we want from life—" He pounds his fist on the glass top of his large, circular coffee table. "—We *want friends*.

"In a lifetime most people only have one or two decent friends, constant friends. I have five, maybe even six. And a decent marriage, and children, plus the work that you want to do, plus the fans that accumulate around that work—Lord, it's a *complete* life, isn't it—but the screenwriters never have it, and it's terribly sad.

"Or the Harold Robbinses of the world—I mean, probably a nice gent. But *no one cares*, no one cares that he wrote those books, because they're commercial books, and there's no moment of truth that speaks to the heart. The grandeur and exhilaration of certain days is missing—those gorgeous days when you walk out and it's enough just to be *alive*, the sunlight goes right in your nostrils and out your ears, hah? *That's* the stuff. All the rest, the figuring out of the designs, for how to do a bestseller—what a bore that is.

"Lord, I'd kill myself, I really would, I couldn't live that way. And I'm not being moralistic. I'm speaking from the secret wellsprings of the nervous system. I can't do those things, not because it's morally wrong and unvirtuous, but because the gut system can't take it, finally, being untrue to the gift of life. If you turn away from natural gifts that God has given you, or the universe has given you, however you want to describe it in your own terms, you're going to grow old too soon. You're going to get sour, get cynical, because you yourself are a sublime cynic for having done what you've done. You're going to die before you die. That's no way to live."

He speaks in a rich, powerful voice—indeed, a hot-gospel voice—as he delivers this inspirational sermon. He may be adopting a slightly more incisive style than usual for the purposes of this interview, and he may be using a little overstatement to emphasize his outlook; but there can be no doubt of his sincerity. Those passages of ecstatic prose in his fiction, paying homage to the vibrant images of childhood, the glorious fury of flaming rockets, the exquisite mystery of Mars, the all-around wonderfulness of the universe in general—he truly seems to experience life in these terms.

He allows that intellectual control and cold, hard reason have a place, too; but they must give way to emotion, during the creative process:

"It takes a day to write a short story. At the end of the day, you say, that seems to work, what parts don't? Well, there's a scene here that's not real, now, what's missing? Okay, the intellect can help you here. Then, the next day, you go back to it, and you explode again, based on what you learned the night before from your intellect. But it's got to be a total explosion, over in a few hours, in order to be honest.

"Intellectualizing is a great danger. It can get in the way of doing anything. Our intellect is there to protect us from destroying ourselves—from falling off cliffs, or from bad relationships—love affairs where we need the brains not to be involved. That's what the intellect is for. But it should not be the center of things. If you try to make your intellect the center of your life you're going to spoil all the fun, hah? You're going to get out of bed with people before you ever get into bed with them. So if that happens—the whole world would die, we'd never have any children!" He laughs. "You'd never start any relationships, you'd be afraid of all friendships, and become paranoid. The intellect can make you paranoid about everything, including creativity, if you're not careful. So why not delay thinking 'til the act is over? It doesn't hurt anything."

I feel that Bradbury's outlook, and his stories, are unashamedly romantic. But when I use this label, he doesn't seem at all comfortable with it.

"I'm not quite sure I know what it means. If certain things make you laugh or cry, how can you help that? You're only describing a process. I went down to Cape Canaveral for the first time three years ago. I walked into it, and yes, I thought, this is my hometown! Here is where I came from, and it's all been built in the last twenty years behind my back. I walk into the Vehicle Assembly Building, which is 400 feet high, and I go up in the elevator and look down—and the tears burst from my eyes. They absolutely *burst* from my eyes! I'm just full of the same awe that I have when I visit Chartres or go into Notre Dame or St. Peter's. The size of this cathedral where the rockets take off to go to the Moon is so amazing, I don't know how to describe it. On the way out, in tears, I turn to my driver and I say, 'How the hell do I write that down? It was like walking around in Shakespeare's head,' And as soon as I said it I knew that was the metaphor. That night on the train I got out my typewriter and I wrote a seven-page poem, which is in my last book of poetry, about my experience at Canaveral walking around inside Shakespeare's head.

"Now, if that's romantic, I was born with romantic genes. I cry more, I suppose—I'm easy to tears, I'm easy to laughter, I try to go with that and not suppress it. So if that's romantic, well, then, I guess I'm a romantic, but I really don't know what that term means. I've heard it applied to people like Byron, and in many ways he was terribly foolish, especially to give his life away, the way he did, at the end. I hate that, when I see someone needlessly lost to the world. We should have had him for another five years—or how about twenty? I felt he was foolishly romantic, but I don't know his life that completely. I'm a mixture; I don't think George Bernard Shaw was all that much of a romanticist, and yet I'm a huge fan of

Shaw's. He's influenced me deeply, along with people like Shakespeare, or Melville. I'm mad for Shaw; I carry him with me everywhere. I reread his prefaces all the time."

Quite apart from what I still feel is a romantic outlook, Bradbury is distinctive as a writer who shows a recurring sense of nostalgia in his work. Many stories look back to bygone times when everything was simpler, and technology had not yet disrupted the basics of small-town life. I ask him if he knows the source of this affection for simplicity.

"I grew up in Waukegan, Illinois, which had a population of around 32,000, and in a town like that you walk everywhere when you're a child. We didn't have a car till I was twelve years old. So I didn't drive in automobiles much until I came west when I was fourteen, to live in Los Angeles. We didn't have a telephone in our family until I was about fifteen, in high school. A lot of things, we didn't have; we were a very poor family. So you start with basics, and you respect them. You respect walking, you respect a small town, you respect the library, where you went for your education—which I started doing when I was nine or ten. I've always been a great swimmer and a great walker, and a bicyclist. I've discovered every time I'm depressed or worried by anything, swimming or walking or bicycling will generally cure it. You get the blood clean and the mind clean, and then you're ready to go back to work again."

He goes on to talk about his early ambitions:

"My interests were diverse. I always wanted to be a cartoonist, and I wanted to have my own comic strip. And I wanted to make films, and be on the stage, and be an architect—I was madly in love with the architecture of the future that I saw in photographs of various world's fairs which preceded my birth. And then, reading Edgar Rice Burroughs when I was ten or eleven, I wanted to write Martian stories. So when I began to write, when I was twelve, that was the first thing I did. I wrote a sequel to an Edgar Rice Burroughs book.

"When I was seventeen years old, in Los Angeles, I used to go to science-fantasy meetings, downtown. We'd go to Clifton's Cafeteria; Forrest Ackerman and his friends would organize the group there every Thursday night, and you could go there and meet Henry Kuttner, and C. L. Moore, and Jack Williamson, and Edmond Hamilton, and Leigh Brackett—my God, how beautiful, I was seventeen years old, I wanted heroes, and they treated me beautifully. They accepted me. I still know practically everyone in the field, at least from the old days. I love them all. Robert Heinlein was my teacher, when I was nineteen...but you can't stay with that sort of thing, a family has to grow. Just as you let your children out into the world—I have four daughters—you don't say, 'here is the boundary, you can't go out there.' So at the age of nineteen I began to grow. By the time I was twenty I was moving into little theatre groups and I was beginning to experiment with other fictional forms. I still kept up my contacts with the science-fiction groups, but I mustn't stay in just that.

"When I was around twenty-four, I was trying to sell stories to *Colliers* and *Harper's* and *The Atlantic*, and I wanted to be in *The Best American Short Stories*. But it wasn't happening. I had a friend who knew a psychiatrist. I said, 'Can I borrow your psychiatrist for an afternoon?' One hour cost twenty dollars! That was my salary for the whole week to go to this guy for an hour. So I went to him and he said, 'Mr. Bradbury, what's your problem?' And I said, 'Well, hell, nothing's happening.' So he said, 'What do you want to happen?' And I said, 'Well, gee, I want to be the greatest writer that ever lived.' And he said, 'That's going to take a little time, then, isn't it?' He said, 'Do you ever read the encyclopedia? Go down to the library and read the lives of Balzac and Du Maupassant and Dickens and Tolstoy, and see how long it took them to become what they became.' So I went and read and discovered that they had to wait, too. And a year later I began to sell to the *American Mercury*, and *Colliers*, and I appeared in *The Best American Short Stories* when I was twenty-six. I still wasn't making any money, but I was getting the recognition that I wanted, the love that I wanted from people I looked up to. The intellectual elite in America was beginning to say, 'Hey, you're okay, you're all right, and you're going to make it.' And then my girlfriend Maggie told me the same thing. And then it didn't matter whether the people around me sneered at me. I was willing to wait."

In fact, Bradbury must have received wider critical recognition, during the late 1950s and into the 1960s, than any other science-fiction author. His work used very little technical jargon, which made it easy for "outsiders" to digest, and he acquired a reputation as a stylist, if only because so few science-fiction authors at that time showed any awareness of style at all.

Within the science-fiction field, however, Bradbury has never received as much acclaim, measured (for example) by the annual awards. Does this irk him?

"That's a very dangerous thing to talk about." He pauses. Up till this moment, he has talked readily, with absolute confidence. Now, he seems ill-at-ease. "I left the family, you see. And that's a danger...to them. Because, they haven't got out of the house. It's like when your older brother leaves home suddenly—*how dare he leave me*, hah? *My hero, that I depended on to protect me.* There's some of that feeling. I don't know how to describe it. But once you're out and you look back and they've got their noses pressed against the glass, you want to say, 'Hey, come on, it's not that hard, come on out.' But each of us has a different capacity for foolhardiness at a certain time. It takes a certain amount of—it's not bravery—it's experimentation. Because I'm really, basically, a coward. I'm afraid of heights, I don't fly, I don't drive. So you see I can't really claim to be a brave person. But the part of me that's a writer wanted to experiment out in the bigger world, and couldn't help myself, I just had to go out there.

"I knew that I had to write a certain way, and take my chances. I sold newspapers on a street corner, for three or four years, from the time I was nineteen till I was twenty-two or twenty-three years old. I made ten dollars a week at it, which was *nothing*, and meant that I couldn't take girls out and give them a halfway decent evening. I could give them a ten-cent malted milk and a cheap movie, and then walk them home. We couldn't take the bus, there was no money left. But, again, this was no virtuous selection on my part. It was pure instinct. I knew exactly how to keep myself well.

"I began to write for *Weird Tales* in my early twenties, sold my short stories there, got twenty or thirty dollars apiece for them. You know everything that's in *The Martian Chronicles*, except two stories, sold for forty, fifty dollars apiece, originally.

"I met Maggie when I was twenty-five. She worked in a bookstore in downtown Los Angeles, and her views were so much like mine—she was interested in books, in language, in literature—and she *wasn't* interested in having a rich boyfriend; which was great, because I wasn't! We got married two years later and in thirty-two years of marriage we have had only one problem with money. One incident, with a play. The rest of the time we have never discussed it. We knew we didn't have any money in the bank, so why discuss something you don't have, hah?

"We lived in Venice, California, our little apartment, thirty dollars a month, for a couple of years, and our first children came along, which terrified us because we had no money, and then God began to provide. As soon as the first child arrived my income went up from fifty dollars a week to ninety dollars a week. By the time I was thirty-three I was making $110 a week. And then John Huston came along, and gave me *Moby Dick* [a film for which Bradbury wrote the screenplay] and my income went up precipitously in one year—and then went back down the next year, because I chose not to do any more screenplays for three years after that, it was a conscious choice and an intuitive one, to write more books and establish a reputation. Because, as I said earlier, no one remembers who wrote *Moby Dick* for the screen.

"Los Angeles has been great for me, because it was a collision of Hollywood—motion pictures—and the birthing of certain technologies. I've been madly in love with film since I was three year old. I'm not a pure science-fiction writer, I'm a film maniac at heart, and it infests all of my work. Many of my short stories can be shot right off the page. When I first met Sam Peckinpah, eight or nine years ago, and we started a friendship, and he wanted to do *Something Wicked This Way Comes*, I said, 'How are you going to do it?' And he said, 'I'm going to rip the pages out of your book and stuff them in the camera.' He was absolutely correct. Since I'm a bastard son of Erich von Stroheim out of Lon Chaney—a child of the cinema—hah!—it's only natural that almost all of my work is photogenic."

Is he happy with the way his stories have been made into movies?

"I was happy with *Fahrenheit 451*. I think it's a beautiful film, with a gorgeous ending. A great ending by Truffaut. *The Illustrated Man* I detested; a horrible film. I now have the rights back, and we'll do it over again, some time, in the next few years. *Moby Dick*—I'm immensely moved by it. I'm very happy with it. I see things I could do now, twenty-five years later, that I understand better, about Shakespeare and the Bible—who, after all, instructed Melville at his activities. Without the Bible and Shakespeare, *Moby Dick* would never have been born. Nevertheless, with all the flaws, and with the problem of Gregory Peck not being quite right as Ahab—I wanted someone like Olivier; it would have been fantastic to see Olivier—all that to one side, I'm still very pleased."

In the past few years Bradbury has turned increasingly toward writing poetry as opposed to short stories. Not all of this poetry has been well received. I ask him if he suffers from that most irritating criticism: people telling him that his early work was better.

"Oh, yes, and they're—they're *wrong*, of course. Steinbeck had to put up with that. I remember hearing him say this. And it's nonsense. I'm doing work in my poems, now, that I could never have done thirty years ago. And I'm very proud. Some of the poems that have popped out of my head in the last two years are

incredible. I don't know where in hell they came from, but—good
God, they're *good*! I have written at least three poems that are going
to be around seventy years, a hundred years from now. Just three
poems, you say? But the reputation of most of the great poets are
based on only one or two poems. I mean, when you think of Yeats,
you think of "Sailing to Byzantium," and then I defy you, unless
you're a Yeats fiend, to name six other poems.

"To be able to write *one* poem in a lifetime, that you feel is *so
good* it's going to be around for a while...and I've done that, damn
it, I've done it—at least three poems—and a lot of short stories. I
did a short story a year ago called "Gotcha," that is, damn it, boy
that's good. Another thing, called "The Burning Man," which I did
two years ago...and then some of my new plays, the new *Fahrenheit
451*, a totally original new play based on what my characters are
giving me, at the typewriter. I'm not in control of them. They're
living their lives all over again, twenty-nine years later, and they're
saying good stuff. So long as I can keep the channels open between
my subconscious and my outer self, it's going to stay good.

"I don't know how I do anything that I do, in poetry. Again,
it's instinctive, from years and years and years of reading
Shakespeare, and Pope—I'm a great admirer of Pope—and Dylan
Thomas, I don't know what in hell he's saying, a lot of times, but
God it sounds good, Jesus, it rings, doesn't it, hah? It's as clear as
crystal. And then you look closely and you say, it's crystal—but I
don't know how it's cut. But you don't care! Again, it's
unconscious, for me. People come up and say, oh, you did an
Alexandrian couplet here. And I say, oh, did I? I was so dumb, I
thought an Alexandrian couplet had to do with Alexander Pope!

"But from reading poetry every day of your life, you pick up
rhythms, you pick up beats, you pick up inner rhymes. And then,
some day in your forty-fifth year, your subconscious brings you a
surprise. You finally do something decent. But it took me thirty,
thirty-five years of writing, before I wrote one poem that I liked."

There is no denying this man's energy and his enthusiasm. It's so directly expressed, and so guileless, it makes him likable and charming regardless of whether you identify with his outlook or share his opinions. He projects a mixture of innocence and sincerity; he looks at you directly as he speaks, as if trying to win you over and catalyze you into sharing his enthusiasm. He is a tanned, handsome figure, with white hair and, often, white or light-colored clothing. The first time I ever saw him, at a science-fiction convention, he seemed almost regal, standing in his white suit, surrounded by a mass of scruffy adolescent fans in dowdy T-shirts and jeans. Yet he seemed to empathize with them. Despite his healthy ego he is not condescending toward his younger admirers, perhaps because he still feels (and looks) so young at heart himself. He has a child's sense of wonder and naive, idealistic spirit, as he goes around marveling at the world. He has not become jaded or disillusioned either about science fiction or about its most central subject matter, travel into space.

"We have had this remarkable thing occurring during the last ten years, when the children of the world began to educate the teachers, and said, 'Here is science fiction, read it'; and they read it and they said, 'Hey, it's not bad,' and began to teach it. Only in the last seven or eight years has science fiction gotten respectable.

"Orwell's *1984* came out thirty years ago this summer. Not a mention of space travel in it, as an alternative to Big Brother, a way to get away from him. That proves how myopic the intellectuals of the 1930s and 1940s were about the future. They didn't want to see something as exciting and as soul-opening and as revelatory as space travel. Because we *can* escape, and escape is very important, very tonic, for the human spirit. We escaped Europe 400 years ago and it was all to the good, and then from what we learned, by escaping, we could come back and say, 'We're going to refresh you, we got our revolution, now maybe we can all revolt together against certain things.' My point is that intellectual snobbishness permeated everything, including all the novels, *except* in science fiction. It's only in the last ten years we can look back and say, 'Oh, my God, we really were beat up all the time by these people, and it's a miracle we survived.'"

But, I suggest, a lot of the mythic quality of space travel has been lost, now that NASA has made it an everyday reality.

"I believe that any great activity finally bores a lot of people," he replies, "and it's up to us 'romantics'—hmm?" (he makes it clear, he still dislikes the term) "to continue the endeavor. Because *my* enthusiasm remains constant. From the time I saw my first space covers on *Science and Invention*, or *Wonder Stories*, when I was eight or nine years old—that stuff is still in me. Carl Sagan, a friend of mine, *he's* a 'romantic,' he loves Edgar Rice Burroughs—I know, he's *told* me. And Bruce Murray, who's another friend of mine, who's become president of Jet Propulsion Laboratories—first time I've ever known someone who became president of anything!—and he's a human being, that's the first thing, and he happens, second, to be the president of a large company that's sending our rockets out to Jupiter and Mars. I don't think it's been demystified. I think a lot of people were not mystified *to begin with*, and that's a shame."

Is Bradbury happy with the growth of science fiction? Does he like modern commercial exploitation of the genre—as in movies like *Star Wars*?

"*Star Wars*—idiotic but beautiful, a gorgeously dumb movie. Like being in love with a really stupid woman." He gives a shout of laughter, delighted by his own metaphor. "But you can't keep your hands off her, that's what *Star Wars* is. And then *Close Encounters* comes along, and it's got a brain, so you get to go to bed with a beautiful film. And then something like *Alien* comes along, and it's a horror film in outer space, and it has a gorgeous look to it, a *gorgeous* look. So wherever we can get help we take it, but the dream remains the same: survival in space and moving on out, and caring about the whole history of the human race, with all our stupidities, all the dumb things that we are, the idiotic creatures, fragile, broken creatures. I try to accept that; I say, okay, we are *also* the ghosts of Shakespeare, Plato, Euripides and Aristotle,

Machiavelli and Da Vinci, and a lot of amazing people who cared enough to try and help us. Those are the things that give me hope in the midst of stupidity. So what we are going to try and do is move on out to the moon, get on out to Mars, move on out to Alpha Centauri, and we'll do it in the next 500 years, which is a very short period of time; maybe even sooner, in 200 years. And then, survive forever, that is the great thing. Oh, God, I would love to come back every 100 years and watch us.

"So there it is, there's the essence of optimism—that I believe we'll make it, and we'll be proud, and we'll still be stupid and make all the dumb mistakes, and part of the time we'll hate ourselves; but then the rest of the time we'll celebrate."

Historical Context

It wasn't easy to get an interview with Ray Bradbury. Initially he sent back my written request with a note scribbled at the bottom saying that he didn't feel like "giving away any more pieces of myself at this time."

Still, one thing I have learned in journalism is that it pays to be persistent. I was friendly with Harlan Ellison in those days, and asked if he felt willing to put in a word for me with Ray.

In retrospect, I have a feeling that Ellison and Bradbury were not close friends. Still, they were on good terms, and Bradbury agreed to visit Ellison's house when I was staying there a few weeks later. The only problem was that Bradbury doesn't drive a car. I had to go to his home, pick him up, and bring him back.

The journey was a little awkward. Bradbury immediately grabbed the dashboard with one hand and maintained a death grip, no matter how slowly I proceeded. Maybe it helped him to feel a little more secure, or maybe it was his way of letting me know that he wanted me to be very, very careful.

When we reached Ellison's house, he relaxed visibly. Soon he was smiling and chatting as Ellison took him on a tour, swapping

116

anecdotes and giving the backstory on each ornament and framed piece of artwork. "Wonderful house," said Bradbury, when the tour was complete. "Wonderful!"

He seemed to be getting ready to leave. "So, about that interview," I said.

He turned to me. Unexpectedly, he reached out with one hand and grabbed me by the neck. He gave me a little shake, like a cat checking to see if a mouse was still alive. He was grinning, though. "All right, all right," he said, and we made an appointment for the next evening.

When I visited him, he sat on the floor throughout the interview, sometimes leaning forward with his elbows on a coffee table. I felt awkward, looking down from my vantage point while sitting on a chair, but this seemed to be the way he wanted it. He evidently didn't feel comfortable in cars, so maybe he didn't feel comfortable on chairs.

He gave a good performance, even though I think he still didn't really want to do it. From his point of view, there was nothing to be gained. My interview wouldn't make him any more famous than he already was, and wouldn't sell any more of his books. But I think he still felt some empathy with writers who were less successful than himself, and he was a genuinely nice guy who had difficulty saying "no."

The only other time I saw him in person was many years later, shortly before he died. He was in a wheelchair, having suffered a stroke, yet seemed vigorous and cheerful while giving a speech in a college auditorium. His best-loved works were still the ones that he had written decades ago—but so be it. To him, they were not as important as his later work, but at least they enabled him to continue enjoying himself in front of the audience that he loved.

He died in June, 2012.

A. E. van Vogt

Los Angeles, California, May 15, 1979

SUNSHINE ON SWARMS of gleaming machines. White highways, blue sky; white beaches, blue sea; white buildings; houses scattered up across hazy hills of mauve and brown. Bare feet, blond hair, tanned bodies, faded jeans. Restless motion, teeming life in a fever-dream valley.

Lawn sprinklers casting rainbows; multicolored birds on power lines; lizards basking on the patio. Concrete, steel, and glass, among the bountiful vegetation: evergreens and succulents, jungle foliage nourished by perpetual sun.

Belden Drive is a narrow concrete road that snakes up into the hills. Mounded bushes, shrubs, and cacti surround Mediterranean-style houses at each bend in the street. The air is vibrant. Insects buzz and hum.

A. E. van Vogt's house is a Spanish villa with red-tiled roof and stucco walls. It stands in a niche on the hillside, not very far below the old HOLLYWOOD sign. The veranda overlooks a slope of lush greenery, down to the wide, flat valley of Los Angeles. To my eastern eyes it's a Pacific paradise transformed by wealth and technology into a new-world composite of Life and Future.

---

[2] Photo from *Reflections of A. E. van Vogt*.

118

Charles Platt

But I feel van Vogt is oblivious to his surroundings. He is not a Californian; he might as well be living in a log cabin, or a cave. The bright scenery of the West Coast seems irrelevant to his interests and his work, because its vivid images are trivial compared to the power of the resonant landscapes inside his mind.

Of course, many fantasists pursue their imaginations oblivious to reality around them. But this is especially true of van Vogt, first because he works more intimately with his subconscious than most writers, and second because much of his life has been spent looking inward, studying psychology and human behavior, primarily through Dianetics and hypnosis.

His science fiction is concerned with the power of rationality, and disciplines such as general semantics. But really, his talent has nothing to do with science or logic. It's an intuitive, wild talent, remarkable for its strangeness. When you open one of his novels, you open the subconscious. He writes dreams.

And by a weird method that he will explain in a moment, he dreams his writing. First, however, he describes how he originally became a writer, while still very young, in Canada (where he was born in 1912):

"A man called John W. Gallishaw wrote a book called *The Only Two Ways to Write a Short Story*. I borrowed it from the Winnipeg library, and I read it all the way through. It's an incredibly hard book to read; it's so long. It gave all kinds of examples. He had twenty stories in there, which he had numbered and analyzed line by line. He had an idea of writing a story in scenes of about 800 words, and each scene had five steps in it. If all those steps aren't there in their proper way, then there's something wrong with that scene. First, you let the reader know where this is taking place. Then you establish the purpose of the main character or the purpose of that scene. Then you have the interaction of his trying to accomplish that purpose. The fourth step is, make it clear: did he or did he not accomplish that purpose? Then the fifth step is that, in all the early scenes, no matter whether he achieves that purpose or

119

not, things are going to get worse."

Van Vogt adopted this system, and has always used it, making him one of the few successful professional authors to have built his career on a popular "how-to" guide. He also learned to write in what Gallishaw called "fictional sentences":

"Every type of story has its own type of fictional sentence. I started by writing 'confession' stories [for women's magazines]. These stories have to have emotion in every sentence. You don't say, 'I lived at 323 Grand Street.' You say something like 'Tears came to my eyes as I thought of my little room at 323 Grand Street.' And the next sentence, and the next sentence. I did that with the very first story that I ever wrote for them, which I called 'I Lived in the Streets,' about a girl who was put out of her room during the Depression. I went to the library every day and wrote one scene. I had just come back from a stint of working for the civil service in Ottawa, on the 1931 census."

It took him nine days of visiting the library to complete this story, and he sold it for $110. He was soon writing and selling more stories to "Confession" magazines.

"I wrote one story for a contest, and won the $1,000 first prize. It was a 9,000-word story. I would say that that would automatically mean between 1,000 and 1,200 sentences. It's not impossible to write 1,000 or 1,200 emotional sentences. It's impossible for an unorganized person, but not for somebody who thinks by a system."

The $1,000 first prize was worth a great deal in the early 1930s—it was equivalent to almost a year's salary in his civil service job. However, he became tired of this genre. He started writing plays for Canadian radio, at ten dollars a time. And then, a couple of years later, almost arbitrarily, he decided to try writing science fiction. His first story sold to *Astounding Science Fiction*, the most prestigious magazine in the field.

Once again, he developed a system:

"In science fiction you have to have a little bit of a 'hang-up' in each sentence. Let's suppose, for example: The hero looks up toward the door." Van Vogt gestures toward the sunlit screen door of his living room, leading out onto the veranda. "He hears a *sound* over there. And *something* comes in. It looks like a man wearing a cloak. You don't quite know what's going on. Then, you realize this is not a human being. This creature or this being, whoever it is, has a sort of manlike shape. And this creature reaches into what now looks like a *fold of its skin*. It draws out a *gleaming metal object*. It points it at you. Is this a weapon? It looks like a weapon, but you don't know that for sure. It's a *hang-up*, you see. The author furnishes the information, but each sentence in itself has a little *hang-up* in it."

As he has been talking, almost hypnotically, with an eerie gleam in his eye, he has created such a mood of menace that, for a moment, the California sunshine seems less bright and the dreamlike description is nibbling at the edges of reality. He would say, perhaps, that this is through the power of his system, but I think it has more to do with the power of his personality and his intuitively shrewd choice of words and images. A system on its own is dull and mechanical, without inspiration to fuel it. Van Vogt goes on to describe how he realized his source for this inspiration:

"I didn't notice, right away, what I was doing. In science fiction I was writing for only one cent a word, so because I work slowly I would wake up anxious, thinking, *work out my story*. I'd go back to sleep, wake up anxious, each time thinking about my story. Then in 1943 in Toronto I suddenly realized. It took me all that time to realize what I'd been doing all those years. Had I been Cyril Kornbluth [who died aged thirty-five] I might never have found out how I wrote. It's a good thing my life went past a certain point!

"I took the family alarm clock and went into the spare bedroom that night, and set it for an hour and a half. And thereafter, when I was working on a story, I would awaken myself every hour and a half, through the night—force myself to wake up, think of the story, try to solve it, and even as I was thinking about it

I would fall back asleep. And in the morning, there would be a solution, for that particular story problem. Now, that's penetrating the subconscious, in my opinion. It's penetrating it in a way that I don't think they'll be able to do any better, thirty centuries from now."

And so van Vogt derived his inspiration through his sleep, filling his science-fiction adventures with fantastic images, symbolic figures, a constant sense of discovery and revelation, and free, flying motion (aided by those telegraphic 800-word scenes, which enforced a fast pace). Some critics, such as Damon Knight, complained that van Vogt's plots didn't make logical sense, and consequently his books were failures. This seems as misguided to me as criticizing a dream on grounds of implausibility. Dreams are powerful *because* they are so full of change and contradictions, in violation of laws of everyday life.

Although his science fiction was highly successful, van Vogt stopped writing it rather suddenly in the 1950s. I ask him exactly what happened.

"I'm a system-thinker, as I think I told you. I had observed that writers got passé, they became old-fashioned to the readers. Another generation comes up and it's about a ten-year cycle. So at the end of my first ten years in science fiction I thought, Well, the ten-year period is over, and all I can do now, is...I'm back in that earlier quaint reality, and there's a new reality coming up, and it'll be as real to the people reading those stories as if God said it Himself; you know, this is the reality of *now*. I thought, What should I do?

"Among other things, I wrote *The Hypnotism Handbook*, for a psychologist. That was in late 1949, though it was not published until 1950. Having written that book I thought I'd looked into human behavior a little bit, I must have gotten something out of it. Then I began to get letters from L. Ron Hubbard ['interviewed' elsewhere in this volume]. In 1950, shortly after the hypnotism book was published, he began to phone me, long-distance from

New Jersey, every morning, and talk for an hour to get me interested in Dianetics. That kind of phone-calling, long distance, was completely out of my reality. It was beyond my conception that anybody was phoning that often, and talking that long, from 3,000 miles away.

"He made a statement around the seventeenth morning he called me, that 'We've got all kinds of people who want to send money to somebody out there, and there's nobody to send it to,' and I said, 'Tell them to send it to me and I'll guard it for you!' and I think I got altogether $3,400 in the next couple of weeks. It was sent for a course that they were going to give out here. Three days later a letter arrived appointing me head of the California Dianetics operation.

"The organization spent $500,000 in nine months and went broke, because at that time there were a tremendous number of attacks on Dianetics. We [in California] were the only branch that never did go into bankruptcy, because I don't believe in being involved in bankruptcy. An attorney friend and I went to see all the creditors, and they let us just fold it and pay what we could.

"One of the reasons why the book *Dianetics* impressed me was the fact that it had not one line of mysticism in it that I could detect. I didn't know, at that time, [editor John W.] Campbell had dissuaded Hubbard from putting any into it. You see previously I had met Hubbard in 1945; I had dinner with him and about a dozen other persons, and it became apparent to me that he was *very* mystically oriented. So when there was, later, not a line of that in the book I thought, by God, this has really got to be a good system, because it has already knocked that out of him!"

Dianetics has since been "incorporated into the framework of Scientology, as an earlier phase you have to go through," according to van Vogt, but he remains uninterested in Scientology, because of its mystical/religious aspects. He retains faith in the principles of Dianetics, and is still president of the Californian Association of Dianetic Auditors. He recalls personal experiences using the system:

"My wife [E. Mayne Hull] had been ill, and had had operations about every two years, starting almost within a year of our marriage, in 1939. She made her will at least six times during that period. When I talked to the doctors, every time they said, 'It looks like cancer.' In 1951 there was another doctor that examined her, and said to me, We've got to watch out, that has all the sound of cancer.

"But right in there she got some [Dianetic] auditing, and the problem all faded away just like it never was. She was not sick again, she didn't go to a doctor, until we went to a funeral of a friend who had died of cancer in Phoenix in 1970. On he way back she said, 'It's like the end of an era;' and she burst into tears. One month later she had blood in her urine and they examined her and this time they said, 'It *is* cancer.' The point is, it had been put aside somehow by the Dianetic thing. Dianetics is essentially based upon Freudian therapy, but Freud allowed the patient to freely associate, and he never concentrated upon one incident. Dianetics concentrated upon one incident, going through it again and again. When that was done, things seemed to fade away. Certain incidents that my wife ran seemed to be keyed to her health; clearly they were not erased, they were just put back, you might say, into some slot."

Van Vogt recalls his work in Hubbard's Dianetic Research Foundation: "Hubbard, having a naval background, had his staff meetings at seven a.m. and I closed that place up at one o'clock at night, when he'd been gone many hours. I went home and went to bed at five-thirty or something like that.

"After the organization went broke, Mayne and I decided to open up our own Dianetics center here in Los Angeles. I partly supported it by putting books together from earlier short stories, because I charged very little at the center—seventy-five dollars for thirty hours of what we called project auditing. In the end I signed off somewhere around 1961."

124

But van Vogt didn't stop thinking about psychology, and inventing his own theories. At one point he realized that his system of tapping the subconscious, in order to write science fiction, could also be used as a kind of therapy.

"If you take an incident of severe, traumatic emotion, and wake yourself up every hour and a half, and think about it, go through it in your mind, and fall back asleep while you're doing that, it takes about two weeks, for a severe incident, before it fades.

"I have a book here which I ordered from the Department of Health and Welfare—their book on sleep and dreaming—and I read the summarization of all the discoveries that had been made, and it was quite evident, first of all, that my ninety-minute cycle was the correct one. I'd just chosen that automatically; an hour seemed too short. What the brain does, in the first hour and a half, it deals with the previous day: when they wake people up they're dreaming about the previous day. And then in the subsequent ninety-minute periods it's all back history, going into childhood. I would guess that the mind is trying to throw off the shock of the past, and keeps associating from one to the other to the other, and can never dispose of any of it. When it took me two weeks to dispose of a fear incident in my childhood, that seemed a very significant observation and discovery to have made. It faded, and another incident came into view, and I went on and on like that, working with fear incidents.

"The effectiveness of it is not easy to prove, but here's what happened when I was reading up on the background of Naples for a novel I wrote called *The Darkness of Diamondia*. I had a planet many light-years distant, called Diamondia, which had been settled by Italians, and they had sort of rebuilt Italy there. There was a place called New Naples, and they build it right under Vesuvius II, that kind of thing. So I read up on the history of Naples. It's a history of massacres, assassinations, murders, horrible continuous killing. It didn't bother me because I'd been reading before about human nature. But I ran across one incident that bothered me. Two

125

fourteen-year-old boys were turned in as traitors and beheaded. For some reason or other that disturbed me. The next day, I couldn't seem to write, I felt distracted. And the next day, and the next. Two weeks went by, and I thought, my God, this thing is still running around—vivid images, running through my head. And so I thought, why don't I try the dream therapy on that?

"By this time, I was using an industrial timer and a cassette recorder, not an alarm clock. An alarm clock you have to rewind and reset, whereas this works automatically every hour and a half."

I interrupt to ask him what the tape recorder says, when the timer turns it on.

"First of all it says *wake up* a few times, and, *remember, you're doing dream therapy—on this subject!*—because I could wake up with the alarm clock and not know what I was dealing with; completely blank.

"Anyway, so I put the memory of those two executions through my mind, went back to sleep; and again; and by six o'clock the feeling had faded. And it never came back. This was a small example of the effectiveness of the system. It's purely my own system. A complete invention of my own."

I ask him if he ever suggested to the Dianetics or Scientology people that they might be able to use this system.

"No, and I'll tell you why—because I don't see how anybody could charge for it!" He laughs. "It's not for a large organization with overhead expenses. It should be used as a supplement to daytime psychotherapy."

"My own feeling," he goes on, "is that psychiatry's going to have to be saved. I may try to save psychiatry, if you'll pardon the, ah...there is an MD who writes science fiction occasionally under the name T. J. Bass. He wrote a book called *Half Past Human*. It's loaded with good information. He runs thirty miles every day. He has overage patients. They start, they can barely stagger into the office, age seventy-three, they've heard about him and his system. And then they run the first 150 feet, and lie down, or whatever, and at the end of a certain period of time they're running with him thirty miles a day. I sent out an inquiry to many science-fiction writers asking, had they invented any new sciences of their own. His answer was, 'I think I've got the beginning of the science of immortality.'

"Now, in 1968 I had a beautiful one-year-old dog; she wanted to go out every morning, she'd come in and wake me up at eight o'clock, which was an unheard-of hour for me. I thought, well now's my time to conduct the experiment I've been planning for fifteen years. The Exercise Experiment. I went out with her on the eighth morning—after you've had somebody wake you up by licking your face with a big wet tongue eight mornings in a row, finally the thought penetrates, all right, the time has come for an experiment. So we went out.

"My theory was that exhaustion is an association with a past illness. Basically it's a Freudian-oriented theory. We started to jog. At the end of 150 feet I was absolutely exhausted. Theoretically *I* should have lain down and rested for a while. But the theory said no—the stress of that moment had forced an association with a disturbance from the past. I thought, What can this be, it's got to be some kind of an association from the past, by my theory, forced by the stress into the here-and-now, just as nervousness overtakes the person who's faced with public speaking. So I thought of an incident when I was aged eleven. I had been out with a bunch of kids on a very hot Saturday afternoon and we'd gone some distance. Coming back, I suddenly had a hard time breathing. In fact I couldn't stand up. I sat down beside the road, and just sat there for about an hour, totally exhausted. So I remembered this incident and mentally went through it a few times by the Dianetic scanning method, and the feeling of exhaustion faded! Then 150 or 200 feet later I felt another type of exhaustion, another feeling, and what was this? Well, all my illnesses kept coming into view, and particularly a fall that I had at age two-and-a-half—I was unconscious for three days at two-and-a-half, from falling out of a second-story window. So anyway, I continued to run, and we ran along this street here, Belden Drive, and then down on Beechwood, and the only time we stopped was when the dog stopped and when we came to the foot of the hill leading up to my house. I looked at that hill and I thought, well, let's consider that the human heart should not be put under total stress the first day or the second day, that kind of thing. So I walked up the hill, and I stopped six times on the way up, each time that I felt the exhaustion, and considered what it could be, and dealt with it, counting the pictures past my mind's eye.

"Now, I'm talking about saving psychiatry. See, I don't believe in running thirty miles a day. The mere thought makes me quail. I seem to remember that the world's record for thirty miles is about two hours and three-quarters. I do not propose to get involved in anything like that. It would be more like four and a half hours. Doing that every day sounds totally mad!

"However: if a psychiatrist were to have half a dozen patients, at so much an hour, running with him, and dealing with their cases as they went along, and then at night had them do dream therapy, a combination of these two things, I think that they could get a lot done. Running, if you're up to it, is an *automatic-gain* situation: a person is going to get a little healthier, no matter what's going on in his head. So I believe that that's the direction that psychiatrists should take."

I imagine a team of out-patients jogging around the Hollywood hills, accompanied by their therapist; one by one, the jogging neurotics experience exhaustion and make insightful mental leaps back to significant childhood traumas, which are exorcised in this sudden flash of association. But there seems to be a practical problem, in this scenario of jogging therapy. Isn't it awfully hard to run and talk to your psychiatrist at the same time? And even if you can gasp out your symptoms—what are the rest of the patients doing?

Van Vogt seems slightly irritated by such a mundane objection. "Well, they'd stop for a moment—some of them would keep on running back and forth, while he's talking to one guy. They could just go back and forth, and then everybody moves forward again."

But this conversation has taken us rather a long way from science fiction. I ask van Vogt how he returned to the field.

"I met Frederik Pohl in the early 1960s. He said, 'Why don't you write for *Galaxy*' [the magazine that Pohl was then editing] so I wrote, first of all, 'The Expendables,' and then 'The Silkie'; and meanwhile I was working on a book called *The Money Personality*. I had gotten another system going. I had discovered that three men that I had known when I was in my teens had all gotten wealthy in Canada. That seemed incredible to me. So I went over it in my mind; how come *they* had made it into wealth, and here I am still working sixteen hours a day?"

I try another angle to get us back to science fiction again. Does he ever try to take advantage of living in Los Angeles, to write for the movies?

"I operate by systems, and until I have a system for writing screenplays, none will ever turn up from my pen. Many times have I had lunch with a story editor or director, and each time they require an outline [a description of the script that may be written]. An outline I cannot write, but I tried, each time. I would then present this unfinished (as it turned out) outline, which they couldn't make head or tail of, in their world. Then a few years later I would come across this thing, and I'd think, well, I can write a short story around this, which I would then do.

"I don't know what the problem is. You see I work a story out as I go along...."

Couldn't he work an outline out as he goes along?

"No, I don't seem to be able to do that. That's not the way I work. But I joined the Writers' Guild at the beginning of this year. They announced a course, once a month, where some of their great writers of screenplays would explain the writing of these things. I took my retired attorney friend with me and we went and listened, and a couple of thoughts have penetrated, up here." He taps his head. "The beginning of a system. Now, if I ever *get* a system, they'd better *watch out!*"

And the funny thing is, he's probably right; after all, his "systems" have enabled him to achieve considerable success in the fields of writing that he has tackled in the past.

After the interview, he invites me to a meal down at a restaurant in the valley. He has recently received large royalties from sales of his work in France, where he is an extremely popular writer; I think he feels like sharing a little of the largesse. Also, I sense he does not receive too many visitors these days, and since the sad death of his wife, the house feels a bit empty. (This interview was prior to Mr. van Vogt's second marriage, later in 1979.)

So we walk out to his car, which is an aging black Cadillac—old enough to possess tail fins. The car's license plate reads NOT A. Van Vogt comments that people stop alongside him in traffic and ask, "Not a *what?*" But of course the cryptic statement refers to his two novels about "non-Aristotelian" (i.e. multivalue) logic—which is another system he advocates.

We drive, extremely cautiously, down the narrow, winding road, in the giant old car. The tentativeness of this foray into the outside world seems to emphasize my impression that he has no special love or need for the California landscape bursting with life all around us.

Over the very pleasant, neutrally American meal, he remarks that "Were it not for having run into science fiction and gained some consciousness-expansion, I would have ended up a clerk in the Canadian government."

He sounds, as always, logical and matter-of-fact about it, but I know that this impression is misleading—for logic means a different thing to van Vogt from what it means to me, as does reality. Nor does it end here, because, as we will see in the next profile, van Vogt's visions have influenced other writers in the science-fiction field. His strange dreams, themselves a distortion of the world, have been used as a mere starting point for fiction that goes still further into metaphysical realms—and yet, paradoxically, also returns closer to everyday life.

Note: in describing van Vogt's decision to join Dianetics, I have inserted within the taped monologue three sentences drawn from his own small autobiographical book, *Reflections of A. E. van Vogt* (Fictioneer Books, 1975). The sentences were added for the sake of clarity.

Historical Context

The movie *Alien* was released very shortly after I interviewed A. E. van Vogt. When he saw it, he felt convinced that it was derived from his very first published science-fiction story, "Black Destroyer," which appeared in *Astounding Stories* in 1939. It described the invasion of a spaceship by an alien creature, and set a new standard for the depiction of alien life forms with a detailed set of attributes and a complex biology.

Although Twentieth Century Fox denied that *Alien* was derived from any of van Vogt's work, they settled out of court in 1980 for a reported $50,000.

He was single when I met him, but met his second wife, Lydia Bereginsky, when he advertised for native speakers of foreign languages in connection with a system he had devised that would help people to learn languages quickly. She was a former model and still a very elegant woman.

In subsequent years I saw them a couple of times at science-fiction events, where dowdiness was the norm and T-shirts and jeans were common. Van Vogt always wore a dark-blue suit, while his wife was elaborately coiffured, wearing a floor-length dress and jewelry. They drifted through the scruffy crowd like visitors from another planet.

In the early 1990s, when he was diagnosed with Alzheimer's disease, his wife demonstrated her devotion to him by maintaining his business affairs and basically managing his life until he died in 2000.

My original profile mentioned that Damon Knight had criticized van Vogt's work, but the full significance of this requires some additional explanation. Knight's highly influential book about science fiction, *In Search of Wonder*, included a chapter-long essay (reprinted from a fanzine) which damaged van Vogt's reputation in the field for many years. Titled "Cosmic Jerrybuilder: A. E. van Vogt," it was such an intemperate diatribe, it might have cast aspersions on Knight's abilities as a critic if he had not already established himself as an arbiter of taste in science fiction. He described *The World of Null-A* as "one of the worst allegedly-adult science fiction stories ever published," and characterized van Vogt as "a pygmy who has learned to operate an overgrown typewriter."

Van Vogt was sufficiently disturbed by the critique that he actually revised the book for a subsequent edition and added a new introduction, in which he wrote:

> *Singlehandedly, Knight took on this novel and my work at age 23-1/2, and, as Algis Budrys puts it, brought about my "destruction."*
>
> *So what's the problem? Why am I now revising World [of Null-A]? Am I doing all this for one critic?*
>
> *Yep. But why?——you ask.*
>
> *Well, on this planet you have to recognize where the power is.*

"On this planet" was hyperbole, but in science fiction, van Vogt was correct about Knight's influence at that time.

The destructiveness of the attack was surprising. I think that Philip K. Dick had it right when he gave this mild-mannered but accurate rebuttal while being interviewed for a little magazine named Vortex, in February 1974:

Damon feels that it's bad artistry when you build those funky universes where people fall through the floor. It's like he's viewing a story the way a building inspector would when he's building your house. But reality really is a mess, and yet it's exciting. The basic thing is, how frightened are you of chaos? And how happy are you with order? Van Vogt influenced me so much because he made me appreciate a mysterious chaotic quality in the universe which is not to be feared.

I love the comparison of Damon Knight to a building inspector who fusses about code violations instead of admiring the originality of the architecture. I think there's some truth in that. And I love the idea of a "funky universe" in which nothing quite adds up.

The work of A. E. van Vogt enthralled me when I first discovered it, and even now, if I read just the opening page of "Black Destroyer" (which was incorporated with other stories in the book titled *The Voyage of the Space Beagle*), the text still exerts a mysterious power. He had a very unusual talent.

He died in January 26, 2000 after suffering Alzheimer's for many years.

Philip K. Dick

Santa Ana, California, May 17, 1979

THE AIM OF the speculative writer should be to see what other people have not seen. The few who manage this offer more than entertainment, more than inventiveness. They give the reader a sense of revelation.

It takes a trace of genius or insanity to see what nobody else has seen, and it takes formidable writing talent to present such visions in realistic, human terms. The work of Philip K. Dick displays this talent, and a bit of genius, or craziness, or both. His best books are revelatory in a mystical sense.

Much of his work starts with the basic assumption that there cannot be one, single, objective reality. Everything is a matter of perception. The ground is liable to shift under your feet. A protagonist may find himself living out another person's dream, or he may enter a drug-induced state that actually makes better sense than the real world, or he may cross into a different universe completely. Cosmic Law is subject to sudden revision (by God, or whoever happens to be acting that role) and there are multiple truths.

---

[3] Photograph by "C.C."

These surreal ideas, and the hallucinatory quality of his writing, led to Dick being labeled an "acid-head" author. His obsessive anxiety about forces of political oppression resulted in his being dismissed as "paranoid." Ultimately, his claim to have experienced mystical experiences prompted many of his contemporaries to refer to him as mentally unbalanced.

When I went to visit him in Santa Ana, just south of the vast sprawl of Los Angeles, I wanted to pin down the truth in these matters. Foolishly, I went looking for objective clarification from a man who does not believe in objectivity. A few hours later I came away feeling as if my mind had been warped. Like a character in one of Dick's paradoxical, unresolved novels, I was left with more questions at the end than I had at the beginning.

I found Mr. Dick to be a dignified, thoughtful, slightly portly figure, with black hair, graying beard, and an informal but distinguished presence. He is erudite, intimidatingly well-read, but has none of the pretensions or detachment of an academic. He lives in a plain, modest apartment with two cats, some slightly run-down contemporary furniture, heaps of reference books, and an expensive stereo system. As I unpack my tape recorder I realize that he has already set up his own; a high-quality Shure microphone is on the black-glass tabletop, and he will be recording me at the same time that I record him. He seems slightly evasive about this, and says casually that he always makes his own tape whenever he is interviewed. I suppose one could regard this as paranoid behavior; I don't, but it does look as if he is intending to check up on me, to see if my tape transcript is accurate—or am *I* being paranoid now?

We begin by talking about his life when he first started writing science fiction, as a student at Berkeley who was also working part-time in a radio-TV retail store.

"I was in a curious position. I had read science fiction since I was twelve years old, and was really addicted. I just loved it. I also was reading what the Berkeley intellectual community was reading. For example, Proust or Joyce. So I occupied two worlds right there which normally did not intersect. Then, working in the retail store, the people I knew were TV salesmen and repairmen; they considered me peculiar for reading at *all*. I spent time in all kinds of different groups; I knew a lot of homosexuals; there was a whole homosexual community in the Bay Area even then, in the 1940s. I knew some very fine poets, and I was very proud of them as my friends. *They* thought of me as strange because I wasn't gay, and the people in my store thought I was strange because I knew gay people and read books, and my Communist friends thought I was odd because I wouldn't join the Communist Party...so being involved in science fiction didn't make all that much difference. Henry Miller said in one of his books, other children threw stones at him when they saw him. I had that same feeling. I managed to become universally despised wherever I went. I think that I must have thrived on it, because it kept happening so many times in so many ways.

"I got married when I nineteen, and it wasn't until a little later that I really began to write. I got married again when I was twenty-one. A point came when I began to feel that science fiction was very important. Van Vogt's *The World of Null-A*—there was something about that which absolutely fascinated me. It had a mysterious quality, it alluded to things unseen, there were puzzles presented which were never adequately explained. I found in it a numinous quality; I began to get an idea of a mysterious quality in the universe which could be dealt with in science fiction. I realize now that what I was sensing was a kind of metaphysical medieval world, an invisible realm of things half-seen, essentially what medieval people sensed as the transcendent world, the next world. I had no religious background. I was raised in a Quaker school—they're about the only group in the world that I don't have some grievance against; there's no hassle between me and the Quakers—but the Quaker thing was just a lifestyle. And in Berkeley there was no religious spirit at all.

"I don't know if van Vogt would agree that he's essentially

dealing with the supernatural, but that's what was happening in me. I was beginning to sense that what we perceived was not what was actually there. I was interested in Jung's idea of projection—what we experience as external to us may really be projected from our unconscious, which means of course that each person's world has to be somewhat different from everybody else's, because the contents of each person's unconscious will be to a certain extent unique. I began a series of stories in which people experienced worlds which were a projection of their own psyches. My first published story was a perfect example of this."

For a while Dick attempted to work both inside and outside of the science-fiction field: "I wrote many novels which were not science fiction or fantasy. They all contained the element of the projected personal unconscious, or projected collective unconscious, which made them simply incomprehensible to anyone who read them, because they required the reader to accept my premise that each of us lives in a unique world."

Such books proved difficult to sell. One, *Confessions of a Crap Artist*, was finally brought out in 1975; the rest have never been published. [Subsequent to this interview, all have appeared.] "There are nine or ten manuscripts extant, over at the Fullerton special collections library," he says, apparently without rancor. I ask him if he is really as philosophical about this situation as he seems. "Well, when *Confessions of a Crap Artist* appeared, that took the sting out of it, and I didn't feel so bad. But of course it did take nineteen years to get that published. It's been a long road; but science fiction offered me a route by which I *could* publish the kind of thing that I wanted to write. *Martian Time-Slip* is exactly what I wanted to write. It deals with the premise that was, to me, so important—not just that we each live in a somewhat unique world of our own psychological content, but that the subjective world of one rather powerful person can infringe on the world of another person. If I can make you see the world the way I see it, then you will automatically think the way I think. You will come to the conclusions that I come to. And the greatest power one human being can exert over others is to control their perceptions of reality, and infringe on the integrity and individuality of their world.

"This is done, for instance, in psychotherapy. I went through attack-therapy in Canada. You get a lot of people all yelling at you, and suddenly the mystery of the Moscow purge trials of the 1930s becomes very clear—what could possibly make a person get up and say in a most sincere manner that he had committed a crime, the penalty for which was execution. Well, the answer lies in the incredible power of a group of human beings to invade a man's world and determine his image of himself so that he can actually believe their view of him. I remember in attack-therapy there was one guy dressed kind of nattily, and he was French. They said, 'you look like a homosexual.' Within half an hour they had him convinced that he was a homosexual. He started crying. I thought, this is very strange, because I know this guy is *not* homosexual. And yet he's crying and admitting to this thing—not to cause the abuse to stop, the screams of these people all yelling at him, 'You fairy, you fruit, you homo, admit what you are.' By confessing to it he didn't cause them to stop, he caused them to yell louder and say, 'We were right, we were right.' He was simply beginning to agree with them.

"All this can be viewed politically or psychologically. To me it was all viewed dramatically in my writing, as the eerie and uncanny invasion of one person's world by another person's world. If I invade your world you will probably sense something alien, because my world is different from yours. You must, of course, fight it. But often we don't because a lot of it is subtle; we just have intimations that our worlds are being invaded, we don't know where this invasion of our personal integrity is coming from. It comes from authority figures in general.

"The greatest menace in the twentieth century is the totalitarian state. It can take many forms: left-wing fascism, psychological movements, religious movements, drug rehabilitation places, powerful people, manipulative people; or it can be in a relationship with someone who is more powerful than you psychologically. Essentially, I'm pleading the case of those people who are not strong. If I were strong myself I would probably not feel this as such a menace. I identify with the weak person; this is one reason why my fictional protagonists are essentially anti-heroes. They're almost losers, yet I try to equip them with qualities by which they can survive. At the same time I don't want to see them develop counter-aggressive tactics where they, too, become exploitative and manipulative."

I ask him what his response is when people tell him he is being overanxious about authority figures and is simply paranoid. In reply he refers to the harassment he suffered while he was an antiwar activist, culminating in a bizarre break-in at his home, which local police in effect refused to investigate. "I was told I was paranoid before my house was hit. Then I remember opening the door, and finding nothing but ruins everywhere, windows and doors smashed in, files blown open, all my papers missing, all my cancelled checks gone, my stereo gone, and I remember thinking, Well, it sure is a hell of a mess, but there goes that 'paranoid' theory.

"Actually I was told by a fairly good analyst that I'm not cold-blooded enough to be paranoid. He said to me, 'you're melodramatic and you're full of illusions about life, but you're too sentimental to be paranoid.'

"I took the Minnesota Multiphasic psychological profile test once, and I tested out as paranoid, cyclothymiac, neurotic, schizophrenic…I was so high on some of the scales that the dot was up in the instructions part. But I also tested out as an incorrigible liar! You see, they'll give you the same question phrased in several different ways. They'll say something like: 'There is a divine deity that rules the world.' And I'd say, yeah, there probably is. Later on they'll say: 'I don't think there is a divine deity that rules the world.' And I'd say, that's probably correct, I can see a lot of reasons for agreeing with that. And later they'll say: 'I'm not sure if there's a divine deity that rules the world.' And I'd say, yeah, that's about right.

"In every case I was sincere. I think philosophically I fit in with some of the very late pre-Socratic people around the time of Zeno and Diogenes, the Cynics, in the Greek sense, those who live like dogs. I am inevitably persuaded by every argument that is brought to bear. If you were to suggest to me at this moment that we go out for Chinese food I would immediately agree it was the best idea I ever heard; in fact, I would say, 'You've got to let me pay for it.' If you were to say suddenly, 'Don't you think that Chinese food is overpriced, has *very* little nourishment, you have to go a *long* way to get it, and when you bring it home it's *cold*,' I'd say, you're right, I can't abide the stuff. This is a sign of a very weak ego, I guess.

"However—if my view that each person has his unique world is correct, then if you say Chinese food is good, in your world it's good, and if someone else says it's bad, in his world it's bad. I'm a complete relativist in that for me the answer to the question, 'Is Chinese food good or bad?' is semantically meaningless. Now, this is *my* view. If your view is that this view is incorrect, *you* might be right. In which case, I would be willing to agree with you."

He sits back, happy with his exercise at eliminating any foundation for an objective structure of values. He has talked easily, engagingly, as if entertained by his own conversation. A lot of what he says sounds playful at the same time that it seems sincere.

I ask how much of his thinking was influenced by LSD experiences, and which of his books, if any, are derived from acid trips.

"I wrote *Time Out of Joint* in the 1950s, before I had even heard of LSD. In that book a guy walks up to a lemonade stand in the park, and it turns into a slip of paper marked Soft Drink Stand, and he puts the slip of paper in his pocket. Far-fucking out, spacey, that's an 'acid experience.' If I didn't know better I'd say that this author had turned on many times, and his universe was coming unglued—he's obviously living in a *fake universe*.

"What I was trying to do in that book was account for the diversity of worlds that people live in. I had not read Heraclitus then, I didn't know his concept of *ideos kosmos*, the private world, versus *koinos kosmos*, which we all share. I didn't know that the pre-Socratics had begun to discern these things.

"There's a scene in the book where the protagonist goes into his bathroom, reaches in the dark for a pull-cord, and suddenly realizes there is no cord, there's a switch on the wall, and he can't remember when he ever had a bathroom where there was a cord hanging down. Now, that actually happened to me, and it was what caused me to write the book. It reminded me of the idea that van Vogt had dealt with, of artificial memory, as it occurs in *The World of Null-A* where a person has false memories implanted. A lot of what I wrote, which looks like the result of taking acid, is really the result of taking van Vogt very seriously! I *believed* van Vogt, I mean, *he wrote it*, you know, he was an authority figure. He said that people can be other than whom they remember themselves to be, and I found this fascinating. You have a massive suspension of disbelief on my part."

I ask to what extent he was ever, really, into drugs.

"The only drugs I took regularly were amphetamines, in order to be able to write as much as I had to write to make a living. I was being paid so little per book that I had to turn out a very large number of books. I had an extremely expensive wife and children. She would see a new car that she liked the looks of and just go off and buy it...under California law I was legally bound by her debts and I just wrote like mad. I think I turned out sixteen novels in five years at one point. I did sixty finished pages a day, and the only way I could write that much was to take amphetamines, which were prescribed for me. I finally stopped taking them, and I don't write as much as I used to.

"I used to talk like I was really into acid. But the fact of the matter is that I took it two times, and the second time it was so weak a dose, it may not have even been acid. The first time, though, it was Sandoz acid, a giant capsule I got from the University of California, a friend and I split it, it must have been a whole milligram of it, we bought it for five dollars, and I'll tell ya, I went straight to hell, was what happened. The landscape froze over, there were huge boulders, there was a deep thumping, it was the day of wrath and God was judging me as a sinner. This lasted for thousands of years and didn't get any better, it just got worse and worse. I felt terrible physical pain and all I could talk in was Latin. Most embarrassing, because the girl I was with thought I was doing it to annoy her. I was whining like some poor dog that's been left out in the rain all night and finally the girl said, *Oh, barf*, and walked out of the room in disgust.

"About a month later I got the galley proofs for *The Three Sigmata of Palmer Eldritch* to read over, and I thought, oh dear, I can't read these, they're too scary. That book of course is my classic 'LSD novel' even though all I had had to go on when I wrote it was an article by Aldous Huxley about LSD. But all the horrible things I had written seemed to have come true under acid.

"That was in 1964. I used to beg people not to take acid. There was one girl who came over one night, and I made her an amateur Rorschach ink-blot, and she said, 'I see an evil shape coming to kill me.' I said, 'You'd be a damned fool to take acid.' So she didn't take it then, but she did take it later, and she tried to kill herself and was hospitalized and became chronically psychotic. I saw her in 1970 and her mind was gone, it had destroyed her. She said that taking the acid had destroyed her.

"I regarded drugs as dangerous and potentially lethal, but I had a cat's curiosity. It was my interest in the human mind that made me curious about psychotropic drugs. These were essentially religious strivings that were appearing in me. By the time of *Three Sigmata* I had became a convert to the Episcopal Church...."

I interrupt a moment, to ask, why Episcopal?

He adopts the gruff expression that I suspect means he's putting me on—or maybe just the opposite—or maybe he's not actually sure himself. "My wife said if I didn't join the church she'd bust my nose. She says, 'if we're going to know judges and district attorneys and important people, we have to be Episcopalian.'"

If this anecdote is told half in fun, it's the last joke of the interview, because at this point he continues in a kind of confessional, which I suspect he planned to make at this time if only to see what reaction he would elicit from me, as a relative stranger.

"I was walking along one day." His tone is sincere, now. "I looked up in the sky and there was this face staring down at me, a giant face with slotted eyes, the face I describe in *Three Stigmata*. This was 1963. It was an evil, horrible-looking thing. I didn't clearly see it; but it was there. I finally identified it, years later; I was looking through a copy of *Life* magazine and I came across a picture of some French forts from World War I. They were observation cupolas made out of iron, with slots where the soldiers could look out and see the Germans. My father had fought at the second battle of the Marne, he was in the Fifth U.S. Marines, and when I was a little kid he used to show me all of his military equipment. He would put on his gas mask and his eyes would disappear, and he would tell me about the battle of the Marne, and the horrors he went through. He told me, a little four-year-old child, about men with their guts blown out, and he showed me his gun and everything, and told me how they fired till their guns were red-hot. He had been under gas attacks, and he told me of the terrible fear as the charcoal in the masks would become saturated with the gas and they would panic and tear their masks off. My father was a big handsome man, a football player, tennis player. I've read what the U.S. Marines did in that war, and those farm boys underwent what Remarque describes in *All Quiet on the Western Front* as unspeakable valor, unspeakable horrors. And there it was in 1963 looking down at me, a goddamned fortification from the Marne. My father may even have drawn a sketch or had photographs of it, for all I know.

"I actually sought refuge in Christianity from what I saw in the sky. Seeing it as an evil deity I wanted the reassurance that there was a benign deity more powerful. My priest actually said that perhaps I could become a Lutheran because I seemed to actually sense the presence of Satan. And this has continued to plague me, as an intimation that the god of this world is evil. The Buddha, seeing the evil of the world, came to the conclusion that there could be no creator god, because if there were, it could not be this way, there could not be so much evil and suffering; I had come to the conclusion that there *was* a deity in this world, and he was evil. I had formulated the problem again and again in books like *Maze of Death* and *Ubik* and *Three Stigmata* and *Eye in the Sky*.

"During World War II, when I was a kid, I remember seeing in a theater a newsreel film of a Japanese soldier who had been hit by a flamethrower by the Americans, and he was burning to death and running, and burning and running, and burning and running, and the audience cheered and laughed and I was dazed with horror at the sight of the man on the screen and at the audience's reaction, and I thought, *something is terribly wrong*.

"Years later when I was in my thirties and living in the country I had to kill a rat that had gotten into the children's bedroom. Rats are hard to kill. I set a trap for it. In the night it got into the trap, and the next morning, when I got up, it heard me coming, and it screamed. I took the trap out with a pitchfork and sprung the trap and let the rat go out in the pasture, and it came out of the trap and its neck was broken. I took the pitchfork and drove the tines into the rat, and it *still* didn't die. Here was this rat, it had tried only to come in and get food, it was poisoned, its neck was broken, it was stabbed, and it was still alive. At that point I simply went crazy with horror. I ran in and filled a tub with water and drowned it. And I buried it and I took the St. Christopher medal that I wore and buried that with the rat. And the soul of that rat I carry on me from then on, as a question and as a problem about the condition of living creatures on this world. I could not exorcise the spirit of that rat which had died so horribly. In my novel, *Flow My Tears, the Policeman*

144

Said, the armed posse is approaching a building where Jason Taverner is shut up in the dark. He hears them and he screams, and that is the rat screaming when it heard me coming. Even in 1974 I was still remembering that rat screaming.

"And then, at the trough of my life, where I saw only inexplicable suffering, there came to me a beatific vision which calmed all my sense of horror and my sense of the transcendent power of evil. My mental anguish was simply removed from me as if by a divine fiat, in an intervention of a psychological-mystical type, which I describe in my new book, *Valis*. Some transcendent divine power which was not evil, but benign, intervened to restore my mind and heal my body and give me a sense of the beauty, the joy, the sanity of the world. And out of this I forged a concept which is relatively simple and possibly unique in theology, and that is, the *irrational* is the primordial stratum of the universe, it comes first in time and is primary in ontology—in levels of essence. And it evolves into rationality. The history of the universe is a movement from irrationality—chaos, cruelty, blindness, pointlessness—to a rational structure which is harmonious, interlinked in a way which is orderly and beautiful. The primordial creative deity was essentially *deranged* from our standpoint; we are, as humans, an evolution above the primordial deity, we are pygmies but we stand on the shoulders of giants and therefore we see more than they see. We human beings are created and yet we are more rational than the creator himself who spawned us.

"This outlook is based not on faith but on an actual encounter that I had in 1974, when I experienced an invasion of my mind by a transcendentally rational mind, as if I had been insane all my life and suddenly I had become sane. Now, I have actually thought of that as a possibility, that I had been psychotic from 1928, when I was born, until March of 1974. But I don't think that's the case. I may have been somewhat whacked-out and eccentric for years and years, but I know I wasn't all that crazy, because I'd been given Rorschach tests and so on.

"This rational mind was not human. It was more like an artificial intelligence. On Thursdays and Saturdays I would think it was God, on Tuesdays and Wednesdays I would think it was extraterrestrial, sometimes I would think it was the Soviet Union Academy of Sciences trying out their psychotronic microwave telepathic transmitter. I tried every theory, I thought of the Rosicrucians, I thought of Christ.... It invaded my mind and assumed control of my motor centers and did my acting and thinking for me. I was a spectator to it. It set about healing me physically and my four-year-old boy, who had an undiagnosed life-threatening birth defect that no one had been aware of. This mind, whose identity was totally obscure to me, was equipped with tremendous technical knowledge—engineering, medical, cosmological, philosophical knowledge. It had memories dating back over two thousand years, it spoke Greek, Hebrew, Sanskrit, there wasn't anything that it didn't seem to know.

"It immediately set about putting my affairs in order. It fired my agent and my publisher. It remargined my typewriter. It was very practical; it decided that the apartment had not been vacuumed recently enough; it decided that I should stop drinking wine because of the sediment—it turned out I had an abundance of uric acid in my system—and it switched me to beer. It made elementary mistakes such as calling the dog 'he' and the cat 'she,' which annoyed my wife; and it kept calling her 'ma'am.'"

At this point I interrupt, just to be sure I'm getting this right: the presence, the voice that he heard in his head, took over control of his body, his speech, and his decisions?

"That's right."

My first impulse is to suspend judgment. My second notion is to look for a second opinion. In March of 1974, Mr. Dick was married: what did his wife think about all of this?

"My wife was impressed," he says, "by the fact that, because of the tremendous pressure this mind put on people in my business, I made quite a lot of money very rapidly. We began to get checks for thousands of dollars—money that was owed me, which the mind was conscious existed in New York but had never been coughed up. And it got me to the doctor, who confirmed its diagnoses of various ailments that I had…it did everything but paper the walls of the apartment. It also said it would stay on as my tutelary spirit. I had to look up 'tutelary' to find out what it meant.

"I have almost 500,000 words of notes on all this. I'm quite reticent about it, normally. I've talked to my [Episcopalian] priest about it, and a couple of close friends. I tried to discuss it with Ursula Le Guin, and she just wrote and said, 'I think you're crazy.' She returned the material I had sent her. Of course, when *Valis* comes out, a lot of this will be in the book. *Valis* is an attempt to formulate my vision in some rational structure which can be conveyed to other people."

I have been listening to all this in a state of confusion. I came to the apartment for what I assumed was just another in a series of interviews about the business of writing science fiction, and now I find myself caught up in a Dickian reality-warp. I'm listening to what sounds like wild fantasy but is being narrated as fact, with obvious, self-conscious sincerity. I don't know what to believe; my world—my *ideos kosmos*—has been invaded by his, as if I have become a character in one of his novels, and he is Palmer Eldritch, dreaming up a new reality for me to live in.

But I can't live in it, because I can't accept it. I can't suddenly believe that there really are extraterrestrial entities invading the minds of men. I can't believe you can learn secrets of the universe by visiting a science-fiction author in Santa Ana.

And yet he is so plausible! In print it may sound absurd; but sitting listening to his shy, matter-of-fact description of events that are totally real to him, I would like to find a way to accept it all, if only because I find him so immensely likeable, and because I have so much respect for his intellect. As his recent books have shown, he has a practical, lucid insight into the workings of the world. In no way is he a seer or a "psychic" delivering a messianic message or recipe for salvation. He admits readily to his tendency to dramatize life, but basically he is a carefully rational man who questions any concept with persistent logic. He is quite ready to discuss the possibility that his paranormal experience might be nothing more than one half of his brain talking to the other half; he's reluctant to accept this explanation only because it doesn't adequately explain all the facts of his experience.

These facts are numerous. I can't begin to summarize them. He's had five years to live with the phenomenon of the "presence" that temporarily invaded his mind (and still communicates with him intermittently). He has accumulated notes and records, all kinds of research data, so much of it that, no matter what you ask or what objection you raise, he's already ahead of you, with relentlessly logical deductions, and data of every description.

I myself have never seen evidence to make me believe in any psychic phenomenon or pseudoscience, from telepathy to UFOs. My faith is that the universe is random and godless. I am the last person to believe that there is a higher intelligence, and that Philip K. Dick has a private connection with it.

I do believe that something remarkable happened to him, if only psychologically; and I do believe that the experience has inspired a rather beautiful vision of the universe (or *koinos kosmos*) and a strange, unique book which may enhance the lives of its readers. This is the minimum with which Dick must be credited. To debate his "mental stability" is missing the point; what matters is the worth of his insight, regardless of its source. There have been men far more deranged than Philip K. Dick who nevertheless produced great art of lasting relevance to the lives of millions of un-deranged readers.

Dick remains much the same personality as before his vision. He has not metamorphosed into a religious zealot. His perceptions, and his ironic, skeptical wit, are as sharp as ever.

A couple of days after the interview, I returned for a purely social visit, without tape recorders (so my remaining reportage is from unaided memory). During our conversation I mentioned a whimsical notion I enjoy, that if I'm far away from somewhere, and can't see or touch it, it doesn't really exist.

"Oh, sure," he said, "they only build as much of the world as they need to, to convince you it's real. You see, it's kind of a low-budget operation: those countries you read about, like Japan, or Australia, they don't really exist. There's nothing out there. Unless of course *you* decide to go out there, in which case they have to put it all together, all the scenery, the buildings, and the people, in time for you to see it. They have to work real fast."

At this point, I was treading carefully. "Let's get this straight," I said. "Are you describing, now, a fictional concept, such as might occur in one of your novels? Or is this...serious?"

"You mean, do I believe it?" he asked in apparent surprise. "Why, no, of course not. You'd have to be crazy to believe in something like *that!*" And then he laughed.

Historical Context

I didn't know Philip K. Dick very well when I interviewed him, but we'd had some professional interactions. While I was the science-fiction editor at Avon Books in the early 1970s, I strongly advised the publisher to buy paperback rights to the novel *Flow My Tears, the Policeman Said*. They refused, partly because they didn't care for the title.

In retrospect I can see their point of view. The title would, in fact, create a marketing problem if the book was to be packaged as science fiction.

This wasn't so clear to me then, and wasn't clear to Phil. He had thought that after *The Man in the High Castle* won a Hugo award, his value as a writer had increased dramatically and permanently. But the only publisher that even made an offer for paperback rights to *Flow My Tears, the Policeman Said* was DAW Books, and I think they got it for $1,500—the same kind of royalty advance that the president and founder of DAW, Donald Wollheim, had paid for novels by Phil that had been published in the old Ace Double format, many years previously.

For me, the experience demonstrated that I was never going to be happy as a commercial editor, so I told Avon that I was quitting, and I told Phil that Avon's refusal to buy his book had been the last straw. I think he felt that I was quitting as a gesture of solidarity with him, which was partly true.

Subsequently, when David Hartwell was compiling a series of classic science-fiction novels for Gregg Press, he asked me to write an introduction for one of Phil's lesser works, *The Zap Gun*. I loved that book, which dealt with the some of the same themes as Vonnegut's *Slaughterhouse Five* but with fewer pretensions and much more imagination. I wrote the introduction and sent a copy to Phil, who was effusive in his appreciation.

Bearing in mind this history, he must have categorized me as a person who was sympathetic to his work and could be trusted. Consequently, when I asked for an interview, this presented him with an ideal opportunity. He had only talked about his mystical experiences to a few friends, and must have been wondering how to present them to a larger audience. Here was the answer: Charles Platt could be the enabler for his coming-out ceremony.

His judgment was good, because I had far too much respect for his intellect and his work to write anything that would invite mockery. On the other hand, from my perspective he put me in a terrible situation. During the interview, he was erudite, charming, funny, smart, and self-deprecating—but sounded utterly delusional. Worse, when I returned to talk to him some more a couple of days later, he sounded even more delusional. One of his claims, for instance, was that he had been nominated by some cosmic force to bring down the Nixon Administration. He told me quite seriously that he was the key figure who had precipitated the Watergate investigation.

He was aware that he sounded irrational, and he was struggling for some objective detachment. He eventually addressed this problem in his novel *Valis*, but at the time I spoke to him, it remained unresolved. He just passed it along to me and said, in effect, "You deal with it."

What was I supposed to do?

For the first and only time in my life, I decided to shield an interviewee from his own statements. I omitted some of the initial interview and almost all of our subsequent conversation, to protect him from ridicule.

Today, this is no longer an issue. Phil gradually revealed all of his experiences and theories to the world, and a significant chunk of the "Exegesis" that he referred to during my interview was eventually published as *The Exegesis of Philip K Dick*, long after his death.

The only part that still remains unclear is where his visions came from. Personally, I am inclined to accept a theory propounded by Kim Stanley Robinson, that Phil experienced some small strokes which created hallucinatory experiences—until a big stroke, followed by a heart attack, eventually killed him.

In the sadly brief period between my interview with Phil and his death in March, 1982 I kept in contact by phone and visited him a couple more times in Southern California. During the last of those visits, I suggested that we could go out to some local bar or coffee shop, as I was getting tired of sitting in the same old Santa Ana apartment, with its dusty stacks of papers, dim lighting, a persistent smell of cat litter, and a carpet that looked as if it had not been touched by a vacuum cleaner in many years. I now thought of Phil as a friend, and he treated me that way, although I suspect he was effusively warm to many people who were thus encouraged to believe that they were his friends.

My suggestion to venture onto the streets made him immediately cautious. First he took most of his money and his credit cards out of his wallet, in case we might be robbed. Then he hesitated and agonized over our possible destination. When we finally reached the sidewalk, he was visibly nervous.

We ended up in a bar that looked as if it had been a counter-culture hangout in the 1970s but was now on hard times. A couple of bad guitarists were playing live music, and as soon as we sat down, they started into Buffalo Springfield's "There's Something Happening Here."

"Oh my God," said Phil. "I really hate this song."

Indeed, the lyrics sounded as if they had been written just for him. "There's a man with a gun over there / Telling me I got to beware," the musicians sang. And as the song progressed: "Paranoia strikes deep / Into your life it will creep."

At this point I realized that Phil was a living validation of the theory that in some inexplicable way, paranoid people act as magnets for precisely the kind of thing they are paranoid about.

We didn't stay in the bar long. It was obviously bad for his state of mind.

After we got back to his apartment, he added a typically surreal twist by telling me that he had been elected by the local tenants' association to monitor the residential complex for criminal activity. "You mean—you're like a rent-a-cop?" I asked.

He gave me his mock-serious look, which looked so serious, he could almost con you into thinking that he really was serious. "You better believe it," he said. "I'm the law around here."

As we talked some more, he also mentioned that he'd had a new religious revelation. According to his tutelary spirit, the core concepts of Christianity were all entirely true.

"Let me get this straight," I said. "For most of your life you have been a nonconformist rebel, and you have been deeply skeptical about the traditional concept of a benevolent Christian God. Now that you are in a very conventional position of authority, your tutelary spirit has convinced you to embrace religious dogma that is also entirely conventional. Are you telling me this is purely a coincidence?"

This was one of the few times I ever found myself a step ahead of Phil intellectually. He was silent for a long moment, pondering the juxtaposition that I had thrown at him. "Well," he said finally, "whatever it is up there," he gestured heavenward, "it's certainly responsive to me."

I last spoke to Phil on the phone a few days before he died. I'd never heard him sound so cheerful. *Blade Runner*, derived from *Do Androids Dream of Electric Sheep?*, would be released in just a few months' time, and he liked the final version of the script. He mentioned his upcoming trip to New York and to Metz, for events where he would be warmly welcomed. He chided me for running a "scurrilous magazine" (*The Patchin Review*), and warned me the persons unnamed were going to deal with me. "You know what they're saying?" he said. "Charles Platt's ass is grass. They're gonna get you, mark my words." Then he said I could come sleep on his living-room floor when I'd succeeded in alienating all my friends.

"Thanks," I said, "but only if you vacuum it first."

I told him that I had been commissioned to write an article about him for *Horizon* magazine, and we agreed that I should call him later for some quotes to put into the piece. But by that time, it was all over.

Today, Phil has achieved far more success than he ever knew while he was alive. It's no exaggeration to say that he has become a cult figure. His books and stories have been made into numerous movies. His work has become the subject for endless analyses by academics seeking to justify their tenure. Alas, the academics know only the work, not the man, and they tend to lack the self-deprecating sense of humor which was such a vital part of Phil's persona.

Nor do they realize the extent to which his life was regulated by the same commercial realities afflicting anyone who tries to make a living by writing category fiction.

When Phil was planning his novel *Valis*, he had a lot of trouble developing a fictional context for his experiences. He literally didn't know how to begin—but was under contract to deliver the book, and had spent all the advance money. In fact he was many months past the delivery date when he still hadn't written a single page.

He told me that in a last-ditch effort to placate his editor, he rolled a blank sheet into his typewriter and put an arbitrary number at the top, something like 374. "Then I started typing the first thing that came into my head," he said. "I began in the middle of a sentence and I just ran on to the end of the page. Then I photocopied it and sent it in, with a letter saying, 'As you can see from this sample page, I'm getting very close to the end, and you should have the whole book within a week or two.'" He smiled reflectively. "That kept them off my back for a few more months."

Such are the realities of being a writer. Even when you're a literary genius, and you believe you have a personal connection with God—you still have to pay the rent.

Charles Platt

E. C. Tubb

London, England, July 3, 1979

I WISH TO take a brief rest from discussing philosophy and meaning. Likewise, I will set aside social relevance, stylistic nuance, and the general stock-in-trade of literary criticism. I want to talk about two fundamental traditions in science fiction: action and adventure.

After all, Flash Gordon lives—as Perry Rhodan, or even as Luke Skywalker. A lot of books of pure entertainment are still being written, without any pretensions or high ambition, and most of us can still yield to the romance of it all if we let ourselves.

Many authors of these stirring stories of quest and combat remain relatively obscure. Not for them, bestseller status or Hugo awards. In fact, this kind of writer is likely to be cynical about such tokens of literary prestige.

My book would not be complete if I failed to include the viewpoint of one such author. His name is not famous, but his expertise as a prolific story-teller is beyond question.

His name is E. C. Tubb. In the thirty years he has been writing (almost always part time) he has produced hundreds of short stories, and 102 novels ("Not a lot," he says with a shrug). Much of Tubb's work has been published under other names; he has been everyone from Charles Grey to Volsted Gridban (yes, Volsted

155

Gridban, which is one of my all-time favorite pseudonyms). Most recently, under his real name, in Britain and America, he has published a series of adventures of Dumarest of Terra: a tall, lean hero with brooding eyes and a blaster at his hip, searching for the mythical lost home-world of the human race. There have been twenty-one Dumarest novels so far, and the hero's quest is still by no means over.

To Tubb, writing science fiction is not an intense creative experience. It is simply a matter of doing his job, as a skilled storyteller, as well as he can. He is suspicious of writers who claim anything more than this. In his own inimitable words: "There are three grades of author. There's the bestseller, who writes one book and lives on the proceeds. There's the hack [a category in which Tubb includes himself] who has to write like a job, and cannot afford to write only one book. And then you get the 'artistic' sod, who has to live in a cottage in Scotland for three years, and he produces one book about an owl, which nobody buys...but he writes for himself. You'd think you couldn't afford to live like that, but they always seem to have friends who lend them cottages, and wives who work, and knit them garments. God knows what they use to write on—toilet paper that comes from the local library? Or sugar bags on the train? And then when the book comes out, they always launch it with a literary dinner, and all the critics laud it, you know. They had a thing on TV about a bloke like that, and I reckoned he had written one word a day. Even I can do better than that."

Tubb used to work successfully as a salesman, and he still talks with a salesman's rapid, fluent cadences. But he becomes self-conscious and modest when he's asked to talk about himself. In fact he had never been interviewed until, one summer evening, I set up my tape recorder in his family home in southwest London.

He begins by telling me that he thinks the interview is a misguided idea, because the details of an author's life cannot possibly be relevant to a reader:

"I've always sent back forms from these people who want to know the date of your birth, grandparents' marital status, everything about you. I think it's a lot of nonsense. Who the hell cares? If an author ran a brothel in Istanbul when he was fourteen, does that improve his writing? It doesn't, does it. There's a curiosity about how old the man is; does that help you, when you read a real good sword-and-sorcery novel, to know he's a doddering old octogenarian, sniffing at little girls? But to be serious—I started writing science fiction just previous to the war [World War II], sold the first story in 1950, and went on from there. I started writing, as most authors do, first through love, and then through money; and I'm afraid, like the majority of authors, the love starts vanishing and the money stays."

I interrupt to ask him if he's sure he means the majority of authors.

"The way they talk, it must do. You can get any bunch of authors together and what are they talking about? They're not talking about improving their work, they're talking about how high an advance they can screw out of the publisher. They're working, fair enough; the only trouble is, like politicians they tend to inflate their own value, and then start saying, 'I wouldn't write a word unless I got X income for it.' Why the hell publishers ride along with this is a mystery to me. How can one man get, say, $1,000, and some one else $100,000? His book is not a hundred times better. It can't be. In fact some of your best-sellers are a damned sight worse. So when authors start believing they are wonderful, because they're paid so much, they're living in a fool's paradise.

"In the science-fiction field, reputations are easy to come by. Someone writes a book and there seems to be a conspiracy to say how good this book is. No one ever stops to read what the man's written. I mean *read* it. They're looking at the name.

"Heinlein is a perfect example. I mention that man because I think he's done himself a tremendous disservice. This may sound sour-grapish but I liked Heinlein—lik*ed* him. I well remember reading *Stranger in a Strange Land* and telling myself all the way through, Heinlein wrote this, it has to be good, there's going to be a great reward for wading through this Christ-legend crap...and unfortunately, there wasn't. I don't think Heinlein is to blame for this. I think there's too many plaudits—and the trouble is, he might believe them—that *Stranger in a Strange Land*, or the ones that came after it, are good. They're not good. He's lost all critical faculties if he thinks they're good.

"I suppose another case is Samuel Delany, with his *Dhalgren*, which is a monument of unreadability. It does seem that whenever you read the books that have been chosen for the Nebula awards, you can only explain this choice by knowing how the choice was made, which is by twelve people in a smoke-filled room saying, 'Ah, to hell with Sam, he's no good, but nobody hates Harry, so we'll give it to Harry.'"

Does Tubb really feel the award system is as corrupt as that?

"Corrupt in the sense that it's not honest. It cannot be honest. No one can read everything that's going and make an unbiased vote on it. I well remember when I was a member of the Science Fiction Writers of America [the organization which sponsors the Nebula awards], I was getting voting forms through the post at a time which was later than the date when I was supposed to return them. They'd taken six weeks on a boat, getting to me. So I couldn't even vote, which was a convenient way of making sure that I didn't. Now, I'm not saying that this was deliberate. But there was such a thing as air mail, and still is, I believe.

"I feel that the Nebulas have been tremendously inflated as regards importance, and they are important in that every publisher plasters 'Nebula Award Winner' on the cover. I think it's detrimental, because we're all writing in a small field and we were all at one time honest enough to admit that half of what we turned out was sheer crap for the market. That was the money aspect, though you could even like doing that. In the early days the pay was so low it was ludicrous, but this is where you cut your teeth. A lot of young authors, now, never knew this. They've come into a market that's paid higher from the beginning. And whether this is good or bad, I don't know, but if you start by getting a wad of cash for your first book, you're very slow in taking less for the next one. And this makes the advance a status symbol. How good is he? Well, what money did he get?"

In case this diatribe might make it seem that E. C. Tubb is embittered or envious, I must say that I don't think that this is so. His complaints are delivered in a wry, offhand style, with a shrug and a grin. When he mentions the success of some well-known author, he usually adds "and good luck to him!" on the principle that there's nothing wrong with getting what you can. Tubb himself seems to live comfortably off his writing and his other work; there's an air of middle-class prosperity about his home, with its new decor and furnishings, a video recorder sitting beneath the color TV, wall-to-wall carpets throughout.

Of course, it wasn't always this easy.

"I started selling printing machines at the same time I started writing. I did it on and off for the next seventeen years. They ended up bribing me to become manager; it nearly drove me mad. Then I did demonstrating; reached my peak selling knives and kitchen equipment. Did quite well at that. I've found it a great asset to be working as well as writing. I'm not a 100 percent full-time writer. You get stale, and it's blasted boring, living in one room with a world of your imagination, and a typewriter. The job you can leave any time, because you've got another source of income. As for the writing you can say, 'Not today'; really, that's the only way to stay sane.

"I've always been somewhat numbed to realize that I am an author. I suppose it's a feeling of inferiority that could stem from never having had a proper education. Not only was I trying to learn English, and how to spell, but also trying learning how to write. I left elementary school at age fourteen and went out and got a job. I gave my parents all my money, whatever it was, twelve shillings a week, and they gave me back two, for fares, and this went on until the war came and stirred everything up. I'd always been an avid reader of science fiction. We read it for escape, because life was very depressed before the war. I feel that this separates people of my generation from young science-fiction people, because the incentive to read it was different. It was a golden age inasmuch as for a few coppers you could escape into worlds of fantasy which were unobtainable anywhere else.

"Just after the war, the army had gone, I was freshly married—it's always funny to talk this way, because people think you're exaggerating. Even my children do. They say, 'How did you start?' Well, we started in one room, no larger than this, about ten by eight. We had a baby in one corner, in a cot, and a sink in one corner, and a gas stove in the other, and a double bed, and that was home. This was so common; but you talk to people now and they'll say, 'You can't have lived like that, the council [local British government] wouldn't have allowed it.' It's like saying, 'You couldn't have worked for such little money—you'd have got more on social security [British welfare handouts].' They don't realize, there wasn't any social security then, no easy handouts. I don't think there's any intrinsic virtue in pain at all, and I don't think there's any virtue in doing without. But I do feel there is character-forming. It's like being thrown in the deep end: you hate it, but by Christ you learn to swim. If there is nothing for you except what you're going to get, you get it. So, you counterbalance the misery against the development of guts, if you like.

"In the early days, when I was selling to magazines, I was an extremely prolific author. I didn't exactly write the entire contents of one magazine, but I came damn near it. Ted Carnell was short of material so he put two or three of mine in one issue, and invented a few names for me, among them Charles Grey. With three magazines running at the same time, and me producing far more than three stories a month, Ted got in the habit of using noms-de-plume. When I became editor of *Authentic* [a now-defunct British magazine] it wouldn't do for an editor to keep printing his own stuff, so I still had to use noms-de-plume. I practically wrote it from cover to cover, one issue, not because of love of money, but—I never would have believed this, before I'd done the job—you were getting rubbish in, and you had a deadline to meet, so you thought, 'I've got to do something to fill out this 2,000 word gap,' so you wrote one. We were paying pretty low, and I could always sell myself cheaper to make the budget go further. I was doing the book reviews and the articles for free, as well as anything else.

"The next thing that happened to me was that I went on to writing cheap paperback books. Got robbed, but, it's all education. In the early 1950s I met a friendly fellow who came along to the pub, and he was a reader for Curtis Warren. He said, 'You write the story, and I'll put it in as mine, and that way it's certain to sell.' Now, it's the oldest con job out; he took all the money, I only got paid for one book out of the three. He still owes me fifty-four pounds, wherever he is. Not fifty-four pounds for each novel—for the pair! I suppose it was about four weeks' work. Anyway, that was my first education—trust no one!

"Later on, they wanted a complementary name to Vargo Statten [a pseudonym used for years by the late British writer John Russell Fearn] so they invented Volsted Gridban, which was me. Oh, I was doing westerns and God knows what—one of my prime books was about the Foreign Legion. I knew absolutely nothing about it; all I'd read was Beau Geste. So all I knew was 'Mon Capitain.' It was all done under phony names. I even did one detective novel, which was a very poor, third-rate Chandler. I'd written the story, and I liked it; but there was no way anyone could have committed the crime. I had to throw half of it away and invent a character halfway through who was the villain. Until I did that, no one could have done the murder—they were all accounted for. So I realized that plots are my weakness. And that is the trouble, plots are my weakness. I start writing the story and then have to plot it as I go along, which means an awful lot of rewriting. If I take six weeks to do a book, I think that's an awful long time. Mind you, of course, I don't do a book every six weeks; there're gaps in between.

"At the moment, I'm working. I've got an ordinary job, which I suppose I'll get somewhat tired of. I'm doing it because I'll get so fed up I'll want to write a book. I've done this before; I think there were two years when I didn't write a word.

"I'm married, I've got two daughters, five grandchildren, but I don't think anyone's interested, frankly. There's no reason whatsoever why I should not be open about biographical detail, it's simply that I think it's so uninteresting, to me, it must be boring as hell to other people. You feel inadequate when you've done nothing special.

"I'll always remember the most off-putting moment, when I met John W. Campbell at a convention. He looked me in the eye— and I'd sold to this man, though I didn't expect him to remember me—and he says, 'Tubb,' he says, 'tell me something about yourself.' And I shrivelled. How the hell can you answer a question like that, and be honest? They must ask questions like that deliberately. They can't possibly be interested. They can't be. For one thing, I've done all the things that authors are supposed to do. I did all this scad of different jobs—in those days, you did a lot of jobs because you didn't stay in one very long. Unless you were a good boy, you got sacked. I was an errand boy, delivered a handkerchief at the front door, by the time I got back I was sacked—because you never deliver a handkerchief at the front door, you should go around to the tradesmen's entrance. That actually happened to me. Then I washed up and worked in hotels, I was a short-order cook—literally!—I was, for all of ten days. I got the push. But still, that's not the point, you write all this down and people will think, 'No, I can't believe this, it's a cliché, it's too much of a pattern.' So I'm very reluctant to talk about it. I'm trying to think of some other things...well, whatever I say, you've got to lie, so why bother. Authors are professional liars; anything you read about an author is bound to be a bit of a lie, after all. He's going to gloss himself up, he's going to polish things. Like: 'I married a beautiful White Russian countess, that was my first wife, I was sixteen and she was twenty-one, and she promised me an estate in Estonia ... that poor woman, never shall I forget, the red smear under the bus.' And then the balalaikas play, and they say, 'Ah, that man's lived, hasn't he! That man's lived!'"

Historical Context

I knew E. C. Tubb as "Ted" while I was part of the British science-fiction field. I admired his writing, but I don't think he ever quite believed it.

I had become actively involved with *New Worlds* magazine, first as a writer, then as a graphic designer, and finally as its editor until I emigrated to the United States in 1970. *New Worlds* published a lot of stories that broke the traditional boundaries of science fiction, and it was a haven for people who expressed strident criticism of adventure-story formulas. Ted was an old-school writer who was out of sympathy with the new regime, and may have resented the way that the new fiction displaced the old.

Personally I was never entirely happy with the inwardness and pessimism inherent in a lot of the new stories, and I retained a great deal of affection for the work that had gone before. Much of it had been unpretentiously optimistic, and made up for its lack of subtlety with a rich stream of ideas. Ted was probably the best British exponent of this form.

Dumarest remains his best-known protagonist, but Ted was much dismayed when his American publisher, DAW books, cancelled the series following the death of company's founder, Donald Wollheim. The quest remained in limbo until it was allowed to approach completion in a novel titled *The Return*, first published in French as *Le Retour* in 1992, subsequently appearing in English in 1997 from Gryphon Books, a small press in New York.

The conclusion of the series was not reached until *Child of Earth* appeared from another small publisher, Homeworld Press, in 2009.

Ted died in 2010 at the age of 90. My fondest memories are of his appearances at British science-fiction conventions, where he gave extemporaneous speeches and performances. His facility with language was far more exceptional than his self-deprecating style suggests.

Charles Platt

Alfred Bester

London, England, September 1, 1979

NEW YORK, MARCH, 1971: I was sitting in my sleazy
little thirty-dollar-a-month room, on my thrift-shop chair, at a table
I had dragged in from the street. Trucks on the avenue were roaring
past, belching diesel fumes. Puerto Rican kids were on the roof of
my building, pounding conga drums. Next door a radio was blaring
WABC bubblegum music. But I was blissfully unaware of these
low-rent surroundings—unaware, even, of the ninety-degree heat.
I was fully absorbed in reading, for the eighth or ninth time, *The
Stars My Destination* by Alfred Bester.

When I reached the end and returned to reality I wished, as
always, that Bester had written more. Only two science-fiction
novels, and a dozen or so short stories, during the 1950s—a
handful of work which had been so unusual and so excellent, it had
made him one of the enduringly important names in science fiction.
Few of his contemporaries had ever matched his vitality, and no
others—none at all—had matched his innovation, sophistication,
and wit. Bester alone experimented freely with typography (in both
of his novels, and short stories such as *The Pi Man*), and even
combined first, second, and third-person voices in a multiple-
viewpoint narrative (*Fondly Fahrenheit*). He alone, among science-
fiction writers of his generation, seemed truly keyed into modern

media and the arts, urban style, and fashion. One sensed that he must have contacts on Madison Avenue; that he would be a connoisseur of wine, and he'd dress rakishly.

I wondered why he had never received much critical attention. Heinlein or Bradbury had been checklisted, indexed, surveyed, and critiqued to the point of total boredom, yet I had never seen an appreciation of Bester's work, or any explanation for why he had stopped writing science fiction.

On impulse, I picked up the Manhattan phone book. Sure enough, his name was listed. I hesitated, and then I dialed the number.

He answered right away, brightly: "Hi, this is Alfie Bester."

I was an odd moment. A disembodied author-figure had suddenly become real; I might just as well have gotten through to Santa Claus.

I told him who I was, and, to provide an excuse for the phone call I mentioned I would like to interview him some time for *New Worlds* magazine.

"Why certainly, when do you want to do it? How about now?" It was a playful challenge, very New York-style, as if saying—you mean it? You seriously want to do it? Then why procrastinate? What's stopping you?

So I went over and met him. It turned out he not only had Madison Avenue contacts, he *lived* on Madison Avenue. He got me drunk, delivered a virtuoso renaissance-man monologue strewn with first names of the famous (from "Sir Larry" Olivier on down), told me a simple formula which I should use in writing my article, and sent me home. I have been using that formula ever since to write most of my nonfiction, including the profiles in this book.

Nine years have passed. Alfie (as I now know him) has grown even more opinionated, slightly more eccentric, and no less challenging. In fact, his strength of character and identity would be hard to take were it not buffered with such friendly, gentle charm. We should remember that this man was not only science fiction's

166

first stylistic innovator, but did it entirely alone in the 1950s. He had no movement, coterie, or clique to tell him that he was right and his techniques were valid. He was a solitary radical, who recalls that his classic novel *The Demolished Man* was at first turned down by "every publisher in New York" because it was so different from anything that had been done before. It takes a lot of willpower to pursue that kind of career. When I went and met him in 1971 and asked him how he coped psychologically with having his work rejected, his response was, "Drink more!"

Today, he still seems to want to be an innovator and polemicist. While others of his generation have either retired or slowed down, Bester has returned to science fiction, aiming high, refusing to repeat himself, and experimenting with unorthodox methods which he freely admits are a gamble. His most recent work, *Golem 100*, is a truly visual novel, incorporating collages and some artwork that he originally drew himself. As for his next novel, he says (name-dropping incorrigibly, as always): "It's based on the old philosophical concept of *anima mundi*—the soul of the world. In the book, everything is alive. The furniture, the pictures, the people, the chairs you sit on. It's going to be pretty wild. I was talking to Steve King about it, I said, Steve, the philosophic concept says that flowers talk to us, furniture, everything has this world soul, and the only reason we don't hear them is because either they talk too slow or too fast, which I buy, that's fine, that's wonderful, but Christ, typographically how am I going to do it? I still haven't decided."

He talks energetically, jovially, often using early-1960s hip slang, like a New York sophisticate of that era who refuses to grow old. His return to science fiction in 1974 came after years of working on *Holiday* magazine: "I had my ten years with *Holiday*, and that was enough. Curtis Magazines fell apart completely—*Saturday Evening Post* went out of business, and *Holiday* was bought by some cockamamie manufacturer from Indianapolis who had made a fortune manufacturing housemaid plastic aprons. They asked me to go out to Indianapolis, and I went and took one look and said, Forget it, I'm quitting. I can't work with second-rate people, I really can't. And these people were *fifth*-rate.

"I went back to science fiction to try a few experiments and stuff like that, and my first experiment was a disaster, as you know. That confounded book *The Computer Connection* [titled *Extro* in Britain]. There is something vitally wrong with that book, and I knew it when I finished it, and I couldn't patch it then, and to this day I think about it, because there's no point in making a mistake unless you understand the mistake so that you don't make it again. I don't understand it, so I can't profit by it. It's infuriating. Of course my redheaded old lady, and a few other people, say 'No, no, it's much better than you think', and I say, thanks a lot, but—I think of it as Beethoven's Fourth Symphony. It comes between the Third and the Fifth. I hope."

Having written for many other genres and almost every branch of the media, Bester still retains a fundamental loyalty toward science fiction: "It's the one literary medium left in which we have a free hand. We can do any damn thing we please. And we know we have a creative reading public who will go along with us. You're not, shall I say, stunning them with the unexpected. They may disagree with your unexpected, but they're not stunned by it, whereas the constant reader of, let's say, women's magazines and women's fiction, if she or he tries to read science fiction, will be absolutely bewildered, flabbergasted, won't know what to make of it."

For many years, Bester has relied on other fields such as TV scriptwriting as his primary source of income. Science fiction he writes for fun, rather than profit.

"I feel very sorry for so many first-rate, splendid writers who earn their livings solely through science fiction and as a result have to turn out an awful lot of junk, because the rates have been very low in the past. Fortunately I have not been forced to do that."

Rates of payment in science fiction are much higher now; does he approve of this?

"Yes, that's splendid."

But surely, the commercialization of science fiction, with larger sums being offered by publishers, tempts an author even more to write for the money and produce whatever seems appropriate to the market.

"Of course they will," he says, cheerfully. He refuses to be baited by my line of questioning, and goes on into an ingenuous laissez-faire philosophy: "Sometimes, I imagine, an author will be writing exactly what he or she thinks the market wants, and without their knowledge they're turning out a masterpiece. As for second-rate, commercial writing—ass-licking writing, as it were— what's the harm in that? Good god, people who read books in subways don't want to be startled too much, they like nice convenient stories, and these *are* convenient stories. Good for them, good for all of them, that's great."

I remark that this sounds a very optimistic outlook. "I am afraid I'm an unregenerate optimist. What can I do? You know, it's so easy to be sour and to beef about things—stuff like that—well, I think that's just a sign of frustration, that's all, and since I don't happen to be a particularly frustrated guy, I'm very happy to let anybody else do anything they damn well please. Fine, great, have a good time."

I ask who the writers are whom he particularly admires. "Harlan Ellison is just the greatest. Even when Harlan goofs, I just love everything he does, because, by god, he goes for hell and high water, to do something different, startle you. It's like Heinlein, once I said, come on, how do you write, kid? And Robert said, I'll tell you what I do. He said, it's like a man in the street is passing by; I reach out, I grab him by the lapels, and I pull him into a doorway, and shake him until his teeth rattle. And that's what Harlan does, and I admire him tremendously.

"There's a marvelous writer named Ballard—what is it, A.G., E.G. Ballard? Jesus Christ, that son of a bitch could write. Christ he's written some stories I wish I had written. There's one called *The Voices of Time*. Whew! What a piece of work. It makes no sense to me at all, but I am absolutely enchanted by it, it's great. And of course *The Crystal World* is a hell of a novel.

"Brian Aldiss—brilliant—*too* brilliant. I've had this argument with Brian for ages. I say, look, Brian, if I can't understand you half the time—and I can't—how the hell do you expect your readers to understand you? But Brian's off on this brilliance kick, I don't know why. I think his greatest novel was *Hothouse* [also titled *The Long Afternoon of Earth*]. You know, Bob Mills, when he was editing *Fantasy and Science Fiction* magazine, received the manuscript and was terribly worried, and sent it up to me and said, Alfie, should I print it or not? I read it and said, If you don't print it you're a damn fool, it's one of the greatest things that's ever been done. He said, 'But, it's so different.' I said, that's exactly *why*. Some of my contemporaries who started with me, I think—I don't want to mention any names—have either been repeating themselves over and over, which I think is criminal, or else have lost their energy, lost their drive. And some of them fortunately have quit writing altogether. And I'm sorry about that." He looks embarrassed at where his conversation has taken him. "Crikey, I don't know what to say."

I suggest that he seems to be setting himself just a little apart from the rest of science fiction, as if it is a world he doesn't really fit into easily.

"It's true, I don't. In Brighton [at the World Science Fiction Convention in 1979] I felt terribly out of place and rather embarrassed by it. This is a tough one, because I'll be accused of snobbism; but the truth of the matter is that my background is the entertainment business—studios, the theatre, publishing offices, *Holiday* magazine, where I was senior editor. As a result, the science-fiction colleagues of mine—I mention no names—seem rather sophomoric to me, and their jokes [at the convention] were rather like fraternity jokes from my freshman year, and the fans of

170

course with their dressing-up and costumes seemed just like overgrown kids, so of course I felt out of place. One might say, 'Oh, Alfie, come one, don't be a snob.' But the truth is that all that's way behind me, and I can't get into the swing of it with any ease." He pauses, almost shyly. "So, I drink too much." And he laughs.

"The few times I spoke to the kids [at the convention] I just leveled with them. I talked plain, ordinary, realistic shop to them, as I would—for example, Peter Benchley came in with a piece that he had written down in DC on sharks, and nobody in the *Holiday* office wanted it, and I was new in the office, and I loved it. I had a violent battle with the art director and my editor-in-chief, I fought for it, so they took it. Then Peter came in, and I leveled with him, I said now, Peter, this is a hell of a piece, but this is the first chapter of a novel. Now, are you going to put your back into it, and do the goddamn novel, or are you going to let it go at this, and go on being a drifter, writing odd pieces for *Holiday*? This is the same way I talked to the kids at the convention. Well, Peter took my advice and put his back into it, and turned out, of course, as you know, *Jaws*. For which I take no credit at all; I just use him as an example of the way I talk to all my colleagues on a professional level, and the way I talked to the kids at Brighton. I don't know whether the kids at Brighton understood. But you've got to do your best."

And he does always seem to be trying to do his best; trying to top himself, in his fiction, to the point where it sometimes seems a self-conscious duty for him to be dazzling and memorable. The result could be embarrassingly pretentious, were it not coupled with his characteristic charm and severe self-criticism.

"I am my own worst editor," he says. "I'm my worst critic, I'm a son of a bitch when it comes to me. My father, who was born and raised in Chicago, never really learned to speak Eastern English, he spoke Chicago English, and he always pronounced my name 'Alford', and when he was very angry with me he would say [Bester goes into a deep, solemn voice] 'Alfoord, what have you done now?'—that sort of thing. Well I now use that for myself, when I've let myself down. I look at myself and say, 'Alfoord, you have to do better next time, Alfoord.'"

There's a pause at this point, as I try to decide which line of questions I want to pursue next. Bester seizes on this pause as a sign of lethargy on my part. "What, have I run you out of gas?" he exclaims happily. "Come on!" I think he likes the idea of being twice my age (he was born in 1913) but still as quick-witted, or more so.

I ask what his ambitions were, when he started out as a writer. Did he ever imagine he might end up well known? Did he aim for that?

"I was an apprentice trying to learn my craft, that's all. I broke into writing for pulp magazines—detective magazines, science fiction, too, adventure—I used to write for a magazine called *South Sea Stories*. Oh boy, my South Sea stories were really something! And then from there, a couple of my editors got brought over to a brand-new thing called comic books, where there was a desperate need for writers. It was a new medium, a new challenge. From there I went on to ghosting *Mandrake the Magician* and *The Shadow* for Lee Falk for a couple of years, and from there I went on to radio. By that time I had been trained in compression, and writing to the point. Of course I'm obsessed with simplicity and compression, which is one of my big hangups."

I remark that a danger of it is that it can oversimplify fiction—especially characters and their motivations.

"Yes, sometimes. Sometimes I condense too much, and oversimplify too much. But you know, I write in two, three, four, five, or six drafts. I go back and I look it over and I say, a little too fast baby; now take it easy."

How would he ideally like his readers to respond to his fiction?

"All I want to do is entertain them so that when they're finished, they say, Jesus Christ, wow, hey, crazy! And then go about their business doing what they always do."

And yet Bester's work sometimes seems to have a message in

it. For example, I point out, the idealistic ending to *The Stars My Destination*.

"That's one of the big headaches. I remember I discussed it with Paddy Chayefsky once, after he had finished *The Tenth Man*, which went kind of philosophic at the ending. I said to him, Paddy, I know why you did it, you build to a certain climax, and there's no way to go to finish it off, except mystic. Is there any other way, Paddy? I haven't been able to find it. And he said, me neither, you gotta go mystic, it's all you can do. And he's right, you know."

This facile and irreverent explanation doesn't convince me, because I sense Bester is rewriting history, refusing to take his old work as seriously as he used to. I point out that when I talked to him in 1971 about the climax of *The Stars My Destination*, and its message, he told me then that he believed in that message quite sincerely.

He looks slightly chagrined. "Well, I forget the message. What the hell was it?" I remind him that at the climax, his hero distributes a superweapon among the common people, telling them that they can transcend themselves.

"Oh, well, I may have believed it then. Now, I don't know. I have great faith in the people on the one hand, but on the other hand I think there are an awful lot of idiots running around. I think maybe today what I'm looking for is a new educational system that'll grow people up a little more, I don't know. At least, the American people. I can't speak for the Continent, or England; they may be a hell of a lot more adult than we are in the States, where three-quarters of us are children, children with delusions."

At this point he seizes the microphone that rests on the table between us, and turns it around. "Now, let me interview you." He's playfully aggressive, and it reminds me of when he once told me that he tends to resort to "attack-escape": escaping from a problem by attacking it.

I protest I haven't yet finished interviewing him. He brushes my objections aside. He spent most of his ten years on *Holiday* magazine conducting interviews, mainly with celebrities. He's a lot more experienced at this than I am. I'm in the position of a filmmaker trying to photograph Orson Welles.

Bester starts quizzing me about the various people I have interviewed so far, and my interview techniques: "How do you cope with people who only say 'yep' and 'nope' to questions?" (I tell him that I don't have this problem, because most writers are extremely articulate and voluble, just like him.) "Now, the toughest thing when you interview people who've really been interviewed a lot, I find that they have canned replies for everything, and I need at least two interviews to break past that and get down to basics. How about you?" (I say that most of the people I've talked to haven't been interviewed that much, with the exception of Kurt Vonnegut, whose replies I still haven't entirely figured out.).

Throughout this, I keep turning the microphone toward Bester, and he keeps turning it toward me. It's ludicrous. Finally I turn it halfway back to him, and he accepts that as a compromise. He continues:

"I find it best to establish some sort of bridge of common interest with the interviewee, no matter what it is." This sounds as if he is about to tell me his formula for interviews, just as he once told me his formula for nonfiction. "The funniest bridge that was ever established with me was when I was interviewing Kim Novak," he goes on. "Somebody had loaned her an apartment in New York on the East Side, and I would go over there, two or three times, and it was always very guarded and careful; she was on her best behavior. The third time I went over there, at three or four in the afternoon, she put some records on. She said, do you want to dance. Come on. So we danced for fifteen or twenty minutes. And after that everything was *fine*. I was very curious; I went back to the *Holiday* office and told them about this, and I said, *Why*, for god's sake? They said, that was the only way she could test you, to see if you were a right guy, with a little physical contact. You know she was a simple kid, like a high-school sophomore from Chicago. But

174

as a result of my going back to the office and telling them about the incident, they were convinced—wrongly!—that I had had an affair with Kim Novak. I said, oh, come on, fellas, it's so *unprofessional*, I could never do that."

These days, Bester's interviewing work is taking him away from show business, into the sciences. *Omni* magazine has given him a list of Nobel Prize winners whom they want him to talk to. He says it's a lot harder to set up a meeting with an eminent scientist than it is with a personality who wants the publicity; but he's pursuing it.

I remark that he never seems to run out of new projects, and new things to try, in general. He agrees: "I'm always looking for new adventures. For example, we went to the Royal Albert Hall, I'd *never* been there to a concert before; it was marvelous. Or I remember in Paris last year, we were walking where they were jackhammering, digging up the cobblestones, so I said, in my broken French, that I would like to try it. So the guy handed the thing to me, and I dug up the street in Paris. You know, you try anything, there's always a new adventure to have, you just have to be willing to take a chance on making a damn fool of yourself, which I *am* willing to do, all of the time."

Does he ever plan to retire? "Retire? Yeah, I want to die with my head in the typewriter. That's my idea of retirement. Arthur Clarke told me that he's retiring, and he's going to do nothing but underwater photography. I said, Oh, Arthur, really, you and your deep-sea photography! Preposterous! Go write another book. But he wouldn't listen."

Historical Context

When I wrote this profile of Alfred Bester, I felt shy about revealing all the details of my first encounter with him in 1971. That visit to his Madison Avenue brownstone had been a thoroughly disorientating experience. Alfie (as he insisted that I call him) loved an audience, and as a self-conscious 25-year-old British writer wannabe, I provided him with a golden opportunity. He started striding up and down his living room, holding a quart of vodka and swigging out of the bottle as he lectured me on how I should write my profile of him. Then he took me downstairs to a second apartment that served as his studio, where a brass telescope, an astrolabe, a Bunsen burner, and test tubes shared space with his old black portable typewriter. It was like a minimal version of a Hollywood set for a 1930s mad-scientist movie. He opened a drawer and took out a (totally illegal) revolver that he referred to as "my little baby," told me his loathing for pigeons, and suddenly threw open the window, shouting, "Let's get that one right there!"

It was a bravura performance. He proved himself to be larger than life; and that, of course, was the whole point.

In 1971 he was still on his long vacation from science fiction. The field had seemed tacky and trivial to a man who enjoyed the rewards of writing for radio, TV, and mass-circulation magazines. He also confessed to me that he found most science-fiction people naïve, uncivilized and physically unappealing. *Holiday* magazine paid him to go wherever he liked and interview whomever he chose, which was a far more tempting prospect than the hard toil of building imaginary worlds for a cliquish readership of nerds and misfits.

He returned to science fiction in 1972, when it was acquiring unprecedented popularity. Bester was aware of his status as the author of two science-fiction classics, and must have felt that he should be able to compete on equal terms with a writer such as Heinlein. So he wrote *The Computer Connection*, which he admitted was an imperfect novel, and then tried to redeem himself with *Golem 100*, a much more ambitious piece of work. Later he confided to me that he considered it the best of all his books, but it received poor reviews and turned out to be a commercial failure.

I believe this was the biggest disappointment of his writing career. Despite his protestations of not being a frustrated kind of

176

guy, he blamed his publisher for not promoting *Golem 100* properly, and he blamed his readers for not appreciating the book.

Late one night in January 1984, five years after I had written his profile for *Dream Makers*, I was a guest at his old farmhouse in Pennsylvania. He drank more than usual, and fell into an introspective mood. "They don't understand," he told me. He seized a poker and jabbed it into the logs in the fireplace. "They don't understand!" Then he gave me a crooked smile, as if acknowledging that he was turning into a cranky old man. He turned his back and went upstairs to bed.

At this point he had abandoned his New York apartment and his house on Fire Island and was living full-time in the Pennsylvania retreat. His former wife Rolly had died, and he was writing a stage-play version of his story Fondly Fahrenheit, even though he was certain that the script would never find a producer.

In the evenings he would hang out with a bunch of misogynistic country boys at a local tavern. "Don't say anything about black people or Mexicans," he warned me before he took me there.

"Do they know that you're Jewish?" I asked him.

He gave me a stern look. "We will not say *anything* about that."

As soon as he sat down at the bar, the bartender put a brandy snifter and a brandy bottle in front of him, and the all-male locals, most of whom were half-drunk, greeted him as one of their own. As the evening wore on they started playing unlisted obscene 45s on the old jukebox, and two guys in checked flannel shirts and baseball caps got into an endless drunken argument about whose turn it was to shoot in a game of pool. A couple of times the phone rang, and the bartender would hand it to one of the locals, who would tell his wife she should give him a break and quit nagging, for chrissake. Complaining about wives seemed to be a primary topic of conversation at the bar.

Alfie found this a source of entertainment. Getting smashed

with the local white trash seemed good therapy for a writer in his seventies who was wealthy enough not to work and didn't feel inclined to waste time trying to satisfy fickle readers anymore.

Soon after that, he developed a bleeding ulcer that resulted in being admitted technically DOA at the local hospital. After a blood transfusion, he returned home and continued drinking. He fell, twice, and sustained serious injuries. He ended up in a nursing home, and according to his friend Judith McQuown (who saw the death certificate) his cause of death was malnutrition. This does not necessarily mean that he was poorly cared for, since many elderly people lose interest in eating when they reach a point where their lives offer insufficient pleasure to be worthwhile.

In a gesture that must have had some humor in it, Alfie willed his house, his money, and his entire literary estate to his bartender.

Before he died I persuaded him to give me the only copy of a manuscript that he had written a couple of decades previously and had been unable to publish. It was a roman-à-clef set in New York City in the late 1950s. When I asked if I could try to place it for him, he shrugged and said I should do whatever I liked with it, because he had no interest in it anymore. I shopped it around, and it finally appeared from Tafford Publishing under the title *Tender Loving Rage* a few years after his death.

That book is the definitive guide to the world in which Alfie spent his most productive years. Alas, the social milieu was disintegrating even as he depicted it. The whole happening scene of the late 1950s—hipsters and hop-heads, beat poets and be-bop, Mad-Ave and action painting—was already experiencing tremors that would culminate in the seismic upheavals of the 1960s. Alfie's characters, so smug in their sophistication, were as ill equipped to make the transition as he was himself.

When he gave the book to me, I assumed his indifference to it indicated that he felt it wasn't very good. Subsequently I realized that this was not the case at all, and *Tender Loving Rage* had been a major bid for serious literary acceptance. Unlike his earlier non-science-fiction novel *Who He?*, it was sensitive in its depiction of real people with real fears and dreams. Indeed, its very human portrait of a scientist is exceptional in modern fiction.

Near the end of *Tender Loving Rage*, the story describes a party thrown by a publisher to promote a new novel. It's a star-studded affair, pure Hollywood, complete with a full-size replica of a yacht. Such largesse is vanishingly rare in the low-rent reality of book publishing, yet Alfie described it as if it was the kind of thing any reasonably successful writer might expect.

If he had hoped for something similar for his own work, he was unrewarded. Twenty-five years later, when I suggested submitting his manuscript to a small press, this may have seemed the final insult to his ambitions. No wonder he told me I could take it and do what I liked. He no longer cared what happened to it, because he had cared too much.

As a courageous innovator, Alfred Bester took risks that no one else had the nerve or the wit to take. Alas, in the end, some of the risks led to failure. In 1971, when I asked how he dealt with so much rejection and he advised me to "Drink more!" we could both laugh about it. The last time I saw him it was no longer a laughing matter, for there was nothing left but the drinking.

When I was a teenager, I had the juvenile ambition "to write like Alfred Bester." I revered his novels. As an adult, I realized that I not only lacked the talent, but also the courage to pursue a career that required so much ambition and defiance.

One of the wonderful aspects of science fiction in the 1960s and 1970s was that a reader could easily meet the writers whose work seemed so full of significance. I felt very fortunate to enjoy the opportunity of getting to know Alfred Bester.

Brian Aldiss

London, England, September 6, 1979

THIS IS THE man who once locked me in a wardrobe because I wrote a bad review of one of his books. Was he overreacting to negative criticism? Not really. The fact is, many offensive, twenty-year-old self-styled critics (as I then was) deserve to be locked in wardrobes. It's a pity there are so few writers with the initiative to take this kind of prompt corrective action.

I'm not attempting to embarrass Brian Aldiss with this anecdote. It would be hard to embarrass a man whose spontaneous nature has provoked so many unusual scenes.

However, I am straying away from the point. The point about Brian Aldiss is that, though he is in every sense a gentleman, one should not be fooled by his respectable British manner. He is also an impulsive character, an iconoclast who has the energy and the initiative to go ahead and *do it*—make the grand gesture—even if he risks looking foolish afterwards. His impulsive spirit has led him into more important situations than the odd social fracas. It

---

[4] Photograph by Geoff Goode.

prompted him, for instance, to go out and get funding for *New Worlds* magazine in the form of a literary grant from the Arts Council of Great Britain. (Has anyone else in the West ever managed to subsidize a science-fiction magazine with government money?) And it has led him to write unpredictable, unconventional books, marking a zig-zag career which by American standards would seem to be commercial suicide. Yet, in the end, somehow, even Aldiss's most whimsical work sells, and he has the satisfaction of staying true to his spontaneous nature, without ever having had to compromise.

He is probably our most all-around literate science-fiction author, measured by his command of language and his critical facilities. He has written a literary history of imaginative fiction (*Billion-Year Spree*); copublished a small critical review long before science-fiction criticism was taken seriously by the rest of the world; and for many years he was a regular critic for *The Oxford Mail*. Moreover, Aldiss is unique in that he moves just as easily in higher levels of the literary establishment as he does among fellow science-fiction writers. He is not a literary snob, however. Quite the opposite:

"Having seen what are supposedly the big fish in the big pond, at the Booker Prize dinner, I thought what an awful giveaway mainstream literature was. I felt, then, very intensely, the virtues of the science-fiction field. The Booker Prize is the most prestigious prize for literature in Britain. The year that I went to the award dinner, it was won by Iris Murdoch for *The Sea, The Sea*. There were a lot of tables, about ten people to a table. At my table, of the six books that were runners-up, I think I'd read one, someone else had read two, and nobody else had read any of them. There was such an air of weariness and uninterest in what went on, and I thought the speeches were very poor. The reservations of the judges, concerning the winners, I felt were an awful let-down—enthusiasm is a valuable quality. You couldn't help comparing it with the Hugo awards, which maybe you've always looked down on simply because they're part of the science-fiction family, or whatever you call it—the tribe. But if you go to the Hugo ceremony, everyone's read the novels, and they're saying, you know, my *God*, if X doesn't win this year, I'll *shoot* myself. The partisanship is tremendous. It may be misdirected, but it's *there*, and I did feel, after the Booker Prize, that we in science fiction really have the edge in a lot of ways.

"Come on, I mean, take the world convention at Brighton; how many people were there, 4,000? Where else would you find such an event? The enthusiasm is quite extraordinary. One of the BBC people filming the convention said to me, 'I can't remember when I went to an event where there were more intelligent and interesting people that I want to talk to.' Well, he wouldn't have found them at the Booker Prize dinner. I have to say it. You know, I was one of the 'Don't knock the mainstream' brigade for a very long time. I don't say I've changed my tune, but—well, maybe I *have* changed my tune."

Indeed, Aldiss seems a little mellower these days than he used to be. Ten years ago, he was extremely critical of what he saw as the many flaws in conventional science fiction, and he was solidly behind the radical spirit that fueled the "new wave" in general and *New Worlds* magazine in particular.

"I think it had a benevolent effect," he says. "I believe that what *New Worlds* did was not create a new audience—the audience was there; but you gave them something to focus on. Heaven help us, but we could liken this to Hugo Gernsback! When he started that first science-fiction magazine in 1926 he found there was an audience; it was there, it just needs something to focus on. And I think that's what we found, in the 1960s."

Aldiss is talking to me in my flat in London, on one of his fairly frequent visits to the city. It's more a conversation than an interview; he's in his usual convivial humor and obviously prefers an informal chat to a carefully worded question-and-answer session. He asks me about the other people I have interviewed, and we talk about the strange sense of community that there is among science-fiction writers and fans—what Algis Budrys refers to as the "brotherhood."

Here again, Aldiss delights in making comparisons with the world of serious literature. "Let's say you were doing a book of profiles of modern English writers," he says. "It wouldn't be quite the same, would it? I mean—shacking up with Beryl Bainbridge? It's a different kettle of fish! But I can tell you I know mainstream writers who would be better for the sort of understanding that exists among science-fiction people. Take J. G. Farrell—another Booker Prize winner, by the way. I met him once or twice. I used to go and lobby in the House of Commons, for the P.L.R. [Public Lending Rights, a proposal to pay authors a small royalty rate whenever their books are taken out of public libraries]. Farrell was there, such an intelligent but lonely man, he didn't know any writers, didn't feel anything in common with them. I think it would be hard for a science-fiction writer to be in that position. I mean, wherever you go—if you wound up in Tokyo, instead of landing in skid row, you'd look up the nearest science-fiction fan, and you'd be all right. The devil taking care of his own."

All this talk of unity and brotherhood warms the soul, but of course, the fact is, there have been obvious differences of outlook and method between Aldiss, and, say, most American science-fiction writers. The insults and invective have long since died down, it's true; but some of the differences remain, as Aldiss himself agrees:

"I believe that in science fiction as we've seen it over the last three or four decades, there are two methods of writing, which struggle for supremacy. One always wins, and that is the heritage of the pulp magazines, where what you really have is *plot*—you've got a guy in trouble and he's got to get out of it. This is the formula. It requires a narrative hook at the beginning, and lots of excitement, and finally a startling conclusion. I believe the other way to approach a story, or a novel, is to think of some scenes that are going to be telling something that the reader will remember; and you've got to have people who are in some way memorable. No, 'memorable' is an easy word. Let's say, people whom you readily distinguish. This is rather more tricky, actually, than thinking of a plot, but I believe that if you have creditable characters and powerful scenes, the plot springs from that, while remaining subordinate to it. This is the difference. I prefer the second method; it's the method I work on. Now and then I have thought of a plot and have used it, but I don't think the results have been as good."

I ask Aldiss which authors, in the science-fiction field, he feels particularly close to.

"I think there are a lot of people for whom I feel—is 'comradeship' the word? Maybe it is. At the end of a long campaign you get to know your friends and the enemies, not that it's quite the end of the campaign, yet, by any manner of means. But let me list them. I suppose of course I have to start with Jimmy Ballard and Mike Moorcock; that's obviously the case. I always liked what Jimmy did, and we both started in the same little hole, in *New Worlds* when it was edited by Carnell.

"One of the things I like about Ballard is that he can conjure up foreign backgrounds. This is, of course, a result of his experience in the Far East, and it stood him in good stead. One of the things I first liked about science fiction was that it did give me strange backgrounds; for instance, in the early work of Ray Bradbury. But after a time I realized he was really talking about things in his own backyard, and the novelty wears off. The same with Clifford Simak: I thought Simak's backgrounds were fantastic. But then it seemed to me that they were all the same and were actually his back yard, or front porch."

Aldiss himself started writing in the 1950s. Did he have specific ambitions back then?

He thinks about it, but can't seem to decide. "Whatever I say is loaded and probably doesn't represent the truth anyway," he says. "I really can't remember; I think I was full of modesty and full of ambition at the same time. I'd wanted to be a poet, but then I'd started reading modern poetry, and decided, right, well, that was out. You know I was so lucky that Faber [a British hardcover publisher] wrote to *me*, and asked me to write my first novel—extraordinary!—but perhaps that's why I've been so wayward ever since. Actually I would like to have written social comedy, and perhaps if Kingsley Amis hadn't been around just a few years earlier, I would have done that. My first book, *The Brightfount Diaries*, was social comedy; it had appeared in chunks in a periodical, and Faber wrote to me and said, 'Would you like to put these things together and make me a book?' And within the next six weeks, six other publishers wrote to me with the same request. Amazing! Then after the first book, Faber said, 'What are you going to do for an encore?' and I said, 'Well, I also write science-fiction stories.' 'Oh, good!' they said, *'we're* science-fiction fans.' And that was true: Sir Geoffrey Faber, Ann Faber, Charles Montieth." Aldiss shakes his head and laughs at how easy it seems, in retrospect.

I ask him if he's happy, overall, about the way his career worked out.

He immediately looks evasive. "Beware the furies," he says. "I'm still working on my career. I think I've been very fortunate. I always have a sense of having escaped slavery. I spent ten years working in bookshops, before I could afford the price of petrol to drive away from that depressed area. Even before that, I had escaped from my father's loathsome gents' outfitters establishment, and I had escaped with one bound from my uncles' architecture firm. There was little that I was qualified to do, I wasn't even very good at digging roads. But I'd always had the urge to write, and I've been able to do it, now, securely, for, oh, however long it is. Twenty-five years? Twenty-one years? Been jolly lucky. And you know, I still enjoy it."

At the same time, of course, Aldiss has had his problems, especially in America, where some of his work has not sold well, and he remains underrated.

"Well, it's true I've had troubles," he agrees, "but that's something to do with my rather cavalier attitude, I think. I've felt like this mainly with *The Malacia Tapestry*; before that, I felt it was all someone else's fault, and that's never a good thing to feel. If you're in there pitching, then it's your fault, ultimately, if things don't go well. I felt *The Malacia Tapestry* was a good book. It was published first of all in hardcover by Harper & Row. It didn't sell very well and no one would buy the paperback rights, until Ace Books picked it up, very cheaply. Well, it's done quite well through Ace, but there was a certain sense of deja-vu in being published by them again, where I'd begun twenty years before, and for about the same size of royalty advance, to be candid. You know, it's time to think again, when that happens. So in a certain sense I suppose I am, in rather a lazy way, reforming myself now. I've got a rather ambitious scheme on, for quite a hefty novel called *Helliconia*. I think that will be good, and this time I'm going to get a commitment from a publisher, get it laid on the production line, as it were, ahead of time. You have to work with the publishing system, not against it. In Britain I think it's still, rather, pleasurably, a cottage industry. In the States publishing is mechanized. The message has got through to me, I think.

"Another problem has been that my science fiction is never involved with high technology. And that's something of the difference between the United States and Britain. Science fiction in America is much more involved with high technology, that's where the cutting edge is. That I think is a positive point; the negative side is that the media have a great grip in the States, and so you get hogwash like *Star Trek*, with its bright—well, it's *not* very bright, actually—this tinsel view of the future, and the galaxy, which has to be optimistic. I did once manage to see an episode all the way through, and at the end Captain Kirk says to the—the chap with the ears—'Well, this proves that the galaxy's too small for white men and green men to fight one another,' and Spock nods and says, 'that's right,' and they clap each other on the shoulder, and up comes the music. Well, what Spock should have said was, 'Why the fuck shouldn't white men and green men fight together? Of course there's plenty of room.' Liberal platitudes do distress me.

"And yet I remember having this argument with some quite high-powered chaps, and they said, 'That's a very subversive point of view, you may think these are platitudes, but they actually do a lot of good.' But I still think that science fiction *should* be subversive, it shouldn't be in the game of consolations, it should shake people up, I suppose because that's what it did to me when I started reading it, and that was valuable. It should question things. I have to say, I owe a lot to John W. Campbell and his damned editorials in *Analog*. I *believe* that you should challenge everything, you know? Occasionally, in my more manic moods, I still carry that early Campbell banner: Science fiction should tell you things you don't want to know."

Does Aldiss feel that the American publishing scene is growing still more media-dominated, with little room for offbeat material?

"I think it's difficult to say whether it's getting worse. It seems worse, but perhaps if you came into it now you wouldn't see it that way. It's like everything else, when you've known it for some while, it seems worse. *London* seems to me worse than it was in the 1960s, but if I was discovering it now, I'd think it was a glorious place. All I can say is that I have produced some eccentric books, and somehow or other they have been published here and in the States—even my new collection of essays, *This World and Nearer Ones*, is going to be at least marginally published by St. Martin's Press. So there's room for hope.

"You know, I have faith in doing what you think is best. Go down with all guns firing—maybe you won't go down at all. Also we have the very good example of John Wyndham. Whenever it was, 1952? Suddenly on the way to Damascus he saw the light and stopped being John Beynon Harris, a hack writing for American magazines, and decided that he would become John Wyndham, and write in an English style. It was actually rather a tea-cosy style, I know. But it was just amazing, the success he had with *The Day of the Triffids*. I knew him a bit, he used to come to the early meetings of the science-fiction luncheon club, in the days when I didn't dare to say a word to anyone. He was very popular. He would always rise and make the same speech, which was, 'Why do they call it science fiction? It's such a *nasty* name.' It was quite a long speech, and he would never suggest an alternative. He was a sort of instinctive writer, but he did convince everyone, I think, that you *could* write science fiction in an English idiom—whatever the hell that means, I'm not quite sure. It means, actually, rather a dated idiom, I think. The Wells tradition? Yes, but I believe that the ideas Wells had were important, whereas Wyndham's ideas weren't important. But his example was quite important."

Is Aldiss in favor of recent trends such as teaching science fiction in schools and colleges?

"What education should do, to my mind, is inculcate imagination, without which we all die. And imagination is something that you get pouring out of your ears if you read science fiction. It hits you, at the age of what—fifteen? Twelve? Eighteen? It blows your mind. If you aren't taught it, you'll still read it anyway, so it seems to me quite a good thing that it's on the curriculum.

"The bad side of this, I suppose, is obvious to everyone: you get a lot of academics who teach it and don't care about it. But why should they care it in the way that you and I care about it? They haven't got that sort of commitment. I met someone who was to have taught a course on Dryden, but no one had enlisted in the Dryden course, so she was teaching Heinlein and van Vogt, poor lady. Well I'm not sure whether I would want to read a lot of van Vogt *or* a lot of Dryden, but I can see the impulse that lies behind that sort of mischief.

"I can also see another mischief, in that it's led some science-fiction writers to tramp off on the university beat, giving lectures, and eventually writing…this is a fascinating phenomenon, you know, science fiction can do anything. To its detriment. We now have the science-fiction college-campus novel. The John Barths of our field. Someone like *Delany*, you know. Very interesting!" There is a slightly wicked gleam in Aldiss's eye.

"But I don't see that it does much *harm*, you know. If you look at it with wider perspective, you see that this is inevitably part of a process: eventually I suppose science fiction will fossilize the way the modern novel has fossilized. At the same time, we're very aware about this business of fossilization, and formularization. Certainly when *New Worlds* appeared, with one bound, we were free, as it were. But I can also remember when this seemed to happen with the publication of *Fantasy and Science Fiction*, and *Galaxy*."

When Aldiss writes, does he have any specific idea of the audience he is writing for?

"I do recall thinking when I began, that I would like to write for everyone, and not a narrow audience. It struck me, for instance, that half the population of these isles was female, and it would be rather nice, wouldn't it, if more women read science fiction. That was not actually a target, but it was an area in which I thought. I remember when I wrote *Non-Stop* [his first novel, retitled *Starship* in America] I was rather uncertain of my audience. I put in—whatever you call them—human touches, which I felt were often lacking in the science fiction of the time. And I wasn't sure how well they would go down, because I wasn't sure whether anyone but the science-fiction audience would read the damn book. You know I'm getting to that John Fowles stage where I'd like to rewrite *Non-Stop* with a preface that would be longer than the novel." He laughs.

"But I think in a way it's an exemplar for much of my fiction since. The idea of people imprisoned by circumstances—in that case, a giant spaceship—has been one of my themes. I can't think why, really, because I don't regard myself as imprisoned by circumstances, but I think I did as a child, and you know you always draw on that reservoir of experience."

189

What has Aldiss been doing recently?

"I was Chairman of the Society of Authors, the year before last, and that actually occupied my whole year. I didn't do anything else except write *Pile*, which is an epic poem I wrote in a week. I was so involved with the Society of Authors, getting them unionized and doing various other good or bad things, that I was offered a place on the Literature Advisory Panel at the Arts Council of Great Britain. I decided that things couldn't be any worse, so I might as well do it. Now I'm coming to the end of my stint with them, and I'm rather disillusioned. There's nothing much you can do; you mainly seem to be okaying grants to a lot of people who don't work. *They don't work very hard*; you know, that's the damned answer, never mind whether they're good or not. And I don't much approve of that.

"Also I don't like the way in which there are assumptions at the Arts Council about everyone there being, if not able, prepared to distinguish between what is good and valuable and what isn't. That gets very boring. I tried to get an Arts Council grant for the world science-fiction convention, you see; I thought that might be an interesting exercise. There were going to be 4,000 avid readers down there at Brighton—why not? Why not put some money up front, to be repaid later if the thing made a profit? I thought it would be a token of something or other, God knows what, or why one should care. And of course they wouldn't do it, the Arts Council said the machinery didn't exist. There were various difficulties, I don't know what the underlying assumptions were, but I didn't care for them anyhow.

"My next novel to be published is in fact a contemporary novel, set in that somewhat mythical year, 1978, and it's due out early in 1980. It's very ambitious, it's called *Life in the West*, and I regard it as taking my science fiction a stage further. It's my Iris Murdoch, in a way, if you like. I put into an ordinary novel, or attempted to, the perspectives that I use in my science fiction, talking about today and seeing it as a period rather late on in the

Byzantine II history of the West. I regard that as rather important—you always do, when the things are in the works, you know. Terribly important. I shall be sad when, eventually, it appears and floats off into the haze of all the other books.

"I fancy people will find it pretentious. I'm rather concerned with this whole business of pretentiousness; I actually hate pretentiousness in others, and think it's a good subject for comedy. But I also think that because I'm so interested in it, I must be rather pretentious myself. I mean if you're interested in a subject, and knock it, that must mean you have an element of it in you.

"You can evade pretentiousness by using metaphor, in fiction. A lot of science fiction is metaphor: you can put up a grand picture, as it were, without being pretentious. You give the reader a chance to interpret the picture in his own way. That's one thing I like about science fiction, and perhaps it's what I *don't* like about the ordinary novel, which is pinned to realism, and therefore lacks the metaphorical quality that good science fiction has.

"You know, despite all its failures, science fiction is not myopic. It does try to see things in a wide-screen way. That's what you like about it. Christ, where else do you go? Perhaps that's why I seem mellower, these days. I have seen that there are other literary places to go. But I no longer think that they're much better."

Historical Context

When I'm interviewing someone whom I know well, you might think that this would give me a significant advantage. Surely, the profile that I derive from the interview should be especially revelatory.

Well—yes and no. The problem is that if a friendship exists before the interview, I will be hoping that it still exists after the interview. I will be tempted to tread lightly on some sensitive topics, while avoiding others completely.

This was my situation when I talked to Brian Aldiss. Having

known him for many years, I was aware that although he is a wonderfully amiable person, he is quite sensitive to criticism. Of course, no writer enjoys negative comments about his work, but Brian's reactions have sometimes been extreme. Indeed, that was why he locked me in a wardrobe on that memorable occasion when we first met.

One topic that I barely touched during my interview with him was the more enduring success of his earlier work. This topic seemed guaranteed to cause trouble, just as it troubled Ray Bradbury when I mentioned it to him. Another topic where I exercised some caution was intellectual elitism. I don't actually see Brian as an intellectual elitist, but he has been accused of it, and I would have been pushier about pursuing that if I hadn't known him so well.

Lastly, I would have been less willing to accept his very diplomatic answers when I tried to get at his attitudes toward other writers. I knew, for instance, that he felt ambivalent about J. G. Ballard, with perhaps some professional jealousy thrown in, but there was not a hint of this in his little eulogy.

This, then, was the public persona of Brian Aldiss—the diplomat who sees two sides of most questions, and the best in everyone. He also interrupted my flow of questions by asking questions of me in return. Control of the interview slipped away from me, and we ended up by having a friendly chat.

A good interview should never be too friendly. It should be energized with tension. Still, while Brian was only willing to present his public persona, I think my profile of him captured that well enough. He really can be exceptionally charming, erudite, witty, and entertaining, especially when he's in a friendly mood— and all the more so if he is speaking on the record.

As for his life and times in the years since I interviewed him, I used to run into him at the Conference on the Fantastic in the Arts, where he would make a regular appearance in accordance with what I see as his love-hate relationship with academia. He had a celebrity status at those events, and being greeted as a celebrity is hard for any writer to resist, especially when attractive, unattached female English professors are present.

After I interviewed him, he spent the first half of the 1980s working on his *Helliconia* trilogy, an epic saga depicting the struggles of a society on an alien world locked into long cycles of catastrophic climatic upheaval. The trilogy reestablished his popular status in the United States and was extremely successful in Britain. Subsequently, he co-wrote *Trillion-Year Spree*, his sequel to *Billion-Year Spree*. It remains possibly the most definitive history of science fiction.

Brian continued writing science fiction in his eighties, some of it seeming an attempt to reach a broader audience, such as HARM (2007), a politically controversial novel set in a dystopian British near future. While his sales in the United States lapsed after the *Helliconia* series, he remains (in the words of the Encyclopedia of Science Fiction) "the central man of letters" in the field of speculative literature.

J. G. Ballard

Shepperton, England, September 9, 1979

Return to Forever. Today I must journey to an enchanted landscape of mystery and stasis. I must follow a private odyssey to the lagoons where iguanas bask beneath a reborn sun; to beaches of archaeopsychic time, where the solitary figure of an aviator, a refugee from some dislocated future, wanders beside the dark water as if tracing an invisible contour inside his own mind. I am drawn there with a sense of inevitability—to the mud flats, the sand banks, the dunes, the drained lakes—the terrain of primordial resonances and apocalyptic fulfillment.

As if it is keyed to a countdown of cosmic time, my hypothalamus is stirring; my subconscious is throwing up images of that mythic zone—that coded landscape—the landscape of Shepperton, Middlesex.

The Architecture of Entropy. So I get out my bicycle, on a cloudy Sunday morning, and I set off with my satchel containing tape recorder, picnic lunch of bread and cheese, ordnance-survey map, and bicycle-tire puncture-repair outfit. Shepperton is about

---

[5] Photograph by Fay Godwin.

194

fifteen miles from the small apartment that I maintain in London. Shepperton, glorified, immortalized in the work of J. G. Ballard, as the nirvana of surreal dreams.

In reality, Shepperton consists of a few little streets of nondescript semi-detached houses and bungalows, some man-made reservoirs, an airport nearby, and gravel pits where rusty dredging equipment stands mired in oily mud. The visitor who has read Ballard and expects a world of inspirational imagery—of terminal beaches and vermilion sands—will be disappointed.

Only one strange figure fits the fantasies. He is a messiah wandering through his private zone of glittering faceted light and strange symbols of the apocalypse. The Prophet of Shepperton: Ballard himself.

Locus Solus. By bicycle my trip takes a little over an hour, westward to the extreme edge of Greater London. It's flat country. There are interminable streets of two-story houses, here and there a petrol station, or a newsagent with an ice-cream sign outside and kids sitting on the curb looking bored. There is an occasional red double-deck bus, an occasional lorry, then a high-street of more small shops—launderette, Wimpy Bar, electrical supplies, tobacconist, betting shop, post office, chemist—all closed, of course, on Sunday.

Flanked by unsuspecting suburban neighbors, Ballard's house blends in unobtrusively. Its only distinguishing feature (not visible from the street) is a pair of small home-made abstract cement sculptures, standing out in the back garden like enigmatic delegates from a nation peopled by emblems of surrealistic art. They seem to be waiting, watching him as he works in the living room, by the window, seated on an old wooden chair at a 1950s-vintage dining table. Here, looking as if he is camping out in makeshift quarters, he conjures his visions of mythic beauty and strange power—the literary equivalent of paintings by Ernst and Dali.

195

Surely You Don't Plan to Stay Here, Doctor? In Ballard's early short stories he dwelled on visions of stasis, where time could be perceived as a tangible quantity, suffusing the landscape. In his first four novels, the world was overcome by various natural catastrophes, wiping away civilization and literally turning the clock back. His heroes were solitary figures, courting the apocalypse and ultimately seduced by it. To them, a private, mystical union with a ruined world was more attractive than the pretense of a "normal" lifestyle among organized bands of survivors.

Since the 1960s Ballard's obsessions have broadened to include modern myth-figures (Kennedy, Monroe, Reagan) and a contemporary urban scenario of automobiles, concrete, and perverse eroticism. His fiction has catalogued the sex crimes of technology and has lab-tested the death dreams of fashion models and housewives. His heroes, however, remain as serenely detached as ever, still opting for isolation, much as Ballard himself shuns the social worlds of Central London and chooses to maroon himself in his Shepperton retreat.

The Abandoned City. "I'm completely out of sympathy with the whole antitechnology movement," Ballard tells me. "Everything from the Club of Rome on the one hand to Friends of the Earth on the other—all these doomsayers and echo-watchers—their prescriptions for disaster always strike me as simply wrong, factually, and also appallingly defeatist, expressing some sort of latent sense of failure. I feel very *optimistic* about science and technology. And yet almost my entire fiction has been an illustration of the opposite. I show all these entropic universes with everything running down. I think it has a lot to do with my childhood in Shanghai during the war. Shanghai was a huge, wide open city full of political gangsters, criminals of every conceivable kind, a melting pot for refugees from Europe, and white Russians, refugees from the Russian revolution—it was a city with absolutely no restraints on anything. Gambling, racketeering, prostitution, and

everything that comes from the collisions between the very rich—
there were thousands of millionaires—and the very poor—no one
was ever poorer than the Shanghai proletariat.

"On top of that, superimpose World War II. I had led a fairly
settled childhood as the son of a fairly well-to-do businessman.
After Pearl Harbor we were suddenly taken from these huge
houses, and suddenly our family was living in a room about half this
size"—he gestures at his small Shepperton living room—"for three
years, in a camp.

"And then the war ended and there was another huge jolt. In
many ways the period after Hiroshima was more confusing than
anything that had happened before; it took so long for the
Americans to come in and stabilize things. All that, and those
extraordinary inversions taking place all the time....

"I mean, I remember this little boy, his name was Patrick
Mulvaney, he was my best friend, he lived in an apartment block in
the French concession, and I remember going there and suddenly
finding that the building was totally empty, and wandering around
all those empty flats with the furniture still in place, total silence,
just the odd window swinging in the wind...it's difficult to identify
exactly the impact of that kind of thing. I mean, all those drained
swimming pools that I write about in my fiction were *there*, I
remember going around looking at drained swimming pools by the
dozen. Or, I used to go down to the waterfront where the great
long line of big banks, and hotels, and commercial houses looked
out over a wide promenade to the river frontage; one day, you'd
see the familiar scene of freighters and small steamers at their
moorings, and the next day the damn things would all be sunk—the
Japs had sunk them, to form a boom. I remember rowing out to
these ships, and walking onto the decks, with water swilling
through the staterooms.

"Given the stability of the society we now live in, this is very
difficult to convey. You've got to imagine something like the Watts
riots on a kind of continental scale. The Watts riot dislocated the

197

United States, but how long did they last? Two or three days? I lived in Shanghai from my birth in 1930, till I left in 1946—a period covering several wars, including a world war, and all these extraordinary inversions, the transformation of a huge city...I think all that was fed into my psyche and when I started writing science fiction and looking at the future, the imaginative elements I was trying to extract from any given situation tended to be those that corresponded to the experience that I'd had earlier."

A Language of the Unconscious. Ballard speaks deliberately, forcefully, as if he is putting the key phrases in italics. And he pauses often, to choose the most powerful image or metaphor. Likewise, in his fiction: he is a deliberate, forceful writer, who has never produced an underplayed or unambitious story. His fiction may sometimes seem "obscure," but even if the reader can't see the literal meaning of a piece of Ballard's work, the power of its mood and imagery is always undeniable. He expresses himself via potent, surreal symbols, or metaphors, like recurring dreams. The dunes, crashed cars, enigmatic women, lost astronauts, and abandoned buildings are intended as signposts, keys to the meaning of technology, the structure of the unconscious, and the promise of the Future.

Reality by Inversion; Fulfillment through Oblivion. "Just as, say, reason rationalizes reality for us, so conventional life places its own glaze over everything, a sort of varnish though which the reality is muffled. In Shanghai, what had been a conventional world for me was exposed as no more than a stage set whose cast could disappear overnight; so I saw the fragility of everything, the transience of everything, but also, in a way, the *reality* of everything, as the glaze of conventional life was removed. I think it's the same sort of situation you experience, going around a silent factory—or an abandoned factory. Even a crashed automobile has a reality, and a poignancy, and *a unique identity* that no showroom car ever has.

"In the novel I'm writing at the moment, the United States, 100 years in the future, has been abandoned, and people are returning to it. They find Lincoln sitting in his memorial with sand up to his knees, all this kind of stuff. I think that this presents a sharper image of what the United States is *now*."

Regardless of his reasons for dwelling on scenarios of decay and devastation, Ballard's obsessions have inevitably been labeled "pessimistic," especially since the heroes of books such as *The Drowned World* and *The Crystal World* choose to sacrifice themselves to the catastrophes that have taken over the planet. Ballard responds: "Most of my fiction, whatever its setting may be, is not pessimistic. It's *fiction of psychological fulfillment*. Most people think that I write fiction of unhappy endings, but it's not true. The hero of *The Drowned World*, who goes south toward and sun and self-oblivion, is choosing a sensible course of action that will result in absolute psychological fulfillment for himself. In a sense—he has—sort of—hit the jackpot! He has; he's won the psychological sweepstakes. I mean, the book makes no sense, and the hero's behavior is meaningless, if you don't see it that way. It's the same thing in *Crash* [his traumatic novel of perversion, violence, and the automobile]. The whole dynamic of that book, I suppose, leads toward the ultimate car crash, which we all celebrate; something like that. All my fiction describes the merging of the self in the ultimate metaphor, the ultimate image, and that's psychologically fulfilling. It seems to me to be the only recipe for happiness we know."

Inner Space. Ballard started writing in the 1950s, and sold his first stories to the British magazine *New Worlds*. These early stories used the jargon of orthodox science fiction, and his early style seemed influenced by the slickness of Americans such as Pohl and Bester. But Ballard never showed any interest in the usual subject matter of science fiction—rockets, aliens, and other planets.

Sputnik I had just been launched, opening up the space age, but Ballard ignored outer space and concentrated on what he called "inner space." E. J. Carnell, who edited *New Worlds* in the 1950s, encouraged Ballard to follow his own direction, despite protests from readers who didn't enjoy this kind of innovation. Within a few years it became clear that Ballard was writing stories which were quite different from anything anyone else was doing; they continued to be published in science-fiction magazines simply because that was the only genre with which they had any affinity at all.

An Unexplored Literary Continent. "I went to Canada with the British Air Force and was stuck on bases on Moose Jaw, Saskatchewan, and so on, where there was nothing to read, no national newspapers, very few news magazines—*Time* magazine was regarded as wildly highbrow. I discovered that the racks of every bus depot, or in the cafeteria, on the base, were loaded with science-fiction magazines, and their contents were more sophisticated than their covers suggested. So I spent about six months reading science fiction, and then I effectively stopped reading it and started writing it.

"The flight of Sputnik I seemed to confirm all the age-old dreams of science fiction in the 1930s and 1940s, but I was convinced, against all the evidence, that that phase was already *over*, and modern science fiction had exhausted its own material, and had lost that very vitality and relevance to the present day that it once had.

"I was interested in the visual arts, and pop-art was born in England soon after I started writing. I went to that famous exhibition, *This is Tomorrow*, at the Whitechapel Gallery, where Eduardo Paolozzi exhibited, and where Richard Hamilton exhibited I think the *first* pop painting ever, and it struck me then that the very things that these pop-artists found so exciting about science fiction actually belonged to the science fiction of the 1930s and 1940s—not, as should have been the case, to the science fiction of the 1950s. Science fiction had exhausted itself and was now just feeding on itself. When you started reading it, once the first flush of novelty had passed, you then began to see that, Oh, God, here they are permutating another time-travel variation, or whatever; and the whole thing needed loosening up."

I ask Ballard if any science-fiction writers influenced his early work.

"I don't honestly think so. Possibly Bradbury, though I don't know, I haven't read anything of his for twenty years now. I think one influence was Bernard Wolfe's *Limbo 90*, which encouraged me to go ahead, because that had sophistication and irony, and a genuine imaginative and literary dimension explored for its own sake, which was missing in all the others. Bradbury in his way was the genius of science fiction but he was kind of naive, and you don't expect any element of irony and self-consciousness in a naive writer. But *Limbo 90* encouraged me to feel that it was possible within commercial science fiction, which was another important consideration to me; I wanted to write within a form of fiction which was read by a reasonably wide audience.

"I felt that I was moving into a largely unexplored literary continent. Here was a unique literary form that had all sorts of things going for it—its popularity, its reliance on strong story lines, its very traditional short-story form and techniques, much closer to de Maupassant and O'Henry, Chekhov, or the Victorian and Edwardian ghost-story writers—much closer to them than to the elliptical, modern *New Yorker* short stories. It had popular imagery and it was about the real world: the transformation of the present and the future by science and technology was something that would affect everybody, whereas the concerns of so much so-called mainstream novels weren't those that would affect society at large. So almost by definition, science fiction was a popular art form. I thought this was tremendously exciting—but nobody, I felt, then, had really made serious *use* of science fiction. It was like going to an amusement park and finding people toying with aeroplanes and electric light and computers, in a world where aviation and electricity didn't exist. I felt then, and still do feel, that science fiction is a sort of playground, a huge amusement park with all sorts of exciting possibilities that need to be taken out and *applied*, to the real world.

"Also I felt a conscious reaction against what was, in Britain at that time, an extremely sterile literary scene. In the mid- to late 1950s the angry young men appeared on the scene—John Osborne's *Look Back in Anger,* Amis's *Lucky Jim,* Sillitoe, all the rest. I felt they were a totally parochial phenomenon, they didn't shake the literary establishment in any serious way whatever. They were all soon annexed into it. I felt, and still do, that the sort of realist social mainstream novel that's been written in England since World War II needs the shot of adrenaline that can be provided by the kinds of fiction that are bought and sold on the marketplace, just as the cinema can benefit enormously from the shot of adrenaline that, say, the Hollywood thriller has. I've always been a great believer in the strong story. I don't believe in a fiction of nuance."

Image Quanta. In 1964, *The Terminal Beach* was published. This was Ballard's most experimental story thus far, depicting the dreams and memories of a solitary bomber pilot stranded on an abandoned Pacific atoll, formerly an H-bomb test site. This strange, ominous journey through a landscape prefiguring Armageddon was written in disconnected sections—like a movie made up of long, separate shots, some of them flashbacks. It was a transitional story which marked the beginning of a new phase in Ballard's writing. He was to develop its impressionistic form much further, and sever his last links with orthodox science fiction and fantasy.

In June 1966 *New Worlds* published *You:Coma:Marilyn Monroe,* the first of what Ballard was to call (with characteristic overstatement) "condensed novels." He had removed all the usual elements of fiction writing—the routines of moving characters around, giving them things to say, developing conflicts and resolving them. All that remained were images, metaphor, landscape, message, and myth figures—some of them imaginary, others drawn from the powerful contemporary media of advertising, movies, and television.

Ultimately, fifteen of these "condensed novels" were collected in one volume: *Love and Napalm: Export U.S.A.* (British title: *The Atrocity Exhibition*). Almost all of the stories consisted of short sections of text, with bold subheadings (the same format that I have borrowed for this profile). The text sections were slices of spacetime; quanta of experience, coexisting on the page, as memories coexist in one's mind. The overall effect was a montage whose parts interlocked; an overall statement derived from many different perspectives.

Dislocation. "In the early 1960s I felt I'd done enough extrapolative fiction set in abandoned Londons of the future or strange research establishments out in the desert. The future had *arrived* by the mid-1960s, so it seemed to me that the main subject matter for the science fiction writer was the present day. And I think I was right. We were *in* tomorrow, and I felt that I had to write about it, and it seemed to me there was no other way of doing it than the way I used the *The Atrocity Exhibition* stories. I couldn't have handled all that material, the subject matter of those pieces, otherwise.

"They were very much a product of all those dislocations and communication overlays that ran through everything from 1965 to 1970. We've moved from a period of high excitement to a period of low excitement, and it's very hard for people who are younger to realize just how flat life is today, and how pedestrian are people's concerns. Leading politicians, trade-union leaders—in the British General election, for example, you'd expect there'd be some appeal to the imagination, even if only on the level of Kennedy, and yet all they're talking about is getting inflation down from seventeen percent to twelve percent. It's like going to a shareholders' meeting of some large insurance company and listening to a lot of accountants quibbling over decimal points. Everything is far flatter now; the 1970s have been enormously flat; the technique of the *The Atrocity Exhibition* stories seems too crowded, in a sense, for the present day. I think if the 1960s had continued and not turned into the 1970s, the stories wouldn't seem so strange.

"Also, one reason why those stories may now seem to be an experiment that hasn't worked is that we're now so mentally lazy. I think if Borges were published for the first time now, people would say it's far too literary and too complicated. It's a good thing he established his reputation in the late 1960s when people were still prepared to make a bit of an effort. People are amazingly lazy now; it's difficult to imagine a film like *Star Wars* being the success in the 1960s that it has been in the 1970s. I think critical judgments were sharper then."

Disaster Area. In Britain and other European countries, especially Germany and France, Ballard has a wide readership, a loyal following, and a strong reputation. Almost all of his novels and story collections remain in print in paperback. He has found much less success in America—ironically, since a lot of the images and obsessions in his work are drawn from the American scene. I ask him if he knows why his work is not well-received by the American audience.

"It's mysterious, I can't really say; you know the American scene better than I do. I think it's easy for an English writer like myself, who doesn't really know the American publishers and readers, to overestimate the literary interests of a huge market like that. I think the readership of fiction generally, in the United States, is far less sensitive and open than one realizes, over here. That sounds bitchy, and I certainly don't intend to be; but I read American novelists who have a high literary reputation—let's say, that school of writers like Roth and Vonnegut. *The New York Review of Books* goes overboard on them, *Time* magazine brackets them with Hemingway and Faulkner. But they're middlebrow writers who don't stretch their readers' imaginations in any way whatever. They're serious writers in the sense that somebody like Daphne du Maurier is serious. Or those writers of the 1930s, like A. J. Cronin. It seems to me it is possible for a writer here to overestimate the literary capacity of the American market."

Beach Head. Still Ballard's new work continues to appear in America, through important hardcover publishers. And he continues to write ambitious, powerful novels. It is more than twenty-five years since his fiction first appeared in print, but, if anything, there is more energy in his work today than there was then. His three children are now away at university, and as a single parent, he is left with considerable time in which to write. He seems happy to be alone out there in his Shepperton retreat. He is amiable, slightly shy (despite his uncompromisingly stated opinions), and not especially sociable: "I'm not a gregarious character. I go in to London on average once a week, I suppose; most of my friends are in London."

He claims that, in his eyes, Shepperton really is a world of beaches and lagoons, an inspirational landscape of mystery. Indeed, this is how he describes it in his novel of metamorphosis and messianism, *The Unlimited Dream Company*. To me, Shepperton will always be a rather grubby little suburb surrounded by a derelict wasteland of mud and refuse. But then, Ballard is a visionary. His style can be imitated, his obsessions can be mocked, but his imagination and insight are unique. His surreal, vibrant images of apocalyptic fulfillment endure—as an enrichment of life, and as a strange kind of prophesy.

Historical Context

When I started reading J. G. Ballard's short stories in the late 1960s, I felt that I had stumbled upon a writer whose work had a revelatory quality. Even now, when I revisit a novel such as *The Crystal World* or his "Vermilion Sands" stories, they have a strangely seductive power. I find myself wanting to live in that fin-de-siècle zone, sliding gently into oblivion alongside the well-mannered men and genteel women who constitute his usual cast of characters.

My association with *New Worlds* magazine brought me into contact with him many times. He preferred to be called "Jimmy," which seemed odd for man who was so reserved and formal in many respects. But that was the least of the contradictions.

I had known him for more than ten years by the time I interviewed him for *Dream Makers*, yet I wasn't sure I really knew him at all. He had not yet written his breakthrough novel, *Empire of the Sun*, which subsequently became a Spielberg movie. Consequently I knew nothing about his childhood in Shanghai, and had never even heard him talk about it until he mentioned it during my interview with him.

Clearly, when his earlier books such as *High Rise* or *Concrete Island* portrayed everyday people losing their protective veneer of civilization, he was transliterating his early experiences from a war zone. But other dark aspects of his work seem to have nothing to do with Shanghai. His novel *Crash*, in particular, looks to me like the result of dredging his own unconscious. It was a uniquely perverse, disturbing and disturbed adventure into sadism and death, and I still remember him laughing happily when he told me that a woman who was paid by his publisher to read the book had concluded that he was "beyond clinical help."

The novel was largely written around a character named Vaughan, who is very clearly modeled on a scientist at the National Physical Laboratory named Christopher Evans. At the time he wrote the novel, Ballard referred to Evans as his closest friend, although I suspect that a "close" conversation between them would have sounded more like a strategy meeting. During one of my visits to England, I asked Jimmy how Evans had felt about seeing himself as the central character in *Crash*, especially bearing in mind the scene where the narrator subjects Vaughan to anal rape. "I've often wondered about that myself," Jimmy said, "but I never asked him. And he never said anything about it."

This struck me as amazingly British: to write a novel in which you describe a fictionalized version of yourself inserting your penis in the rectum of your closest pal, and then continue your friendship without either person saying a word about it. But it was also typical of Jimmy's reluctance to get too personal. He happily went public with statements such as this quote from an interview he gave to *Re/Search* magazine: "What we're getting is a whole new order of sexual fantasies, involving a different order of experiences, like car crashes...." But he didn't talk about his own sexual fantasies.

In reality, his interest in death and dismemberment had long preceded *Crash*. In 1967, when actress Jayne Mansfield died in a car accident that decapitated her, Mike Moorcock called Jimmy to tell him the news. "The poor kid!" Jimmy exclaimed (according to Moorcock). There was a brief pause. "Any photographs?" Jimmy asked hopefully.

His attitude toward women was a mess of contradictions. One time I was walking with him across a field near his home in Shepperton, while my girlfriend walked ahead of us with Claire, and a dog ran to and fro. Because the two women were deep in conversation, they didn't realize that they were heading toward a corner of the field that was entirely walled in by hedgerows. "Look at those women," Jimmy said to me. "That *dog* is more intelligent than those women." He raised his voice. "Over here!" He shouted the words as if he was trying to communicate with someone who was cognitively impaired. "The gate, is, over, here!"

Still, the book he wrote after *Empire of the Sun* was titled *The Kindness of Women*, and was a semiautobiographical love letter to those who had been close to him. He also seemed to be a wonderful father to his two daughters, whom he raised single-handedly after the death of his wife. His relationship with them was playful, completely uncontaminated by the dark obsessions of his writing.

I recall that the daughters had a pet rat, which they surreptitiously brought with them into the car one day when we were going to drive somewhere. Jimmy was about to start the car when something triggered his suspicions. He turned and gave the girls a penetrating look. "There's a rat in this car," he said.

"No, no there isn't," one of them protested.

"Yes there is. He has to go back in the house."

"Oh no, Daddeee, please let him come with us!"

"No, no, back into the house. No rats in the car."

Of course, this was the same car which he turned over, not so many months later, in an impromptu real-life recapitulation of the accident that he described in his novel.

He knew that his life seemed a mix of contradictions to outsiders. We corresponded intermittently, after I had relocated in the United States, and in one of his letters he mentioned that he was waiting for a French journalist to arrive at the house. He had given street directions over the phone, explaining how to find Shepperton. "Yes, yes, just like in your book, *Crash!*" the journalist exclaimed.

In his letter to me, Jimmy wondered how the journalist would react when he turned up at the modest suburban home on that Sunday afternoon, where he would find a haven of domestic tranquility, with three children playing in the back yard and Claire putting roast beef in the oven. *Move along, nothing to see, no trace of mutilation, anal rape, or drug abuse here.* So where, then, did it all come from?

The plot of *Crash* entails a plan by Vaughan to die in a head-on collision with Elizabeth Taylor. Jimmy had referred to the actress in some of his stories, but in *Crash* she was featured as an actual character. His use of public figures in works of fiction had begun four years earlier, in 1969, when I took over as the editor of *New Worlds*. The magazine was not doing well, and had lost some of its more notable contributors. I made a phone call to Jimmy, begging him for a story. He had always been rather kind to me, and obviously wanted to help, but was in a creative dead spot. To deal with it, he went into London and spent a whole afternoon in Foyle's, the biggest bookshop in England, looking for inspiration.

He found it in a clinical textbook by a plastic surgeon. Jimmy had been to medical school, and retained an interest in medicine that seemed morbid to me, although probably he would have said that he was merely recognizing aspects that most people preferred to ignore. Perhaps the plastic-surgery text appealed to him because of its seemingly contradictory mix, as it described procedures to make someone more beautiful by slicing up human flesh. He especially enjoyed one line that he found in the book: "In the experience of this surgeon, skin is never in short supply."

But how could he turn this into a story? The answer came soon enough, under the title "Princess Margaret's Facelift." It was written entirely in clinical terms, as if the procedure really had been applied to the daughter of the Queen of England.

This created not just one but two possible threats of legal action. First, the magazine might be sued by the Royal Family for defamation, and they might have a good chance of winning under punitive British libel law. Second, Jimmy had copied sentences from the surgical book word-for-word, revising them only to insert Princess Margaret as the patient. His favorite quote from the surgeon was used without modification as the last line in the story. Could this be viewed as plagiarism?

There was only one way to find out. Michael Moorcock, who still owned the magazine, agreed that we should publish the story, although as unobtrusively as possible. I managed to fit it into a single page, and we were relieved when we suffered no consequences.

Jimmy, meanwhile, started writing more stories in which

famous personalities were transplanted into fictitious scenarios. They included "Mae West's Reduction Mammoplasty" and, most infamously, "Why I Want to Fuck Ronald Reagan." I think this thread of his work can all be traced back to that afternoon in Foyle's, and part of me feels happy to have served as an enabler.

Then I have to step back and wonder why I should feel that way. What, exactly, was my relationship with this man's work? When he wrote an opinion piece in the 1960s in which he mentioned, casually, that most people would rather be involved in a sex crime than in conventional sex, why did I find this plausible? When he claimed that he was merely exposing the impulses that everyone shared beneath their deceptively civilized exterior, why did I feel intuitively sure that this was correct, while anyone who claimed otherwise was in a state of denial?

I never nailed down the answers to these questions. Maybe Jimmy was right, and a suburb such as the one in which he lived was nothing more than a cover story, concealing dark desires that are common to all human beings. Or maybe he really was delusional, tormented by pathological impulses, and "beyond clinical help" as the woman who evaluated *Crash* had said. John Baxter, who wrote a biography of Jimmy that was published in 2011, certainly subscribed to that theory, portraying Jimmy as a psychopath who was obsessed with pornography, was prone to violent episodes, and was habitually evasive. "Jim's skill was to speculate and fantasize, evade and lie," according to Baxter.

The one thing I feel sure of is that Jimmy was a bona-fide literary genius whose work still has the power to shock, amaze, and excite the imagination.

He died in April 2009 of prostate cancer, at the age of 78.

John Sladek

London, England, February 26, 1981

TO ME, SOMETHING vital is missing from visions of the future by writers such as Clarke and Asimov. There's no sense of humor.

So I turn now to John Sladek, our shyest, slyest satirist, unable to take anything seriously for long, up to and including his own career. He's veered playfully from one literary joke to another—all the way from science-fiction parodies to a book that revealed the "missing" thirteenth sign of the zodiac so convincingly that it even fooled some professional astrologers.

Sladek is as serious about our technology-driven future as any other futurist. But he sees it mismanaged, messed up and malfunctioning. He sees corporations obsessed with idiot objectives, fail-safe systems that do fail and aren't safe, and machines that misunderstand their masters and refuse to turn themselves off.

His recent novel, *Roderick*, is a clever, funny parable about the world's first human-like robot, built secretly with embezzled NASA funds on the whim of an eccentric bureaucrat. Abandoned by his makers when the money runs out, Roderick wanders into the world like a mutant Horatio Alger, with nothing but a set of Boolean-algebra truth-tables and a thorough knowledge of TV soap operas to help him understand human behavior. The result is more than whimsy, much more than farce. It raises some awkward questions about what we're going to do when the dividing line blurs between human and machine intelligence, and why we seem so interested in making gadgets that imitate us in the first place.

For the most part, Sladek's humor overshadows these serious messages. Yet they are the point of the book, so far as he's concerned, and he seems happy to start our interview with a little lecture on this subject (the laughs come later).

"It's clear that we're very uneasy about humanoid machines. We either relegate them to jokes, or to horror stories. There doesn't seem to be any ground in between, where we feel comfortable with the idea. And yet we're very certainly going to build the corny, classic robots that go clanking around in science fiction.

"Artificial intelligence researchers say we're not going to build them, because it wouldn't be practical—there's no rational reason to fit an artificial brain with arms and legs and have it behave like a human being. But rational reasons have nothing to do with it. We're going to build robots because we like the idea of building robots.

"The idea of the robot is much more deeply embedded in our culture than people realize. The notion of machines that look or act like people has been a guiding aesthetic principle for inventions going back to Greek times. Greek mythology is full of robot stories—Prometheus making a clay man and someone else criticizing it and saying he should have left a window in the chest so people could see what it was thinking, for instance. The Chinese were building very elaborate puppet theaters, automatic orchestras and so on, about 300 A.D. There are also stories about statues coming to life—Pygmalion is the classic example—and the sexual side of robots was pretty evident in that story. There were also stories of robot soldiers, guards, or defenders—such as Talos, the bronze man who was supposed to fire himself up to glowing heat and then embrace people to kill them. Then there was plenty of building of clockwork automatons at various times throughout Eastern and Western culture, as soon as clockwork had been invented.

"It seems to me that there must be some reason that people are endlessly fascinated with imitations of the human form. Since we're primed psychologically to recognize other individuals and distinguish them as separate from the rest of the world, the notion of artificial people calls that whole distinction into question. If they're artificial, how can they be people? If they act like people, how can they be separate from humanity? I think that these questions are going to get much more interesting in the next few years, as all the predictions that we're not going to have robots don't come true. I think robots are going to be built in large numbers, as servants, playmates, teachers, sex objects, and just for company.

"When I started thinking about all this, it seemed to me that it hadn't ever been dealt with properly in science fiction. It seemed to me that robots had been," he chuckles, "badly treated in science fiction. People keep talking about, you know, Isaac Asimov's three laws of robotics, but that's not the way it's going to be at all. Those laws are supposed to be logic laws, but really they're just legal laws. They depend on interpretation. The first law says a robot may not harm a human being or allow a person to come to harm; well, in that case, a robot's got to know what a human being is, so it's got to have built into it a whole lot of the stuff that we've got built into us, to be able to identify another human being. So it's going to be a very good imitation of us, in which case it may well have a lot of trouble telling the difference between human beings and other robots, built like itself.

"Asimov's first law is unrealistic, anyway. If a millionaire builds a robot, his first thought will be to protect his investment. So the robot's first law will be to protect itself—not other people. And since a principal interest in building robots is likely to be military, those robots are certainly going to harm human beings as much as they can. So I would say that, when and if robots are built, they're going to be much more like Philip K. Dick's imaginations than Isaac Asimov's."

And this brings him to the *Roderick* books.

"I set out to make Roderick a learning machine, whose job is to learn how to be human. If you wanted to make a very human-like robot, that would be the way to go about it, rather than by pre-programming.

"But I found that the book was turning into something else as I wrote it. I found myself contrasting the machine-like lives of the people with the rather human life of the robot." He grins, enjoying the irony.

So his serious novel turned into a surreal situation comedy, a blend of black humor and playfulness, as if by Franz Kafka under the influence of nitrous oxide.

In Sladek's next novel, he plans to make more of the darker implications, and hold back the humor, while still dealing with the same subject.

"It's provisionally titled *Tik-Tok*, set about fifty years from now, when people have recreational, home-use robots and they give them awful-cute names like 'Tik-Tok.' Tik-Tok begins by committing a hideous murder in the first chapter, and then...." Sladek shakes his head with fatherly regret. "I'm sorry to say, he goes downhill from then on. You see, I really can't imagine robots being incapable of wrongdoing; it's so built into our conception of what it means to be human. Even people who dote on animals prefer those animals that will naturally tend to disobey them, and have to be trained like children. I mean, not many people dote on worms, or insects, you know?

"I do mean eventually to stop writing about robots. But the whole field of computer science is so important, and people are so ignorant of it generally, there's a lot of material that needs to be dealt with. Right now most people seem to think that microchip

Charles Platt

technology is just a good way of building videogames, as if videogames were the end product. And of course they're just the beginning."

Sladek lives in London and has been there for fourteen years. But he was born in Minnesota, in 1937. He looks back on his American childhood with a mixture of laughter and loathing, and still uses the mid-American cultural wasteland to pathetic and ludicrous effect in his comic novels.

He first started writing with the encouragement of fellow Midwesterner Thomas M. Disch.

"Tom and I collaborated on a few short stories, in the first instance. Then I wrote some of my own, and sold the first to Harlan Ellison for *Dangerous Visions*. Tom and I collaborated on *Black Alice* [a modern murder mystery] and on a terrible gothic novel, and I wrote another gothic myself, under a pseudonym. Then we went traveling, and while Tom was writing *Camp Concentration*, I wrote *The Reproductive System*." [Published in the U.S. under the title *Mechasm*.]

This book pits a mob of earnest, dedicated, small-town buffoons against the totally ruthless Dr. Smilax, maddest of all mad scientists, whose favorite relaxation is to sit in his custom-built dentist chair and drill and fill his own teeth. Smilax plans to rule the world via his "reproductive system": intelligent machines that build replicas of themselves and adapt to any challenge or contingency. The plot grows ever more complex, and manages to ridicule, with some affection, every science-fictional cliché ever invented.

"I've never specifically wanted to write science fiction," Sladek recalls. "I just wanted to write stuff, get it published, and make a living out of it. Science fiction did seem to be a good way of starting out; and I suppose I ended up a science-fiction writer because what I write won't fit anywhere else. It's a more tolerant genre than the others."

He arrived in England just when science fiction's "new wave" was emerging in the British magazine *New Worlds*. A lot of his work

215

began appearing there, though he never felt part of the movement.

"I've never really understood schools of writing and literary categories. I just liked the idea that there was this fantastic magazine, the most experimental publishing venture around, I guess, taking all my stories. I read everybody else's work in it, but I can't say I identified with any of it. Not even Ballard, though he was and is one of my favorite writers."

It was in *New Worlds* that Sladek published his classic novelette "Masterson and the Clerks," a surreal fantasy about small-time businesses with delusions of grandeur, enticing them farther and farther from sanity. Since then, Sladek has repeatedly satirized the corporate mentality.

"I actually worked at various jobs for small companies like that, with maniac bosses. Lots of things in "Masterson and the Clerks" really happened. I got interested in the way companies and people in them set about dehumanizing themselves, in this idiotic rearrangement of human lives, this curtailment of human sensibilities, just for the purposes of some silly organization. I suppose this sounds depressing, but comedy is always the other side of tragedy. Not that any of my stuff approaches tragedy—I'm mainly concerned with pathos, I suppose. With wasted lives." He laughs happily. "Wasted lives can be wonderfully funny—if they're appearing in fiction."

After *The Reproductive System*, Sladek's next seriously satirical novel was *The Müller-Fokker Effect*, which he says "vanished without trace." Perhaps because he felt disillusioned by this failure, he spent the next ten years following whatever literary whim came into his head, with total disregard for building any kind of coherent career.

First he devoted two-and-a-half years to researching *The New Apocrypha*, a nonfiction source-book that methodically debunks every possible pseudoscience, crank cult, and mystical belief, from parapsychology to perpetual motion. "I kind of suspected that book wouldn't be too successful," he says, "because people don't really like books which tell them that things aren't true.

"So after it was published, and it didn't do very well, I decided that if I couldn't sell books by telling people the facts as I saw them, I would try—well, lying to people! I picked the most outrageous lie I could imagine, which was that there are thirteen signs in the zodiac. I figured out all kinds of evidence to prove that the thirteenth sign had once existed, and had been suppressed. I called it Arachne, the sign of the spider."

He published this as Arachne Rising, by "James Vogh," a secret identity that has not been revealed until now.

"It certainly did better than *The New Apocrypha*. It was a good exercise, actually, in finding out what believing this nonsense is like, because I had to convince myself it was true, so that while I was writing the book I was completely caught up in the notion. It gave me some insight into what makes lunatics write lunatic books.

"It's not at all different from the kind of belief that I think scientists have in their ideas and theories. The only difference is that pseudoscientists drop all pretense at criticizing their own work and at trying to make it fit reality. They simply promote what they're doing.

"And it's really kind of fun being obsessed in this way. If there were nothing else in my life, and I'd come up with this one idea that there was a thirteenth sign in the zodiac, I suppose I would go on promoting it for the rest of my life.

"I fooled quite a few astrologers. Stan Gooch, he's a writer on astrology and the paranormal. And several British newspaper astrologers. They wrote to me, and I met a couple of them—as James Vogh."

Friends of Sladek, who were in on the joke, told him this was all good fun, but a long way from the serious fiction he should be working on. Sladek responded to this helpful advice by writing, of all things, an old-fashioned British murder mystery.

"I had written a short mystery story for a contest in *The Times*, and won the contest. So"—he chuckles at the absurdity of it—"I got a contract to do a full-length detective novel. I wrote that, and enjoyed it, so I did another one. But by this time, even if publishers had been thinking of reviving the detective novel, they changed their minds. It wasn't going to take off.

"So I decided finally to get down to work, and *Roderick* was the next project. That represents what I ought to be doing."

But he still has a wayward, obsessive intelligence that gets hung up on almost any kind of distraction, from Rubik's Cube to the Rosetta Stone. Games, codes, and logic problems can lure him into a single-minded state that lasts for days or months. Partly because of this, he often seems withdrawn. Receiving visitors, he stops for a moment with a momentary blank look, as if some kind of recognition system is being powered up; and then—"Oh, hi," he says, with a shy smile, emerging (part way) from whatever conundrum he's been mulling over. The visitors are invited in, and he's friendly and funny, but still not entirely present, as if he's running a mental program labeled "Polite social conversation," while most of his mind is busily thinking: "Maybe if we substitute X for A and invert the matrix, and then...."

He lives with his British wife and young daughter in an anonymous, system-built housing development on the north-east edge of London.

"Just lately I've been realizing," he says, as if with a sense of revelation, "how my horizons have shrunk. You know, the United States disappeared a few years ago, then the rest of Britain disappeared and I was left with London, and now during the last year most of London has gone, and I'm just down to Tottenham, and during the last week or so—well, I've hardly left the house! I guess I have gotten more and more reclusive. I suppose I'm alienated from the everyday world; after all, I've chosen to live in a foreign country. But I don't know what effect it has on my work. I don't trust analogies from my life to my work. I like to think of my work as being just invention. Anyway," he shrugs it all off, "I'm not that self-analytical.

"I'm perfectly happy for my work to be published as science

fiction, if people will buy it and read it. But I don't know if it is science fiction. I suppose if I had to define it, I'd say I'm writing 'classy' science fiction." He laughs at the idea. "It's good quality, no shoddy materials, the workmanship is all there to be seen. Something like that.

"A lot of science fiction does strike me as junk-food writing. I think Isaac Asimov is a very good example, and Robert Heinlein is another, and Ray Bradbury. The old clan there. Of those three, Bradbury is the only one who ever could write, really. I suppose Heinlein did one or two things which I'd have to say I liked a lot. But even his good stuff is really marred by bad writing. And Isaac Asimov, I don't think, ever cared to do anything else but pulp writing, and would probably be perfectly pleased to be known as a bad pulp writer. Wouldn't he? It's ideas that he's interested in, I suppose, so he probably figures that doesn't mind how he gets them across."

Does Sladek like modern fantasy any better?

"It's just a matter of taking a background of Grimm's fairy tales, Arthurian legends, and cranking out adventure stories. At least, stuff I've seen looks like that. It seems to me very much like the Western; the rules are very restrictive. More so than science fiction. I guess it'll be popular for a while, and then die out."

So what does he like?

"John Barth, William Gaddis—I think Gaddis is very important. His novels deal with large ideas. I can't lump together all the books I like, except to say that they're not conventional novels. I think the conventional novel must be dead by now; I can't imagine anyone sitting down and writing a conventional novel and making anything important out of it."

If he prefers to read non-category fiction, does he mind having his own work categorized?

"The fact that 'science fiction' is stamped on a book cover will probably guarantee a certain sale. That's to my benefit. But I'm really sorry that people feel it necessary to be told the books are science fiction before they'll buy them—or that other people will avoid books because they're science fiction. Probably a lot of my stuff isn't taken seriously enough by non-science-fiction people because it has that label on it. That doesn't bother me too much; it would be nice if it weren't so, but I don't see the categories breaking down."

He sounds uncomfortable, as if he finds it hard to deal with this kind of businesslike topic, and would much rather be talking about abstractions—like computer programming, or mathematical games, or (of course) robots. I get the impression that he prefers to avoid practicalities altogether. Did he, in fact, ever have any realistic plans about where his writing would lead?

"No." There is a long silence. He laughs. "I bet you like helpful answers like that! But I guess I'm not terribly ambitious. Everybody who writes would love to be lionized, to be a famous writer, to be at the top of whatever pyramid it is, and of course I would too. But I'm not very good at gauging where I am. I know I'm not at the very bottom, and I certainly know I'm not at the very top. I don't have any idea about the levels in between and I don't indulge too much in charting my career. I just decide what I'm going to do next—and do it."

Historical Context

I first got to know John Sladek when he rented a room in the squalid tenement where I lived with my girlfriend in London's Portobello Road, during the late 1960s. Sometimes on a Saturday night we would go out to the local pub with some saucepans, ask the bartender to fill them with draught beer, bring them home, and get drunk with John's girlfriend Pamela. We would talk about story ideas (which were never developed) and grand plans to create best-sellers (which were never written), and we would play word games, which Pamela often won by cheating. For me it was one of those brief, precious times when pleasure is abundant and the future is not something that anyone takes very seriously.

John was a wonderful lodger, because he was so much fun to talk to. He seemed to view the British in general, and London in particular, as an endless source of amusement. I never heard him argue with anyone, and we shared a mutual weakness for games and puzzles that sucked up hours of our time.

I created a code; he broke it. He showed me the anagrams he had made from his name; I spent an afternoon coming up with Ralph T. Castle as an anagram of mine. At the same time, during that slightly magical period while he was falling in love with Pamela and I was working on the floor above, doing page layouts for *New Worlds*, John wrote probably the best short stories of his career.

I think the most ambitious was "The Master Plan," exploring the last moments in the life of a U.S. military general, written as a complex set of nested threads representing the general's thoughts as his mind ranged backward in time. On the typewritten manuscript, John distinguished the threads by underlining each of them with a different color—about ten in all. I suggested that when we published the story we could make the distinction by using different typefaces, although this would be a major challenge for the typesetter. We did it, the typesetter cooperated, and it worked.

You could read the story as samples from layers of consciousness, but John contrived the segments so that they would also fit together as a conventional linear narrative. This was the fun part, the game: to write a single piece of text that could be read in two totally different modes. It was a tour-de-force, but was difficult for a reader to follow, as well as being difficult for a typesetter to typeset, and was quickly forgotten.

John pulled off a similar stunt with "Alien Territory," consisting of 36 separate paragraphs that you could read in literally thousands of different sequences. These "life quanta" made some kind of sense no matter which path you followed—or you could treat the story as a conventional linear narrative, beginning with paragraph 1 and continuing sequentially to paragraph 36. The story ended with the phrase, "...he wrote it across their backs in lead." Depending which paragraphs you had read previously, this referred either to a massacre or to a person inscribing a pencilled caption on the back of a photograph.

I loved John's literary playfulness and tried to emulate it with my own multiple-choice narratives, one of which, titled "Norman vs. America," was published in the short-lived science-fiction quarterly *Quark/*. I think John and I were equally aware there was no real future in this kind of foolishness, but even after I relocated in the United States, we couldn't resist some word play or mathematical games. We returned several times to the challenge of finding a pseudonym that was an anagram of each person's name, or the shortest possible sentence that contained every letter in the English language. My greatest achievement was "zephyrs just vex dumb quacking fowl." I don't remember what John's was.

John never did find a really productive niche as a writer. He was too clever to write straightforward science fiction, yet not pretentious enough about his cleverness to become a darling of critics and academics. He was an entertainer who told esoteric, self-deprecating jokes; a word-gamer who expected readers to recognize a palindrome when they saw one.

His novel *Roderick* (1980) had been conceived as one long book but was divided into two volumes in the U.K., the second being titled *Roderick at Random* (1983). In the U.S. the publisher planned to publish it as a trilogy, with two-thirds of the first U.K. book constituting the first U.S. volume. Unfortunately the project was abandoned before volumes two and three ever appeared. *The Complete Roderick* (published in the U.S. in 2002) restored the whole text in one volume, but John never lived to see it.

Neither *Roderick* nor *Tik-Tok* was a commercial success.

In *The SF Encyclopedia*, critic John Clute describes John Sladek as "the most formally inventive, the funniest, and very nearly the most melancholy of modern American sf writers." I think this underlying quality of pathos interfered with the success of John's work, quite apart from the complexity of his humor, which eschewed the simple absurdism that made a writer such as Douglas Adams so popular.

John returned to Minneapolis where he became a technical writer for a large company, although he still continued to produce short stories on the side. After a long period in which I lost touch with him, we renewed our friendship via email. He and his second wife made plans to visit me in Arizona in 1999, but then decided that they couldn't spare the time or the money. Tragically, one year later, at the age of 62, John died of idiopathic pulmonary fibrosis.

For most of his life he had known that his health was problematic, although he seldom talked about it. His good company once seemed as plentiful as beer from the pub on Portobello Road; but that, alas, was as illusory as the gamefulness of life itself.

Harry Harrison

New York City, April 28, 1981

THE YOUNG HIGH-TECH hero of 1950s science fiction seems a little quaint these days. His little lectures on physics and engineering strain the attention span of readers reared on the rhythms of TV commercials and video games. Science fiction should have computers in it, and fancy gadgets and so forth...but we don't really need to know how all that stuff *works*, do we? Thrust aside the complexities of that computer bombsight, Luke; close your eyes and go with the flow of the Force. It's easier than Yankee ingenuity, and less time consuming than the scientific method.

Technologically accurate adventure fiction isn't dead, of course—it still survives in the pages of *Analog* magazine, its birthplace, and in occasional paperbacks from publishers such as Baen Books. But Robert Heinlein, the garrulous guardian who nurtured it to maturity, abandoned the form years ago. Many other writers also left it in favor of fiction that was more remunerative, offered more immediate escapism, or was simply easier to write.

The rewards for accurately researched science fiction were always small. You had to stay scientifically up-to-date, you were paid a pittance, and serious critics ignored you. No matter how well you did it, you were still writing category fiction of few literary virtues. If you took extra trouble to get the science right, that was largely between you and your conscience—reviewers in *The New*

York Times certainly wouldn't notice.

So it is that Harry Harrison has been relatively rarely reviewed, revered, or even remembered by critics. Harrison has stayed steadfastly within the technologically oriented, action-packed school. That he has exploited its potential more sensitively and resourcefully than most of his contemporaries has often been overlooked.

Of his more than thirty novels, he remains best known for *Deathworld* and *The Stainless Steel Rat*, both of which grew into series; and for *Make Room! Make Room!* which was debased into the movie *Soylent Green*. He has been writing science fiction for more than thirty years: methodically, persistently—and uneconomically, for much of that time. Science fiction in the 1980s can be lucrative for some, including those who, like Harrison, manage to keep their earlier books in print. But back in the 1950s and 1960s, there were only two ways to make a decent living: by turning out large quantities very fast, or by treating science fiction as a labor of love and earning a living by writing other stuff on the side.

For many years, Harrison chose that second option.

"I spent ten years writing Flash Gordon, to stay alive," he recalls. "The syndicated strip. Every daily and Sunday for ten years, from 1958 to 1968, every one of those scripts was mine. I also ghost-wrote a lot of stuff. I ghosted comics for Leslie Charteris for years. I wrote for confession magazines; I did 'I was an Iron Lung Baby.' I did men's adventures such as 'I Went Down in My Submarine,' right through 1957, for a nickel a word—maximum!

"But my science-fiction novels have always been novels that I wanted to write. Every single book. That's what's great about science fiction; you can write a book for fun, and get it published.

"The *Stainless Steel Rat* books I almost write for money. I sign the contract and think, 'Not another one.' But once I start writing I sit there laughing and enjoying myself."

Harrison talks in restless, staccato bursts, moving the conversation along as fast as the action in some of his novels. He's a series of contradictions: raconteur and drinking buddy, yet secretly shy; aggressive, yet an old-fashioned liberal and pacifist. He advocates ground-breaking experiments in fiction, at the same time that his own writing stays true to time-honored techniques. He made his career as a writer, but for the first ten years he worked as an artist:

"I went to art school, I found working in art really tremendous. I did classical painting—easel painting—but then I went into commercial art because I knew I'd never make a living at fine-art painting. I wasn't that good. But I was pretty first-rate as a comic artist. I broke into comics with Wallace Wood. We were in art school together and we penciled and inked together, early stuff. Horror was very big then, Bill Gaines was doing horror comics, we were doing westerns for him, some horror for him.

"Then I illustrated science-fiction magazines. I illustrated for *Galaxy*, I did some book jackets for Gnome Press, I did that mostly for a hobby, I got ten dollars for a drawing, was still making a living off comics. I got to know all the science-fiction writers because I was Harry the Artist, doing all this. Then I was packaging comics, editing comics, when the *putsch* came, when the comics went from 680 to 200 titles a month, a lot of artists were walking the streets. It seemed like the end of the world.

"So I started editing pulp magazines. I did *Rocket Stories* and *Sea Stories* and *Private Eye*, and Lester del Rey was doing *Science Fiction Adventures* for the same company, he got fired and I took over the magazine. I think I sold my first story around then, in 1951, to Damon Knight; I said, 'what do you think of this story, Damon?' And he gave me a hundred dollars for it.

"But I was still doing other stuff, in New York, to earn a living. I was writing confessions stories, anything, freelance. Bruce Elliot was an old friend of mine, I used to give him work when I was an editor, he'd give me work when he was an editor; in the old days you had to pass work around, there wasn't much work so you gave it to your friends. *Nepotism ruled okay,* you know? I had to get out. I didn't want to be art director—if you're art director you have to read all the crap in the magazine. And I was tired of writing it, so I got about two hundred dollars, gave up my job, my wife Joan gave up her job, we had an old Ford Anglia, took that to Mexico, put the baby in the back, one year old. Never came back to New York except on visits."

Harrison has traveled a lot, since then, living all over Europe and writing an average of one science-fiction novel a year. His first, *Deathworld*, was a deliberate attempt to write a story of non-stop danger and action. It was an instant classic and he followed it with several more in the same vein.

"I did *Deathworld* about seven or eight times in various ways. Once I got the formula right I disguised it with different kinds of titles. *Deathworld* had worked, I knew I could make money off that formula.

"But in the end I had to get out of the routine, so I wrote *Bill, the Galactic Hero*."

This was Harrison's comic novel satirizing many of the storytelling traditions of science fiction. It was rejected by Berkley, the first publisher Harrison submitted it to.

"I gave Damon Knight, who was reading for Berkley Books, a couple of chapters and an outline with some vague idea of where it would go, and thought he'd give me like $1,500, $750 of that on signing the contract. But when it came in he bounced it, saying 'It's an okay book but you made a mistake, it's an action novel, go through it and take out the jokes.'" Harrison rolls his eyes in despair at the memory. "So I submitted it to Doubleday, and they bought it. But it was very heart-stopping for a while, there; I feared all along that I'd written a book that no one wanted, and for a while it seemed I was right, no one wanted it. I got so shocked by that that I went back to doing *Deathworld* again, or something like it, and built up slowly, to the work it would take to get *Make Room! Make Room!* done."

In that novel, written at a time when few people took

overpopulation very seriously, Harrison projected as carefully and thoroughly as possible the future effects of an uncontrolled birth rate. The job took five years, and he has not tackled anything with that degree of social relevance since then.

However, his lighter novels often contain underlying political or social messages, on a less ambitious level, and Harrison seems to be the only high-tech science-fiction writer who espouses a left-wing ideology as opposed to the conservatism of others such as Heinlein, Pournelle, Niven, or Bova.

"Well, most engineers *are* pretty right-wing. But being right-wing is just a native American fashion. We always had it. We've also had native American socialism. We almost had a socialist president—Eugene Debs was two million votes from being elected president. That's what frightened the far right in America, who gave us what we have now, no liberal press, no liberal thought, and a disaster like the present president. Oh, you'll say there are a few liberal outlets around, but suppose you live in the small town of Asshole, Texas. You get a Hearst paper in the morning, a Hearst paper at night, a Hearst TV station, and if that's not enough you can read *Time* and *Newsweek*. What do you know about nine-tenths of the world? Americans are just as uninformed as *Pravda* readers in Russia, from the opposite point of view. We have freedom in this country, no one's denying that, but freedom of information is something else altogether. When you're getting nothing but one political attitude all your life, you have no real freedom of choice. And you wonder why they elected Reagan?"

Harrison himself has now settled outside of his native America, in Ireland. "I very rarely go to science-fiction conventions, I never do the big hoo hoo and the big ha ha, and they don't know that I'm alive, that little clique that wins those bought-and-paid-for prizes like the Hugo and Nebula. I'm not part of it; *Skyfall*, a book of mine that sold a quarter of a million copies—they printed about 350,000 and actually sold a quarter of a million—never received one nomination for a Hugo or a Nebula. So I have a strong suspicion that someone's buying and someone's reading, but someone else altogether is nominating.

"The Hugo and Nebula mean a lot as far as money goes, if you mention them on a book cover. But one award, I won't tell you which, I really have seen won by ballot-box stuffing. But we really don't want to go into print about Nebulas and Hugos, do we? I mean are they important to the world? They're no different from, say, the Oscars, which are also bought and paid for—they must be, if really rotten pictures like *The Deer Hunter* win and good pictures are ignored. Something rotten always wins awards; which is why Brian Aldiss and I founded the Campbell award, which is voted by a handful of people who have critical, writing, or editing experience, enjoy science fiction, and also have experience of literature outside of science fiction."

I mention that some people regard the Campbell award as being cliquish.

"It's no more cliquish than a Nobel Prize. We have one judge in Sweden, two in England, one in Ireland, one in Germany, three or four in the United States, and for six months we correspond intensely, and then we use the Australian system to vote. Where's the clique? If anything it's the direct opposite. What does Tom Shippey have in common with Jim Gunn? And Kingsley Amis is a new judge. That's a clique? Come on now."

Judges of the Campbell Award have also been criticized for picking books which editor John W. Campbell, after whom the award was named, would have found unreadably modern. It seems odd that Harrison, who sold most of his early work to Campbell's magazine, should continue to write straightforward storytelling himself, at the same time that he advocates breaking the old storytelling rules. Of the "new wave" of the sixties, he remarks:

"I could never write that kind of thing. I couldn't afford to write it, I am a slow writer, which means I have to be a commercial writer, because if I'm only doing one book a year I can't afford to have that book not sell. So as a writer I have a specifically defined area that I can work in. As a reader and as an editor I have a much larger one."

And as a reader, his tastes are not satisfied by much of the science fiction currently being published.

"I think it's pretty rotten for the most part. Badly written, completely derivative, digging out old plots—rewriting Edgar Rice Burroughs, if that's possible. And this whole new move to fantasy; it's so easy to write fantasy. You're not really writing science fiction when you take a world so far in the future that it's completely isolated from everything we know.

"I love female writers, I always try to anthologize women who write, some really fantastic people like Kate Wilhelm and Kit Reed and Sonya Dorman, but they don't write enough, so instead we have what I can only describe as the 'tears and Tampax' school of science fiction, prizes for dream snakes and dragons, that kind of stuff. You've read it, or at least you've held it in your hand. Have you ever read one? All the way through? Hmm, strong fellow! Did you enjoy every word of it? Well, tell me later, off the record, eh?

"Not too long ago I was on television in Britain with four or five writers, one of whom shall be nameless, and people were saying how wonderful he was and I was sitting there very quiet. Then someone read the jacket copy of his book and it said, 'More ideas than in six other science-fiction novels.' And I said—'Yes, all the ideas taken from six other science-fiction novels.' So now he's not talking to me anymore. But you know you get a little fed up after a while. You pick up a book and you read the first chapter, and you know what's going to happen. The writer's fairly incompetent, can't handle the English language at all. Juvenile, puerile, repetitious—and ninety-five percent are that way."

Does he think that there must be good manuscripts that are not being bought by editors for some reason?

"*Everything's* being bought. That's the worst part of it. I was so glad when science fiction expanded, I thought there'd be so much more printed and a residual amount of good stuff would be there.

But now it's expanded, it turns out nothing residual is any good. The new writers coming in don't seem to know how to write at all. And by new writers I don't mean people like Tom Disch, who is still referred to as 'new' even though he's been around for fifteen years. Who's come along since him? Very few of any consequence."

I ask what Harrison's own ambitions were, when he was a new writer himself, starting out. Looking back he seems to come to the conclusion that ambition never really came into the picture. It was more a matter of surviving on a day-to-day basis.

"I was born in Stamford, Connecticut, in 1925. When I was two years old I moved to New York. My father was a printer, stone broke during the Depression, moving house in midnight flits every three months, beans-and-tea, all that kind of thing.

"My generation was a draftee generation. We knew the second we turned eighteen, we'd be in the army. I went in 1943, and we didn't even know if we'd win the war or not. So we never looked ahead; you'd fart around in school, try to chase girls, couldn't get near them in those days. And you saw it coming, a sort of a feeling of doom, you never really thought where you were going to go, except stay alive; get through high school and a week later you're in the army.

"I came out of the army, I was happy to be alive, but it was a tremendous thing to readjust to civilian life. It wasn't a matter of ambition, it was just staying alive again. People forget, you know, the shell-shock from the war. A lot of guys became alcoholics, couldn't readjust. You're shaped by the army, that horrible, stupid institution. I couldn't even read; I worked down to the *Daily News*, there was nothing I could read that was more complicated, and then one day I found I couldn't even read that. Well, if you're in an emotional position where you can't read the *Daily News*, you've got trouble, buddy!

"I worked out of it, you know, drank a bit more, the usual solutions you go through. Nobody could afford shrinks in those days. I went to art school, became a comics artist. That field was pretty cheap, though, so it was still a matter of staying alive. But I experienced the joys of reading science fiction, and meeting the writers and the artists and the editors in the field, the bunch of drunkards.

"I never had any big ambitions except to stay alive as an artist rather than have a job. I loathed jobs. Mild aims. Staying alive with a family is enough, without high-flown literary ambitions. Yes, you want your novels to be accepted, you want Book of the Month Club. But also, being a science-fiction writer, you're always being knocked down, you're in plenty of hubris, let me tell you. My novel *Captive Universe* went through three editors at Book of the Month Club. One of them loved the book; the other said 'Yeah, we'll take it I guess'; and the last one said, 'It's science fiction, we can't take it.' Two months later they took *The Andromeda Strain*, packaged as being 'not science fiction.' You get enough experiences like that, you expect no justice, you know.

"I've written books that tried to get out of the field. Like *The Technicolor Time Machine*, which almost got out of it. Every fourth or fifth book I take a deep breath and write one that can bridge—and no one notices it. With *Make Room! Make Room!* I tried to get out, and Doubleday said, 'No, Harry, if we do it as a straight novel we'll sell three hundred copies.' They wouldn't have promoted it or anything. I sold it to the films years later by accident. There was a lawyer who wanted to buy it, and once he bought it he sold it to MGM for a dollar—he was fronting for MGM all the time. They don't want to give the author anything. That's the history of film. You think publishing is ruthless; try those swine out there in Hollywood. You have to be just like they are, go for the throat, tear it out, show no mercy!

"Someone once sent me a clipping from some magazine, an interview with George Lucas, saying 'I grew up reading science fiction, I really was a fan of science fiction, but I didn't like things written by people like Heinlein or Bradbury, I thought Harry Harrison was my god, and I enjoyed everything he wrote.' That kind of thing. I thought, 'Well! Why the hell didn't you write to me and have me do a god damned script for you, you know, if *that's* what you feel, *old son*, I'd be very happy to come over and make some money from this rotten field.' Oh, there's no justice in this field. But I earn a living in it, I live abroad, I have all my novels in print in English, all thirty of them, and in twenty-one other languages as well. I get a lot reversions of rights and sell them again, my kids are growing up, the financial pressures get less. I was screwed blind a couple of times, we've all been screwed blind by publishers, but they can't screw me anymore. Films screwed me once but can't screw me again. And I'm making a living at it, I'm not going to suffer over it, you know, I'm not going to fall into the syndrome of another of our friends who spends his time worrying about money he didn't earn. Eat, drink, and be merry."

Historical Context

My interview with Harry Harrison took place in my apartment in New York. He had settled in Ireland a few years previously, but was visiting the city to meet some editors. He was a gregarious person, yet he seemed to view editors as his opponents in a never-ending fight where his objective was to wrestle them to the mat and extract as much money from them as possible.

While many writers share this outlook to some extent, Harry had an unusually combative personality. He talked fast and his eyes moved restlessly as if he was always checking for a possible competitive advantage.

During my brief tenure as an editor at Avon Books, I mentioned Harry's name once to senior editor Robert Wyatt. He had never bought anything by Harry, but he certainly remembered having lunch with him. He recalled that before the meal began, Harry had ordered and consumed three cocktails in very rapid succession. "His objective seemed to be to drink as much as possible at my expense," Wyatt said, shaking his head at the memory. Yes, that sounded about right to me.

Harry was also highly competitive. At the time of my interview with him I was learning computer programming and had written a twenty-question general knowledge quiz as an exercise. It was obviously not a serious program, as it included questions such as "Which toilet tissue is softest?" and "What is the sound of one hand clapping?" Still, I always asked guests to try it, because their reactions were interesting.

Harry approached it in the same style that he approached editors. I remember him hunching over the keyboard, peering at the screen, then shooting me quick, suspicious glances as he muttered to himself, complaining about the questions, demanding clarifications, and trying to gauge what I might have programmed as the correct answer. He got eighteen right out of twenty, but even that wasn't enough to satisfy him. He argued with me over the remaining two questions, and suggested strongly that I should revise his score upward to 100 percent.

At the same time, he could be wonderful company and was a great raconteur. It's unfortunate that he didn't apply his formidable intelligence and breadth of knowledge to more books that were challenging. Perhaps he would have said that he satisfied that ambition in *Make Room, Make Room!* Or the *Eden* series of novels, beginning with *West of Eden* in 1984. Yet I always felt that the old cadences from his past as a comic-book writer were just below the surface.

Harry had a liberal political orientation and was very serious about international cooperation, like his contemporaries Frederik Pohl and Brian W. Aldiss. He founded World SF in collaboration with them and the Swedish writer Sam Lundwall. He travelled widely, lived in several different countries during his life, and spoke Esperanto.

After a decade in which he wrote relatively little, Harry died in England in August, 2012 at the age of 87.

Charles Platt

6

Theodore Sturgeon

Los Angeles, California, September 16, 1981

THE GLASS TOWERS of downtown Los Angeles stand less than a mile away, hazy in the smog, but this little street of Spanish-style houses is a backwater untouched by urban redevelopment. I climb stone steps, pass through an archway, penetrate a tunnel of unkempt foliage, and emerge in a small courtyard. Old-fashioned, three-story apartment buildings stand on either side, their sandy-brown walls half hidden behind cacti, shrubs, and palms. Insects buzz and hum in the hot morning sun.

I locate a tiny door into the basement of one of the buildings. The door is no more than four feet high—as if built for children, or gnomes. There's no name, and no bell. I knock.

The door opens and a gaunt, pale, gray-bearded figure squints up into the harsh light of day. He reaches for my hand and draws me down the steps into his subterranean refuge. I have to bend double to squeeze through the doorway; and then I find myself in a tiny cluttered place barely bigger than an elevator. "Sit down," says Theodore Sturgeon, watching me steadily with his pale blue eyes, "and make yourself at home." He smiles a secret smile as he closes the door, cutting off the daylight.

---

[6] Photograph by Marc Zicree.

235

A water bed takes up more than half the space of this cubicle. A ventilation fan hums steadily. The one tiny window is heavily curtained; a metal-shaded lamp sheds dim yellow light; boxes of books are piled in the corner, in the shadows. A doorway leads through to a tiny toilet and a metal shower stall to the left, and a miniature kitchen to the right.

There's hardly room to turn around; I feel like Alice in Wonderland, a giant in a shrinking house. Sturgeon describes it as his "crash pad"—one of three dwellings he maintains on the West Coast. He suggested we do the interview here, because he feels it is best reflects his personality. Some would probably classify it as fit for monks or prisoners in solitary confinement, but he seems to enjoy it—perhaps because it embodies some of the virtues he values most. It makes do with less, it's home-renovated, and it's quite eccentric.

While I set up my tape recorder, he tells me how little he had to pay to make this dwelling habitable. The water bed was a mere fifty dollars. His work-table was improvised from salvaged wood and packing crates. The carpet was found on the street. The paint for walls and ceiling was ninety-nine cents for one gallon, because the color had been discontinued. Halfway through the paint job, he realized he hadn't bought enough, so he had to dilute what was left with white. It still wasn't enough, so he had to dilute it again, and so the ceiling fades from beige at one side to off-white at the other. "Do you realize how much you'd have to pay an interior decorator, to get that kind of effect?" he asks me, and waits attentively for me to affirm his judgment.

He lights his pipe, explaining that he only smokes because it induces vasoconstriction—shrinking of the blood vessels, which, he says, alleviates his low blood pressure and enables him to think better. He goes on into some of his other theories about health, involving herbal remedies, spices, vegetarianism, and vitamins. And then, on another tangent, he mentions a gadget he made recently, to hold a book with its pages open, so he can read without suffering from tired arms. The gadget consists of a piece of coat hanger and a couple of paper clips. He shows me. "Do you realize how little that cost to make?" he says, amazed by his own ingenuity.

I realize that I am not, after all, in Wonderland. This must be Looking Glass Land, because the man sitting opposite me, watching me with those strangely steady, pale blue eyes, can be none other than the White Knight. At any moment, he will demonstrate an upside-down cookie box that keeps the rain out.

I don't mean to make fun. It simply seems that Theodore Sturgeon loves being an eccentric, and delights in his noncomformist ideas, any one of which he can justify with impeccable logic. It's all part of the rich (albeit recycled) tapestry of a life full of fantasy.

Since he seems to avoid the obvious and orthodox, I ask him if he could be described as an unreformed radical.

"Radical? Perhaps, in a way—in my refusal to accept certain things. Most people are constantly in the habit of accepting things which are totally nonsensical. For instance, until recently, when an airplane was flying across the state of Kansas, they couldn't serve drinks. Did you know this was the last touch of the Ptolemaic universe in the law? Because it had to do with a static earth with a sun that traveled around it. You could logically own land from the center of the earth to the zenith.

"We're surrounded by this kind of thing. People obey laws which have no real rationale behind them; or customs, or so-called morality. But morality is just the leftovers from ethical thinkers. There's a very important distinction between morals and ethics. Ethics are really species-survival oriented. But morality is a static thing. When an ethical thinker comes up with something new, they usually crucify him or cut his head off or crush him under a stone or evict him. But ultimately the idea survives and it trickles down into the morality, which gradually absorbs it. And most of our moral structure has come to be that way.

"We're constantly faced with things that simply don't make

any sense. And we don't sharpen our tools and our lenses and what-not to observe these things. And I *do*. And it's gotten me into some very interesting trouble—and I wouldn't have missed a minute of it."

He speaks softly, gently, persistently, in a lulling rhythm. He pauses and smiles, still watching me intently, as if trying to discern whether I'm with him—whether he's dealing with a kindred spirit.

I say that he seems to be describing a world in which a few enlightened individuals perceive things more clearly than large conformist groups. Does he see life in terms of us-versus-them?

"No! I do my best never to think in those terms. I don't think I'm special by blood or by...I have a talent. A huge talent. But that's like a guy I knew one time who was six-feet-four and weighed 230 pounds. If it was convenient for him, he'd crook his elbow and rip his shirt up the back. But he had nothing to brag about, he didn't do a *thing* to get that way. Talent is just the same, like eye color, or anything else that's given to you.

"My feeling about 'us and them' is: When you come right down to human nature, if you get an ardent Russian communist and a real right-wing American, and they're both in agriculture, and you dump them together, I doubt they're going to get into a political dialogue. They're going to talk about seed corn.

"I'll never forget what one of the astronauts said, when they looked down from 163 miles: 'I don't see any lines.' I love that. 'I don't see any lines.' People are people.

"I'm not a joiner. I belong to very few organizations. Politically, I usually vote for what seems to be more or less liberal; I voted Libertarian last time, and before that I voted Peace-and-Freedom. Libertarian, at the moment, feels more like home to me than anything else.

"I have a certain amount of scorn for people who don't vote and then complain about what the government does to them. You realize Ronald Reagan was elected by twenty-two percent of the registered voters in the United States? And then you get the

238

screaming and hollering that's going on now.

"My favorite all-purpose bumper sticker is, 'Keep the Faith and Reelect Nobody.' You like that? Hmm? I think that is an operating political principle. It's right in line with my feeling that the entire universe is in flux, and we ought to be, too. Build nothing that we can consider permanent. Long-lasting? Sure. Solid? I agree. Forever? No."

I interrupt this flow of axioms and epigrams to suggest that, even if he's unsure about the term "radical," he could still be called rebellious.

"Yes. That's true. I have a right to my own life-style, and I don't like yahoos coming along to correct me. I happen to be of a nudist persuasion, and I don't wear clothes unless I have to. The one thing that really bugs me the most is if somebody knocks on the door, and it's a stranger, then I have to go put some pants on before I open the door. The essence of that is that I am being forced to obey somebody else's rules on my own turf.

"I do insist on my own life-style, and I like to protect my own way of thinking. At the same time, I constantly attack the stasis that overcomes people. You know, when someone says, 'Uh-uh, I don't want to hear that, I don't want to know that.' Well, that person just died. You've noticed the symbol that I use on all my correspondence?" (It looks like a Q with its tail elongated into an arrow.) "It means *ask the next question.* I counsel people to do that, because the moment they stop doing that, they die, and then they walk around with all the millions of other zombies you see walking down the street, who just don't care anymore."

I manage to interrupt to inquire whether I may, in fact, ask the next question.

He smiles self-deprecatingly. "Of course, go ahead. I tend to ramble on, I know."

I mention another personality trait that I sense in his work: an almost paradoxical mix of grim visions and lyrical sentimentality.

"I am a highly tactile person. And I'm a lover, I believe in that.

You mention the word 'sentimental'; this is a pejorative in England, among English critics particularly."

I try to object that, although originally British myself, I didn't mean "sentimental" as a put-down. But he continues:

"Expressions of sex and love embarrass the British very much. They take refuge in words like 'mawkish'—I've had that used against me, and I can't even define it. I think it essentially means feelings of love, which embarrass them. But love does not embarrass *me*, and it never has. James Blish once wrote an appreciation of my work in which he said that many writers are afraid to say certain things 'in case momma might see,' but Sturgeon apparently doesn't give a damn. And that's true. That's why I don't, for example, hide my association with *Hustler* magazine." (At the time of this interview, he was writing a regular review column for *Hustler*.) "I admire Larry Flynt. He is honest and he is devoted and he has absolutely no tolerance for sticky-fingered politicians and blue-nosed moralists—like the right-to-life people, for example, who want the state to move in and protect any conceivable speck of life, even though the state then puts a number on this speck of life when it is 18 years old and sends it out to get its head blown off. This is the kind of inconsistency which I insist on fighting, and Larry Flynt feels much the same way. His magazine is vulgar and gross, but he does not like people who beat on women, or people who beat on children, and as far as kiddie-porn is concerned, he has no patience with it. Well, he'll hint at it, maybe, and it will sell magazines, but his own convictions are totally, strongly against that kind of thing."

Interesting. But I would like to talk more about Theodore Sturgeon's fiction—and science fiction in general.

Of course, he's happy to do so; happy to talk on any topic. I begin to feel as if he has anecdotes at hand for every possible occasion.

"As far as science fiction is concerned," he tells me, "I want to proclaim my everlasting love and devotion to it, because outside of poetry it is the only form of literature which has no parameters whatsoever. There's no ceiling, there's no fence, there's no horizon, you can go anywhere. I refuse to let any definitions of science fiction limit me, because I have my own definition of science, which derives from *scientia*, which is the Latin word that means knowledge. To me, science fiction is *knowledge fiction*, and it's knowledge not only of physical and chemical laws but also the quasi- and soft sciences, and also matters of the human heart and mind. This is all knowledge, and so to me it's all legitimate science fiction.

"You know one of the most exciting things I've ever thought of in my life is that someday there'll be a generation ship [a starship that takes several generations to reach its destination] and on that ship, by statistical necessity, there will be a science-fiction writer. What will he be writing about? What *will* he be writing about? I think science fiction is the cutting edge of the human psyche. Isaac Asimov once said that there are only three basic science fiction stories: *What if?* and *If only!* and *If this goes on*, and I truly believe that.

"It is also what I call the 'pigs and wings' form of fiction. We know perfectly well that pigs don't have wings, and probably can't, but we can *conceive* of them, and the fact that we can conceive of absolute impossibilities, and even construct whole narratives around them, is a very special thing that I think our species has."

But to turn from the general to the specific for a moment: Are there any trends in modern science fiction that Sturgeon dislikes or disapproves of?

"The proliferation of series, right now, saddens me a lot. It's a nice comfy thing for a writer to fall into a contract which will guarantee for sure he's going to be able to sell four books. But I think that in itself is pretty sad. After all, where is the real importance in science fiction? It's always in people who *break* the trends. Ray Bradbury wrote Ray Bradbury right from the beginning, when nobody was about to buy things like that. He would not—and could not, I think—write what other people wrote. He wrote Bradbury until ultimately the markets opened up for this snowstorm of manuscripts, and let him in.

"I was just sent a huge book from one of the universities, for my comments. And I'm sending it back, refusing comment. Article after article, essay after essay, each striving to be the one which comes up with the ideal cubbyhole in which to put a particular kind of thinking. I find it insupportable. There are too many people in the world—and most of them seem to be in academia—who feel that an application of handles is an understanding of what you are handling. And it isn't. It is not. Nobody alive now seems capable of reading a novel by simply sidling up to it, and saying, 'Hey, tell me a story.' No, they have to put a label on it. They want to know if it's a mystery, science fiction, romance, or what. *What's it about?* And to find out, they read the book jackets, which are generally written by people who haven't read the books properly anyhow, and give away part of the plot. The author who structures his book very carefully and takes trouble to place all his surprises, has his surprises taken away from him. What use is fiction without surprises?

"For years I have avoided any book that has the word 'sword' in its title. What gets me about sword-and-sorcery fiction is that there is a very basic lack of surprise in these stories. I don't care how exciting and bloody they get; the hero always wins. He may get limbs lopped off, but he will always win in the end, and I prefer the kind of suspense where you cannot be sure whether he is going to survive."

As regards Sturgeon's own work, we've seen little from him in the last decade, although he continues to publish short stories and reviews, from *Omni* to *The Los Angeles Times*. I ask if readers and critics sill typecast him as the man who once wrote *More Than Human*.

"You get that all the time. My first story was sold forty-three years ago; but some of my recent work has been very much appreciated. 'Slow Sculpture' won both the Hugo and Nebula awards," he reminds me.

"Of course, *More Than Human* still goes on. It's now under film option from Robert Gordon, a film editor, who edited *Blue Lagoon*, which might have been a stupid picture, but was a beautiful one. So we may also end up with a stupid picture, but I guarantee it's going to be a beautiful one.

"At the moment, Jayne [his wife] and I have been asked to write a sequel to *Alien*. We have a marvelous plot for it. I am at the moment doing a narrative for the most expensive and elaborate Laserium show ever. Laserium is an unforgettable experience. Have you ever seen it? Almost beyond description! This will be syndicated all over the United States and probably Europe as well."

And he says he is still working on his epic novel, *Godbody*, which has been in progress for ten years but which he cares about too much to finish by a specific deadline. In addition, he has contracted to write an entirely new science-fiction novel, *Star Anguish*.

Of course, life wasn't always quite like this.

"In order to stay alive, I have done all kinds of different things. I'm a very skilled short-order cook for example. I'm a Class A heavy equipment operator—I can run anything with tracks or a boom on it. I have five ratings in the Merchant Marine. I play enough guitar to do three-chord work with a bluegrass band. And I trained as a circus performer. When I was twelve, in high school, I was the original ninety-seven-pound weakling, the brunt of all kinds of bullies. Within one year I gained about sixty pounds and grew about four inches, became fascinated by gymnastics, and ended up with an A.A.U. title on the horizontal bar and a free scholarship to the most advanced gymnastic organization in the city, and I was going to be a flyer at Barnum and Bailey. Writing was the last thing in my mind.

"Then one fine day I woke up with a 105-degree fever. My stepfather would not permit me to be sick, so I dragged myself to school. Same thing on the second day. On the third day I couldn't get out of bed at all. I had acute rheumatic fever, and a sixteen percent enlargement of the heart, every joint in my body hurt, and my brains were fried by holding that high fever for so long. This was 1934, so there were no miracle drugs, just aspirin and bed rest.

"After four months in bed I was able to walk, but that was the end of gymnastics for me. However, within six months I passed a physical examination for nautical school.

"I learned something there that I will never forget: that people in authority will purposely amuse themselves by hurting others. I mean, standing at attention with a piece of rock salt in your mouth until you collapse; stuff like that. I took absolutely all that was coming to me as a fourth-classman, moved into third class, and then ran away—I was not going to quit under fire.

"On the basis of having been a cadet, I had no problem getting seaman's papers, and that's when I took off on merchant ships.

"In 1939, I was in the merchant marine, and by then slogging away at trying to become a writer. We docked in New York and there was mail waiting for me—a letter of acceptance for a story I had sent to a newspaper syndicate. Not a science-fiction story. I was so excited, I quit my job and went ashore.

"They paid me five dollars for this story. For the next four-and-a-half months I wrote for that syndicate, and they would buy no more than one or two stories a week, so I made five and sometimes ten dollars a week. Now, my room cost me seven, and any money that I could save, I could use to eat. Have you ever noticed that pound cake has no crusts? Well, what do you think happens to the crusts? At that time, Cushman's Bakery used to sell a shopping bag full for a nickel. That's one of the things I survived on.

"My room was on Sixty-third Street, where Lincoln Center is now. My brother lived in Brooklyn, and I used to go and see him—walk all the way, downtown and across the Brooklyn Bridge. Subways then were a nickel, so I'm telling you what I learned about saving money in those days.

244

"But then somebody showed me the first issue of *Unknown*, and I was just thrilled. I ended up selling so much to John W. Campbell that at one time I had four of my stories in his two magazines. This is why I used pseudonyms at that time: one was E. Waldo Hunter, and the other was E. Hunter Waldo, because Campbell remembered it wrongly from the time he'd used it before.

"He was the strongest influence on my writing, my best friend and my worst enemy, in that he kept me in science fiction when this category was indeed a ghetto, and it was very hard for me to get decent attention from any serious critic.

"Then later I suffered writer's blocks; I wrote nothing between 1940 and 1946 except "Killdozer." I had a wife and two kids at the time, and things got very tough, very hard indeed. Later, when I married Marion, and we had four children, things got terribly hard, and I finally had a major breakdown in 1965. I almost didn't make it that time.

"But things have been much better since then. Recently I feel I've paid my dues and it's all coming back to me now. One of the most important things that has happened to me, as far as my head is concerned, is est training. I went through est in October of 1979. It's a hugely effective course, it is not what people think it is, it is not fascistic. I'm seriously considering going back and taking it again, now that I have a little more consciousness of what it's all about."

He pauses, finally. It's almost mid-day, which was our agreed cut-off time for the interview. Throughout the past ninety minutes, Theodore Sturgeon has maintained his intense focus on me, while talking in his gentle, persistent rhythm, and tolerating very few interruptions. At first, I think he was watching to discern whether I was simpatico. But I think it meant more than that. His epigrams and axioms seem like phrases from a manifesto, outlining a whole belief system—a system that Sturgeon seems to be offering as an invitation, for those willing to shed the conformist preconceptions of the straight world, and join him.

If this is the case, I suppose I haven't been a very cooperative subject. I've maintained an interviewer's detachment, neither agreeing nor disagreeing. And so as I leave his little hideaway, I have the odd feeling that I've just rejected a gentle but persuasive invitation to some sort of philosophical communion.

Historical Context

In his novel *God Bless You, Mr. Rosewater* Kurt Vonnegut introduced the character of a penniless science-fiction writer named Kilgore Trout, which he said later was based on Theodore Sturgeon. Vonnegut and Sturgeon had met in 1957 when both were living in Cape Cod and Vonnegut was working as a salesman in a Saab dealership (which later went out of business). Although *Player Piano* had been published, Vonnegut would not achieve serious recognition until many years later.

Sturgeon was an odd choice as a model for a stereotypical pulp-magazine wordsmith whose novels had awful titles and were full of wacky ideas. Many other science-fiction writers in the 1950s wrote more prolifically and on a more formulaic basis. Sturgeon, in fact, went through long periods in which he was unable to write at all, and when he did write, his work was highly unconventional in its explorations of sexuality and its emotional power.

Rock critic Paul Williams was a great admirer of Sturgeon, and speculated that his tendency to procrastinate resulted from lacking a mature awareness of time. "Ted is living—not in the past, but in an eternal present," Williams wrote in 1976, but also noted that Sturgeon's unproductive periods were associated with conflicting feelings about his own work: "Contracts go unsigned, letters of reversion and copyright renewal go unwritten, he has this master plan that he does little to implement but meanwhile he tries to prevent his books from being reissued so they won't interfere with the plan. He relishes the dream of having all his work available in a uniform edition. But deep inside him, I have to believe, there's something that feels much safer knowing people can't read what he's written."

After Sturgeon's death, Williams obtained permission to compile The Complete Stories of Theodore Sturgeon, a multi-volume collection providing the comprehensive overview that Sturgeon had resisted for many years.

I only met Sturgeon the one time, myself, when I interviewed him for *Dream Makers*. Still, Paul Williams' description of his ambivalence rings true to me, especially coupled with comments that I heard over the years from editors who despaired of obtaining work that was promised but seldom delivered. There is no doubt that Theodore Sturgeon was a difficult writer to get along with. He was also complex, to the extent that even he seemed to have trouble understanding himself, although he would have been the last person to agree with that assessment.

For many years he was unwilling or unable to finish writing his last novel, *Godbody*. A version of the manuscript was found after he died and was published in 1986. Describing a messianic figure "healing" a small town of sexually repressed and twisted people, it recapitulated themes that Sturgeon had dealt with during his most productive period in the 1950s.

Theodore Sturgeon died of lung fibrosis in 1985.

Jerry Pournelle

Studio City, California, September 16, 1981

JERRY POURNELLE HAS been to the 1980s what Robert Heinlein was to the 1950s; and I'm not just talking about his talent for technological invention and sociological projection. I'm speaking of his politics.

As the tide of American liberalism receded from its high-water mark in the late 1960s and revealed the bedrock of conservative thinking that had always lurked beneath, Jerry Pournelle's work began to seem more and more relevant—vogueish, even. In story after story, novel after novel, he has campaigned for those traditional American traits that Ronald Reagan helped the nation to rediscover, and that Pournelle had held true to all along: rugged individualism, the profit motive, deregulation, personal freedom, an armed citizenry (that most of all!)...plus good old Yankee Ingenuity to save us from the low-tech, zero-growth drudgery that ecofreaks and no-nuke nitwits would wish upon the world.

Sometimes he reminds me of the right-wing bumper stickers that go beyond ideology and into self-satire. Like, "Warning: I Don't Brake for Liberals!" or "More Nukes, Less Kooks!" or "Peace—Through Superior Firepower!" In fact, this last slogan is available on a T-shirt from *Soldier of Fortune* magazine, for which Jerry Pournelle is a contributing editor.

Do I exaggerate? Only a little. In Pournelle's novel *The*

Mercenary, soldier-hero John Christian Falkenberg remarks, "After all, war is the normal state of affairs, isn't it? Peace is the ideal we deduce from the fact that there have been interludes between wars." (And in case you object that this is merely a fictional character talking, as opposed to Pournelle himself, check out his introduction to David Drake's story collection, *Hammer's Slammers*. Falkenberg and Pournelle share almost exactly the same phrasing.)

Or there's this quote from *Exiles to Glory*, in which an enlightened scientist is trying to recruit a reluctant student for a space-industrialization project to save mankind:

"Farrington sighed. 'You've been brought up to think somebody will take care of you. Social Security, National Health Plan, Federal Burial Insurance, Family Assistance, Food Stamps, Welfare. Union representatives to speak for you. And I'm talking about a place where it's all up to you, where you take care of yourself because nobody's going to do it for you. I guess that can be scary to modern kids....'"

If Jerry Pournelle had started publishing novels back in the 1960s, he might have found his market restricted to Goldwater loyalists over fifty. Young readers of that era would have dismissed him as some kind of silent-majority crackpot extremist.

Times, however, have changed. Pournelle's novels written with Larry Niven (*The Mote in God's Eye*, *Lucifer's Hammer*, *Oath of Fealty*) are among the most successful science fiction in print. Admittedly, the political angle in these collaborations is played down. But his solo-written books are becoming almost as popular, and their messages are stated so strongly that they would seem like propaganda if the ideas weren't so provocative and the stories weren't so tightly told.

Personally, I admire the solid science and careful extrapolation in his work, while I view his success with some dismay. By my scale of values, anyone who refers to the "inevitability" of war is helping to promote it as a self-fulfilling prophecy. And an inefficient but compassionate bureaucracy seems more tolerable to me than totally uncontrolled, ruthless free enterprise. Not every individual is *capable* of being rugged; those that can't should be cared for. And military atrocities will always overshadow, in my mind, the military virtues of which Jerry Pournelle writes so often and so warmly.

So when I go to talk to him for this book, I'm not sure whether to expect an interview or a confrontation. Bearing in mind one slightly explosive encounter that he and I have already had in the past, I think he may be looking forward to our meeting in the same sort of wary spirit as I am.

Jerry Pournelle and his wife live in a large, old, white-painted wooden house in a white-collar residential neighborhood just outside the City of Los Angeles. Other members of the family include his three children, his research assistant, and a menacing dog that eyes me calculatingly and sniffs me carefully before I'm allowed through the front door. "Don't worry," says Jerry. "He only bites pacifists."

The office/study, where the work is done, turns out to be an unpretentiously makeshift mixture of old and new, function and ornament. A modern swivel chair stands in front of a grand old desk that dominates the center of the room. The desk is piled untidily with papers; the walls are hidden behind tall shelves crammed with books and more papers; a computer video monitor stands on a small typing table; the shades are pulled halfway down over the windows, and outside them the lush Californian foliage is dappled with sunlight.

Pournelle himself is a big man, tall and broad-shouldered. Coupled with his commanding voice, this can make him seem bombastic or even intimidating. But he welcomes me into his home with a friendly smile that allays some of my apprehensions, and he seems very ready to sit and talk at length, in an easygoing fashion, over a series of glasses of sherry.

I feel honor-bound to tackle some of the aspects of his work that bother me the most. For instance, I feel that his books suggest

250

to young readers that complex social problems can be solved by using brute force. Does he ever worry about encouraging kids to indulge in power fantasies?

"If you are trying to tell me that I should not depict realistically the attractions of a properly run military outfit," he replies, "you're a fool. Because it can be damned attractive. Do you think I should exercise self-censorship and not let people know? In the movie version of *Faustus*, Richard Burton is on horseback in armor and he says, 'Is it not a pleasant thing to be a king and ride in triumph to Samarkand?' Should that line have been suppressed? Are you telling me that I shouldn't tell people that there *is* a share of glory? It's a damned attractive life; if it wasn't, why would so many people want it?"

I reply that it is the presentation of violence as an easy answer that bothers me most. In *The Mercenary*, for instance, a planet's deadbeats and social parasites are threatening the survival of their own society. The hero solves this problem by luring the civilians into a giant stadium, where they are massacred by mercenaries.

Pournelle, however, does not see this as advocating violence as a permanent solution. "In the stadium scene, the politician turns to the soldier and says, 'You saved our world.' But the soldier says, 'God damn you, don't say things like that, I've bought you a little time, that's all I could do, and it's up to you to do the rest, and God help you if you don't.' Now, I don't think that that is saying he has solved their problems, or anything like it. The politician may think his problems have been solved because his opposition has been temporarily eliminated. The soldier knows better.

"I think I have a realistic view of human nature. Isaac Asimov has an asinine motto, 'Violence is the last refuge of the incompetent.' I agree with it completely—if it's read properly. That is, only the incompetent wait until it's the last resort!

"If you don't believe that violence can be an effective means of changing destiny, then I invite you to ask the Carthaginians their opinion. Or the Knights Templar; they were among the most successful international corporations in the history of mankind, and were suppressed with bloody awful violence and horror. I guess what I have to tell you is that there is a terrible truth to Goering's remark that the noblest of spirits, the highest of aspirations, may be silenced if their bearer is beaten to death with a rubber truncheon. One doesn't have to like that to admit it's got a lot of truth to it."

But isn't there a danger that armed preparedness becomes a self-fulfilling prophecy? Surely, the very existence of weapons is an encouragement to use them.

"You sit here in an area which has the lowest crime rate in Los Angeles," he tells me. "Well, there may be a reason for this." He reaches under his desk. For a moment I'm not sure what to expect. Then he pulls out an enormous stainless-steel revolver, and brandishes it meaningly, at the same time taking care to keep his finger off the trigger and the gun pointed at the ceiling—for which I'm grateful.

"Probably everybody on this block can do what I just did," he continues, replacing the gun in its hiding place and relaxing back in his chair. "And yet there hasn't been a gunshot fired on this block since I've been here, and that's fifteen years. I teach my children, as soon as they're old enough, what weapons are—they all know where they are in this house, and they never touch them. There are four rules: All guns are always loaded. You must never put your finger on the trigger unless you're prepared to fire it. You never point a gun at anything you don't intend to shoot. And you never shoot anything you don't intend to kill. Now, given these rules, how could anyone get hurt, if you obey them? The people that terrify me are the *amateurs*. My kids will never shoot anyone accidentally. I don't say, however, that they will never shoot anyone.

"I have looked through history, and I've found only two periods of sustained peace, spanning generations, in the history of mankind. Do you find more? One was the Pax Romana, which was enforced essentially by a unilateral supremacy of Rome. The other was the Pax Britannica, which was enforced essentially by the unilateral supremacy of the British fleet and marines.

"Even a country like Switzerland has not had long periods of peace. Switzerland has a fairly decent record, but look at the cost— 'cost' in your terms, not mine. They have universal military training, brutally enforced—do you know the penalty for refusing military service in Switzerland? The alternative is ten years in prison, or permanent exile. You don't have to guess that every Swiss household has weapons; you *know* they do. And they include not merely sporting rifles and pistols, but automatic weapons, mortars, and military equipment. And yet the Swiss crime rate is lower than ours—their violent crime rate is almost nonexistent. So I put it to you that here is a society which is not thought of as oppressive or overtly violent—it is said to be dull. But it is more thoroughly armed than you can conceive of.

"My view of gun control is that we ought to implement the Swiss system in the United States. Every citizen of this country should go through at least weapons familiarity and some kind of basic training and be required to keep weapons. I don't think that anyone will invade us, after that, and we might be able to do away with some of our strategic weapons, although not all of them.

"I think the harnessing of violence, and the understanding of the price you pay if you are unwilling to participate in your own defense, is all wrapped up with my view of gun control: I prefer to reduce the agentry of the State. You know, during most of the period of the Roman republic, it had only twenty-four paid policemen: the bodyguards of the consuls. For the rest, court decisions were almost self-enforcing. Citizens were expected to aid the magistrate.

"It is very hard for the State to be oppressive when it must get such active participation of the citizenry to enforce its decisions. I think that would be much preferable to agentry—to hiring people to enforce decrees for you. Have you ever been to a cop house and talked to them, and listened to what they think of civilians?"

This sounds a fundamentally democratic kind of system—all citizens equally armed—and yet, in his fiction, Jerry Pournelle tends to portray a small group imposing its will on the masses, for their own good. And in *The Mote in God's Eye* a cyclical view of history is used to justify an eventual return to an aristocratic monarchy—which the book seems to suggest is not entirely a bad idea.

"Representative democracy is not the be-all and end-all," he replies. "In fact I don't give a damn if the political system is monarchical or elective, so long as it has large areas in which it leaves me alone. And my suspicion is, by the way, that a king has less power over me than a president. Read your Rousseau on the subject; his theory of the general will. The general will is the will of all, and thus if you oppose what the government says, you are really opposing your own will, and therefore *you may be forced to be free*, hmm? That strikes me as being the ultimate rationale for something even worse than fascism, because fascism at least understood that there are differences between people and said, basically, 'You are going to compromise your differences and work together.' I'm talking about Italian fascism, not German National Socialism, which is an entirely different matter and was not based on any rational view of anything.

"The communist system is based on Rousseau's ideas of the general will. The Marxists say that we'll just eliminate all the classes but one. So I still think that fascists are considerably less enemies to traditional Western civilization than communists, so long as we clearly distinguish between German National Socialism and Ibero-Italian fascism. Mussolini not only made the railroads run on time, he *built* them. Whatever you want to say, Italy would probably be better off under him than it is under whatever the hell it has now.

"I don't know, I'm not an Italian, and in many respects I have no right to an opinion on the subject; but I just look at their economic development pattern in the 1920s, starting with a much lower base than they have now. And I find that the Italian anti-fascist writers do not have the verve of the German anti-Nazi writers; they find it harder to find something to hate. I mean, the guy who makes you drink castor oil is certainly not being very nice to you, but that's entirely different from his putting you in a goddamn camp, or cutting your balls off, or making a lamp shade out of you.

"I think it is very possible that Mussolini could have made a different decision and become an ally of the West. He almost was; he kept Austria from being absorbed by Germany for many years, and could to this day be a hero. After all, Stalin is still thought of in some heroic terms, and yet that son of a bitch managed to knock off more people than Hitler ever did, and I'm not talking about during the Second World War, I mean the phony famine in the Ukraine, and all the rest of it. He racked up a score that Genghis Khan would envy."

I break in here, to object that there can't be many people who admire Stalin any more.

"What about most professors of philosophy over age fifty?" he responds. "After all, don't we still think of Marcuse as a legitimate philosopher? And yet what is he but a Stalinist apologist? He takes Erich Fromm's theory of alienation, and uses it to become an apologist for the worst excesses of the Stalinist regime. Do you find that rational? Do you find his book *readable*, for that matter? Yet he was a tenured professor at a California university supported by the taxpayers.

"You know, I don't find this country in terrible danger of losing all its freedoms, when it will pay a man as *dull* as Marcuse to be a professor at one of its leading universities." He smiles wickedly.

Still on politics—since so much of his writing is political, and since Jerry Pournelle himself obviously loves a political debate—I can't resist mentioning that I heard he was, at one time, a member of the Communist Party.

He pauses and looks rueful and abashed. "That was a long time ago. After I got out of the Korean War, and came back and was an undergraduate. I fell into the hands of those who kept telling us that Marxism was within the Western tradition, and so forth. I was also victim of the snigger-theory of philosophy, which is that if you admire anyone other than a leftist then you're barely tolerated in the university department, and they laugh at you. I had been through a pretty miserable war; the communists promised to do something, and it didn't look to me as if anyone else was going to do anything." He shrugs. "Misplaced idealism.

"Being a communist was a matter of selective blindness. You adopt a system of looking at things, and if you interpret what you see in those terms, and in no other way, it's easy to delude yourself. You cut yourself off from almost everyone else, your only close friends are people who are part of that movement. If you try to quit they throw you out in such a way that people who used to be your best friends will cross the street to avoid you.

"I've studied formal philosophy, and quite a lot of it. I wasn't converted to the materialist view of things for some time; I found it unsatisfactory. On the other hand, communism didn't give me an incentive for doing anything. To march in step with the flywheel of history is about the only inducement that Marx gives you for being loyal to his cause. 'What is going to be, is inevitable; and therefore you ought to be for it, because that's what's good.' That seems to be nothing but the rather contemptible worship of power. And yet, the modern American intellectual finds communism more acceptable than fascism."

Unlike many science-fiction writers who postulate future social history and interstellar empires, Jerry Pournelle has some first-hand experience of that on which he speculates. Prior to becoming a full-time freelance writer in the early 1970s, he worked for local city government: "I was director of research for the City of Los Angeles, which was a political plum in some respects—I wrote the Mayor's speeches for him, and that was the one thing I really *had* to do."

And before that, he spent many years in the aerospace industry: "I had a very senior position for someone my age, in North American Aviation, which at that time was the outfit that was building Apollo. I was a Space Scientist; my position was to find things within the company that I thought I could contribute to, and go work on them. The last professional assignment I had was to work on the experimental design for Apollo 21. But there wasn't going to be any Apollo 21, it became fairly obvious, and at the same time the management said, 'We've got to trim the number of people who are senior scientists.' They offered me a position with actually a raise in salary, as a manager in the operations research department, which is what I'm supposed to know most about, in scientific disciplines. But I would have been supervising two-hundred-and-something employees, which would have been a disaster. I have never been a supervisor of any large group."

And so, after moving into the political work and various other activities, he chose to become a writer: a job in which one manages—and answers to—no one but oneself. Pournelle remains active in real-world politics, however, particularly where the space program is involved. "Very early on, when I was managing the human factors laboratories at Boeing, it had become obvious to me that the space program wasn't really going anywhere. Kennedy's announcement just committed us to a specific goal; it was not a program of designing fundamental building blocks to exploit the space medium. We have yet to do that.

"There were, and are, no *technical* problems in doing what seemed then, and seems now, so very obvious that we ought to be doing. The problems were all political. So, already possessing a doctorate in psychology, I went out and got another one in political science, to study politics and learn how to manipulate those levers.

"This, I suppose, is one reason why I'm now a writer; I can reach considerably more people. I'm not conceited enough to think that I was that good in the systems analysis business; I have no great illusions that my value to the space program in a professional capacity would be that much greater now than, perhaps, my son, who has more recently been to the universities. So I prefer to get my message across by having a lot of readers."

At the same time, he is secretary of the L5 Society—a privately funded group advocating space colonies along the lines suggested by Gerard O'Neill—and he is co-founder of The Citizens' Advisory Council on National Space Policy. This latter group has hosted meetings of notables including aerospace engineers, company presidents, the Administrator of NASA, and the Presidential Science Advisor, and has submitted its recommendations to the government. Most notably, it has been influential in developing and promoting concepts that became embodied in the Strategic Defense Initiative.

But Pournelle's main interest—and a formidable source of income—is still his writing.

"The best way I know, to be persuasive, is to be read by a very large number of people. They pay you lots of money for being read by a large number of people. I call it doing well by doing good. I certainly do well; it's up to you as to whether I do good. I certainly think I'm being fairly effective.

"*Lucifer's Hammer*, for example, put across a stronger pro-technology message than you might think. It said that civilization is fragile, and it's worth keeping, which is a relevant message in these times when a large number of people seem to think that the benefits of civilization come free-flowing from heaven with no work on anyone's part. People have about as much understanding of where these benefits come from as my dog has of where the canned dog food comes from. I think that's tragic.

"The book put forth a legitimate message, and it did it without any of its characters, save one, knowing what the message was. I think that's the right way to write ideological fiction, if you want to call it that. I don't think the characters ought to know what the message is. That's my quarrel with Ayn Rand, other than that I don't agree with her message anyway."

Since his collaborations with Larry Niven have become true best sellers, I ask Jerry Pournelle if he doesn't worry that his "blockbuster" system in publishing draws resources away from other, less-commercial books by new authors—who may find it increasingly difficult to get published, as a result.

"I completely agree," he says. "But what am I to do?"

Does it bother him when the large sums of money that his books earn, or the books themselves, provoke criticism?

"I can get in the mail twelve favorable reviews in major publications, and one bad review in an amateur magazine that is circulated to twenty-six people, nine of whom don't read it...and I will brood over that bad review all day." He smiles and shrugs; and I get the impression that although he is indeed sensitive to criticism, it will take more than bad reviews to deflect him from his sense of purpose.

I ask if, as a writer of scientifically accurate, predictive fiction, he disapproves of the trend toward fantasy.

"I know very little about fantasy. If I ever wrote it, I would have to come up with a very self-consistent mythology in which to place the story. I would be cheating my readers if I did not give them what they expect: a fairly ruthless internal consistency.

"I'll tell you that, of twentieth century authors, I probably admire C. S. Lewis more than any other, and I suppose in a sense *The Great Divorce* is one of my favorite works—which we stole from outrageously for *Inferno*, by the way. Lewis did it better than we did, I'll be the first to admit, although we made it maybe a little more exciting. So I like good fantasy, but I have not been willing to work hard enough to come up with an epic book. I guess I would have to do an epic-proportioned fantasy; I don't know how to do little tales.

"Some fantasy is unutterably trivial. You know, you may criticize *The Mercenary*, but what about John Norman?" (Author of numerous slightly erotic fantasy novels featuring male barbarian warriors with female slaves.) "I think my wife would not even be civil to Mr. Norman if she were to meet him at a cocktail party. I've been married to the most liberated woman you've ever met, for twenty-something years. She is in the top one percent of salaried women in the country, she is an expert at what she does, she may be the world's best at what she does. She teaches reading to jailed teenagers. Her students are all illiterate, over thirteen years old. She has not yet failed to teach one to read, though she gets them with documentation and tests from psychologists proving it's impossible. So you see I have a different view of women than that in the John Norman novels, which I find fairly boring. Norman—like Marcuse—is both ethically horrifying and *dull*. In the first place, to be quite blunt about it, the idea of sex with a woman confined in a rape-rack does not appeal to me enormously. I guess that was almost the first thing that struck me in reading those books, how little fun that would be." He hesitates for a moment. "I'm not sure I want that quoted...but maybe I do."

Leaving aside fantasy, what of science fiction? Does he feel that, despite the vast increase in the quantity of books, innovation in the field is declining?

"In some respects science fiction is becoming bankrupt; we're not studying much science, and most writers are way out of date on what's going on.

"But isn't part of the problem also that at least a portion of the field takes it literally that works have to be depressing in order to be good? As in Vonnegut's view of life, which is that inevitably you get stepped on. I don't find that to be historically true, and I don't find it to be true of my own life.

"I admire Brian Aldiss greatly, but I have never heard a more outrageous statement than his defense of giving the first Campbell Award—the one then given by Harry Harrison and his groupies— to Barry Malzberg for *Beyond Apollo*, which is probably the one novel which you could be absolutely certain that John W. Campbell would never have bought or have read more than ten pages of. Aldiss said that the book recognizes the fallen state of man and the

260

tragic view of life which is essential to all literature. I simply cannot buy that; I cannot agree that literature must be tragic or that man's fallen state has to be the central thesis. It's the central thesis of Christianity, but the Christian sects that I find most admirable dwell upon that less than they do upon the idea of *redemption*.

"I prefer to think that mankind has a 100-billion-year future, and I try to write in such a way as to help bring that about. Can you believe that we are no more than a million years old—if that—and we have ahead of us 100 billion years? Hell, ours may be the last generation not to be immortal! So how can you be depressed? We have this whole universe, with trillions of stars in it, to conquer. It's all ours, as far as we can tell.

"I am absolutely certain that if you'd let me invest in the kind of future that I want to bring about, then I can give you whatever you want, even a little enclave in which you make your living literally by the sweat of your brow, and putter in your garden and have your own vine and your own fig tree—the biblical recipe for happiness. I guess what I am trying to say is, what *do* you want?

"Suppose that life is meaningless in that we really are merely the dance of the atoms—which I find an enormously improbable thing to believe; you can't calculate the odds against it. But even if this is so, don't you find it exciting that there are 100 billion years ahead of us, and we've just started? Who knows what we can build. Maybe what we're doing is creating God."

I comment that, to the writer or the reader weighed down with everyday woes, taking the long view is not always easy.

"But how can you have anything *but* a long view? Perhaps you can't understand what it was like to grow up in a town in which the ice man really came around in a horse and buggy. I literally went from riding horses and jumping over fences, supervising tenant farmers in cotton fields, who were only a degree removed from slavery...to seeing people land on the Moon. Now, that's a transition. We live in a marvelous time, and it's getting better. So people have to invent reasons for being unhappy. Well, if you're trying to tell me that you see no purpose to life, then I can only tell you that you haven't looked very hard."

I notice that he has been referring increasingly to theological concepts; and this prompts me to suggest that the strength with which he holds and defends his views reflects a quality that some find in short supply these days: faith.

"I've read the book of common prayer, and was brought up around it. I attend church—Church of England. Our boys go to church schools, if that means anything. And they're respectful, they're polite, they do not seem to be particularly unhappy or rebellious, and they don't sit around and brood and stare at their navels. My daughter is an officer in the paratroops, and was, by the way, the first in her class, which ain't too bad." With quiet pride he points to a picture of her, in her uniform, on the wall.

"People tell me ways I ought to live," he goes on, referring perhaps to criticism that he has received because of his political views or his apparent intractability. "But I look at them, and they don't seem to be as content as I am—or to have as many reasons to be content as I do."

This may sound complacent, but I think it reflects a sincere belief in his values—and a real concern for the future.

I can't say that my visit with Jerry Pournelle has remade me as a member of the Right. But anyone should be impressed, I think, by some of the points he makes, either in person or in print. He demonstrates beyond debate the benefits that technology can bring. He argues from a broader historical perspective than most of us maintain. And he is, in the end, an idealist. He seems to feel no equivocation; there is right, and there is wrong, and you defend your principles with all the physical and mental resources that you possess.

The core of it, I think, is his sense of community. Again and again, throughout his work, a small, cohesive unit looks after its own with great compassion, while arming itself against outsiders, who are always viewed with suspicion.

The small, cohesive unit may be a bunch of colonists on an alien planet, or (in the super-city of *Oath of Fealty*) a vast gathering of American families. Most often, though, the unit that looks after its own is a military unit. Near the beginning of *The Mercenary*, when Falkenberg is a young recruit who has just joined the space marines, he's rescued from the clutches of a corrupt bureaucrat by a petty officer. Pournelle writes:

"The petty officer was twice his age, and no one ever called John 'sir' before. It gave John Falkenberg a sense of belonging, a sense of having found something he had searched for all his life."

This, I think, is the very human yearning behind the nationalism and the rugged rhetoric. And it's a yearning which Jerry Pournelle's fiction itself satisfies, among alienated young readers all across America. His books offer a sense of belonging: to an ethos, or a vision of the future. And that is something which transcends politics.

Historical Context

Before I visited Jerry Pournelle to interview him, our initial meeting had been at a science-fiction convention. This was not a friendly encounter, as I had recently written a book review in which I referred to him as a fascist. As we came face to face and he saw my name badge, he glared at me with disdain. "I didn't realize you were a pipsqueak," he said. He whipped off his glasses. "I'll take your head off right now!"

Some of this was theater, but I wasn't sure how much. I tried to apologize for my inappropriate use of words, but even after he reconsidered his threat of summary decapitation, he was in no mood to be placated. "Maybe I should sue you and attach your income for the rest of your life," he said.

Norman Spinrad happened to be walking past us. "Not worth it, Jerry," he remarked.

Jerry Pournelle, however, is a Southern Gentleman. I don't

pretend to understand every aspect of that code, but I have found that behind the bluster, there may be more tolerance than one might expect. A few weeks after our encounter, I summoned the nerve to write to him, asking if I could interview him for my collection of profiles, provided I pledged to present his views in a fair and balanced manner. He responded by inviting me to his home for a prolonged and cordial conversation.

Would the stereotypical liberal have done the same, if I had been a hardcore member of the NRA and had written a review denouncing him as a communist? I wonder. My former East Coast compatriots could learn some manners, at least, from the gun-totin' flag worshippers of the western states.

In retrospect, perhaps Jerry was curious about me and viewed me as a challenge. Probably he wanted to demonstrate that he was in no sense a fascist—and in that, he succeeded. In fact he was more successful at presenting his political views than he could have expected, because I was already making a gradual transition away from modern liberal politics, and my conversation with him hastened the process.

My initial mistake had been to think of him as being "right wing." Even now, most journalists, academics, and democratic voters on both of the American coasts seem to assume that if someone isn't left wing, there's only one alternative, because it's a binary choice.

In fact a more suitable label for Jerry (if a label is necessary) might be "libertarian." When I suggested this to him a couple of years later, he shrugged and said, "Yes, but with a small L," not wanting to be identified as an actual member of the Libertarian Party.

Of course, just because he has laissez-faire beliefs doesn't necessarily mean that he's an easy guy to get along with. He was on his best behavior when I interviewed him, but he is just as often as bombastic, confrontational, loud, and abrasive as when we first met.

Unfortunately this means that many people (including myself) have responded more to the sound of his diatribes than to the content.

Even when he receives an apology, he can be a pain the ass. Years after *Dream Makers* had been published, I ran into him at a conference hosted by the American Association for the Advancement of Science and decided it was time to pay my debt. "You may find this hard to believe," I said, "but I have reached the conclusion that on many of the topics we talked about, you were right."

"I was right, eh?" He gave me a withering look. "Well, hell, I knew *that*."

7

Piers Anthony

Inverness, Florida, March 16, 1982

IT'S LIKE IOWA with palm trees, this sleepy little town of Inverness, Florida, with stores selling fertilizer, feed, and farm equipment, and pickup trucks parked outside at the curb. Why would a science-fiction writer choose to move out here?

I run a quick mental inventory of all the facts and rumor that I know about Piers Anthony. Born 1934. He sold his first stories in the late 1960s. Acquired a reputation as a "difficult" author who has had occasional fights with publishers, some of whom he accused of blacklisting him and his work. Prolific; he has produced ambitious science fiction (*Macroscope*, *Tarot*) with high stress on pure concepts, characters functioning symbolically in complex games and equations. More recently, has produced numerous fantasy novels (especially the *Xanth* series) that are pure entertainment appealing primarily to young readers, and have begun to make the bestseller lists.

He's a strict vegetarian—won't eat *or wear* anything derived from dead animals. And he seems somewhat reclusive: many people I know in the science-fiction field, including a number of editors, have never met Piers Anthony, and even Keith Laumer, who lives

---

[7] Photograph by Charles Platt.

less than twenty miles away, hasn't seen him in fifteen years.

I drive along blacktop country roads, past fertile farmland and small patches of forest. Following complex route instructions, I take an unpaved road into a wooded area that's been remade as a residential development. But the developer's sign out front looks worn and faded, as if the scheme never took off quite as planned, and the area has a funky, low-rent look.

"If you're willing to brave the wilds," Piers Anthony wrote to me, replying to my request for an interview, "I'm free any time, except at horse-feeding time...."

The dirt road turns into an even smaller dirt road. Simple wooden houses are scattered here and there among the trees. It looks as if human beings have hardly touched the land.

Piers Anthony's house is the only two-story building. A Volkswagen microbus and a Ford Fiesta are parked on the grass outside. There's a corral at the back with horses in it, and a pen full of dogs. Small outbuildings stand amid tall grass and succulent plants.

I stop the car. Here he is, running toward me from out of the woods, a wild-eyed bearded man in red T-shirt and old jeans, looking like some hippie-hobo of the forest. "How long are you going to be here?" are his first words after I've introduced myself and am closing the car door. "What I want to do is answer the questions, or whatever you have," he goes on, "and then there are some questions which I've written down, which I have to ask you." He talks quickly, nervously, as if he just got word of some impending disaster, and we don't have much time.

I meet his wife, who seems quiet, thoughtful, and slow-moving by comparison, and then Anthony leads me—quickly, quickly!—past the corral and the dogs and the chickens, out to his workshop, a small barn set well back from his home. Inside it's very rustic, like a summer house, but with lots of bookshelves. I barely have time to turn on the tape recorder before he starts talking, eager to maximize every moment.

267

"Just make sure any questions that you have get answered," he warns me. "I can talk—I overflow—I can write—I mean, I write more than almost anybody, last year it was 480,000 words of manuscripts turned in to the publisher, and I do three drafts, on a manual typewriter, I paid $450 for it at the time, I could have had a Selectric for the same price, but I don't want to be hung up by a power failure, and sometimes you can have them for four hours! This machine, office machine, has never let me down, and when I'm ready to go, I *go*, at my speed. That's why I use the special keyboard layout." (The keys are arranged by frequency of use, rather than in the standard Q-W-E-R-T-sequence.) "It's the world's fastest keyboard; I'm not the world's fastest typist, when I'm going well it may be thirty words a minute, partly because my brain is the limiting thing, and I do first drafts on this clipboard—see, it has a box behind it, where the sheets that I've written can be put inside, with spare paper. I have upon occasion done as much as a thousand words in an hour, in longhand. I used to type first drafts, but my little girl was born, she's fourteen years old now, but back when she was six months old, my wife went back to work, I wasn't earning enough as a writer, the number-one thing you need if you're a writer is a wife to earn your living until you can make it, and so I took care of my little girl, I changed her diapers and so on, fed her, everything, I couldn't take my eyes off that little girl, she was precocious, she was hyperactive, she would get into trouble, so I had to find a way to do any work and watch her too, and I moved to the self-contained clipboard. So she affected my whole writing career, but in a positive way, as it turned out, because I always have the clipboard now, if I wake up in the night, or go anywhere, any time, I can write. If I'm standing in line waiting for something, like my driver's license, I'm writing several hundred words. I don't care if people think it's strange, some people think that maybe I'm an FBI man making notes, I don't care, I keep going, I'm working literally almost all the time that's available, if I'm not sleeping, or eating—actually, I write when I'm eating. And I have never been to a science-fiction convention, I don't travel, I stay home, and if I'm not writing I'm answering fan mail. I answered thirty-three fan letters last month, this is the consequence of popularity, this is recent, I mean, in earlier years I'd get about one fan letter a week—"

I manage to break in here to ask if his wife doesn't mind this non-stop work obsession.

"No, my wife understands, I mean, she had to quit her job because it got to the point where her total wages went to pay the tax on my income, and she got disgusted with that. You see, I used to earn $500 a year, $1,000, and then $5,000, but when I started earning $70,000, and then $100,000, and I suspect it'll be about $150,000 this year, I have launched into the big time. I used to have arguments, I had one with Dean Koontz, he was saying he was earning almost $100,000, and he didn't need to pay attention to nitwits like me. Well, I don't know how Dean Koontz is doing now, he's writing cheap novels pseudonymously, so I suspect the positions are reversed. I am now earning it, but I don't make any claims to being suddenly a genius because I make a lot of money. The money, as you know, is likely to be inversely proportional to merit, and my most thoughtful pieces are likely to earn less than my least thoughtful. When I'm doing a *Xanth* novel, I go through it about double the rate of anything else. For Avon Books I write science fiction, for Del Rey Books I write fantasy, I wrote *A Spell for Chameleon* for them, it won the British Fantasy Award, and then the subsequent one started selling better and better, and started paying. It's nice to write what you like, but you don't necessarily get rich on it. I may be one of the most commercial writers you'll interview, in the sense that I write the cheap stuff that sells big. By training—I have a degree in creative writing—by education—I was born in England, my parents each graduated from Oxford University, and I have the background, the literary background, and what am I doing? Light entertainment. But, I mean, the money—after struggling along all these years, at low-paying stuff, or trying to, I've made the shift. And I can't say I regret it. I regret it in the intellectual sense that I wish I could have done a piece of such quality that I would get an award from the Nobel committee, but the compensation for this is money, and I'll *take* the money! At the same time, I still make myself do some serious stuff, because I want to keep in touch, I want to be in good mental condition just as I want to be in good physical condition, which is the reason I exercise, I'm physically—one of my controversial statements!—I regard myself as one of the *healthiest* science-fiction writers of my age. You can see dirt-marks on that last beam over there, I do my chin-ups there, and in light clothing I can do twenty-five chins, which is twice as many as I could do in high school. Yesterday I did my run on schedule and I broke my record for my three-mile run, I'm very much into physical fitness, health, partly because I'm forty-seven years old, I'm middle-aged, and this is about the time when people become aware of this."

He pauses to take a breath. While he's been talking I've been taking in my surroundings. This large hut, or small barn, smells of sun-baked wood and dusty books. The peaked roof is of bare boards and beams. The working area is walled in with steel shelves of reference volumes on history, geography, science, and politics. We're sitting talking at the far end, on an old convertible couch. Behind me, the wood paneling is warm from the sun outside.

I'm interested by Anthony's frank talk about his fantasy novels, but not entirely convinced. Surely, a serious novel like his *Macroscope* earns more in the long term than a lightweight fantasy that's soon forgotten?

"Okay, *Macroscope* was published in 1969, and it has brought me a total of about $28,000, I can look up the exact figure if you like, I'm very careful about such things. *Source of Magic*, which was published in 1979, ten years later than *Macroscope*, has already brought me $31,000. And I buzzed it out in a hurry, just because it went fast, and was fun.

"The kind of thing that you can spend five years working on,

270

and end up with a hundred pages—there should be a place in the market for this, as well as for the stuff that you spend ten days writing and it sells 250,000 copies. I do both; the trouble is, I fail on the quality material, and so I am now known, probably, for the lightest material that I do. I'm sure that you assumed that I would defend the light material and say how great it is, but I don't defend it, I say it's great for money, it's great for fun, but I wouldn't call it great literature."

I ask him who he blames for this state of affairs. Himself? His readers? His publisher? The distributors?

"Everybody. Oh, there's blame to go *everywhere*. I struggle with this, I say 'Why-why-why?' and I beat my head against the wall. But I try to judge by my own reactions, when I'm watching television, and I don't eschew television, it may be a 'vast wasteland', but when I hear that said I always think of the desert, which is a wasteland, but if you look you'll find it has its own ecology, there are things in the desert that don't exist elsewhere and should continue, so that 'wasteland' just means that human beings don't have much use for it, the animals and insects that are there do, it's not a wasteland to them.

"Anyway, what do I watch when I have complete freedom to watch anything on TV that I want to? That was the question I was trying to address by my circuitous route. Well, likely as not it will be some cheap, junk thing, Magnum, P.I., something like that, when I could be watching the New York Philharmonic. But when I've done hard work, I want to relax, I don't want something that's going to try my intellect, I want something where it doesn't matter whether I pay attention to it or whether I don't. I want it *because* it is junk. Same thing with my readers, I don't think they are determinedly negative or low-brow, it's that they're tired when they come home, they don't want to read *War and Peace*, they just want to relax and be entertained, without any strain on body or mind, and TV is geared to do this, and so is some fiction."

But now that he's become successful, couldn't he write

something more challenging and hope this time that it will sell purely on the basis of his name?

"Well, the series I'm about to sell to Avon, called *Bio of a Space Tyrant*, is a space opera, deliberately, and yet I discover as I write it in first draft that I'm going to get into more direct social comment than ever before in my life. I'm not saying, 'Here's my name and reputation, pay attention to what I say,' I'm sneaking it in.

"I put it to the publisher: 'Supposing someone who *really can write* tried space opera?' You realize, a lot of what I say sounds conceited, and yet I believe it, I believe in myself, I *can* write, I don't claim I'm the finest writer, but I'm one of the good ones. I can do your kind of writing, I can do commercial writing, I can do it all, and not many people can do it all. I can do the lightest, funniest fantasy that's on the market—nobody's even competing with my fantasy, I've got that market to myself. And I can do the most deadly serious writing. *Bio of a Space Tyrant* is based on the Vietnamese boat people, really. They left Vietnam, they came up to Thailand, they weren't rescued. The men were killed, the women were raped, kids thrown overboard. The women would be raped ten times before they finally get to land, only two survivors, and nobody will believe them—they say 'Where are your witnesses?' All the witnesses were killed. I said to myself, 'Supposing that happened in space?' And my mind started working, and I've now got a five-novel series going. I've set it in the solar system, my people are Spanish-speaking, and they finally get to Jupiter, the land of plenty, 'Send me your homeless,' and so forth, but the people say 'Sorry, there's a new administration, the policy has changed, we will tow you back out to space.' This is the Reagan policy, you understand. If he had his way he would tow them back out into the ocean and not worry about them."

I can't help wondering if everyone will take this series as seriously as he does—critics, in particular. Does Piers Anthony feel that he has been mistreated in the past by his critics?

"Yes and no. When I had trouble with Ballantine Books, which blacklisted me rather than be honest—and because I actually went to a lawyer, I can say this, if anybody was going to sue, I was going to sue. They sold a book in England, they sold a book in Holland, and in Germany. Not only didn't they pay me, they didn't even put it on their statements. I got angry, and I sent them a detailed letter. I understand that Betty Ballantine said it was the most offensive letter she had ever received in her life. All I did was demand a correct accounting. But I should add that reports at Ballantine Books are now made honestly.

"Anyway, this is where the trouble started, because I started getting blacklisted, and this went into criticism. There are still areas where I can't get reviewed, because people heard stories about what a bad person I was."

I get the impression from this that he feels publishers are liable to cheat anyone they can, simply for the money; and he tends to be careful of those he deals with in the outside world. Does this have anything to do with the childhood alienation that so many science-fiction writers talk about?

"When I was growing up I was small. When I graduated in ninth grade I weighed a hundred pounds and I was five feet tall. I was the smallest, shortest person, male or female, in my class, in Westown School, in Pennsylvania.

"In addition to being small, I came to this country when I was six years old, from England, and they were trying to correct my English accent, and I resisted it. So, outsider? Yes. And one who was small. I understand it.

"But, you see, I grew. From five feet to about five-eleven after that. I have some questionable pleasures, but one was at the twenty-fifth class reunion, and a man I stood next to there, he was about six feet and had gotten fat and paunchy and so on, and I was there with my little girl and picked her up, and he said 'Careful, she weights a lot.' The pleasure in this was that he was the class bully. He was six feet back then, when I was five feet. He was beating me up. And twenty-five years later, he couldn't even *catch* me if he wanted to. If he did, he wouldn't be able to take me. I had a very sinister pleasure knowing that I knew it and that he knew it."

I also get a sense that he is a compulsive achiever, from his self-imposed work schedule to his physical-fitness program. When he talks, he stresses all the verbs—especially words like "can," "will," or "do."

"It's true that, even when I run, I try to break my own records, even though I know intellectually that I'm just doing it for the exercise. If I run ten-minute miles, I know I'll get the exercise. Why, then, am I running seven-minute miles?

"I do get compulsive. When I get into something, I do drive, I like to do the best I can do in whatever I do. I do my work, I do my homework, you see all the reference books here.

"When I don't write, sometimes I find myself going into a depression, when I spend two days answering fan mail and not writing. It creeps up on me. I want to write. I feel a compulsion. And when I am writing I feel happy, I feel satisfied."

But where does this compulsion come from? "I don't know. I look at animals and I see puppies raised together—we have two, and one is compulsive, always competing, and the other takes it easy. It's not anything we did, it's not the environment, it comes from the genes.

"My grandfather was called the Mushroom King of Pennsylvania. Half the mushrooms this country produces are still produced in that area. He sold out two weeks before the crash of 1929, but the people he trained went into business for themselves. He was dedicated to business and making money.

"But my *father* went into education. He taught Spanish, he became the intellectual and therefore was not rich. Now here I am; my father certainly wasn't going to shove me into business, he rejects the business ethic, the idea of driving hard to make money repelled him—understandably. I myself don't go for business that much, but I do have the drive, and I'm making the sort of money my grandfather used to. I am not foolish about money at all. I don't waste it, you don't see me going off and buying Cadillacs, no you see me out there splitting wood, because we have a wood-burning stove, and solar-powered water heating, if the sun doesn't shine we don't bother with hot water, because I don't like to pay fuel bills. I'm a miser! I like to think that if my grandfather were alive today, and looked to see who has the attitude that mostly approximates his—it would be mine."

At this point, his wife buzzes us on an intercom from the house and says that lunch is ready. He's been talking for about an hour and a half (I have included, here, perhaps one-third of all that was actually said) and seems unhappy about stopping.

We walk out into the sun. I notice ants in the sandy soil, moving relentlessly to and fro, carrying enormous grains of sand in their mandibles. It seems appropriate, somehow, that Piers Anthony should work right next door to an ant hill. I imagine him figuring out some way to rate his work-day against theirs, so he can find out who's ahead.

The inside of this home is a cheerful but total shambles. He explains that they were cheated by a dishonest builder who gave them a galvanized steel roof instead of the everlasting stainless-steel one that they'd paid for. They sued the builder, he went bankrupt, and the house was never completed. That was four years ago. So the floor is of unfinished concrete, the ceiling of unfinished wood, and when I use the bathroom I notice that, although there's a shower fixture, the bath has never been installed. Instead, there's a huge mound of newspapers and magazines.

Piers Anthony explains more of his philosophy as we eat cheese omelettes together. He's used his royalties not on his own home (which looks, indeed, like a hippie commune displaced from Northern California). Instead, he's been buying up land all around the house; he says that he and his wife "don't care to gamble on the quality of neighbors who might move in. So we buy all the land we can, to prevent it from being settled." They've accumulated thirty acres, so far.

After lunch, his wife, who used to work as a programmer, unearths their Atari home computer from beneath some plastic placemats that protect it from dust, and she demonstrates the word-processing program—which Piers Anthony doesn't use, because the Atari has a conventional typewriter keyboard, and he's adapted himself to the special layout on his manual typewriter. And anyway, computers are vulnerable to power cuts. He'd rather stick with his strictly non-electrical system.

He quizzes me for New York gossip, and tells me how helplessly naive I am for believing that most publishers are honest and most editors can be trusted. "Most publishers are amoral. They don't believe what they do is wrong, but the writer had better beware."

And on this ominous note it's time for me to leave; because, this same afternoon, I must now go and interview Keith Laumer.

Historical Context

Every writer featured in the original pair of *Dream Makers* books was allowed to review my text and request corrections. Very few of them took advantage of this option to any significant extent.

André Norton and Jack Vance were two exceptions. They were displeased with some of my observations, and demanded revisions. Piers Anthony was likewise unhappy about the way in which I portrayed him, but as a matter of principle he chose not to infringe on my right to say what I wanted. Instead, he made his point by applying the same process to me that he felt had been applied to him. He wrote a mini-profile of me, satirizing my style and my habit of drawing inferences from a relatively small amount of evidence.

This was an uncomfortable experience, because there was just enough truth in his complaint to make me question my own judgment. When I got to know him better subsequently, I did conclude that my original characterization of him had been fairly accurate. Still, I now feel obliged to mention his complaint. I hadn't met him before I wrote my profile of him, and it was based on just a few hours of conversation.

The way he responded to me was characteristic of his dealings with people in book publishing. If he feels he has not been fairly treated, he can become quite combative. On the other hand, if someone has behaved decently toward him, he can be one of the most helpful people I know. As we continued to communicate and achieved a better understanding, I discovered how generous he could be.

In 1986, a friend of mine who had recently acquired an editorial position was desperate for books by "name authors." He asked me if I thought I could obtain permission to write a sequel to a Piers Anthony novel. I had never tried to do anything on this basis before, but Piers's novel *Chthon* had always fascinated me, because I felt it was full of dark impulses and desires that were not explicitly developed. I could definitely imagine making them a little more explicit in a sequel.

When I asked his permission, he readily agreed. In fact he gave me creative control of the project, and even refused to accept payment. I negotiated an agreement with New American Library and was ready to begin work when I received a letter from him reminding me that he had already written a sequel of his own under the title *Phthor*. Presumably, I was aware of this.

Well, actually, no, I wasn't. However, I had signed a contract, so I had to accept the fact that I would be writing a sequel to a sequel.

Piers supplied me with a copy of *Phthor*, at which point I discovered that the situation was even worse than I had expected. At the end of the book, every single character was killed, while the planet on which they lived was vaporized.

In a testy mood, I wrote to Piers and asked him why he had ever agreed that I should write a sequel to an adventure in which everyone was dead on the last page. His answer was simple and succinct: "You think I remembered?"

Eventually I found a workaround using a parallel universe, but the plot became so complicated, even I had difficulty keeping track of it. Unsurprisingly, the sales figures were disappointing.

Undaunted, I embarked on a different kind of joint venture with Piers, inspired by my knowledge that in the early 1970s he had written a book titled *3.97 Erect*. He had sold it to Essex House, a publisher that briefly specialized in erotic science fiction. They went out of business before they could publish the book, and he had been unable to find any other publisher that was willing to deal with it. Just as he had satirized my profile-writing technique, *3.97 Erect* satirized the conventions of pornography. It was a fantastical adventure featuring a protagonist with an exceptionally small penis (3.97 inches long) that created vast quantities of smegma.

This novel seemed guaranteed to please no one. It wouldn't satisfy people who liked to read pornography, and was likely to disgust and offend people who didn't. I have always enjoyed gestures of defiance, so to me, this book absolutely deserved to be in print.

It occurred to me that other writers might have their own novels like *3.97 Erect* that had been considered too unconventional, strange, or offensive to be accepted by conventional publishers. Actually, I already knew of one: *Hog* by Samuel R. Delany, which had also been intended as an Essex House book. Maybe I could start my own small press to publish them all.

The time was right, as Apple had recently introduced the LaserWriter. In conjunction with a Mac running PageMaker software, desktop publishing had become a reality. Instead of paying a printing company, I could generate typesetting myself. The only problem was money: the LaserWriter alone cost $7,000, in 1985 dollars. I figured I needed $10,000 for a complete system.

Piers said he was willing to capitalize my venture on condition that sooner or later, I would return as much of his money as possible. That was a deal I could not refuse, so I bought the equipment, commissioned cover art for *3.97 Erect*, and paid someone to copy-type the manuscript into the computer, optical character recognition being unknown in those days.

I decided to name my venture Black Sheep Books, as every book would be like a black sheep of the family. Finding a new name for *3.97 Erect* was much harder. I really didn't like the title, but Piers didn't like any of my alternatives, until finally I suggested *Pornucopia*, which satisfied him.

Now came the hard work in my venture: Negotiating with a printing company, arranging warehousing, establishing distribution, and all the other chores that are associated with old-fashioned books. While I had been fully aware of them, I had never guessed how much time they would consume. With much chagrin, I found myself gradually forced to admit that I was much more temperamentally suited to being a creative person than a business person.

After consulting Piers, I placed a small ad in *Locus* magazine, looking for someone to pick up the titles that I had planned to publish. I received a response from a very nice man in Texas named Phil Gurlick, who possessed the business acumen that I lacked. His company, Tafford Publishing, did eventually bring *Pornucopia* into print, along with several other novels that had been languishing in obscurity.

I sold all the desktop publishing equipment and sent the proceeds to Piers. He made a loss on the venture, but he got his book into print, and we remained on good terms.

Pornucopia has since been republished by Mundania Press, and has spawned a sequel under the enticing title, *The Magic Fart*. Piers, meanwhile, lives at the same location in Florida where I visited him in 1982, and derives a steady income from a seemingly endless series of Xanth novels. The last time I checked, he was working on number 41.

8

Keith Laumer

Brooksville, Florida, March 16, 1982

THE FIRST TIME I met Keith Laumer, he was tall and strong, a casually capable outdoorsman with an equally formidable intellect and not a shred of false modesty.

He had traveled widely while in the Air Force and while working for the State Department. He had taught himself something about almost everything, from history to language to gourmet cooking to engineering to art, and all that he knew was factually accurate, and most of it was fascinating. He showed a small amount of pity and a fair amount of scorn for anyone who was less demanding than he was—as though he believed that excellence was the only value that truly mattered. He was impatient with people who tolerated weakness or imperfection in themselves.

The second time I met Keith Laumer, one year later, his left side was paralyzed from what doctors had diagnosed as a stroke, and he seemed devastated by the frustration of what had been inflicted upon him. Fate was forcing him to accept the unacceptable: a disability that made a mockery of the code he had lived by.

That was more than ten years ago. As I drive to Laumer's Florida home, now, I have no idea what has happened during the

---

[8] Photograph by Jay Kay Klein

Charles Platt

intervening decade. He lives in wild, empty country. Down an unpaved back-road of fine, pale gray dust, between stunted trees and swamp grass; the telephone poles carry a single wire, and a single lonely bird is sitting on it.

I reach his driveway. And here is a strange, enigmatic sight: For some reason, the entrance is framed by two dented 1968 Mercury Cougars, abandoned here on flat tires, with numbers scrawled in black paint on their rusty roofs.

Approaching his house—a modern building on a spacious piece of land—I find more junked Cougars parked at the side of the driveway; and more are in the three-car garage; and still more are scattered across the lawn at the back of the house. There must be at least thirty cars altogether, all of the same year and model, all dilapidated, and all numbered in black spray-paint.

Keith Laumer greets me at his front door and we walk through his elegant home. He moves slowly, still encumbered with a leg brace, but he no longer has the air of despair that he showed ten years ago. He seems grim and determined, now, to overcome the catastrophe that almost ruined his life. He tells me how he came to live out here. His father bought large tracts in Florida very cheaply after World War II, and became a real-estate millionaire. When Laumer decided he wanted to build a dream house, his father supplied an idyllic plot surrounded on three sides by a lake, in untouched countryside. Here, on what is virtually an island, Laumer supervised construction according to his own specifications—he was trained as an architect. Outside every window is water, and beyond that, wilderness.

Ever true to his code of self-sufficiency, he then started making his own furniture, to his own designs, in a woodworking shop in his garage.

"When I was out in Rangoon, Burma, in the Diplomatic Service, where the beautiful oriental timbers grow, I shipped home a bunch of slabs of three or four different beautiful woods. I was about halfway though finishing the whole house when I

281

was…temporarily interrupted.

"At first, you know, the medical profession told me, 'The likelihood of any significant recovery is minimal.' In other words, what they were really saying was"—he clenches his fist on the handle of his cane; he grimaces with rage, and raises his voice to a shout—" 'Fuck you, stupid! Assholes like you spend your goddamn lives abusing your fucking bodies sucking on cigarettes and drinking booze and never getting any exercise, and when the goddamn thing finally rots you come crawling in here whining for a miracle. Well, you're not going to get one. Do you realize I'm late for the golf course?'

"And then zap, out the door."

The anger leaves him as abruptly as it came. I realize I'm flinching from him. While he was shouting, the intensity was frightening. But he continues, now, in a normal, conversational tone.

"Well, the fact is, I always took the best conceivable care of myself. I used to do a five-mile run every day, on trails through the woods. And it's almost as though I had a premonition that something was going to happen to me, because every day when I came in I'd turn around and say, 'All right, you sons of bitches, that's another five miles I took away from you. You can't get that back.'

"I never ate too much or too little, I ate good food, and I never did start smoking, so I never had to quit. I enjoy beer or wine, but there isn't any form of hard liquor that I like.

"One day shortly after I got into this horrible state I was reading an issue of *Time* on the subject of CVAs, which means Cerebro-Vascular Accidents, and it had a little checklist there. I scored zero all the way down; *nothing* applied to me. So I got through and I said, 'Okay, it'll never happen to me. So let me out of here!'

"And actually it *didn't* happen to me. What actually happened was a curious thing, to which everybody is subject, to some degree, starting before you are born, as soon as your intellect becomes aware of itself. Your mother bumps against something, and you didn't like that a bit, and you make a decision, 'I do not like to be knocked around, and I have got to be *tough*, so that it cannot happen to me anymore,' Your body responds to that absolute command by hardening itself, in the firm of muscles tightening up.

"Everybody has a tight muscle representing some experience that you subconsciously shunted aside. Say a big black dog comes bounding out onto the lawn when you're three years old. that's too scary, so some part of your mind, way down deep, says 'This is too much!' and shunts that emotional energy into some place where it's safe, way down in a muscle next to the bone of your thigh, perhaps. And little by little you get an accumulation of these things. And apparently in my case I got an accumulation of them and finally crossed a threshold—and something said 'Okay, execute Plan A.' And Plan A was to go—crrrkkkkk. And there I was, all fucked up."

I say that this sounds like the theory of Rolfing.

"The therapy that I'm getting is to Rolfing as champagne is to ditch water. The most visible part of what he does is the massage, using a knuckle or an elbow. He can feel that muscle down there that's harder than rock. When he squeezes out that muscle, it lets go. And I can feel it let go. And the funny thing is that I get the emotion that originally caused it. Either I'm scared shitless or I'm awful sorry for poor little me or I'm so goddamn mad I could kill somebody. The emotion comes flooding out, as fresh as the day it happened. And after that, the muscle can stay normal.

"And once he gets everything out, which is simply a matter of digging and digging at it, then everything will work freely." Keith Laumer says this with absolute, calm conviction. The therapy he is receiving, twice a week, has lasted four years now; but he knows it will work. Obviously, it has to.

"It hurts horribly, but it's just barely within what I can face. It's at least as bad as surgery without anesthetic. It's especially bad when he hits a fear pocket, because then you get terror along with the pain. Like when he starts working down in around the throat. You know goddamn well you're being choked to death, and you're panic stricken, and suffering agonies at the same moment.

"If somebody had tried to tell me about this before I got into this state I would have said, 'Bullshit.' But when it happens to Number One, you can't deny it.

"When I first got into this state, for five years I didn't write anything. Then I slowly got started, doing a few short stories, and then I started writing one of the novels for which I had contracted before. And I have now completed four novels and half-a-dozen short stories, and am just starting a new novel which is due in a few months, and I have just signed a contract to do two more.

"I always used to type. Now, I have to do it in longhand. But I have a gal who comes in once a week to tidy up the place, and she also types up what I've written. So that works fairly well.

"I just turned in a new Retief novel, and before that was *The Star Colony*, and *The Ultimax Man*, which came out some months ago from St. Martin's Press."

Retief is Laumer's favorite hero, an interstellar diplomat whose lot in life is to grapple constantly, and comically, with a galaxy full of incompetents.

"I always enjoyed doing Retief and I still do. The world is so full of bullshit—there's always a fresh supply—and in the Retief stories I try to puncture some of it. And that's always worth doing."

He started writing the stories as a reaction to his time spent in the Diplomatic Service. I ask how long he was with the State Department.

"I was never *with* them," he corrects me grimly, "I was *employed* by them. I was, in fact, against them from the beginning. I was there for about three years; I was a Third Secretary of Embassy of the United States of America in the United States Diplomatic Service, and I was a Vice Consul of Career in the United States Consular Service, and I was a Foreign Service Officer of Class 7 in the United States Foreign Service. I ranked 'with and after a captain', which didn't thrill me because I had already been a captain in the Air Force."

Mentioning these positions reminds him of all the publishers who have printed inaccurate biographical notes of his life. And this brings back his rage. One moment he's mild-mannered Keith, with a sly smile and a taste for gentle irony. And then, in a flash, he's Demon Laumer, screaming and swearing obscenities in vile fury. It's difficult for me to indicate, in print, how wildly he fluctuates to and fro.

"As a result of my going from the Air Force to the Diplomatic Service, and then back to the Air Force, the—*GOD DAMNED ASS HOLES*—who write blurbs on book jackets, instead of asking me, made up some—*CRAZY BULL SHIT*—about how I was some kind of 'diplomatic aide' or some god damned thing. If the—*MOTHERFUCKING ASS HOLES*—had just asked me.... Anybody who knows anything about diplomatic practice would read that and say, 'This guy's a *phony*, because there is no such thing as a diplomatic aide.'

"When I go in there and see them and say a bad word, do you think that does any good? No, they put the same *GOD DAMNED SHIT* on the next book. They make me grind my teeth.

"And then the god damned editor of *If* magazine, when it was running all the Retief stories, constantly got out his *god damned editorial pencil* and changed the little technical niceties to something that seemed to his *god damned brainless mind* to be a little closer to Middle American blah, thereby completely destroying the verisimilitude. So anybody who was actually in the Diplomatic Service reading it would say, 'Well this asshole's never been near the Diplomatic Service.' The *god damned prick*!

"I said, 'Look, when I say the man was a counsellor, I do *NOT* repeat *NOT* mean that he was a member of a *council*. So will you kindly *FUCK OFF* changing the spelling to 'councillor'? It *AIN'T THAT*, see'?"

Laumer relaxes back into his chair.

"But do you think he got it? He didn't understand. Perhaps—perhaps I didn't make it plain enough. Or—maybe he thought I didn't mean it, because I wasn't emphatic enough." He gives me a faint, ironic smile.

"Little things like that. For some reason unknown to anybody the word 'despatch' in the State Department is spelled with an E. So I spelled it with an E and he changed it to an I. I said, 'Will you *FUCKING LAY OFF*'? And he said, 'But I looked in the Web-ber Dick-on-ary....' So I said, 'Look up your *FUCKING ASSHOLE*, jerk! *I* am the guy who was a full-time professional U.S. diplomat.'"

His anger subsides again, and he begins telling me another anecdote.

"One day I had a most interesting letter from somebody at the State Department Foreign Service Institute who asked me if, the next time I was in Washington, I would stop by and address the student body. And he said, 'Personally, I'm sort of a Magnan type myself.'" He chuckles.

"A what type?" I ask, not geting the joke.

"A Magnan type." He sees that my face is still blank. Suddenly, he grabs his cane and slams it against the floor. He lets out a terrifying, full-blooded scream. "You never heard of Magnan! *Gaaarrgh!* He is Retief's sidekick in *every* Retief story. *Aaarrgh! Nyaaarrgh!*"

It's a terrible, frightening sound, like a barbarian war cry. He lets go of his cane, grabs a saber in an ornamental sheath, and strikes it fiercely against the couch where he's sitting. He keeps screaming and scowling at me.

"I thought you said 'magnum'," I try to tell him.

"*Aaarghh! Aaarghh!*"

"I'm sorry Keith, but—"

"*Naaarghhh! Aaaargh!*" He pauses for breath. "Have I made myself clear?" he asks mildly, replacing the saber in its corner. "You see, I think people ought to know that Magnan is the sidekick of Retief," he goes on matter-of-factly, "and is a weak sister, highly ineffectual, and it's pretty funny when this guy put in his letter, 'I'm sort of a Magnan type myself.' I thought that was really charming.

"How are you going to transcribe my roars, off the tape?" he asks reflectively. "I suggest: 'A-R-G-G-G-H-H-H-H.'"

Feeling slightly dazed, at this point, I manage to agree that this sounds like a fine way to spell it. Hoping to put the conversation on safer ground, I ask why he seems so down on the State Department.

"The United States Department of State," he says carefully, "is as *filthy* an organization as ever existed on this planet, up to and including the Gestapo."

No, I object, it can't be that bad.

"*Worse!* It is rotten from the top to the bottom, and if anybody gets into it who isn't rotten, he's pounded on till he is rotten, or he gets out."

Really? *That* bad?

"*WORSE!* Think of something rotten, and they do it. Nothing as wholesome and decent as simply taking money for selling military secrets to the enemy. I mean, any red-blooded American boy might do that. But not these cocksucking bastards, they go way beyond that. If you've read my novel *Embassy*, which is not science fiction, you'll get some idea of my experiences. I poured my life blood into that book. A testament of two-and-a-half to three horrible fucking years out of my life. And editors said, 'Oh, yes, *The Ugly American* with sex.' Gaah! It's a horrible thing that that god damned book *The Ugly American* came out when it did. It was a piss-poor book, and if *The Ugly American* hadn't come out right ahead of mine, it would have sold twelve zillion copies. It should have been reissued when that thing was going on in Iran; because what went on in my book was the same kind of shit, and it showed exactly how it comes to pass, because of the venality and cowardice of the god damned bastards who've been running the American Embassies in the United States Department of State.

"If I were placed in charge, I would disband the department, fire anybody who had worked for it in any capacity, and no one who had worked it would ever be eligible to work for the new Department of Foreign Affairs. Every building that had belonged to that organization would be gotten rid of, every vehicle. That's what it would take to clean it up. Nothing less."

I ask if he feels that bureaucracy is always inherently corrupt and inefficient.

"Of course. It's a concept that has flaws built into it, part of its nature. There are a lot of jokes that embody the truth, like the one: 'In the civil service they promote a man until he reaches a job that he can't do.' It's the fucking truth! Therefore you have an incompetent occupying every position.

"It is absolutely against the interest of any bureaucrat to cut down in any way on the scope of his duties or the number of people that work for him, because his pay is based on these things. So you get one bureaucrat fighting to steal some section away from some other bureaucrat so he can have all these people added to his list, so he can get a raise.

"It's analogous to the U.S. legal system, which places a premium on extending litigation. It's not in the interest of lawyers to shorten litigation, but to prolong it as far as possible."

I ask if his dislike for bureaucracy is so strong as to make him a libertarian.

"No—that's anarchy, and under anarchy the biggest assholes gang up and beat the shit out of everybody else and take everything for themselves, and I'm not interested in that. It's Europe in the Dark Ages."

I mention that Poul Anderson is a libertarian of sorts.

"Well that simply establishes that Poul Anderson doesn't know shit from wild honey. People who express approval of that kind of thing aren't thinking in terms of, all of a sudden, no more TV, no gas in the gas station, no groceries in the grocery store. All of that is the product of a fantastic network of cooperation. If everybody just said 'Fuck it!' it would all stop. You could take off your clothes, go off into the woods, and start looking for nuts and berries."

Laumer's views on modern science fiction are almost as scathing as his views on the political establishment.

"I find it very bad and uninteresting. A lot of it is very pretentious. Science fiction started off as a literature that was created for fun and read for pleasure. Now it's become a channel for social and socialistic ideas from writers who are avant-garde and new-wavy and liberal, and all those things make me puke, so there's just nothing there for me.

"Personally, I never said, 'I am going to write science fiction', I just decided to write something that pleased me. I never even had the intention of becoming a writer; one day, in Rangoon, I told my wife, 'I'm going to stay home from that god damned office today and write a story.' And I did, and I sold it, and all the ones since.

"I went on doing jobs, like going back into the Air Force. It was a long time before it occurred to me that I should quit doing all the other stuff and write full-time. But I finally did, resigned from the Air Force in 1965, came to Florida, and built the house, and settled down to live happily every after. And five years later they tried to kill me. So that has drastically changed the pattern of my life. I've had to devote every waking and sleeping moment to fighting this god damned plague, to recover my life, which I am doing, *and will complete.*"

During the last part of our conversation, we've been eating steak which he insisted on preparing for me—a very fine cut of beef, cooked to perfection. He clings stubbornly to his ideas about excellence. He still has detailed plans for the completion of his house: "Everything properly made, and perfectly maintained," seems to be his motto.

And I learn that the dozens of junked Mercury Cougars that he's collected are a strange part of his obsession with perfection. He's vague about how the collection got started, but he's quite definite about what he's going to do. He'll repair every last one of them, as soon as he gets his strength back. He'll restore them "to new condition—or better." He tells me there are thirty-eight cars in all, and shows me some hood emblems and instrument-panel trim that he's already removed and had re-chromed. "It gives me something to occupy my mind, when I'm not thinking about 'Topic A'," he says quietly.

To me, it seems as if the cars are an externalization of his own condition; he wants to restore their steel bodies as he would heal his own. He shrugs, and doesn't argue the point.

Before I leave, he shows me pictures of his three daughters, one of whom lives in London, the other two in Texas, which is also where his ex-wife is located. "After I have completed the total recovery of my health," he says, "I'm going to marry an absolutely first-class young beauty and have another family. And I'll know a lot more about what I'm doing, the next time."

Then he walks outside with me, into the warm Florida evening.

I remark that the cruelty of what he has experienced would make me doubt the existence of a god, if I were not already agnostic.

"But it has had exactly the opposite effect on me," he says. "Before this happened to me, I was always content, but never happy. Now, I have a whole new view of life. I appreciate life with a depth and scope I would never have imagined. And it cannot be an accident. I believe in God, now, and could not have come to this realization any other way. There is some principle, some force, which is active in controlling the universe, and I definitely believe that this applies to the individual."

For now, at least, he seems to have vented all his resentments. He speaks with a strange kind of equanimity.

"I sure wish some of my old friends would stop by," he goes on, as I get in my rented car. "Though I wouldn't ever tell 'em that," he adds gruffly.

I can see why they stay away, of course. They must dread his spasms of rage, and the way he reminds us of the shadow under which we all live. Keith Laumer was stricken at age forty-five, in excellent physical shape; obviously, then, it could happen to me, or you, or anyone. I suppose it's poor form to emphasize this. Most of us naturally prefer not to dwell on mortality, and it's easy to feel uncomfortable visiting disabled friends, or even reading profiles of them. Pretending to be invulnerable is a common enough way of coping with life.

Keith Laumer, of course, now lacks that option.

Historical Context

After my profile of Keith Laumer was published, I spoke to someone who had known him before I met him and had been with him during an incident where Keith had become disoriented and his speech had become slurred. This incident was the precursor of Keith's mental impairment, and I believe beyond any doubt that it was, in fact, a stroke. I'm not sure why Keith felt such a need to deny that, and I never had a chance to ask him about it. I didn't know him well, and he wasn't easy to talk to on the phone.

He died in January 1993, aged 67. I don't know what happened to his beautiful house and the wrecked cars strewn around it. Tragedy is not my favorite topic. There are some things that I prefer not to know.

L. Ron Hubbard (?)

By mail, April 1982

SOME OF MY more paranoid friends warned me not to try to interview L. Ron Hubbard. They said I'd get my name on "the Scientology hit list," and I'd be the target of mind-games and covert investigations.

They told me than an interview was impossible, anyway, because L. Ron Hubbard lives in perpetual retreat on a huge yacht cruising the Mediterranean, protected by an entourage of fanatical disciples in Scientology—the global religion of which he is the founder.

Of course, I said I was far too sensible to pay attention to wild rumors and hearsay. But as I subsequently became tangled in a tantalizing correspondence with Mr. Hubbard's various officers and agents, I couldn't help wondering if I was acting like some "Skeptical Investigator" in a ghost story—the kind of character who laughs at doomsayers warning him to stop before he rouses the Wrath of Hbbrdu with his reckless investigations. "Heck, I don't believe any of that foolishness," he scoffs. "Why, that's just a lot of—Aaaarrrgghhh!"

And the wise ones shake their heads and say, "We tried to tell him, but he *just wouldn't listen.*"

Forgive me for running off into fantasy. It's hard not to, when dealing with a real-life myth figure whose exact life history is still a subject of some debate. The following facts, however, seem more or less agreed upon:

As a teenager, Hubbard traveled through the Far East. A member of the Explorers Club, he was awarded three Explorers Flags. He became a pilot, proficient in both powered flight and gliders, in which he set records for time aloft. His real career, of course, was as a writer: He wrote screenplays for Hollywood, and he wrote prodigiously for American short-story magazines of the 1930s and 1940s. Much of his work appeared under pseudonyms, much of it was adventure fiction, and some of it was science fiction. His writing was fluent and dramatic, sometimes laconically humorous, and always highly imaginative.

But he stopped publishing fiction in the 1950s. On the basis of some private research he founded Dianetics, the "modern science of mental health," and opened training centers across America. Many of the centers failed when the organization expanded faster than its capital would allow, but Mr. Hubbard regrouped, returned, and became the central figure in the Church of Scientology, which he built into an international organization claiming more than a million members, many of whom regard him as a great spiritual leader.

The controversies surrounding Scientology are not relevant to this book. What interests me is that, thirty years after he left science fiction, Mr. Hubbard returned to it. His 430,000-word novel *Battlefield Earth* was published in the fall of 1982, and is just as vigorous and dramatic as the writing of his youth.

In his introduction to this epic he says that he found himself with time on his hands, so he decided to write a novel. Clearly, he didn't do it for the money; I'm told he was a millionaire even before he started Scientology. Perhaps he was lured by the challenge of writing a science-fiction best seller, on a scale equal to that of his old contemporary Robert Heinlein. Or perhaps he simply couldn't resist marking the fiftieth anniversary of the start of his career as a writer.

My quest for an interview, to answer questions like these, was long and full of mystery—though I was never quite sure how much of the mystery was in my own head. It began at the end of 1981, when I wrote to one of L. Ron Hubbard's literary agents, Forrest J. Ackerman. Ackerman seemed miffed that I didn't want to interview *him*, but he said my request to interview Hubbard had been forwarded—though he didn't specify where. I began to get the impression that people associated with Mr. Hubbard were careful never to state in writing that they had sent something to him or received something from him. Maybe it was just an accident of phrasing; but it fascinated me.

Within a few days I received a letter from Wally Burgess, the International Director at Hubbard's Office of Public Affairs, in Florida. I liked the letterhead—L. Ron Hubbard's name was embossed in gold foil at the top, just like the cover of a best-selling novel. Not exactly subtle, but impressive.

Burgess said he could put me in touch with a Hubbard bibliophile; not with Mr. Hubbard. I wrote back again and repeated my original request.

Next I got a letter from Vaughn Young, another Director of Public Affairs, this time of Author Services, Inc., "Representing the Literary Works of L. Ron Hubbard" in Hollywood, California. Young's letter discreetly implied that *something* might be arranged—though he didn't say what. He told me to send him my interview questions, and wait for developments.

The Author Services letterhead included a Los Angeles phone number. I tried dialing it, and got through to an answering service that claimed never to have heard of Author Services. When I persisted, they went and checked their records and found they did take messages for that company—but they had never heard of Vaughn Young.

This really fed my fantasies. I imagined endless protective layers around L. Ron Hubbard: an infinite series of dummy corporations, false names, and forwarding addresses. I began to feel I was pursuing a science-fictional Howard Hughes.

Anyway, I sent my list of questions to Mr. Young, and he wrote back enigmatically: "I believe I will be able to help you out." He added: "I look forward to the response as much as you."

Note: "the" response, rather than "Mr. Hubbard's" response. Again the phrasing seemed odd—but by this time I was beginning to realize how easy it is to read hidden meaning into any sentence, and how myths can multiply around a myth-figure merely by the fact of his existence.

One week later, Vaughn Young sent me a letter saying— enigmatically, again—"I am pleasantly amazed at what your questions evoked." Well, I was pleasantly amazed, too; because enclosed with his letter were eleven typewritten pages of answers to the questions that I had asked. These pages constituted, in fact, the first interview of any kind that L. Ron Hubbard had given since 1966. Witty, fluent, and full of character, the complete text appears below. I have included, also, most of the text of my questions, because I like the contrast between my somewhat earnest approach and Mr. Hubbard's laconic attitude to the whole affair.

Well, this almost seemed too easy; and maybe it *was* too easy. I started wondering if, in fact, the typed responses were genuine. After all, I didn't know who I was writing to, and I didn't know where the responses had come from. Vaughn Young—assuming there *was* a Vaughn Young—had never specifically stated that he had written to Hubbard, or that he had received anything from him. And so, a trifle nervously, now, and trying to be as tactful as possible, I wrote and asked for proof.

While I was waiting for that, a friend pointed out something to escalate the paranoid fantasies still further. The typewriter used in Vaughn Young's letters to me had a slightly damaged capital "A"; and this was identical to a damaged letter "A" in the typed responses that were supposedly from L. Ron Hubbard. Moreover, the paper had the same distinctive watermark.

Did this mean that "Vaughn Young" had made up all the answers *himself*? Or (a more exciting idea!) was Vaughn Young *really*

L. Ron Hubbard, writing to my under a pseudonym? Or (and this, surely, was the classic piece of conspiracy thinking) had "they" deliberately used the same paper and the same typewriter, hoping I'd notice, so that it would make me paranoid?

Within a few days I received a handwritten authentication from Mr. Hubbard, by express mail, from a P.O. Box in California. I also received another letter from Vaughn Young, explaining that he had used his typewriter merely to transcribe responses that Mr. Hubbard had dictated. Young subsequently telephoned me, and told me that the Author Services letterhead was out of date, and they now have a new phone number listed on a new letterhead. Los Angeles telephone information verified it when I called them a few days later. Finally, Young visited me in person, and played me a cassette tape of songs from *Battlefield Earth* (with cheerful lyrics such as "Kill the humans! Kill the humans!") while he vetted my introduction to Hubbard's interview responses for inaccuracies.

Well, I'm grateful to Mr. Hubbard for taking the trouble to answer my questions, and I'm also indebted to Vaughn Young for acting as go-between and tolerating my skepticism. And yet, it might have been more satisfying, in a way, never to have received a conclusive response, and to have gone around in circles forever, from one mail drop or answering service to the next, building more and more crazy, complex fantasies in the process. Mystery and myth must always be more enticing than dull old reality; paranoid theories are more fun than any rational explanation. At the end of a ghost story, we feel cheated if the Skeptical Investigator emerges unscathed, and proves that there was no ghost at all—merely the night breeze blowing through an open window.

Question: Since Mr. Hubbard was last active in science fiction, it has changed greatly. The magazines have declined while paperback novels have proliferated. Technically accurate, predictive stories have given way to novels of the "soft" sciences. In the last fifteen years, some people complain of a trend toward reworking the old formulas endlessly as if there are no new ideas left. Finally, some science fiction has grown to best seller status and some authors now receive million-dollar royalty advances while the rest still earn only $5,000 to $10,000 for a book. What are Mr. Hubbard's opinions on these various trends?

Response: You reminded me how I came to enter this field.

It was the day I met John W. Campbell, Jr.

I had been called down to that dirty old building on 7th Avenue in New York City by F. Orlin Tremaine and some other top executives of Street and Smith. I didn't know what they wanted but S&S was The Giant of the industry and so such "invitations" were heeded. It was like an audience with the king.

I wasn't the only one. J. Arthur Burks, another top writer, was also there—equally mystified.

Well, Tremaine tells us he wants us to write science fiction.

Burks and I look at each other.

Science fiction? We write about *people*, not monsters and machines.

Exactly the point, Tremaine said. S&S had just bought *Astounding Science Fiction* and sales were unacceptable. What the magazine needed was stories about people written by some headline writers like Burks and myself, but it had to be science fiction.

A special company, A. B. Dick—sort of the Nielsen or Gallup of that day—had found that a few writers sold magazines and Burks and I were among that select group. All we had to do was write science fiction and write it about people, not monsters.

Burks and I may have been successful writers but that was hardly reason to say no to the biggest publisher of the day so we wisely agreed.

Astounding editor Campbell was called in and introduced to two of his newest writers and told that he would print whatever Burks and I wrote—no questions asked.

Campbell didn't like it one bit. He snarled but S&S was calling the shots. He was told to buy our stories and publish them. At our rates, it would ruin his budget. Besides, he had his own idea how science fiction should be done.

But Campbell gave in.

And that is how it began.

John and I became the best of friends and, frankly, I don't know how many of us were foisted off on him or how many he found but he ended up with a stable of writers second to none. He became the Czar of science fiction and he earned it.

"Dangerous Dimension" was the first fruit of my SF effort, followed by "The Tramp".

Rather than BEMs, "Dangerous Dimension" used a philosophic theory that predates Western culture—than an individual's location depends on that person's ideas and not the location.

The story centered on a meek little professor (henpecked by a domineering housekeeper) who stumbles on the secret and finds he is instantly transported anywhere by merely thinking of the location—sometimes to his embarrassment.

The story was unusual for its philosophy, humor, and its emphasis on people and not monsters.

"The Tramp" was a guy who acquires immense mental powers after a brain operation to save his life.

The fans loved it.

The "new trend" began.

Circulation soared and Campbell sighed and put his monsters and robot societies away.

That is history. But Campbell got even.

Although we became good friends, he got the fantasy I wrote out of *Astounding* by starting a brand new magazine to accommodate it—*Unknown*.

That handled that.

Question: In the last ten years, fantasy has emerged as a separate category rivaling science fiction. Is this a healthy trend, or does it imply that readers have come to fear science and prefer to read about medieval societies run by magic?

Response: I am very pleased that you make this distinction for too often fantasy and SF are blurred.

The two genres are quite distinct.

If you mix one with the other, you dilute both.

Fantasy deals with magic, mythology, the supernatural. There are no boundaries in fantasy.

When Einstein came out with his Theory of Relativity and the fixed speed of light, a tremendous barrier had been imposed on SF. No longer could a space ship just whip out to Xnenophean 5 for lunch and zip back for tea.

So SF writers had to come up with new ideas and "Doc" Smith was one of the best. He had to come up with new drive systems to circumnavigate around Einstein more than anything else.

But in fantasy, you don't have that problem.

It's all "magic" in this genre.

You see, "Dangerous Dimension" was actually fantasy because it was based upon a spiritualistic idea. "The Tramp" was science fiction.

So when you ask if readers prefer to read about medieval societies, I think it is more the case that they prefer the freedom of that genre.

Fantasy predates SF.

It is as old as storytelling itself.

One is not necessarily better than the other.

They are just different.

Question: Does Mr. Hubbard have any social or psychological theory to explain why so many people are willing to take ideas seriously which used to be laughed at? Many adults now read about dragons, monsters, or far-off galaxies, whereas twenty years ago that kind of thing was ridiculed as "kids' stuff." Does this reflect a turning away from the problems of real life?

Response: Your question about what was "kids' stuff" twenty years ago brings back memories!

I think if you will look at the trends of the last forty or so years, there was a development towards being very "serious" and "scientific." This happens every now and then as some new theory takes hold—and then passes.

But I think it would be a bit inaccurate to say that just because people today are enjoying SF and fantasy they are "reverting." What they are doing is getting rid of the ideas that were imposed upon this society by the man-is-mud-and-trapped-in-mud practitioners.

Fantasy is as old as Man. It is only in the last century that someone has come along and said that we are made of little wiggly-wogglies. They promise that they'll have it all explained for us any moment as soon as we pour another billion dollars into their lab. But all we've gotten so far is a nuclear nightmare.

SF and fantasy hold out the prospect of possibility and in possibility you have choice and in choice you have freedom and *there* you have touched on the basic nature of every person.

This society offers just the opposite—and I am not singling out any one society.

People walk about knowing that something is wrong but they just can't seem to put their finger on it.

If you really want to be blunt about it, this world we live in with its insanities and madmen ready to blow it up is more unbelievable than any SF or fantasy.

So when one grows up in that kind of world, anything else is easily believable.

Question: My second and third questions, above, relate to levels of faith and belief in the general public. As the founder of Scientology, Mr. Hubbard must have a particularly good perspective on what people believe today and whether mental health, overall, is improving or declining. Does the popularity of science fiction imply that people's minds are more open now than before, or are people less prepared to deal with the real world? Does this mean, in turn, that there is more need today for Scientology as a system to enhance our mental abilities?

Response: I've always found the phrase "deal with the real world" to be amusing.

Pick up a daily newspaper and read the headlines and then look about you and see how the two compare. Which is "real"? To believe the news, every other person is being shot, airplanes are falling like rain, every house is burning down, and tornadoes are as common as clouds.

Are newspapers reporting the "real world"?

I think not.

But you can sure begin to think the world is that way if you read enough papers and watch enough TV and don't LOOK. (And one of the results of too much "news" is that people think it is even dangerous to look!)

So to judge the "mental health" of society, where do we turn?

Do we use the information given by others or should we look around us and judge for ourselves?

A society composed of individuals who can look about and see what is there and see what is NOT there (an equally valuable skill) is healthier than one consisting of people who need Dr. Knowitall of Johnny Journalist to tell them what to believe.

To the degree a Scientologist learns to look for himself, he or she is sane and to that degree the society benefits.

As long as there is a need for sanity, there will be a need for Scientology.

It has made a difference to the degree that it helps the individual to help himself.

Question: Elite secret societies of especially gifted people have been a common theme in science fiction. Often the elite are a jump ahead up the evolutionary ladder. Is this a valid parallel with Dianetics or Scientology? Were any science-fiction books influential on Mr. Hubbard when he conceived of a cohesive organization of gifted individuals using a new mental discipline?

Response: People always enjoy the idea of an "advanced" society but this is always taken in a "vertical" sense—sort of "up"—as compared to an Eastern view that would probably be better described as "horizontal"—expanding out. It is also the difference between one and three dimensions.

Professor Mudge in "Dangerous Dimension" wasn't really all that "advanced" when he discovered how to teleport himself around the galaxy. In fact, he made his discovery by looking not for a "fourth dimension" but a "negative dimension."

Thus Mudge did not move "forward" but "backward."

Mudge's problem was not so much what he found or discovered but his inability to control it.

This is the problem that befalls every "advanced" society—it simply cannot control its creation but is controlled by them.

I found this to be a challenge for the individual for it is there that the battle or struggle is most real.

That is why Mudge and The Tramp are so similar. The two are from totally different backgrounds and both are fairly mundane individuals. But suddenly they "advance" (whatever that means) but they cannot control their newfound abilities. The "gift" was almost Mudge's undoing. It destroyed the hobo.

It was this problem that intrigued me and was what I researched. I knew that there was a mechanism in man that acted like a self-destruct button.

The results appeared in *Dianetics: The Modern Science of Mental Health* in 1950.

Question: Why did Mr. Hubbard return to writing science fiction?

Does he write only to entertain, or to communicate a message or even enlightenment?

Response: *Battlefield Earth* was written to celebrate my fiftieth anniversary as a professional writer.

Possibly, by definition, every story has a message. It is a communication. A story that doesn't communicate isn't much of a story. It is just a question of how much *does* it communicate?

Writers who take their "message" first and then try to weave a story around it make better advertising executives than writers.

Question: What were his original ambitions as a writer? Did he achieve those goals? Why did he stop writing science fiction? Did the obscurity of the field, its low literary status, and its meager rates of pay influence his decision? Where did he write his early work? Was he part of a regional group of writers? Did he feel at home among other science-fiction people?

Response: At first, I wrote on anything I could find—if it took pen or pencil I wrote on it. When I traveled through the Far East (twice) as a teenager, I used old ledgers as well as stationary pads.

The only time I really stopped writing was for the first two years of the Second World War when security prohibited the keeping of diaries.

But I finally found a worn Smith-Corona or a Royal (I forget which) in 1943 and began to write.

My first story in two years was forgettable. It was barely over 1,200 words but it was a story! I was as proud as any neophyte who had just sold his first story.

I limbered up soon enough.

Like remembering how to ride a bicycle, it just takes some refreshing.

But writing for me has always been something more than a profession—and I think you will find this to be true with any true writer. It is a way of life.

So I never really stopped writing, except for those two years.

Looking back on it, it is amazing that all of us from that great period did what we did—given the publishers and the agents. It was a challenge.

But we hung out together and even today I consider them my friends. We traded stories and ideas while jealously wondering if what we described would appear under someone else's by-line.

We yammered and argued and celebrated and watched others come and go while we wrote.

My first professional story was in the *Sportsmans Pilot*, although I had been writing in college before that and while traveling.

So when the old golden anniversary came rolling around, I figured I would celebrate it in the only way I really knew how—I wrote *Battlefield Earth*.

Question: Did he have any inkling that Scientology would become so successful? Has he now achieved all of his ambitions? Is, perhaps, writing a contemporary best seller the last big challenge?

Response: We were all quite surprised at the immediate success of *Dianetics: The Modern Science of Mental Health* in 1950. The publisher was caught flat-footed when the book shot onto the best seller lists and just stayed there. (By the way, the first Dianetics article was NOT in *Astounding* as some contend. The first article was *Terra Incognita: The Mind* and it appeared earlier that year in the winter-spring edition of the *Explorers Journal*.)

As the book was the result of years of hard work supported by writing, I never suspected that I had only scratched the surface of what could be learned about the human condition.

I am very happy with the life I have lived and really regret no part of it. I have had one vocation—to understand life and do something to help my fellow man help himself.

My philosophy has been that wisdom is not something that

304

should be locked away. It belongs to any who seek it and who can use it to benefit their fellows.

My greatest treasure is my many friends.

Question: As a somewhat mysterious and powerful figure, Mr. Hubbard has become a focus of all kinds of rumors—much like the late Howard Hughes. For instance, I have heard that he lives in exclusive luxury on a yacht in the Mediterranean. It's said that he is a multi-millionaire. There is a cynical anecdote that at the last meeting of science-fiction writers which he ever attended, he told them they were crazy to write for a penny a word when they could apply their ideas to the real world. Are any of the stories true?

Response: It is one of those curious phenomena of our times that people are asked to "set the record straight."

Over the years I've learned that it is like the plight of the Sorcerer's Apprentice. With each denial or correction, the rumor splinters into more rumors....

I've just learned to laugh them off.

It's more fun that way anyway.

Question: Will there be more novels by L. Ron Hubbard? Does he have plans for the next five or ten years?

Response: Yes, I am just finishing another science-fiction saga— bigger than *Battlefield Earth*. Plus I just did two screenplays.

I'm planning on doing some cinematography, for the camera has always been one of my loves.

Question: On the personal side: Is Mr. Hubbard married? Does he have children? Does he have hobbies?

Response: Yes, and I am even a grandfather!

As far as recreation—I write!

Additional Response: I would like to comment simply on the title of your book—*Dream Makers.*

It was Descartes who used the dream to establish his certainty of himself and the world and, finally, God. He sought something that could not be doubted—and found himself.

There is a basic truth in that for all of us.

Those who dream give us future.

But in doing so, each man or woman should find themselves.

For dreams are too often pitted against "reality"—as Descartes did—when they might well be more real than this very page.

It was only in this century that dreams lost their value (except to analysts who made a fast buck) and it is a delight to see their value restored.

Dreams are the vision of man's future and it is only the future that will tell us if the vision was true.

Thus I wish you every best success with your second volume of *Dream Makers.*

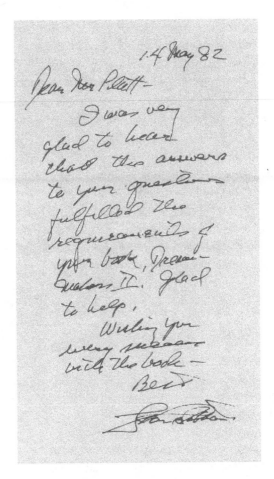

Historical Context

After my Hubbard interview was published, the repercussions continued for many years.

First I was approached by a man named Fred Harris, who was organizing a coordinated effort to promote Hubbard's science fiction. Although Fred never specifically suggested that I owed Hubbard a favor in return for him granting me an interview, he asked me to write a review of *Battlefield Earth* (which was published in 1982) and nagged me repeatedly for advice about the best strategy for winning a Hugo award. I tried to be evasive, which didn't work. I wrote a lukewarm review, which didn't help. Finally I got irritated and wrote a long review of a book denouncing Scientology. I wanted to make it clear that as a writer, I would maintain my independence. Probably this was considered a betrayal.

Fred Harris attended many science-fiction conventions, and at the next one where I saw him, he sat down opposite me at a table in the lobby of a hotel. He appeared to be extremely drunk, which made me nervous. He then picked up an ornamental oil lamp that was standing on the table. This made me even more nervous, as the lamp was made of glass and I could see the lamp oil sloshing around inside its base, while the flame flickered.

"Charles," said Fred, staring fixedly into my eyes. "Is this a lamp?" He held it up in front of me. His arm was swaying from side to side. I had visions of the lamp crashing down and setting fire to the table, Fred Harris, and probably me, too.

"Yes, Fred," I said, nodding quickly. "Yes, it is a lamp." I paused. "Would you like to put the lamp down, Fred?"

He nodded slowly. "I'm glad we can agree on that." He replaced the lamp on the table.

Apparently there is a procedure in Scientology auditing where the auditor asks the subject to agree to some basic facts as a prelude to more complicated issues. I think that's what was going on, although Fred seemed too drunk to get to the complicated issues.

L. Ron Hubbard died in January, 1986. A few weeks later, it was my turn to be a bit drunk at a science-fiction event. "Fred!" I hailed him, as he was heading for the exit of a hotel. "Fred, I need to know. This is important. Are you in contact with Ron's thetan?" As I understood the Church of Scientology teachings, if Fred was a "clear" who had progressed to the upper levels of enlightenment (which seemed likely, even though he had never admitted to being a Scientologist) he should be able to contact Hubbard's thetan, or departed spirit. At the time, these concepts were considered trade secrets by the Church, and I was behaving like a blasphemer quizzing a cardinal about communication with the soul of a deceased pope. Fred gave me a very hard look, and walked away.

Shortly after that I was subjected to a tax audit by an IRS employee who seemed to take a very active delight in the process, even though my income was extremely low that year. I thought he had exactly the personality profile of a Scientologist. He spent literally days investigating me, even visiting the college where I was teaching, in an effort to prove that I had an office there, so that he could disallow my home-office deduction. In fact I had no office at the college, but he disallowed my home-office deduction anyway. The process just went on and on. When I asked why I had been chosen for this special treatment, he grinned and said, "Mr. Platt, it's just like winning the lottery."

I moved to California for six months and requested transfer of the audit there. Then I moved back to New York, and once again asked for transfer of the auditing process. By this time my nemesis had been promoted to investigate organized crime, and I got a "normal" auditor who wrapped things up within just a few hours. He was familiar with my previous auditor, and referred to him with a derogatory nickname, a violation of IRS protocol that my accountant found astonishing.

Time passed. Someone at the Church of Scientology sent me a letter asking to borrow the authentication letter from L. Ron Hubbard, so that the signature could be compared with another signature relating to a fight over Hubbard's assets. I surrendered the letter, because if I didn't, I thought it would be subpoena'd anyway. A while later, the letter came back. Then a Scientologist asked to buy it, apparently because Ron's signature had value regardless of what he had been signing. I sold it for $200.

In February 1995, when a British publisher was thinking of doing a new edition of *Dream Makers*, I decided to reopen the authenticity issue. Usenet was active in those days, so I posted a message on alt.religion.scientology asking for Vaughn Young to contact me if he was still out there.

He was, and he did, although he explained that Vaughn was his middle name and Robert was his real first name, to which he had reverted "when my wife and I fled Scn in 1989." He had defected and had been hiding from the Church for the past six years.

We swapped messages for a while. He said he used to work with Fred Harris (the guy who asked me if the oil lamp was an oil lamp). He assured me that the handwritten letter from Hubbard had been genuine, but he confessed that my suspicions had been correct regarding the answers to my interview questions . "I wrote Elron's answers," he said, "and sent them to him for okay." ("Elron" was the way in which people close to Hubbard referred to him.)

So—the answers had just been made up? "Nope, wasn't 'made up'," he wrote back, "but approved, as described. In that vein, it was Elron. You see, had I not done it that way, it wouldn't have been done at all. He was very much in hiding."

Robert continued: "I was his ghost [writer] for many things. I did all his 'greetings' to the various orgs and even wrote a couple of policy letters that he approved. He liked my style, which was why I was also his editor for the *Mission Earth* series, ghosting parts of that for him too!"

Robert then described how he had left the Church. "I spent 14 months on the RPF [Rehabilitation Project Force], the Scn gulags, under guard, hard labor, etc. There was a power struggle after his death and I was on the losing side. After I was let off of it, I couldn't handle the group and got into an argument with one of the top execs who physically attacked me and threatened to send me back to the gulags. That's when I said, no way, and took my wife and fled."

Shortly after he contacted me, Robert generally came out of hiding to attack the Church of Scientology. He now has a Wikipedia entry, numerous tell-all monographs online, and a large entry on xenu.net, the anti-Scientology site. He also served as a witness in various high-level lawsuits involving Scientology. Search for "Robert Vaughn Young" online and you'll find no shortage of material.

He was diagnosed with metastatic prostate cancer in November 1999, and died in June 2003.

I think, and I hope, this is the end of the story.

Personally, my interest was always very narrow. I didn't care much about Scientology. I only had two goals: to interview L. Ron Hubbard about his science fiction, and then determine whether the responses had been genuine. Thirty-two years after the interview and almost twenty years after my last communication with Robert Vaughn Young, I think I came as close to my goals as I could. Whether it was close enough to count as a "real" interview remains a matter for debate. Hence the (?) which I have appended to Hubbard's name in this edition.

Arthur C. Clarke

By phone to Sri Lanka, April 21, 1982

IT'S A FRESH springtime morning. Seen from the windows of the fifteenth floor, the buildings of Manhattan are a sun-and-shadow masonry mosaic under the bright blue sky.

I'm looking out onto this panorama from a comfortable swivel chair, behind a big desk, in the ample office of an editor who's away for the day, in the headquarters of Berkley Publishing Corporation on Madison Avenue. It's a setting to inspire powerful fantasies and delusions of grandeur, but the truth is that I'm just here to make a free phone call.

I tried to tell my publishers that there was only one way to do this job properly. I should be sent to Arthur Clarke's tropical retreat in Sri Lanka, to meet the man in person. Think of all the background color, I said. Face to face with this legendary seer of the space age in his colonial mansion, chatting in the Trophy Room over a dish of curry and a few cups of locally grown tea, while the houseboys fan us with palm fronds, the monsoon rains patter into the rice paddies, parakeets squawk in the coconut palms, and monkeys chase tarantulas in the front yard—what a profile this would make!

---

[9] Photograph by Charles Adams.

But, as my publishers put it, we had to be realistic. And in the end it turned out that a half-hour international telephone call was as realistic as they were prepared to be.

Well, a phone call would be appropriate in a way: The conversation would be conveyed to Sri Lanka by satellite, and Clarke was the man who invented communications satellites in the first place.

No one took him very seriously, of course, when he wrote that first article about "extraterrestrial relays" for the British magazine *Wireless World* in 1945. Even he didn't take himself very seriously: he didn't try to patent his invention, because he didn't imagine it would be built in his lifetime.

It's hard to remember, now, that in the late 1940s and early 1950s space travel of any kind was nothing more than a vague, wistful fantasy. Most people, including many respectable scientists, openly laughed at the notion. Even the tiny minority who took it seriously, including visionaries such as Clarke and the British Interplanetary Society, tended to assume that it wouldn't happen until decades or even centuries had passed.

But the move into space gathered momentum exponentially. And with it, so did Clarke's career. First, the dull groundwork prior to launch, building his own telescopes as a kid (he couldn't afford professional equipment) and publishing his first stories in amateur magazines. Next, lift-off, in which early work consumed large amounts of energy for small initial gains. Then, as his trajectory lifted him into greater altitudes in the science-fiction medium, he encountered a fast-moving body of high mass, in the form of Stanley Kubrick. And the slingshot effect of this fly-by was the last boost that Clarke needed to accelerate to escape velocity. Suddenly he was free—forever free!—from the gravity-well of category fiction. His mission, now, was to boldly go where no science-fiction writer had ever gone before, into a rarefied realm of luminaries and macrocosmic events: science prizes, bestseller lists, international conferences, congressional speeches, prestigious awards. And he's been coasting in free-fall ever since.

By the 1970s, Clarke found less and less to tempt him away from Sri Lanka (formerly the British colony of Ceylon), where he had relocated originally because of a chance meeting in a London pub with an old friend who got him interested in scuba diving—the nearest thing to zero gravity available on planet Earth.

Finally, in 1980, Clarke renounced writing altogether and retired into permanent tropical hedonism. Interviewed in *Science Digest*, he said he was following the example of the composer Sibelius, who "locked himself up in his study...and said 'I am writing my great work,' and all he did was enjoy himself and drink a bottle of brandy a day and do no work at all. And I admire that."

But Clarke's claims proved premature. Moved by his New York literary agent's heartfelt cry ("You owe it to your readers, Arthur!"), and moved perhaps still further by a million-dollar offer from Del Rey Books, he sat down and wrote what he'd always said could not be written: the sequel to *2001: A Space Odyssey*.

On the date of my phone call, Clarke is doing the final revisions to this sequel. It's nine-thirty a.m., New York time, as I wire my tape recorder to my publisher's telephone and direct-dial Clarke's number halfway around the world. It's ten-and-a-half hours later in Sri Lanka, and he should just be finishing his day's work.

Distant relays click. Impulses leap from one repeater to the next, then take that big stride 22,300 miles up to a communications satellite and down again. Of course, this is just one routine international call out of thousands made every hour; yet still the technology seems impressive. Maybe I'm naive to feel this way, but Clarke himself seems never to have lost his wide-eyed wonder at science and technology, no matter how much it becomes a part of everyday life.

He answers the phone, sounding very British. "Ah. Hang on a second," he says. "I'll just switch off the word processor."

There's a pause, and then he's back on the line, ready to talk.

He sounds close and clear; the only clue that this is an international call is the echo I hear of my own voice, delayed by half a second from having traveled 50,000 miles to Sri Lanka via satellite, and 50,000 miles back again.

Since I'm stuck in New York, unable to witness with my own eyes the Sri Lankan parrots, monkeys, tarantulas, and so forth, I ask Clarke to describe his surroundings.

"I'm sitting in a long room," he says. "What I call the 'ego chamber,' where I work." (His British pronunciation rhymes "ego" with "echo.") "At one end there is a TV set with two video recorders. Then there is an 8mm and 16mm projector, and a 35mm slide projector, and a lot of bookshelves. A door leads through to the lav—on that door there are instructions for using a zero-gravity toilet. From *2001*, I expect you remember.

"Where I am at the moment, at the other end of the room I'm surrounded by my word processor and printer, and telephones. There are windows along one wall, and trees outside. We're near the center of Columbo. This house is quite modern, about twenty years old—one of the last that was built without any concern for expense."

He speaks in quick, precise sentences that end abruptly, as if he doesn't like wasting words. His matter-of-factness reminds me of his writing, which seldom attempts to be stylized, and even now sometimes falls into the idioms of old British boys' adventure fiction. In *2010*, for example, a character exclaims "Phew!" after a moment of danger—an expression I hadn't seen in print since I read *Biggles* novels twenty years ago.

I'm interested that Clarke has stayed so faithful to his original writing style and intentions, unlike some of the other elder statesmen of science fiction who started when he did.

"You mean people like H. G. Wells?" he jokes.

But I'm thinking of, say, Pohl, whose style has changed considerably over the years, or Heinlein, who has experimented with all kinds of different themes and methods.

"I guess I'm just an old conservative," Clarke replies. "Although, really, if I have stayed true to the original form of my writing that's simply because I have a constant commitment to science."

A commitment that still entails that almost childlike quality of wonder?

"Yes, very much," he agrees immediately. "And I'm proud of that. I regard it as something of an achievement not to have become cynical."

Or pessimistic; he seems to retain perpetual faith in the future.

"One must obviously be worried about all sorts of things," he says. "Right now, the Falkland Islands, for example." (At the time of this interview, British troops had just landed.) "And of course the ecological and other well-known possible disasters. The unavoidable ones, as well as avoidable ones like nuclear war. But I do remain an optimist, especially in my fiction, because I hope it may operate as a self-fulfilling prophecy."

The ending of his novel *The Fountains of Paradise* seems a slight exception to this, in that it has a wistful quality, as if Clarke is regretting a far future of space exploration that he will never live to see.

"If the ending of that book does seem wistful, that's only because, at the time I wrote it, for a number of reasons I thought it was my last book. Actually, as regards the space program, I never dreamed I would see this much. I have no gripes, no complaints at all. I never dreamed, for instance, that I would ever know what Jupiter looks like. From a purely personal viewpoint I'm not too bothered by the present lull in the space program. We need time, in a way, to make sense of what we've already learned. On the other hand, I have friends in the program who are suffering now because of the cutbacks in funding."

His novel *2010* depicts manned exploration of Jupiter's moons less than thirty years from now.

"But that's just a continuation of the future we visualized in

316

2001," he explains, "and of course it has already become an impossible future. When we wrote *2001* in 1964, 1965, and 1966, it did not seem unreasonable to imagine that by the end of this century there would be these giant space stations." (Necessary in order to build manned ships to explore interplanetary space.) "But Vietnam and Watergate and all the other things that happened in America changed all that. It will all still happen one day—but not on that time scale.

"I've never attempted to predict the future, and am not interested in doing so, *in my fiction*. Only in my nonfiction.

"Conceiving *2010* was actually rather difficult, because I'd painted myself into a corner in so many ways in *2001*. I think some people were expecting me to bring back Bowman [the astronaut from the first story] in white robes, or something, but I wanted to avoid any cliché of that type. For a long time I didn't see how I could write any kind of a sequel at all."

The novel is dedicated to two Russians: one a cosmonaut, the other a scientist. Clarke has always expressed idealistic yearnings for world peace and cooperation; I ask if he deliberately includes this kind of message.

"As far as putting messages in my fiction is concerned, I'm always fond of quoting Sam Goldwyn, who said, 'If you've got a message, use Western Union!' But of course there is an *implicit* message. No writer can avoid it if he's worth anything at all."

Is there going to be any more to the *2001* saga? Dare one ask—does *2020* come next?

"As a matter of fact, the joke's already going around. Not *2020*, though—it's supposed to be *20001*."

But he's not serious.

"No—except that now I've got this word processor, anything might happen, in five or ten years. I've just started writing articles again, believe it or not. I just sent off a long piece—well, long for me—to my agent, which may cause a lot of controversy. *The Menace of Creationism*. I've even hinted it might be a communist plot. That's tongue-in-cheek, of course, but I wanted to make people think."

I ask him if he still reads any science fiction. But, like so many of the best-known authors in the field, it seems he feels no need to.

"I gave up the magazines years ago, just as a matter of necessity—I didn't have enough time. In fact, I hardly read any fiction these days."

Is it simply a matter of his finding no science fiction now that he feels is worth reading?

"That is indeed a possibility," he says dryly.

The vast amount of money paid for world rights to *2010* is, of course symptomatic of modern publishing: the blockbuster system, which robs attention and money from more minor novels—especially those by new writers.

"I suppose that may be true," he says, as though he hadn't thought too much about this. "I don't know. From my own point of view, I'd naturally prefer to live in a penthouse than a garret."

He's achieved so much, at this point, I can't help wondering whether he can possibly have any ambitions left to fulfill.

"Hardly any. I say half jokingly that I'd like to go in the space shuttle, but I think that's not very probable. Actually, my only remaining ambition which I could fulfill is learning to play the piano. I can play a scale now, which is more than I used to be able to do. Then I have two computers in the house, now, and I'm spending a lot of time learning to use them.

"And of course it's a full-time job just trying to decide how to spend all this money!"

I suppose I should end there. According to the Alfred Bester method, an article should always end with the Best Anecdote, and that one-liner seems to be it.

But that wouldn't be quite fair. Clarke cannot be casually characterized as someone whose main concern is making money. He's delighted by his own successes—in fact, he tends to talk about them at every opportunity. But his intentions as a writer and as a futurist have always been idealistic. Back at the beginning of the 1960s, in his classic nonfiction book *Profiles of the Future*, he wrote:

"Whatever the eventual outcome of our exploration of space we can be reasonably certain of some immediate benefits—and I am deliberately ignoring such 'practical' returns as the multi-billion dollar improvements in weather forecasting and communications.... The creation of wealth is certainly not to be despised, but in the long run the only human activities really worthwhile are the search for knowledge, and the creation of beauty. This is beyond argument; the only point of debate is which comes first."

In the same book, he predicted that communications satellites could foster global unity via totally free, international, educational television.

And so, to Clarke, space exploration was not merely a power fantasy, or escapism, or a profitable investment, or a form of heroism. Rather, it was something through which we could transcend ourselves; something so big that it could eclipse petty differences and unite us all. He has come back to this theme again and again, not only in his nonfiction but in almost all his novels.

Prelude to Space, revised in 1954 but mostly written in the bleak post-war Britain of 1947, includes a lyrical vision of what the first manned lunar landing might mean to humanity:

"Out of the fears and miseries of the Second Dark Age, drawing free—oh, might it be forever!—from the shadows of Belsen and Hiroshima, the world was moving towards its most splendid sunrise. After five hundred years, the Renaissance has come again."

It didn't work out that way, of course, and his sentiments now seem naive. But as Clarke says himself, he is proud not to have become a cynic. If the idealism in his fiction has turned out untrue-to-life, I cannot see this as a failing on his part. I prefer to blame the world leaders whose lack of imagination and spirit molded our real-life future, falling so far short of Clarke's grand vision of how things could have been.

Historical Context

The only time I met Arthur Clarke in person was during the late 1960s at a science-fiction social event in a London pub. Although *2001: A Space Odyssey* had not yet been released, he had finished his work on it and was already feeling like a celebrity. As he moved around the bar chatting briefly with people whom he knew from writing for fanzines in his childhood days, he seemed very self-possessed and casually confident. The only thing that troubled him was deafness in one ear, incurred when he damaged an eardrum while pearl diving off the Great Barrier Reef.

His novel *2010: Odyssey Two* was made into a movie in 1984. He did follow through with his plan to write another sequel, titled *2061: Odyssey Three*, which appeared in 1987. He finished the series with *3001: The Final Odyssey* in 1997. The latter employed the concept of cryonics, speculating that science in 3001 would be capable of rebuilding the brain of an astronaut who has been freeze-dried in space. Clarke once wrote a letter to a cryonics organization stating that "no one can quantify the probability of cryonics working, [but] I estimate it is at least 90%—and certainly nobody can say it is zero!" He made no arrangements for his own cryopreservation, however.

At the age of 85 he began working on a series of novels cowritten with Stephen Baxter, postulating that a race of aliens with almost godlike powers have been inhibiting the evolution of sentient life throughout the universe, with the objective of regulating energy consumption that would otherwise accelerate the process of entropy. His last literary work was a collaboration with Frederik Pohl titled *The Last Theorem*.

Suffering post-polio syndrome, Clarke was forced to use a wheelchair for much of his life after 1988. He died twenty years later of respiratory complications and heart failure.

Charles Platt

Stephen King

Bangor, Maine, May 3, 1982

HE BRINGS OUT a stack of fat, lurid paperbacks. "Look at this. Look what I just went out and bought." He holds one up and growls with heavy melodrama: "*They Thirst!* by Robert McCammon." He shakes his head, as if in regret. "I'm afraid I'm going to love this book. I've got a real taste for crap. I'll probably like it better than this one, *Blood Rubies*." He picks up another paperback. "But I'll probably like *this* one best of all. *Judgment Day* by Nick Sharman. I'll bet at some point somebody will get killed in a bathtub, and they'll turn black, and somebody else's fingers are going to *plunge into their writhing flesh*." He grins cheerfully.

I suppose this is the kind of thing you expect from Stephen King, especially if you've read *Danse Macabre*, his book about himself and horror fiction, in which he plays up his popular tastes and avoids any hint of academic literary analysis—even though he has the background to write it, if he should choose to.

But he chooses not to. He makes it clear that, regardless of his success and his money, he still goes out and buys books and gets off on cheap thrills like any other horror fan. He presents himself as an everyday American, just like the ones he writes about so compellingly and so sensitively in his own novels.

There's the catch, of course. No matter how hard he tries to be a regular guy, his rather special writing talent is still there to prove that he's anything but average. And when I talk of talent, I do not merely mean his flair for shocking people. His novella "Apt Pupil" in the *Different Seasons* collection makes it clear, if there was ever any doubt, that he can write fine prose of subtlety and precision. Personally, I think he's the best popular novelist we have, when it comes to capturing everyday life, truly understanding American character, and building a structure of modern myths on this foundation of gut-level reality. In his verisimilitude and in his fantasies, he expresses the essence of our times.

He might receive more praise from serious critics if he would spoil his books by making them more ponderous, less dramatic, more pretentious, and less fun. But he seems constitutionally opposed to any hint of snob-appeal, in his fiction and likewise in his lifestyle. He continues to live in Maine, and shuns the New York cocktail-party continuum that has served as a breeding ground for so many other effete literary reputations.

"One of the reasons I don't want to live in New York," he says, "is that I see it is a kind of literary party with these dickey birds that crawl all over you saying, 'Hey, come on out and let's have a few beers down at the Lion's Head', Or, 'Let's pop over to my apartment, and we'll do a few lines, and we'll talk about books.' But we won't *write* books, because we'll be doing lines and having a few beers at the Lion's Head.

"What writers really talk about is not art, anyway, but money. They want to know, 'What's your contract like? What kind of advertising budget are you getting?' I have always perceived the worst enemy of the writer to be the guys around him."

So he stays in Bangor, a town that still has some rough-and-ready, frontier feel to it, and he has a grand old house, with steps up to a big front porch with white pillars, and two turrets, one circular, one square—a rambling mansion which, inside, turns out to be furnished with almost anonymously contemporary American taste: nothing cheap, but nothing ostentatious, either.

King is tall, hunches his shoulders slightly as if shy of showing his height, and speaks more readily about reading or writing than about himself. His face is very expressive, switching quickly from mischievous dimples to a hint of melancholy. He sits out with us on the back porch, drinking beer, dressed in an old T-shirt and threadbare pink corduroy pants, while his kids play in the garden. He seems happy to be surrounded by family, and he chats in a deliberately relaxed fashion to myself and Douglas Winter (who arranged this interview and has used some of its material in his book *Faces of Fear*, published by Berkley, New York, 1985).

"Most people think that because I write horror, I must be weird," King tells us. "If they meet me, they take this kind of careful approach, like, 'Are you all right? You're not going to bite me, or anything like that?' A lot of times I feel that I'm disappointing them, in that I seem very mild-mannered and not very threatening. If only I had a little more of the Boris Karloff or Bela Lugosi charm, or something—even Christopher Lee!

"Of course, the other myth is that I must lead a very glamorous life, on the Riviera and all that. Well, it's a nice house, and a comfortable life, but it's not like something out of Rosemary Rogers. It's not the *glitterati*."

Someone as famous as Stephen King, of course, has already been interviewed endlessly, to the point where one might expect that he has nothing new to say. Yet his other interviews (and I've read a dozen of them) barely seem to scratch the surface, and his own *Danse Macabre* is shy of self-analysis.

Some readers may object that King writes horror, not science fiction, and thus has no place in this book. But as I've said before, I regard him as our preeminent modern myth-maker; and his work sometimes strays close to science fiction, even though he eschews its social scene.

"I've been at a couple of science-fiction conventions," he says, "and those people were out in a fucking *void*. There were people there who were literally separated from reality. Fundamentally, it seemed to me that they all felt alien, and maybe that is why they like science fiction. When you have people who belong to this Society for the Preservation of Creative Anachronisms, or whatever it is [a group that acts out medieval fantasies in full costume], I mean, those guys have blown their cogs! They're *gone*! If they didn't have people looking out for them, some of them would be committed."

He leans forward and adds, in self-parodying, confidential style, "A lot of them are *fat*, too. Have you ever noticed that at science-fiction conventions? There's always some dude that comes sort of boiling off the elevator, he's wearing Bib overalls, and he's nine feet wide. The floor shakes!

"I was never part of a fan network. I never had that kind of a support system. I grew up in a little town called Durham, which is about 150 miles from here. In a city, you find other people that are like you and like the same things. Then you get all this talk, talk, talk at club meetings, or conventions, and it's a dangerous thing. Everybody begins to reinforce everybody else, and starts to write about everybody else's characters. You develop a mythos. Whenever anybody develops a mythos, that means that the last ounce of creativity has expired somewhere. Like—Lin Carter forever!" He laughs.

He used to read science fiction, but not so much now.

"If I look at the first page and I see a lot of italics and sentences like, 'He chevvied his hamscammer and frotted over to Billegum'— I don't want to read a book where I have to learn a whole new vocabulary. So many people in the science-fiction field—I don't want to name names—are not very good writers. They're forgiven for writing awkwardly, or unoriginally, or a little bit boringly, because it's science fiction.

"But just because you work in a genre, you shouldn't be allowed to write poor prose. You shouldn't be allowed to say, 'I can write this kind of prose because, in the context of science fiction, it's great writing.'"

Perhaps science-fiction readers will resent this kind of

criticism from the man who's already confessed his weakness for books like *They Thirst*. But I suspect King of being a very analytical reader, even while he's claiming a craving for cheap thrills.

When he first started writing, he wrote science fiction.

"I think I must have been seven or eight. I was sick, just constantly sick, with the same thing I've got now—bronchitis. There was one year I didn't go to school, I just lay there in bed and wrote a lot of stories. I was very aware of how bad I was, so sometimes I would copy other people's stories, till someone told me, 'Oh, Stevie, that's *wrong*! You can go to *jail* for that!'

"I started to submit stuff when I was about twelve, to magazines like *Fantastic* or *Fantasy and Science Fiction*. Those stories had the trappings of science fiction, they were set in outer space, but they were really horror stories. One of the few good ones was about an asteroid miner who discovered a pink cube, and all this stuff started to come out of the cube and drive him back further and further into his little space hut, breaching the airlocks one after another. And the thing got him in the end. All the science-fiction magazines sent it back, because they knew goddamn well there was no science in it, there were no aliens trying to communicate using psionic talents, or anything like that. There was just this big pink thing that was going to eat someone, and it ate him.

"I used to imitate everything that I liked. I would have short stories where I started off sounding like Ray Bradbury and ended up sounding like Clark Ashton Smith. Or even worse, they would start off as James Cain and end as H. P. Lovecraft. I was just silly putty. And still today, there will be reviews that say, 'The kindest thing we can say about Steve King is that he doesn't have much of a style.' I never have, and I know that. But I think there's a lot of critical interest in writing that's pretty, rather than writing that's serviceable, and I'm more interested in stripping down. I don't want people to see my face in the book at all."

In fact he seems to go out of his way to write in the most popular, colloquial idiom, as if anything else would run the risk of seeming pretentious. For some reason that I can't pin down, pretentiousness bothers him a lot. It's the one topic that he is evidently reluctant to talk about.

"When someone tries to make a 'thing' about being a writer, that's bad enough," he says. "What's even worse is if people call you an *author*, and you let them do that. That's terrible!

"In college I would go around with a John D. MacDonald book, or a collection of short stories by Robert Bloch, and some asshole would always say, 'Why are you reading that?' And I'd say, 'Hey, this man is a great writer.' And in fact MacDonald has written a novel called *The End of the Night* which I would argue is one of the greatest American novels of the twentieth century. It ranks with *Death of a Salesman*; it ranks with *An American Tragedy*.

"But people would see the picture on the front, a Gold Medal paperback with some lady with her cakes falling out of her blouse, and they would say, 'It's garbage.' So I'd say, 'Have you read anything by this guy?' 'No, all I gotta do is look at that book, and I know.' Which was my first experience with critics, in this case my teachers at college.

"I always liked that kind of fiction, and that's what I always wanted to write. There ought to be a middle ground, where you can do it with some nobility, instead of either a) being a schlockmeister or b) saying 'Hey, everybody's just *saying* that I'm only a popular writer. They don't understand how sensitive my soul is.' There ought to be a place in the middle where you can say, 'I'm trying to do the best I can with what I've got, and create things that are at least as honest as what any craftsman would make.'"

In his novella "The Body," in the *Different Seasons* collection, King includes what appears to be one of his own very early short stories—and mocks its slightly self-important strivings as being "painfully sophomoric.... Could anything be more *serious*? More *lit'ry*?"—as if that is the ultimate embarrassment.

"The Body" also depicts a seemingly autobiographical childhood among lower-middle-class, dead-end kids: an almost anti-literary background, where there would have been no place for anyone who indulged in affectations.

"In the family that I came from," he says, "there was a high premium on keeping yourself to yourself. I hung out with the kids, I worked on cars, I played sports—I had to play football, because I was big. If you didn't play football, and you were big, that meant you were a fucking faggot, right? Inside, I felt different and unhappy a lot of times. But I kept that part of myself to myself. I never wanted to let anybody get at it. I figured they'd steal it, if they knew what I thought about this or that or the other thing. It wasn't the same thing as being embarrassed about it, so much as wanting to keep it and sort of work it out for myself.

"I could write, and this was the way I defined myself, even as a kid. Maybe I couldn't put one past the centerfielder, and maybe all I was good for in football was left tackle. You know, I used to get cleat marks up my back. But I could write, and that is still how I define myself, and that's a danger, because you tie up you self-image, your masculinity, whatever, in being able to do this, which means that if you lose it, you have nothing left.

"After *Carrie* was published, my wife Tabby got very exasperated with me, saying, 'You've made all this money, you are a success, let's spend some of it.' But I was insecure inside, for a long time, saying, 'Look, I don't trust this. Nobody can do this. You can't do this twice or three times.' My idea was, the success would never happen again, so I should trickle the money out. Maybe the kids would be eating Cheerios and peanut butter for dinner, but—that's okay! Let them! I'll be *writing*."

And then, as if feeling that all this is beginning to sound too serious, he adds:

"I've always regarded being a writer as a twitch, like being able to do this." (He wiggles his thumb, which is double-jointed.) "It so happens that *that*"—he wiggles it again—"doesn't make any money. But the ability or the desire to write everything down is that same kind of a twitch."

I ask him if, like some other writers, he feels he is writing for a particular person.

"I think that there might be. I really think it's myself; but there does seem to be a target that this stuff pours out toward. I am always interested in this idea that a lot of fiction writers write for their fathers, because their fathers are gone." (King's own father left the family when he was an infant.) "I don't know if there is anything to that or not. But there is that feeling of it going out toward a point, when it's the best."

This seems to be as complete a statement about the creative process as anyone could ask for, so we tackle the next topic, which has to be the obvious one: horror novels. What does he feel is the most important element in horror?

"Character. You have got to love the people in the story, because there is no horror without love and without feeling. Horror is the contrasting emotion to our understanding of all the things that are good and normal.

"If you can't bring on characters that people believe and accept as part of the normal spectrum, then you can't write horror. This is a problem that a lot of the supermarket novels have: you don't believe the people, and therefore you don't believe the horror, and you're not scared."

So King's work is almost always about everyday characters in everyday settings with which the reader can identify fully. For some people, though, his work can become a little *too* real.

"I got a really strong reaction to the "Apt Pupil" story in *Different Seasons*. My publisher called and protested. I said, 'Well, do you think it's anti-Semitic?' Because it's about a Nazi war criminal, and he begins to spout all the old bullshit, once the kid in the story gets him going. But that wasn't the problem. It was too *real*. If the same story had been set in outer space, it would have been okay, because then you'd have had that comforting layer of 'This is just make-believe, so we can dismiss it.'

"So they were very disturbed by the piece, and I thought to

myself, 'Gee, I've done it again. I've written something that has really gotten under someone's skin.' And I do like that. I like the feeling that I reached right between somebody's legs"—he makes a graphic, grabbing motion—"like that. There has always been that primitive impulse as part of my writing."

The renewed popularity of horror is still relatively recent, of course. Some writers in *Dream Makers* have complained that their work won't fit the fiction categories, and suffers as a result. King's answer, as things worked out, was to develop a fiction category of his own, to fit his work. He knows how things would have been if he'd been writing at a different time.

"In the 1950s, they would have gotten the manuscript of *'Salem's Lot* and they would have cut it in half and published it as a 'Crime Club' title, and I would have made fifteen hundred dollars. There's a novel by Richardson Matheson, *A Stir of Echoes*, published as a 'Crime Club' in the 1950s. Nobody would touch it. But now they can call it a 'horror novel' and it's commercial. And the critics buy that completely. The critics will buy almost anything that a publicist puts in front of them."

At first, he seems reluctant to complain about criticism that he's received. Yet there are obviously some hard feelings.

"Some critics seem to feel that something very popular can't really be good, because that low common denominator is represented by people like Sidney Sheldon, Jacqueline Susann, people who are not good.

"But I'm convinced that most of the critics who review popular fiction have no understanding of it as a whole. They don't seem to have a grounding in it. They seem almost illiterate in some fields. There's so much popular fiction that nobody even sees, because it doesn't hit the *Times* best seller list. There are books that are not best sellers, that *are* popular fiction, that are wonderful novels, wonderful stories. There's a guy named Don Robertson; I think he's one of the most interesting writers in the country. There's a horror writer that even people in the field haven't read;

he wrote *The Beguiled* and his name is Thomas Culenin, and he's an interesting writer. A Southern gothicist. I mentioned him in *Danse Macabre*. And nobody has ever reviewed a novel by Michael McDowell in the critical press, that I know of, and I think he's one of the top-drawer novelists in the country right now. There is nobody writing any better books in paperback-original than he is; but he's not reviewed.

"I'm not much on the cult of personality, but if you work hard on a book, you hate to see it dismissed in three or four paragraphs, or not reviewed at all. I haven't had a book reviewed in *The New York Times* Sunday book review since *The Stand*, and that review was about three paragraphs long, and I'm morally certain that the guy didn't read the book, or did a skim job.

"After a while, if you live long enough, by the time you're so old that you've begun to parody yourself or have actually begun to degenerate as a writer, and you and your contemporaries have all had your strokes and your heart attacks, *then* people start reviewing you well—mostly because you've survived the demolition derby. That's when you get good reviews: after you've done your important work."

He adds that some critics seem to resent his books simply because publishers pay so much for them. So he sold his next novel *Christine* for a *one-dollar* advance. In due course, it will earn royalties as a percentage of the cover price of each book sold; but there's no money up front for critics to complain about, and he'll be paid only in proportion to the number of people who actually buy the novel.

I feel he'd rather trust the judgment of an average book-buyer than that of a critic—or even an editor, for that matter.

"A lot of hardcover editors seem to me to have very Ivy League sensibilities. It used to be that at least they would bring out decent novels, even if those novels didn't sell much more than 2,000 copies. But now they're saying"—he goes into a snobbish accent—"'Well, all right, we must publish these awful potboilers, so we'll choose them.' And they pick out the worst, most awful, abysmal books to push. I'm not talking about best sellers—I'm talking about the ones that are pushed really hard and do *not* become best sellers. There was one by a guy named William Kinsolving called *Born with the Century*. It has got to be one of the most dreadful pieces of trash. It makes *Princess Daisy* look like *War and Peace*. And yet somebody thought it would be a big money-maker, because they don't have any understanding of popular taste—the understanding that we would have from what we pick out on the newsstands. These editors don't go to the newsstands. Ask a hardcover editor what he's read and in most cases he'll say, 'Well, I've been working my way through Henry James for the fifth time, and otherwise I don't have time to read anything but manuscripts.'

"The truth is that the level of taste, in the general body of people who read in this country, is a little bit higher than most hardcover editors, in their ignorance, are willing to admit. The real bad stuff won't sell. But the American public *will* respond to quality popular literature. For instance, *Watership Down* was a big best seller."

It might seem that someone as successful as Stephen King would no longer have any difficulties dealing with editors, so far as his own work is concerned. And yet success creates new problems of its own.

"I like to write three drafts: a first, a second, and what I think of as the editorial draft, when I sit down and take an editor's criticism and work it through in my own mind, and put the whole book through the typewriter again, and repolish the other stuff as well. But as the successes have mushroomed, it's been tougher and tougher for me to get my editors to give me time to do that third draft. What I'm really afraid of now is that one of them will say, 'I think this is great', just because it fits the publication schedule. Every year, I'm on a faster and faster track. I'm supposed to get proofs of *Different Seasons* today. It's a 600-page book but Viking wants the proofs read in five days, so they can take advantage of coop advertising between the paperback house, themselves, and the movie company that's releasing *Creepshow*. They're going to have Bernie Wrightson's *Creepshow* comic book, and the hardcover of *Different Seasons*, and the paperback of *Cujo*, in 3,200 dump bins, not only in bookstores but Shop 'n' Saves or something. So therefore I am supposed to read the proofs in five days. Now, what if we let a bunch of dumb errors go through? It isn't a matter of creativity, or trying to do the best book possible, that's governing things right now—it's advertising. And that scares the hell out of me, because we'll fuck up real good one of these days, and then people can say 'Steven King writes for money', and at that point *they will be right*.

"In the case of the last couple of books that Viking has done, the hardcover sales have been enormous. There've been like 385,000 copies in hardcover. So we're talking about a gross which would be $13.95 times 385,000. This is important enough so that, at this point, I think that if there was any change suggested to me that I didn't want, all I would need to say would be, 'No. I won't do that.' And it would never be a question of their withdrawing my contract, would it? They'd just finally say, 'Well, okay then, don't do it that way.' Which means, in effect, that if I'm willing to be really intransigent, there'll be no editing at all."

Some writers might see this as an ideal position of power. But King recognizes the dangers of no longer being subject to any editorial feedback.

"It's a terrible position to be in. I think I just have to resolve to take editing, even if I think the changes are wrong. To do otherwise is to become a monster and claim that I'm doing it right, and I don't need any criticism, editorial help, or guidance. And I can't do that.

"On the other hand, I say to myself, 'Well, the things that I do are the things that have made me a success.' And if somebody wants to tamper with that, maybe they're wrong."

The writer-editor relationship has been a recurring theme in *Dream Makers*, as I have tried to show how compromises occur between what a writer wants, and what an editor thinks the readers will want. Stephen King, of course, no longer needs to worry too much about having his work rejected, or having to tailor his books to suit the needs of the market—he *is* the market, or at least a large segment of it. But his comment about allowing himself to be edited demonstrates that, no matter how important a writer becomes, his writing still does not exist in isolation. There is always a subtle interplay; the process by which a book is published still leaves its mark on that book.

Stephen King prefaces his *Different Seasons* collection with the rather modest motto: "It is the tale, not he who tells it." However, as his own profile shows so clearly, the tale *is* he who tells it; and it is also a product of commercial constraints, financial pressures, and other practical factors that poison or fertilize the creative process.

I have tried to pinpoint some of these factors in the profiles I've presented here, as well as portraying the dream makers whose inspiration and talent will always remain the most important factor of all.

Historical Context

Douglas E. Winter, who arranged this interview, was an attorney who worked for Covington and Burling, the highly prestigious law firm in Washington, DC. What he really wanted, though, was to write horror novels. I don't remember how he established contact with Stephen King, but he invited me along, and we agreed that each of us would write his own version of the profile, splitting the taped material 50-50.

I wrote my version first and sent it to Doug, who was somewhat dismayed. "You used all the best quotes," he complained.

"What did you expect?" I said. "Did you think I would just use the less-interesting ones?"

"We were going to split it 50-50."

"Well, I only took half. I just took the good half!"

We resolved this issue on a friendly basis. This entailed me giving up some of the material, which I think made it into Doug's book, *Faces of Fear*, which was the equivalent of *Dream Makers* in the horror genre.

One topic that I didn't include here was the issue of King's first three novels, which had supposedly never been published.

During the interview, when Doug asked about this, King told us to turn off our tape recorders. "All of those books are now in print," he said.

Subsequently the rumor circulated that they had been published under the name Richard Bachman. King was eventually forced to admit it, and when his secret identity was no longer a secret, the novels that had languished in obscurity became immediately successful, confirming the outlook on the publishing industry that he expressed in our interview.

He remains one of my favorite authors, and if his sensitivity and his talent for evoking realism could be emulated by more science-fiction writers, I would be reading more science fiction.

As for my friend Douglas Winter, he wrote the definitive biography of Stephen King, titled *The Art of Darkness*, and he wrote a novel titled *Run* that was published by Knopf in 2000. He also continues to work as an attorney.

Charles Platt

James Tiptree Jr.

McLean, Virginia, June 8, 1982 and subsequently

IN 1967 A woman named Alice Sheldon began writing stories under the name James Tiptree, Jr. She kept her real identity secret from everyone in the world except for her husband. She established a post office box and a bank account for "Tiptree," and she hid behind that name for ten years, while her remarkable stories attracted acclaim and awards. Had it not been for some detective work by a science-fiction fan, she would still be hiding from us now.

Pseudonyms are common enough, of course. Sometimes a writer wants a more glamorous name, or uses different bylines for different categories of fiction. Either way, it's seldom a big secret. Even writers who seek privacy will usually stop short of becoming totally anonymous.

But Alice Sheldon is not like most other writers.

She and her husband live a few miles outside Washington, D.C., close to the headquarters of the CIA, where both of them used to work. Perhaps it's only natural for a one-time agency employee to want to write anonymously. As I journey to interview Alice Sheldon at her home, I wonder if this is the whole explanation, or if there were deeper motives behind the male name. Even now, five years after her identity became known, she has never been interviewed in person.

She turns out to be a strikingly beautiful woman. Only a slight trace of gray at the edges of her curly red hair betrays that she might now be over sixty. She has compassionate eyes, and a quick smile; her manner is forthright, with a touch of elegance. She stands with a scrupulously correct military posture, suggesting a refusal to recognize weakness or adversity.

Together with her husband, whose diffident manner and bushy white beard conceal a sharp mind and wit, she shows me around their home, which they designed themselves. It gives the sense of being outdoors, inside; there are large open spaces, large panels of glass, a floor of polished concrete (aesthetic in its simple practicality), a wood-burning stove, and a huge brick-walled pond of multicolored fish. She shows me how to feed a carp so that it nibbles my fingers.

We walk out into a garden full of exotic flowers and trees. Raccoons live in the woods beyond the lawn; she likes to treat them to dogfood and peanut-buttered crackers. In the pines and willows, birds of blue and scarlet call to one another.

As we exchange the smalltalk of strangers, I sense she is discreetly weighing me up. In addition to working for the CIA, she was a behavioral psychologist. Her fiction has been sometimes playful, sometimes formidably perceptive, and I have a suspicion that the same is true of her.

As if to confirm it, she casually mentions some obscure events in my own past history. She's *checked up on me* somehow, to even the score between interviewer and interviewee. When I ask where she discovered the details, she just laughs teasingly and changes the subject. [This interview was conducted long before the world-wide web enabled anyone to find out about anyone.]

Changing the subject turns out to be one of her greatest talents. A casual comment about goldfish provokes a little lecture on the mechanism of growth-suppressing hormones. Mention of horses inspires a dissertation on the equitation seat and the cruelty of Arab harnesses. By the time we start the actual interview, I've come to realize that these anecdotes are a form of evasion: she's shy of talking about herself, and switches instinctively to any other topic. And then she stops and apologizes. She wants to do the interview properly, because she is, I think, a woman with a strong sense of duty—as becomes obvious after our in-person conversation is over. She writes me letters, she asks for the tape transcript and returns it covered in amendments, she sends me transcripts of subsequent interviews with other people, and I end up recording three more conversations with her over the phone.

Writing this now, I'm faced with 103 pages (25,000 words) of my own tape transcripts, plus an equal quantity of other transcripts and written material from her, including muddy Xeroxes, letters in tiny, neat handwriting on exuberantly colorful stationery, endearing little postcards, a haphazard bibliography—everything annotated with extra remarks in the margins and on slips of paper taped at the bottoms of pages, as if she became more and more obsessed with the task of telling this story truly and completely.

The trouble is, Alice Sheldon's remarkable life is too big for a profile. As she has described it herself, rather modestly in the third person, for *Contemporary Authors*:

> *She found herself interacting with...lepers, black royalty in lion skins, white royalty in tweeds, Arab slaves, functional saints and madmen in power, poets, killers, collared eunuchs, world-famous actors with head colds, blacks who ate their enemies and a white who had eaten his friends; and above all, women: chattel-women deliberately starved, deformed, blinded, and enslaved; women in nuns' habits saving the world; an Englishwoman in bloomers riding out from her castle at the head of personal Moslem army; women, from the routinely tortured, obscenely mutilated slave-wives of the 'advanced' Kikuyu, to the free, propertied Sumatran matriarchs who ran the economy and brought 600 years of peaceful prosperity to the Menang-Kabaui; all these were known before she had a friend or playmate of her own age.*

She was the daughter of Herbert Edwin Bradley, an attorney and explorer, and Mary Wilhelmina Hastings Bradley, a writer who taught herself everything from foreign languages to big-game hunting. With them, she saw more of the world by the time she was ten than most of us will ever see.

"Mother and Father dreamed about Africa when they were in their own youths. They became enamored of Carl Akeley, an ornery, cantankerous man, but a multi-faceted genius—one wing of the American Museum of Natural History in New York City is named after him, and devoted to him. His final expedition was in search of the black gorillas of the mountains of Uganda; Father had made a little money in real estate, and said he would finance Akeley if Akeley would take him plus two scientists from Princeton. Somehow, the two scientists turned into me and Mother.

"We walked 2,700 miles across Africa, and had 250 porters, carrying sixty-pound loads, because that's what it takes to maintain you for a one-year safari, living on the country. No radios or planes or any means of rescue existed then; all roads, phones, and electricity ended at the coast; and in the interior there were no maps, towns, or landmarks, only foot trails made by the slavers.

"In a sense I was badly brought up because, by the age of five, if I dropped something I was quite accustomed to clap my hands and have six large, naked cannibals spring to attention and pick it up for me. And I considered it quite normal to have thirty natives watch me having my hair brushed every morning. My hair was so strange, almost white, they weren't quite sure if I was a child or some kind of goddess.

"Mother wrote thirty-five books, including five about Africa. She was the first to state in print, 'Gorillas are tame, delightful creatures, and we've had lunch sitting within ten feet of a troupe of them.'"

Alice Sheldon goes to one of many shelves of books in the converted sun porch at the back of the house, where she works amid piles of papers and overdue mail stacked in big plastic trays.

One tray is labeled "For God's sake read these and answer them!"

She pulls out one of her mother's books: *Alice in Jungle Land.* "This one she wrote about me. It has my line drawings in it, and photographs—there's me, riding a baby elephant. I had crepe-de-chine bloomers on, and they made me ride the bloody thing.

"Once, I ran away; I got into a good patch of elephant grass, where I made a secret house by crushing the grass down. Mother led a search after me and hauled me back out. You know, being hauled out of my James Tiptree retreat, when everyone found out who I was and I had to go back to being Alice Sheldon, was a similar feeling. I guess I cried, if it doesn't sound too soapy.

"I really don't like people paying attention to me. It probably comes from the experience of growing up in Africa, with my parents and their adult companions; I had the feeling of being on a microscope plate, with these six enormous eyepieces goggling down at me. I was my parents' precious child, and I was never left alone, because they'd lost the other nine through miscarriages— they had an Rh problem. I was a classic example of the 'Hartley Coleridge Bind,' which makes children of high achievers so lucrative to psychotherapists."

She felt obliged to equal the achievements of her remarkable mother. "She was a small, red-haired, blue-eyed person, the kind you help through doors, and then discover she can carry a Springfield rifle and walk forty-five miles hunting elephants, and do it again the next day while her first day's partner is resting up in bed, and then do it the next day, and the day after that. Even as a child, without meaning to, you compete."

At the same time, she tried to meet the expectations of her father—who, she learned later, had always wanted a son. "Every time I did anything boy-like, like going into the Army, Father approved deeply."

To these family pressures were added some traumatic traveling experiences. In India: "I remember the streets of Calcutta, which I saw at age nine. As we went for some morning sweet cake, we'd step over dying people with dying babies in their arms, each living their whole lives on one square yard of sidewalk."

In Africa: "The first people I ever saw dead had been accused of witchcraft or thievery. The belief in witchcraft is the curse of African society; it gives free rein to all the paranoid impulses. These two people had first been tortured, then crucified, on horrible little bushes stuck through their vitals, and flies were crawling over them. At age nine or ten, this makes an impression.

"One effect of this kind of thing," she continues with a smile, as if to downplay it, "is that I have been very gullible and naive all my life. I knew, as facts, so many weird things, that I would believe anything. I had seen people burning their grandmothers on the steppes of the Ganges, so I was honestly a little surprised when my grandmother died and they buried her in a grave in a cemetery instead of burning her on the steppes of the Chicago River."

By the time she was twelve, "I had just about had it. I didn't realize that my parents, in the name of love, had dumped their accumulated nervous tensions onto me. I got razor blades and put them in the back of a five-pound history book, and brought it down, sawed and sawed—I was so stupid, I tried this side first." She shows the top side of her wrist, where even now there are thin white scars. "But," she adds quickly, not wanting to suggest that she was courting sympathy or creating a fuss, "I must add, there wasn't any hurrah. I came to, cleaned up the mess, and went to class."

To escape the parental influence, she asked to go to a Swiss school. "I had an unpleasant tendency to be smart, because that was something Mother and Father praised. I didn't know how to talk or act around people of my own age. I was always the youngest, and I never had the sense to be unobtrusive. My little hand would always shoot up if I knew the answer, and the more desperate I got, the cleverer I acted. Like a rat, when the little food pellets give out—he still goes on punching that same button."

And so she was ostracized by the other kids. "I was lonesome and did a great deal of experimenting with getting killed. I would

340

go down to the railroad track, and see how close I could stand when the train to Geneva went through. Every night I would stand closer, and one night something just brushed me, like a feather, except of course it was going past at about a hundred miles an hour."

Later, at Sarah Lawrence College, she still found it hard to fit in. "I was known as 'That Girl' and nobody would room with me. I wasn't in the art club, for example, although by this time I was a selling painter."

She found a strange consolation in the indifference of the universe.

"I was a great one for running off from parties and finding a local cemetery or lawn, where I would lie down—even if there was snow on the ground—and look up at the stars. I'd think, 'There's Sirius, and Sirius looks on all things, and *Sirius doesn't care.*' My life, my death—Sirius was utterly indifferent. And that was so comforting; the cold indifference of those stars, I actually felt it, all down my front."

She married for the first time while still at Sarah Lawrence. "I was made into a debutante, and I thought that meant I was on the slave block, so I married the first boy that asked me, three days later. I'd seen him for seven hours. He'd been seated on my left at the party, he was certified as a poet and a gentleman by the president of Princeton, so I ran off and married him in Waukegan. Broke my mother's heart, because she'd given me the most expensive debutante party ever seen, in the middle of the Depression, and had intended a grand tour to follow, culminating in my presentation at the English court, to the King, with three feathers on my head. Anyway, I married this beautiful but absolute idiot—what they hadn't mentioned in the documentation was that he was maintaining half the whores in Trenton and was an alcoholic."

She got divorced in 1938. Having published graphic art in *The New Yorker*, she worked to refine her painting in oils, and exhibited and sold her work in Washington, D.C. and Chicago. Then, in

1942, she enlisted in the U.S. Army and was "the first women ever put through Air Force Intelligence School at Harrisburg, with thirty-five men who had nothing better to do than watch me." She became a photo-intelligence officer and started work "literally, in the cellar at the Pentagon," interpreting high-altitude photographs of the Far East for use in bombing sorties.

In 1945, she joined the Air Staff Post-Hostilities Project, devised by its commander, Colonel Huntington D. Sheldon, who had been Deputy Chief of Air Intelligence in the European Theatre. His aim was to seize and bring back to the U.S. as much German secret scientific research and personnel as possible, including atomic physicists, the first operational jet aircraft, and rocket technology. Without his initiative, most of this knowledge and material would have been lost to the Soviet occupation of East Germany.

Alice Hastings Bradley married Huntington D. Sheldon in a French mayor's office, very shortly after she had begun working in his project. They remain married to this day, a very strikingly close and devoted couple.

After the war, she and he left the military and ran their own small business for a while. But in 1952, "They'd been after Ting, and after him, to come back to Washington and help start what was then not yet formed: the CIA. All we'd had 'til then was the OSS, full of aged cowboys who wanted to do it like we did it in Dusseldorf. Ting finally joined the CIA at supergrade level; I was at mere technical level, helping to start up their photo-intelligence capability, which was then evaluating captured German air photography of the U.S.S.R.

"It was an awfully hectic life. Since the Russians are always doing something at two in the morning our time, that blasted loud-ringing telephone would go off, and I'd hear Ting murmuring in the pillow, 'I guess you'd better get the President on this one, John. All right, we'll put the watch staff together.' And then he'd be up and dressing and on his way. And then I would be on my way at eight in the morning to *my* rather harassing job.

"After we had the department set up and running, I got bored with it. So I played games on the clandestine side for a bit."

Wondering if she means that she did actual espionage work, I ask if she was sent out of the country.

"No, no, I was just—on the clandestine side." For the first time, she is shy of speaking. "I stayed in the United States. Mostly I was being trained."

I ask if she's allowed to say what she was actually doing.

"No. Except that it was not James Bondish, really. It probably would have eventuated into a little James Bondism, but...."

Was she commissioning people to go out and get information? Or was she just interpreting results?

"Neither. I was working up files on people. That's the clandestine side; the covert side does all the interpretation and evaluation. That's why the Bay of Pigs happened, because the clandestine side took control, got out from under, because Allen Dulles was the clandestine type, and totally end-ran the evaluation process, which was saying 'No such effort can succeed.'

"My photo-intelligence work had been a clean, harmless contest of skills. No one had been blackmailed or coerced, or even endangered. It had no more moral ambiguity than looking over the neighbor's fence and counting his laundry. But the clandestine side, dealing in assassinations and military operations, actually strikes me as wholly inappropriate to intelligence work, and its long-range effect tends to discredit the nation that employs it with anything less than superhuman care."

So for a little while she was actually out in the field—wherever 'the field' was.

"Well, I—I was around." She laughs. "But after I got started there, I realized that what I wanted to learn was not intelligence of the military sort, in which I include our civilian agency. I wanted to find out secrets that were in *nobody's* head. I wanted to do basic science.

"When I had finished being an artist, I was left with many

questions about perception: why is a spot of orange up in the left-hand corner very good, when a spot of blue wouldn't be? What *is* the perceptual evaluative mechanism? I developed the modest aim of knowing more about visual perception than anybody in the world, before I was dead."

So at this point she went back to college?

"At this point, I said, 'The hell with it.' I left a safe open one night. Twenty minutes later, I checked it, and caught it. But I'd never done that before in my life, and I said, 'My innards are telling me something.' So I wrote a two-line letter of resignation, and ran away from *everybody*. I used the techniques the CIA had taught me, and in half a day I had a false name, a false bank account, a false social security card, and had rented an apartment and moved in. I was somebody else."

I comment that this reminds me of the retreat she built as a child in the elephant grass.

"Yes, very much. I wanted to think. So I thought, then I got back in touch with my husband, and we thought together, and decided we could really work things out.

"To do what I wanted to do, I needed a doctorate in experimental psychology. I was in my late forties, but I was helped into a predoctoral fellowship at the National Institute of Health, the only snag being that I had to get straight A's. You can be young and stupid, or old and smart; I was old, so I had to be smart. I did get a lot of honors—I graduated summa cum laude, and I had a Ph.D. magna cum laude. My husband was an incredible emotional and practical help through all of this, so deeply supportive, I couldn't have done any of it without him. I don't think I'd even be *alive* now, without him.

"I dragged out the predoctoral fellowship, long after I finished my Ph.D. exams, so that I could do four years of solid research, and I'll tell you, there is no greater thrill I've ever had than to stand bare-faced in front of Nature and say, 'I think this is the way your creations work; tell me, am I right?' and Nature grumblingly and reluctantly makes you do—as I did—thirteen different paradigms of the god damned experiment before you get the thing without any uncontrolled variables, and then finally says, in answer to your question, a clear-cut 'Yes.' That is the most thrilling moment I have ever had in my whole life."

The experiment that she devised was to debunk an item of orthodox wisdom which held that, because laboratory rats will cluster around anything new that is put in their cage, animals must be generally attracted to novelty. Alice Sheldon had observed for herself that wild animals *avoided* novelty; her experiment finally established that animals in a safe, familiar environment will go to the novel stimulus, while animals in an unsafe environment prefer things that they know. "This sounds like common sense—which is typical of many behavioral findings that take months or years to prove under strict experimental control."

But behind the experiment was her interest in human perceptions. Why, for example, does the public first shun a painter's work, and then decide that his paintings are worth millions, after he has died a pauper?

Sadly, she was unable to continue her research. "As a new Ph.D. I had to teach monster classes of education students who could barely count their toes." She applied herself to the task with her usual sense of duty. "I tried and I tried. The teaching was emotionally draining. I also had to renew my grant, and grantsmanship is a terrible job. I saw no way to do research again in the next five years, and I just burned out. I was too old. I had to quit for health reasons, which caused me great sadness for two or three years."

But by this time she had sold some science fiction. The first four stories had been written, in a fit of defiant bravado, during her Ph.D. exams.

"We had a torture rite at GW. You took five exams, one every forty-eight hours, each lasting a whole day, on a different field of psychology. One boy lost all his wisdom teeth, another broke out in

345

blood all over his shirt front, other people had less spectacular troubles. I wrote my first science-fiction story."

She had been reading science fiction since she was ten years old. "I always felt a mystic glow about being a science-fiction writer. I've had a story in *The New Yorker*, and I used to write a page of art criticism every week in the *Chicago Sun*, but to be published in that cruddy little blotting-paper magazine sent shivers up and down my spine. People reading *my* story—I still don't believe it, you know? As the rich man's mistress said, 'Even if it is only carbon crystallized under immense pressure and heat—*I want it!*' "

And yet she chose to publish all her fiction behind the most closely-guarded pseudonym. This, of course, was consistent with her desire to retreat and not be observed; 'James Tiptree' was yet another patch of elephant grass.

Why did she choose a *male* name? At first, she ducks this question.

"I thought, well, the editor will send this stuff back, so I'd better use a false name, and then I can try the next story with a different name, so he won't remember having rejected me."

When pressed, she goes further.

"A male name seemed like good camouflage. I had the feeling that a man would slip by less observed. I've had too many experiences in my life of being the first woman in some damned occupation; even when I wasn't the first woman, I was part of a group of first women."

And finally, when I *really* press her on the subject:

"I simply saw the name on some jam pots. Ting was with me; I said, 'James Tiptree' and he says—'Junior!' It was done so quickly, without conscious thought; but I suppose I couldn't have avoided having the thought—although I don't remember it—that the editor would take my stories more seriously."

She was sincerely astonished when all her first stories were accepted. She started spending more time on her writing, and developed deeper themes, which were sometimes complicated by her posing as a man. "I was faced with all these mysterious male drives and conventions that I didn't share, but I squeaked around that by making the male narrator old in most cases. The country of the old was the country of the dead, to most of my readers, who figure life ends about forty, so anything I ascribed to an older man, they would believe. Also, the glandular systems of older men and woman are more alike. Being older myself, I naturally tended to use universal motives, as in that story 'Mother in the Sky with Diamonds,' where a man is trying to save his wretched old mother from a heartless tyranny.

"However, men have so pre-empted the area of human experience that when you write about universal motives, you are assumed to be writing like a man. And so when my identity was revealed, some people said it proved that a woman could write like a man. Now, in the first place, this assumes that I was *trying* to write like a man, which was the last thing I was trying to do. I was writing like myself, with the exception of deliberate male details here and there. Other critics talked about my 'narrative drive' as being a male writing style, but narrative drive is simply intensity, and a desire not to bore. It has never been confined to men. Take one of the first women utterers that we know about: Cassandra. *She* was never accused of a lack of narrative drive. She was just a little before her time, which is often what women's crimes consist of."

"James Tiptree" soon started attracting attention as a new writer of exceptional power and skill, and letters began arriving at the post office box, offering praise—and asking awkward questions. Alice Sheldon was characteristically scrupulous in her replies. "Everything I said to everybody was true, with the exception of the gender implied in the signature. I never *stated* I was a man." And to avoid lying, she gave "Tiptree" her own life history—which was her undoing. In 1977 Jeffrey D. Smith, a fan of the Tiptree stories (and now a close friend) saw an obituary of Alice Sheldon's mother in a Chicago newspaper. The details were too close to the known facts of "Tiptree's" mother to be a coincidence; and so Alice Sheldon was unmasked.

"The feminist world was excited because, merely by having existed unchallenged for ten years, 'Tiptree' had shot the stuffing out of male stereotypes of women writers. At the same time, the more vulnerable males decided that 'Tiptree' had been much overrated. They sullenly retired to practice patronizing smiles."

I ask her if there were any other feminist reactions.

"Ursula Le Guin said it was sort of embarrassing to have kicked me out of the feminist letter that was going around a few years previously. They'd asked me please to leave because, as a man, 'Tiptree' just didn't have the basic sympathy! Also I had started talking about mothers, which none of them liked to talk about. I'm not a mother myself—I was prevented from being a mother by a healthy case of peritonitis which I contracted in the middle of the Mojave Desert one August. But I have great respect for mothers, and a serious interest in the whole subject."

I ask her if she was influenced by any science fiction in particular, when she began writing.

"When you say that, what passes before my mind is simply a marvelous pageant, all mixed up and jumbled together. Sturgeon, especially, and the early Philip K. Dick, and Damon Knight, were big influences. Frederik Pohl helped me enormously. The early Barry Malzberg I liked very much; I corresponded with him when I was a man. And the very freaky stuff—I liked things that I couldn't do. Some of your British people. The Vermilion Sands chap— Ballard. And Moorcock, except that I began to realize that some his work was stunty; the Cornelius stories never rang true.

"Then of course there's the great neglected work, *Bill, the Galactic Hero* by Harry Harrison. What a rodomontade. It's almost *Dr. Strangelove.* Of course, you see, I'm a frustrated comedian, and a really good black comedy, I eat it up. My own early stories, the shallow belly laughs, I esteem rather more than my critics do—a good laugh is rare. Not to be sneered at.

"When I started writing, I felt as if I were peeling away layers

348

of myself, like an onion. I started getting pretty close to the really inside layers, and I felt I'd peeled myself down to the empty core. I wrote 'Slow Music,' which reads like a funeral march, a goodbye. And I meant it that way. I thought I was through, and typically, I was going to kill myself.

"But then it seemed as though there was a little more of me after all. I found another onion."

More recently she has produced some grim and powerful stories, and a gently lyrical series in which the closely observed natural beauty of the Quintana Roo territory of Mexico is infused with a mystical sense of Mayan history. Alice Sheldon herself maintains a small house in that part of the world.

After a hiatus brought about by severe health problems that necessitated open-heart surgery, she resumed working on *Brightness Falls from the Air*, a new novel. She seems reluctant to say very much about the book, but remarks that it represents "a great leap forward in my own writing discipline."

Unsurprisingly, in view of her artistic background, almost all her work is vividly visual. And her interest in behavioral psychology shows itself in many stories where a large social truth is acted out on a small-scale human level—much as an experiment in psychology will demonstrate a law of species behavior.

Her characters are often fiercely independent and forced to fend for themselves; yet her stories lack right-wing or libertarian flavor of the "rugged individualist" school of modern science fiction. I ask if, in fact, she identifies with any political philosophy.

"Around the late 1930s, I can't tell you how much time we wasted defining our differences with Stalinist communism, and Trotskyite communism—I'm sort of burned out on the subject. Only some benevolent dryad kept me from joining a John Reed club; once you do that, you're stamped as a communist front member forever.

"I'm an anarchist if anything. But I figure that the changes we're going to see in our time are going to be brought about more by reactions to external circumstances than by groups of people working *for* one system or another. Most likely is the dropping of the Bomb; short of that, there's ecological devastation, or an economic upheaval in the West. It's not that I have a feeling of helplessness; I think the individual can do a great deal in the world. You're not old enough to remember the real movement toward fascism that there was in this country, but George Dudley Pelley, just before the Second World War, had 10,000 armed men, called Silver Shirts, drilling in New Jersey.

"I joined Friends of Democracy right after the war, a little counter-espionage organization. We used to enroll in hate groups, send away for their literature. They were reasonably discreet to start with, but then they'd send these incredible, mad brochures advocating the sterilization of all Jews and cripples. We traced the movements of people from group to group—they never could resist listing all their founding fathers on their letterheads. I came to the conclusion that there was about a ten percent hardcore paranoid component in this country: those whose natural idea of government, whether impassioned or lethargic, was fascism. I still do believe that; they smolder there like an ember. Reagan started out from a point further toward the middle, but he attracted in his following, of course, a lot of what is politely called the extreme right. He gave the whole thing an impetus and a nourishing ambience, and I think the far right has probably done a good bit of recruiting."

Is she as skeptical of authority in real life as she is in her fiction?

"Yes. Power corrupts, absolute power corrupts absolutely, and as Eric Hoffer said, an absolute religion engenders the most absolute cruelties. Look at the wars in Ireland. But much as I loathe Roman Catholicism as an authoritarian religion, Islam is worse. Mohammed has no compassion, no understanding that man might require forgiveness for anything. He taught that women have no souls. He was a military leader who didn't even have the breadth of spirit that *Eisenhower* had.

"I was brought up on the knowledge that the Inquisition had burned alive two of my great-great-great grandfathers, for the crime of possessing a Bible. They wanted to read the thing in their own hands, without the intermediary of a priest. Man's humanity to man, I do not believe in; women only have the degree of freedom we have now because of these very artificial social circumstances; kindness to the weak does not hold when the war of all against all starts. Our freedoms and privileges will be the first to go. And, as in the case of Rome, the fall of the kingdom will be blamed on our liberties."

I remark that this sounds unmitigatedly pessimistic.

"God simply hasn't come down and told me, 'You will save yourselves.' If we don't actually kill ourselves off, I think we'll end up as a sort of Calcutta. That's what an exponential birth rate means on a finite surface. There are simply too many people."

I still object that she seems to lack faith in our ability to solve problems and change.

"Man does not change his behavior; he adapts to the results of it. This is, to me, the most grisly truth I learned from psychology. It's often the only predictor you need in any given situation, especially for groups, and often for single people. Man believes that, whatever the situation is, it's going to continue. For instance, because science has helped us in the past, we will assume it will continue to do so.

"Being a lifelong atheist, I have had to work out a structure of basic values for myself. My premise is that we like a value which we essentially represent; to a giraffe, for instance, a long neck is *good*; life loves life. Life is a denial of entropy; it's a striking manifestation of *negative* entropy. So I believe it can be shown that things with a high degree of organization, meaning a low degree of entropy, seem good to us. For example, Nazism is a highly entropic form, and democracy is far more complex. An altruistic act is more complex than a selfish one; you can carry these concepts quite a ways, to show that most things we feel to be 'good' in the New Testament sense, and sensible, involve a more organized structure of action. To me, Lucifer is positive entropy, runaway breakdown of the system, the war of all against all, which I think will, unfortunately, recur."

Perhaps it's in the nature of an experimental psychologist to invent a scale against which human values can be measured. Perhaps a quasi-anarchist who has worked at a high level in the CIA will inevitably end up preoccupied with morals and motives. Perhaps any child exposed to countless bizarre cultures will search, as an adult, for a bedrock of truth amid all the chaos; and any precocious adolescent misfit, lacking the intuitive ability to fit in, will turn to logic as a tool to cope with quirks of human behavior.

I don't presume to draw these conclusions myself. I think Alice Sheldon already hinted at them for me. I suspect, in fact, that she picked out beforehand the anecdotes that would provide the best insight into her own character: the story of her little secret home in the elephant grass (which she described right at the start of our very first interview), and her description of finding solace when she would lie alone in a cemetery and contemplate the indifference of the universe. Below her, the exanimate; above her, the inanimate. Dead people and distant stars impose no demands, no perplexing social mores.

I think this makes it discreetly clear that her desire for anonymity, and her exaggerated, naive responses to people's demands, are interlinked. Again and again, she has portrayed herself over-reacting clumsily to what she thought people wanted: from her awkward attempts as a young child to please the adults, to her marriage to the first man who asked her, to her self-inflicted exhaustion as a teacher, coping with the needs of students and sacrificing her career as a psychologist in the process.

Before I met Alice Sheldon, I assumed that her reclusiveness was comparable to that of some other writers I had encountered. By making themselves inaccessible, they impose a little test of

352

dedication on anyone who wants to talk to them. Their act of aloofness is really a power-play, and a hard-to-get courtship ritual.

I now understand that for Alice Sheldon, this was not the case at all. While it lasted, her anonymity was a form of self-preservation—protection from those endlessly perplexing, undeniable social demands.

Now, of course, I'm guilty of eroding her privacy further, with my demands as an interviewer—to which, as usual, she responded with mad excesses of conscientiousness. All I can do at this point is close with what seems to me her most eloquent statement on the subject.

"When I was at Sarah Lawrence College, I used to do all my work at night and leave it on the professor's desk in the morning, like the elves. I'd still like to do that, to be able to write stories on old leaves, or something, and have them flutter down through an editor's window with nobody knowing who did it.

"All that's gone, now. All that wonderful anonymity."

Historical Context

I made many friends among the writers I visited while I was compiling *Dream Makers*, but none was more remarkable than Alice Sheldon. I returned to her home a couple of times, and we spent many hours talking.

Eventually she asked me if I would write the biography of her husband, who had held a very senior position in the CIA as Director of the Office of Current Intelligence, providing assessments of world affairs for Presidents Truman, Eisenhower, and Kennedy. She offered to pay me with her own money, but I said I would be happy to do it if she would just cover my travel expenses. She said she wanted the text primarily for his children and grandchildren. I think she just wanted his achievements to be recorded rather than forgotten.

Ting (as Alice called him) agreed to give it a try, just to keep her happy. He told me with a slightly roguish smile that he was free to tell me anything at all, because no one had ever debriefed him when he left the agency. It had been his job to debrief everyone else.

However, interviewing him turned out to be an exercise in futility. First, he was extremely modest, and was unaccustomed to talking about himself. Second, having spent most of his life keeping secrets, it simply wasn't in his nature to speak freely. I would sit with him in the kitchen while she discreetly retreated to her office, and I would ask questions such as, "Did you take any famous prisoners of war when you were in Germany?"

Alice of course was listening in from the other room, and finally she couldn't stand her husband's modest and minimal responses. She strode into the kitchen. "Why don't you tell Charles about that time when you had Goering naked from the waist up, shovelling shit from the horse stables?" she demanded.

Ting raised his eyebrows. "Well, I—I don't recall any such thing," he said. The roguish smile returned. "And—why, if it had happened, it would have been a violation of the Geneva Convention."

Obviously we weren't going to get very far with the biography, but I did talk to him a lot about world affairs in general, and he became quite enthused to have a listener who admired him and shared some of his more radical opinions. At one point he offered me a beer, which he took from the refrigerator. He hesitated, then took out a second bottle. "I think I'll have one myself," he said. He hesitated again. "Let's add a shot of vodka. Have you ever tried that? You know—it makes beer so much more *interesting*."

A few minutes later, as we were drinking our "interesting" beer, Alice came in. She stopped and stared at him. "You're drinking," she said, sounding deeply upset. I realized, then, that he had been an alcoholic—and also saw how much she played a nurturing role, regardless of her more public persona as a fiercely independent woman.

On another visit, all three of us were standing outside their house on the lawn, on a very beautiful summer day. Ting touched my arm. "Listen," he said. "They're talking to each other."

I realized he was referring to a pair of birds on opposite sides of the garden. One made a call, and the other replied; and the sequence repeated. What a wonderful metaphor, I thought to myself: the former Director of Current Intelligence at the CIA, picking up the communications between two song birds.

Alice and Ting were a devoted couple. One time when I was talking on the phone to her, and I chided her gently for smoking cigarettes, she said, "I'm not concerned about getting cancer. I wouldn't want to live longer than Ting." And I don't think this was hyperbole.

It was during my last phone call to her that she told me he had experienced a hemorrhage which blinded him in both eyes. She was characteristically analytical about it, explaining the biology of the condition, and why it was incurable. But I sensed her strength wavering. "All he does now is sit and listen to classical music," she said. "Very loud. It's getting very difficult, here."

Not long after that, she decided that the pleasurable times in their lives were over, and she telephoned a friend to announce that she and her husband had chosen to die. She used a revolver to shoot him twice in the head. She used the same weapon to kill herself with a single shot.

I still have a photograph of Alice, inscribed to me. I mourn the loss of her, but I respect the decision that she made. Many times during her life she had courted death, and the final consummation was not a surprise.

Charles Platt, by Douglas E. Winter

CHARLES PLATT SETS up his own tape recorder next to mine. I ask him why and he responds with the anxious geniality of a man facing root-canal work: "Well, I want my own tape, to hear what I sound like. I'm used to being on this side of the microphone."

The devil gets his due, it is said, and an interview with the interviewer seems a fitting close to the *Dream Makers* series. Berkley Books agreed when I proposed the encounter, so I find myself sitting across the table from Charles Platt, trying to recapture the first impression I gained of him several years ago, when a call to an anonymous telephone number, in search of *New Worlds* magazine, led me to his door.

After a confused taxi ride through Greenwich Village, I found Platt's apartment nestled in a shadowland alleyway of parallel row-houses, originally built as servants' quarters to an estate long ago vanquished by urban expansion. e. e. cummings once lived here, and the lower-case, cloistered atmosphere of an artists' colony was unmistakable.

At the last row-house, an elderly tenant waved me upstairs as if she knew my destination. My knock was answered by the clank of a security bar. The door rattled inward, and Platt jack-in-the-boxed out of its shadows. An unruly shock of chestnut hair topped his thin face, whose sharp and boyish features were emphasized by mischievous eyes. "Hullo, I'm Charles Platt," he said, and without further ado ushered me in.

At first, I assumed that his apartment was temporary

quarters—there was a spartan and decidedly whimsical quality to its furnishings—but later I saw it as a logical extension of his personality. Books lined three walls of the living room, while a stereo and a stack of records (Dave Edmunds and Nick Lowe albums prominent) stood at the fourth. Beneath one bookshelf were boxes and boxes of Weetabix, a British cereal to which Platt is addicted, and which, along with other eccentric foodstuffs, he will carry on his travels—even, on occasion, when invited to dinner. The apartment's principal feature was a word processor (then. still an innovative tool for a writer); its decor was tacky Americana, ranging from a plastic 3-D Jesus plaque to souvenir plates inscribed with verses to Mother.

As this curious mixture of appurtenances suggests, locating Charles Platt may be easier than defining him. If we look to the public record (and by this I mean the charmingly opaque two-line summations on book jackets) we learn that Platt was born in Scotland in 1949...wait, this one says Tehran in 1944...no, here it says a small English village in 1945, the adopted son of Lord Platt. When I ask about the discrepancies, Platt seems more concerned that I should actually own the books in question. "I can never take anything totally seriously," he says, as if the proposition were not self-evident; but the interview proceeds with candor and a fair modicum of seriousness. At one point, he seemingly apologizes, his expression deadpan: "I promised myself that, as an interviewee, I would do those considerate things that make an interviewer's life easier."

With the question of birthdate unresolved, it seems inevitable that we begin at the beginning. Platt was born in London in 1945 (and Lord Platt, a distinguished physician, was his uncle). At age five, his family moved "to the horrible, dull little town of Letchworth, where I went to a peculiarly permissive and progressive school, which gave its students a totally unrealistic view of life. They all expected things to be extremely easy when they left school, because things had been so easy when they were *at* school.

357

Some of them became disillusioned and bitter; others just remained perpetually naive, which is what happened to me."

He describes his childhood as typical of a science-fiction writer. "I was one of those people who read a book a day and believed in it in that peculiarly intense way that real science-fiction fans have. I wasn't terribly popular socially. I was the youngest in my class—didn't enjoy sports. My idea of a recreation would be plotting a three-dimensional graph and cutting out the little templates and stacking them. I was also interested in astronomy—anything which would entail getting away from being beaten up at school."

Writing science fiction was the inevitable next step. "I wrote comic strips when I was about seven or eight, which I tried to sell to my friends at school. This didn't make me very popular or very rich, but I had *big plans*. I tried to sell a few stories when I was eighteen or nineteen, sending them to *New Worlds*, which at that point was a slightly more literate imitation of the American science-fiction magazines."

In 1963 Platt entered university at Cambridge, intending to study economics, but he quickly dropped out and moved to London. "Almost coincidentally, Michael Moorcock took over editorship of *New Worlds*. I sent him my fifth story, which he liked very much and bought—he made it the cover story, which was a nice way to break into print." (Platt prefers to forget that his first professional sale was in 1964, to *New Worlds's* companion magazine, *Science Fantasy*.) "It also turned out that I was living in an area of London about two blocks from where Moorcock was living, which was very serendipitous." Platt became the designer and later the (unpaid) production manager for *New Worlds*, supporting himself by writing "ridiculous soft-core nonsense." He also played keyboards in several "obscure" rock bands. When Moorcock left *New Worlds* in 1969, Platt took over as editor.

In the late 1960s and early 1970s, *New Worlds* was the focal point for a loose-knit group of writers who brought a brief and startlingly unwelcome "new wave" to science fiction. Platt is still possessed by the idealism of those times: "Largely as a result of *New Worlds*, I discovered literature which lacked the speculative component of science fiction but nevertheless was equally challenging to the imagination. I was woken up to the fact that most science fiction is not terribly well written, and does not offer any great insights into the human psyche—which is something you ignore when you're sixteen years old, because at that age, *you* don't have many insights into the human psyche, either.

I'd always been interested in anything new or experimental, so the idea of experimenting with fiction was just fascinating, There weren't any rules at school, so why should there be any rules in fiction? It struck me as perverse that some of the older writers felt that you could speculate on almost any topic, but when it came to writing your speculation, you had to stay within very rigid stylistic limits. I think writers should be able to try whatever they like, to extend their imaginations or tastes as far as they will go."

Was there a feeling of manifest destiny among the *New Worlds* writers, of bringing a real change to science fiction?

"No one would have said so, of course, because we didn't want to seem too pretentious; but there was. There was also a sense of 'us-versus-them,' which was prevalent in all the arts and in politics. The 1960s were the first time in history that youth had been given much power in anything, and I was youth at the time. We had *our* music, we had *our* clothes. I wanted us to have *our* literature, too. And *New Worlds* was the focus of what was new in this respect.

"We didn't think that we were going to take over the world, but we did think we could push science fiction in our direction a bit. And to some extent we were right; although I never imagined that this slow slide back into conventionality would occur. I thought that innovation in music and writing was just going to keep on growing outward and upward. It never occurred to me that people would really prefer to go back to the same old stuff, after they'd had a taste of more innovative and challenging material. People read science fiction to be surprised, so why would they prefer something *less* surprising?"

When asked what happened, he shakes his head, honestly bemused. "I don't know. I tend to draw analogies with music. Music is no longer a very potent force, but in the late 1960s a lot of people were drawing energy from it. The Beatles really did inspire people, by taking this crass form of popular music and adding orchestras, doing what they liked, breaking all the rules and getting away with it. And when that all fell to pieces—when that band split up, and Jimi Hendrix died, and Bob Dylan had his motorcycle accident and came back giving us country music—that was incredibly disillusioning.

"Then, of course, the anti-war movement was *successful*, and there's nothing like success to defuse things, because you no longer have anything to fight against. And a lot of people got scared. I think Dylan's retreat from all those angry lyrics of the 1960s was a classic case of someone getting scared by what he had opened up. Also, you know, people become more conservative as they grow older, which is another thing I don't understand. So the decline of innovation in science fiction, I think, was wrapped up with all of that."

Between 1966 and 1970, Platt wrote four science-fiction novels. All are out of print, and none was especially successful, except perhaps for *The Gas*, a post-apocalypse satire written for the renowned publisher of erotica, Olympia Press. Haunted by his failure to have written a critically or commercially successful science-fiction novel, Platt rages against the thought of being judged solely on his early books: "They just sounded fun to write. I never imagined them lingering on years later to embarrass me."

Platt left England in 1970, resettling in New York City. The reasons for his move "are contained in any Beach Boys or Chuck Berry song—you know, I wish they all could be California girls, 'or 'Hot dogs and hamburgers...back in the U.S.A.' All the national

360

clichés turn out to be true. People talk more bluntly over here, are less reserved, It's a country which, until now at any rate, hasn't throttled itself with its own history. It's still willing to change abruptly, and I like change. I also like cities, and I think New York is probably the most visually exciting city to be in. I get recharged just by riding my bike around town."

He travelled extensively through America in the early 1970s, and "wrote some undistinguished novels in order to finance an itinerant lifestyle." In 1972 he was appointed consulting editor, specializing in science-fiction, at Avon Books. He compiled their "rediscovery" list of science-fiction classics, and persuaded Avon to publish two new issues of *New Worlds* in book form. He resigned when Avon refused to buy Philip K. Dick's *Flow My Tears, the Policeman Said* because they disliked the title.

Platt has since spent most of his time writing outside of science fiction, producing a versatile assortment of books, including *Outdoor Survival* (a guide for young people), *Sweet Evil* ("a fantasy of Mansonesque decadence"), and three installments of the "Christina" series of erotic novels. He was New York columnist for the *Los Angeles Free Press* (as well as for *The Fetish Times*), taught evening classes at two New York colleges, worked briefly as a magician, and most recently has authored numerous games and utility programs for home computers.

In 1977 he published his best and most serious science-fiction novel, *Twilight of the City*, "using economic theory as a way of building the scenario." Although he has since published only one science-fiction story, he still sees himself as a science-fiction writer: "It's hard not to. I imagine it's the same if you learn country guitar: No matter what style you adopt after that, you still think in certain guitar-picking patterns. Even though I've done relatively little science-fiction writing, I still think of myself as a science-fiction writer, because I'm imprinted that way. I still get ideas for science-fiction books. I have ideas for twenty, at least, written down and stored away."

Platt's major writing influences have been "Alfred Bester, the great innovator of the 1950s, and J. G. Ballard, great innovator of the 1960s," as well as the late C. M. Kornbluth and Algis Budrys (*Michaelmas* was *the* novel of the 1970s"). He remains interested in most forms of experimentation in literature, but holds little hope for a near-term return to it in science fiction.

"American publishing and, to some extent, British publishing have changed so much in the last fifteen years. Then, science fiction was obscure to most publishers, and they let their hireling do whatever he liked; but science fiction is now considered big business if you get the right formula, and thus it is becoming more like television than a small press—those being the opposite ends of the artistic scale. So it's going to be much harder to do anything very surprising."

The problem is compounded, in Platt's view, by the lack of effective criticism of science fiction. "Most of it is inarticulate, and not much of it is very critical. Most of it is saying, 'Oh, here's another fine Gene Wolfe novel. Jolly good. How pleasing it is to see such fine writing.' Well, that is not criticism; that is the sort of response that occurs when one's pleasure centers are inoffensively stimulated.

"It's a miserable job being a critic. You don't get paid much. You have to think at least as hard as if you were writing a short story. Few critics' works are going to be anthologized, so you are really writing something which is almost disposable. So it's not surprising that few good writers bother to write criticism. Why should they? They're much better paid and better loved for writing fiction."

Nevertheless, in recent years, Platt has returned to science fiction primarily as a critic, to tilt at the windmills of its writing and publishing establishments. He assisted in a brief revival of *New Worlds* from 1978 to 1980, financing, editing, and designing one issue himself. In 1980 he began editing and self-publishing *The Patchin Review.* a "little magazine" that "is the only truly radical, skeptical voice within the science-fiction field." The magazine presents serious criticism hand-in-hand with unadulterated gossip and satiric tomfoolery. Platt's editorial tone has led certain writers and critics—not a few of whom have been the subjects of its barbs—to contend that he pursues controversy only for the sake of controversy. He reacts with hurt surprise: "Any area of the arts gets stale unless people try new things. People are not going to try new things if they are constantly congratulated for doing the same old things. I'm not necessarily in favor of newness for its own sake, but I do get bored if there is a conspicuous lack of innovation. Science fiction should be a literature of surprises. We all know each other in this field, with the exception of a very few editors and writers, so naturally we tend to be tactful socially, and even in reviews that are published in professional magazines. This is bad; it leads to complacency, and complacency leads to repetition, low standards, bad habits that are never corrected. So, I think honesty is an antidote. I don't see what's controversial about that.

"Good heavens, this country has freedom of speech written into its constitution. That's another reason I live here. The country I come from does not have that guarantee, so I feel acutely that it's very important free to speak your mind. I'm always surprised when other people want to qualify that. They say, 'Freedom of speech, yes, I completely agree—except, of course, in certain circumstances.' And that, to me, is not a trivial difference at all, That is *all* the difference."

His adamance notwithstanding, trouble seems to follow Platt. In pursuit of his vague ideal of honesty (applied selectively, as witness his revisionist approach to his own history), he holds no truck with tact or diplomacy: "You know, without wanting to sound too profound, sometimes the truth seems more important than a friendship." Indeed, a friend of more than ten years' standing became so upset by his *Dream Makers* profile that he threatened to seek an injunction against publication of the first volume. They have not talked to each other since 1980.

What practical effect does he hope his critical efforts will obtain? Where would he like to see science fiction in ten years?

I'd like there to be less of it. Some politicians scream, 'Get rid of the welfare chiselers.' Well, in my case, I don't object at all to people on welfare, but there are certain writers who are on a kind of 'science-fiction welfare'—they're conceptual parasites, serving no useful function in creative or literary terms. I would like there to be less of such repetitive, derivative writing.

There is also a great need for good rational fiction, because there is so much anti-rational fiction being published. There has been such a retreat from science, just because some of the things that science achieved turned out to have unpleasant side-effects. We now have people who are against nuclear *anything*, rather than being selective. As far as I'm concerned, having gone this far, science is the only thing that can save us. So it's all the more important, now, to see stories which are proper science fiction rather than whimsical fantasy, myth, or whatever you want to call it.

It's a matter of doing the job properly; that is to say, of making it rational—as opposed to fantasy, which is not—and writing it well. Just because it often has not been written well does not mean that's what science fiction is; it just means it has seldom fulfilled its promise."

What about Charles Platt? Where would he like to be, as a writer, in ten years?

"I always wanted to be about ten different things. That's the whole problem. Unfortunately, there's not enough time to do all these things before you die; and, as one passes the age of thirty-five, one stops thinking about how much time has passed and starts thinking about how much time remains."

Platt's renewed ambition is obvious as he discusses his interest in completing a new science-fiction novel by early 1983. "Doing the *Dream Makers* volumes taught me a lot about the methods used by successful writers. And then I began to understand much more about publishing than I ever had. So I now feel I have a better shot at writing something which will please me, something that will please other people too, and will perhaps be moderately successful."

Historical Context

I'M GRATEFUL TO Douglas Winter for allowing the inclusion, here, of the profile that he wrote of me. Looking back at it now, I find that my perception of the publishing industry hasn't changed at all, and most of my predictions about it were accurate.

I was far less prescient regarding my own situation. I don't know what I was referring to, when I talked about finishing a new book in 1983. I suspect that it was never started, let alone finished.

I did eventually write a serious science-fiction novel to the limit of my abilities, titled *The Silicon Man*, which appeared in 1991. It received some nice reviews, most notably in *The New York Times*, but Bantam Spectra Special Editions allowed it to go out of print a few weeks after it was published. Spectra Special Editions specialized in "serious" science fiction. The imprint only lasted for a few years, for the usual obvious reasons in a post-*Star Wars* world.

Fortuitously, a magazine named *Wired* was launched in 1993. It enabled me to write about new technologies and business ventures that might bring us a little closer to some of the exciting futures that I had imagined when I was a teenager. Probably this kind of journalism was what I should have been doing all along.

I became one of three senior writers at *Wired*, until the dotcom bubble burst and the magazine acquired an editor who lacked the imaginative spirit that had energized the magazine. Writing for *Wired* was no longer fun, so I spent a few years working in the field of cryonics, which was the closest I could get to the application of a science-fictional technology. I managed a team of first responders, and despite my lack of formal qualifications, I designed and built equipment for a California laboratory in my own workshop. By this time I had relocated to a Northern Arizona wilderness area.

Currently I write technical books such as *Make:Electronics* that tell young people and hobbyists how components work and what you can do with them. Really I enjoyed myself more as a journalist and as a fiction writer, but technical writing has an attribute which seems important to me: instead of merely providing entertainment, it serves a practical purpose.

I retain great affection for the science fiction that suggested so many possibilities and gave me confidence in the power of technology to enrich our lives. But that was back in the 1960s. When I open those books now, I am overwhelmed with a mixture of nostalgia and pain. Most of the writers are no longer alive, and most of the futures that they described remain unfulfilled. Human beings turned out to be far more cautious and conservative than I expected, and the political process has impeded change. Many people are easily scared by science, while those in political office enjoy more job security if they can discourage disruptive technologies by regulating them.

I gave up reading science fiction in the early 1990s, not because I had fallen out of love with it, but because I loved it too much.

As a writer myself, I was fortunate. I have written more than forty books in a wide variety of genres. Some were trashy, some were informative, some were offensive, many were not as ambitious as they should have been, and a couple were quixotically self-satirical—but with one exception, they all found their way into print. Editors were kind to me.

In the magazine field, persistence coupled with luck and arrogance enabled me to work for *New Worlds* in the late 1960s and *Wired* in the 1990s. I see them as two of the three most exciting publications in the second half of the twentieth century (*Analog* being the third). I'm proud to have been closely associated with them.

The only project I would still enjoy pursuing in science fiction would be a latter-day version of *New Worlds*, mixing fiction, science, and art with the same defiant spirit as in the 1960s. It would be in an electronic format, which would remove length restrictions on features while allowing high-quality color reproduction throughout, with audio and video clips embedded in the text.

The problem is, now that I live in Arizona, I don't feel motivated to tackle a project that would suck up a lot of time. I am much more interested in exploring dirt roads in a 4x4 SUV. The desert is not so different from the surface of Mars, and to a former British citizen, the ecology and the human culture are intriguingly alien. Thus I have come as close as I can to my childhood ambitions to live on an alien planet.

I am making the most of it while I still have the opportunity to do so.

—CP